Praise for *Reasons She Goes to the Woods*

Longlisted for the Baileys Women's Prize for Fiction and shortlisted for the Encore Award

'Pearl is a marvellously contradictory creation, showing the cruelty in children as well as their neediness, their capacity for love and friendship... Davies' novel reads almost like a prose poem.'

Independent on Sunday

'A sexy, contrary book...also a story concerned with morality. The most sustained and challenging aspect of the narrative is its insistence about what a little girl is like.'

Times Literary Supplement

'Exquisite...to be marvelled at.'

Guardian

'A spiky echo of Angela Carter, with whom Ms Davies at her best stands fair comparison... The language is fresh, the imagery striking...and Pearl herself is a rampant, compelling, fully-realised, wild-eyed, teary creation.'

The Scotsman

'Outstanding... Davies is a poet, and this is a poet's novel in the very best sense – every word is pin-sharp and perfectly in its place.'

The Times

'Best for highbrow sun lounging...told with a gothic, sensual style that Angela Carter would be proud of.'

Grazia

'Raw, lyrical, sad, this haunting story packs a deceivingly strong punch.'

Publishers Weekly

'Dark, beautifully descriptive and rather haunting.'

Grazia Daily

'A poetic and strange novel, full of flair.'

Emerald Street

'A rounded, complex portrait of growing-up that has an atmosphere all of its own.'

We Love This Book

ABOUT THE AUTHOR

DEBORAH KAY DAVIES was born in South Wales and began writing as a mature student at Cardiff University, where she earned a PhD in Creative and Critical Writing and taught Creative Writing.

Her first book was a collection of poems, *Things You Think I Don't Know* (Parthian, 2006). This was followed by a collection of short stories, *Grace, Tamar and Laszlo the Beautiful* (Parthian, 2008), which won the 2009 Wales Book of the Year award. After publication of her debut novel, *True Things About Me* (Canongate, 2010), the BBC TV *Culture Show* named Deborah as one of the twelve best new British novelists. Published in the US by Faber in 2011, Lionel Shriver chose the novel as her personal Book of the Year in the *Wall Street Journal*.

Deborah Kay Davies' second novel, *Reasons She Goes to the Woods* (Oneworld, 2014), was longlisted for the 2014 Baileys Women's Prize for Fiction and shortlisted for the 2015 Encore Award. In her review for the *Guardian*, Eimear McBride described the novel as 'exquisite…to be marvelled at'.

Deborah lives in Cardiff with her husband, the poet Norman Schwenk.

TIRZAH AND THE PRINCE OF CROWS

DEBORAH KAY DAVIES

ONEWORLD

A Oneworld Book

First published in Great Britain & Australia
by Oneworld Publications, 2018

ISBN 978-1-78607-444-7
eISBN 978-1-78607-445-4

Typeset by Fakenham Prepress Solutions, Fakenham, Norfolk, NR21 8NL
Printed and bound in Great Britain by Clays Ltd, Elcograf S.p.A.

Oneworld Publications
10 Bloomsbury Street
London WC1B 3SR
England

For Norman,
my indispensable, beloved captain and crew.

I Am a Worm, and No Man

(Psalm 22:6)

Behold, I see the Lord descending as a dove, Pastor says. The gathering of brothers and sisters in the vestry turn their palms up and make encouraging noises. Tirzah is peering at the fanlight above the curtained double doors, her eyes the merest slits. Come, we beseech You, Heavenly Father, Pastor goes on, enfold us in Your wings, transport us to the heights. Sometimes, Tirzah sends herself up to the ledge just under the narrow, grubby window. That's as far as I want to go when I'm in the prayer meeting, thank you, she thinks. It's a nice way of passing the time. Up she goes now, like a spider on a strand of silk, and settles to survey the room. From this angle, some people's hair looks sparse. And that's not only the men; Mrs Stanley's scalp has a broad, straggly seam, the pink flesh breaking through. It's surprising, because at floor level, she has rows of dry, mousy curls crowding her forehead. Vain, she is, thinks Tirzah, watching as she tweaks her fringe. And going bald, poor dab.

Apart from Pastor, who is still doggedly coaxing the Holy Spirit as if it were a nervous budgie, her parents look

1

by far the most holy. Tirzah's mother is smiling tremulously, perched on the edge of her chair, ready to run into the arms of Jesus, should He beckon. Her father is wrestling with something as usual. Although he is quite still, there is a sense of contained movement about him, evidence of a struggle only she can detect. Amen, Lord, he says, at intervals, mechanically. Verily, whispers her mother. Come, oh precious Jesus. We are waiting. Tirzah watches as her mother raises her arms towards the buzzing strip light. Fill us to overflowing, Lord, she calls, and everyone steps up the intensity. Tirzah's armpits prickle at the way her mother's voice throbs for Jesus, and immediately she is back in the circle.

None of the women shows even the smallest glimpse of a knee, and some not even an ankle; the flesh is fallen and the portal for sin. If you give it an inch, Tirzah knows, it will spill out and go rampaging over everything like bindweed in a rose garden. Tirzah's legs are covered with thick black tights. She can feel the rash of woolly bobbles meshing on the insides of her thighs. Across the semicircle, her cousin Biddy is resting on her mother's shoulder. Tirzah has a proper look: Biddy is actually really asleep. Her mouth is relaxed, each outward breath puffing her lips so that it seems as if she is blowing kisses to the room. Biddy has new shoes, with the most lush little heels and buckles. It's just not fair. Tirzah's mother insists she wear boy's lace-ups. We do not follow the world, you silly, shallow child, she always says. We are *in* the world, but not *of* the world. Never forget it. And don't talk to me about Biddy, that girl is spoilt to death. Her mother's antique shoes are maroon leather affairs with fringed tongues on the fronts and stubby stacked heels. In them, her ankles still manage to look like delicate branches from a rare type of tree.

It doesn't matter how much Tirzah explains about the other girls in school, and the tidy two-tone shoes they wear, her mother is unmovable on the subject of suitable footwear for growing feet. These will last you; boy's shoes are sturdier, she states, with little variation, twice-yearly in the shop. And I'll get my money's worth. Then she goes on about all the daft fashions around. You'll thank me one day, madam, she's always saying, when everyone is hobbling out for their old age pension with snaggly tootsies and bunions. All Tirzah can see are her ugly, indestructible boy-shoes, and how fist-like her own woolly ankles look. Some of the sixth form girls are even wearing platforms to school, though they are banned. And meanwhile she has to stomp about in sponge-soled, wipe-clean lace-ups. The idea she is still growing makes her want to weep; the girls in class say she has feet like Olive Oyl already.

She gazes around again. Most of the brethren keep their knees together, as is only polite. All that equipment, Tirzah thinks, straining to see the bulgy crotch of Pastor as he rocks his lean buttocks into a more comfortable position and starts to sing in his nasal voice: *I tried the empty cisterns, Lord, but, ah! the waters failed.* Everyone joins in, swooping up and down over the tune. Tirzah automatically hums the contralto, wondering what a cistern actually is. But, more importantly, what does it look like down there, behind those zips? Hideous, she doesn't doubt. Coiled up, but ready to unleash itself, like that bothersome bindweed maybe, and smother all the sisters, herself included. Dada's legs are always spread apart, though, his boots rooted to the spot. Thank goodness his trousers are so roomy you can't see any bulges or odd shapes under his zip. Otherwise she would swoon regularly at the sight. The hymn continues, and Tirzah ups the volume: *E'en as I stooped to drink they fled, and mocked me as I wailed.* The moment it's finished her mother starts to pray, already gasping between each word, her hat brim rising like a hungry mouth from its hat-pin pivot at the back of her head, her eyes rolling up under quivering lids.

Tirzah counts slowly, and gets to three hundred and twenty-seven before her mother finishes; there are often dips in her flow of praise, but always a quick acceleration before the end, so Tirzah doesn't have to pay too much attention to her counting. She inhales deeply, aware of her mother subsiding, and realises someone has broken wind. How rude, she thinks. And extremely unchristian. The Son of God never broke wind, she's sure. Suddenly she wants to get out. It's disgusting, having to breathe the air from inside someone's behind. Doesn't matter how holy they are. She diverts herself by trying to guess who did it. Some people you just know would not. Mrs Edwards, though. She's looking more restless than usual. And she has covered her nose with an embroidered hankie, shifting around in the too-small chair.

Thinking about Mrs Edwards' soft bottom inside her pants, and the way her fart must have silently curled out from the gusset, Tirzah starts to heave. Immediately her mother's eyes fly open, and she stares at Tirzah. I'm poorly, Tirzah mouths, and startles herself by making the most guttural kind of burping sound. She smacks a hand over her mouth and runs towards the curtained doors. After a fight with the long paisley drapes, she's out, the doors banging shut behind her. Lovely, lovely open air, she thinks, at once feeling more herself. Even though her chin is wet and her hands are sticky, it's only spit. Thank the Lord, she thinks. Being ill in prayer meeting would have been so awkward. She clears a final putty-like wodge from around her tonsils. Ych-y-fi, she says aloud, bending to

4

examine the tiny, glistening mound on the pathway. Human beings are revolting.

She straightens and shakily inhales the cleansing, night-shrouded air. There is another, purer world out here. The graveyard sweeps downhill, the shale path glowing in the dark like the Path to Glory. Amongst the headstones, yew trees mass in black clouds, their secret, slow-beating hearts crouched deep inside. She imagines unloosing from her body again and flut-tering up through the top of her own head like a newly born moth. Leaving behind the stuffy, holy room, the dust-rough curtains and threadbare carpet, she can feel the weight of the moisture-laden air on her millions of wing scales. On she flies until she reaches the graveyard wall. The stones give off a sharp smell, and as she lands, the lichen opens its thousands of tiny blossoms and they explode, sending out spurts of perfumed powder. Tirzah makes believe she has settled in a gap between two stones, and listens to the twig-like scratches of small brown birds hopping on the wall above her. She hears the squelch of fungi spreading along the base of the wall.

This is the kind of God I would like to have, she thinks, surprising herself. Someone who could lie quietly between these stones with me. It is soothing to merge into everything, here in the wet, forsaken graveyard with its lumpy grass and cross-hatching of buried bones. The sky pressing against the mountain's edge is both dark and pinkly glowing, punctuated by a solitary crow that looks like a stab wound in its tender flank. She waits, absorbing the violet's talc-scented breath as it runs around the grave margins, and the sheen on the ridged burdock leaves, and thinks if she is still enough, and small enough, maybe she will learn something important. She can see the spotted, luminous throats of the cuckoo-pint with their columns of berries left over from winter, bright as tiny headlamps. Just as she begins to understand, she is yanked back into her damp dress, somehow still clutching her Bible, still slumped against the chapel wall.

Like a radio being switched off, the shutting doors silence a hymn abruptly. Then Osian is kneeling beside her. You poor little dab, he says, trying to hold her hands. Are you feeling iffy? Tirzah is suddenly tired. Come on, you, he says, heaving her into his arms and standing her upright. No one will know we're together. I slipped out when they were all going at it hammer and tongs. They'll be yonks. Tirzah looks at Osian. He is taller than her now, even though they are the same age. The wing of his black hair falls forward over one eye. She strokes her dress into some sort of order, and wonders how he always knows what to do. They've made you a matter for prayer again, Osian says, his head on one side. Am I in for it? Tirzah asks. Your mother says that even though you appear devout to the world, you have an ungovernable heart, he replies. Those were her exact words. An ungovernable heart? Tirzah asks. That's you, Osian says as he grabs her hand and pulls her towards the path. Now let's go to my house.

Whosoever Shall Smite Thee on Thy Right Cheek

(Matthew 5:39)

Osian wants to put Tirzah's dress to soak in a bowl of water, but she shakes her head. Are you being funny? she says seriously. They're only grass stains. I'll just give them a wipe down for now. He runs a cloth under the hot tap and wrings it out. Can I go to the loo? she asks. He hands her the warm cloth. Upstairs on the landing she tries a few rooms, taking in the lino-clad floors and looming chests of drawers in each; she's never been up here before. In the bathroom, she wipes her face and squeezes out a worm of toothpaste on to her finger, rubbing it all over her teeth. She uses the cloth to wipe her dress. Then she drinks some water. Back in the kitchen, Osian is making a cup of tea. No hot chocolate, of course, he says. Speaking in his father's voice, he booms: Mortify the flesh, wicked boy! Be its master, not its slave! He shrugs, but even with his back to her she can tell he's grinning. From the kitchen table, encased in her damp dress, she gazes at him. What if there was no Osian? Since ever she can remember he's been there, her playmate and buffer in chapel, so it's hard to imagine. But now she sees that he's changed somehow:

his voice is huskier, his mouth mysterious. She is surprised to notice his shoulders are bulkier and his waist slimmer than she remembers. Only his rain-straight, swaying black hair is like it always was. When did this happen?

The kettle starts to shriek, and Osian aims steaming water into the pot, swishes it around, then puts two heaped spoonfuls of sugar in her mug. She watches as he unerringly pours the tea from a height. There you are, your majesty, he says, placing it before her in his own indefinable way. Get that down you – it's thirsty work, being a matter for prayer. He leans against the dresser, hands in his pockets, head to one side, as if waiting for an answer. The boiler pilot light in the corner burps into life, its tiny blue flame like a Pentecostal tongue. Thank you, Osian, Tirzah says over the rim of her mug. Suddenly there are things she wants to ask him, but the words have all scattered like beads from a broken necklace. With the old Osian she would have found it easy to talk. They were comfortable together. Am I like this because of my ungovernable heart? she wonders. Osian is watching her, his eyes crinkling. Aren't you having anything? she asks, looking down into her mug.

When Osian has poured a cup for himself, they sit and drink. The kitchen is dim, with a lingering smell of fried onions. Tirzah wonders what his mother's been cooking. Do you think I'm a bad person? she asks finally, putting her empty mug down. I mean, you know me: am I bad? Osian is serious. Very, he says. You are a lost soul. You must be, running out of the midweek meeting. Tirzah sends up a silent prayer. Don't joke, Osian, she says. This is serious. I'm always trying to be good. Osian laughs again. He thinks for a few seconds. There are more important things than being good, he says, nodding firmly. But, Osian, how can there be? And what about the way we are all guilty worms? Tirzah asks. It's hopeless. I was thinking all sorts of sinful thoughts at the meeting. About bums and bulges, things like that, she adds silently. Osian laughs, laying his forehead down on the table. Honestly! she says, tapping his head. Really, tell me what you think. All I know, he tells her, lifting his head, is that the poor old worms aren't guilty. How can they be? God made them. Besides, all they do is eat earth. And if they're not, neither are you. There, that's settled. He stands up. Come on, we've just about got time. I want to show you something.

In the attic, Osian flicks the light switch. A clear bulb hangs from a dusty cord, its glow grudging. Tirzah sees, laid out on a low table, a whole network of railways, junctions and platforms. Little cows stand on green fabric, tiny people wait for trains. Fuzzy trees dot the boundaries. It's lovely, she says, kneeling down. All aboard, Osian calls, and the train starts to whizz around the tracks. Tirzah is looking at a kidney-shaped blob of blue paint with two minuscule ducks in the middle. Oh, bless him, she thinks. The thought of Osian carefully painting the pool and placing his miniature birds just so makes her heart swell like a note played on the organ. I've been waiting to get it just right before I showed you, he says, towering over his made-up country. Been saving all my chore money. Tirzah wants to be that girl on the platform carrying a basket, always ready to go off on a journey. Osian says: I painted her to look like you. Do you like her? Tirzah nods. The girl has scarlet lips and a copper comma of a ponytail. Where is she off to? she wonders. The train comes to a halt, but the girl is rooted to the spot, still looking down the track. What's the use of being someone who is stuck in one place, always waiting to get on a train that can only go round in circles?

Osian comes to kneel beside her, and together they contemplate the railway. She can feel his warmth against her. I'm glad you like it, he says, leaning his shoulder in. It's very nice, Osian. It must have taken you ages, she says, turning to him. He is silently brooding over his creation, and she studies his nose, his long, half-closed lashes. For the first time she senses her ribs moving as she breathes, and the way her body sits inside her drying dress. Osian, she says, putting her hand on his arm. He turns, and before she can say another word, presses his lips on hers. Tirzah has never kissed anyone this way before. His lips are firm, and his saliva tastes faintly of onions when he pushes the tip of his tongue in. She turns her mouth away and looks sideways at him. Osian's eyes are wide and amused. The train still whirs round, the auburn-haired girl still waits with her basket. I love you, Osian says. And I love you, Tirzah answers. You and Biddy are my best friends. No, he whispers, smiling. I really love you. Tirzah shakes her head. I have to go, she says, making a move to get up; Osian is strange to her. Ah, don't tell me this makes you feel like a guilty worm? he says, his hand pressing on her thigh, preventing her from moving. Yes and no, she answers. I'm not sure.

They hear the front door slamming. Quick, Osian whispers, switching off the light. They make it down the attic ladder as Osian's father gets to the top of the stairs. What have you two been doing all alone up here, may I enquire? he asks, squinting his eyes at them. Here I am, just back from the place of prayer, and this is what I find. He lowers his head like an angry animal and stares at Tirzah. Now, why aren't you in your own home, young lady? It was my idea, Da, Osian says. She was poorly and I looked after her. Osian's father fills the landing, forcing them to take several steps back. His voice seems to bounce off the walls. What am I always saying to you, son? he shouts. My house, my rules. He reaches around Tirzah with a broad hand for Osian and pulls him forward, knocking her off balance. You, girl, to the kitchen this minute. I will inform your parents you were upstairs. Tirzah's ankles are like pieces of stiff wood. She has to take one step down at a time. Behind her she can hear the sound of Osian being smacked hard across the face.

In the kitchen, Osian's mother is lifting a patterned scarf off her gleaming black hair. What were you thinking of? she asks Tirzah sadly. Still, what's done is done, and there's no going back. We were only looking at Osian's train set, Tirzah whispers. Now then, his mother says softly, no stories, please. It will only make matters worse. Osian would never have a train set. His father says such things are a wicked waste of time and money. She puts her hand on Tirzah's shoulder and squeezes. Her eyes are red, and she wipes her nose on an apron corner. Let's see. What about a little bit of toast? she asks, starting to bustle about without doing anything. They are both listening to the sounds of furniture being knocked over and Mr Evans's deep shouting from above. The toast is already under the grill. Sit down by there and have a quick bit of supper, she says, filling the kettle with water. It will do you good after you've been unwell. She butters the toast fiercely, breaking it into pieces. Tirzah looks at Osian's mother, and the plaited bun, luxurious and full of a kind of mystery, which is piled richly on top of her head. It looks too heavy for her to support on such a narrow neck. Tirzah's own throat has shrunk so much that not even a sip would pass, but she struggles to eat some of the charred bread. Thank you, Mrs Evans, she says. She tries to take in what Osian's mother is saying. Always Aunty Margiad to you, little one, she hears. Mrs Evans indeed. Thank you,

Aunty Margiad, Tirzah whispers, the incinerated toast stuck to her tongue like coal dust.

There is the sound of a banging door and then Mr Evans comes downstairs. Everyone should be in bed, he announces, out of breath. This is what happens when one lets down one's guard to the Evil One. Everything else flies out of the window, including Christian bedtimes. His hair has flopped from the slick comb-back he always wears. Tirzah looks at his half-untucked shirt and disarranged tie. It's high time you were in your own home, he says, not meeting her eye. I will step out with you now and have a word with your parents. Tirzah stands up and looks around for her Bible. And we will put you on the altar, young lady, he goes on loudly, as if he were addressing a congregation. Right you are, Trevor dear, Mrs Evans says, and nods encouragingly at Tirzah, eyes glittering against her dead-white skin. A tendril of hair has escaped and is coiled around her small jaw like a drooping plant. Tidy yourself up, Mr Evans shouts. She jumps, and with trembling fingers pushes the hair behind her ear. Off you go, pet, she says to Tirzah, coming over to give her a peck on the cheek. Take care now, and God bless.

Osian's father keeps a hard grasp on Tirzah's elbow as they walk, his breathing still noisy. Does he think I'm going to scarper? she wonders. A growing desire to shove him off is rising inside her. They walk in and out of the pools of lamplight, past the curtained front windows of the terraced houses. Tirzah slows down when she sees her neighbour's black cat arching its way towards her. Mr Evans tightens his grip. Get off me, she says suddenly through narrowed lips. You are hurting my arm, and she shakes herself free. Pussy, puss, she croons, crouching, and the cat makes a small chirrup of greeting. Hello, Blod, she whispers, stroking the cat and ignoring Mr Evans. She can scarcely see, her eyes are so full of tears. Blodwen raises her inky, pointed face and rubs Tirzah's wet cheek. In the quiet street, Tirzah puts both hands on Blod's reverberating back and allows the purring cat to calm her. Mr Evans's black shoes and trouser turn-ups are waiting. Unhurriedly she stands and walks ahead of him, sensing he is struggling to control his anger. He would like to strike me like he struck Osian, she thinks, appalled by the realisation. Briefly she remembers Mrs Evans flinching away from him. Before he can react, she darts ahead and bangs on her suddenly beloved front door. When her father peers out, she pushes past and runs up to her room.

Tirzah lies straight and stiff under the bedclothes, her outline barely making a shape. The unlined curtains are meagre and the street lights stain the room with tints of dark yellow. She can hear Mr Evans shouting downstairs and her father answering him, but she is unable to concentrate. On the wall opposite the bed is a framed embroidery. She sits up. Surrounded by a trail of cornflowers and poppies are the words, *Suffer The Little Children.* This picture has been in her room since she was a baby, so familiar she hasn't really looked at it for years, but now she wonders what it really means. Tonight has been so strange, she begins to think it might be a message. If it means all children, big or little, should suffer, then she understands. And as if a door has swung open to let in freezing blasts of air, she starts to shake, chilled by a mood of utter dejection. She wriggles, trying to find a comfortable spot, and imagines Osian's father being a boy. How did he fall in love with Aunty Margiad? Was he ever handsome? Did he have hands like Osian? Did he stroke Aunty Margiad's long, silky hair and kiss her lips in secret on the mountain? Poor thing, with her trembling fingers and sinewy neck. Was she a lovely girl once? Tirzah considers, and realises Mrs Evans is beautiful, even now. Osian has taken after her, that's plain to see. It's hard to picture Mrs Evans falling in love with that man, but it must have happened somehow. People just don't get married out of the blue.

She remembers the fleshy sound of Osian's face being slapped, his stifled cries, and her own head starts to burn. Is Osian lying on his bed now? How is he feeling? She hopes he's asleep and dreaming a good dream. Tirzah can't imagine Joseph whacking young Jesus about the head. Then she reminds herself: Of course, He was perfect, so it's not the same thing. The Son of God was never a guilty worm. But what trespass have she and Osian committed? Kissing couldn't possibly be a sin. And anyway, how would Mr Evans have known what happened in the attic? She lies back down, her body starting to relax as she warms up. She hears the front door slamming and then there is quiet downstairs. She thinks about the grown-up Osian she glimpsed this evening, realising he has even lost the salty boyish smell she always loved. She punches her pillow, hoping her parents won't want to have things out tonight. And tomorrow there will be ructions; she will be in trouble with everyone. Feeling scoured out inside, she is smitten with the knowledge that she is almost a grown-up too, and deliberately steers her thoughts from the way she returned Osian's kiss, imagining instead that she is drifting with open arms and closed eyes through the huge doorway of the castle of sleep.

The Lust of the Flesh, and the Lust of the Eyes

(1 John 2:16)

Tirzah has escaped to Biddy's house. They sprawl at opposite ends of the new chocolate-brown velour sofa Biddy's mother is so pleased with. Rain throws itself at the sash windows, rattling the frames, and a watery valleys' light coats the glass ornaments in the display cabinet with an unreal sheen. Listen to that old wind, Biddy says, hugging a cushion to her chest and nudging Tirzah with her foot. It's nice to hear it when we're inside, but doesn't part of you want to be out there? Tirzah nods. She likes to think about the mountain when there is a storm. She pictures the rooks being thrown around the sky, and the whinberry bushes shining with raindrops. The ragged sheep will be pushing against the low mossy wall that runs for miles around the edge of the forestry. They press so hard they leave blobs of grubby wool in the wall's crevices. It must be nice for them, sheltering beneath the eaves of the pine trees, nibbling tender spurts of greenery from the wall. The forest floor is dry even in the worst rain. She has sat on the dusty, needle-strewn ground deep in the woods and breathed its trapped, resin-rich smell. Not a single raindrop can get through the huge pine-umbrellas way up above. It's stifling and warm, silent and watchful, in amongst the endless straight trunks. A place no one could ever find you.

Tirzah thinks now of Biddy's back garden, and how much she loves it, even in the rain. Her own father concreted over the earth in theirs two summers ago, when the dandelions were bursting like mini explosions everywhere you looked. He'd been battling the weeds for as long as Tirzah could remember, glad of the chance to explain how God had quite rightly cursed nature since Eve deceived Adam. Mind you, he always liked to add, that Adam must have been a weak one. An apple? I mean. It would've been a very different story if yours truly had been on the scene. Really? A piece of fruit, and he caved in? Sin, sin, sin! he'd shout, making the word sound like something you coughed up, slicing at the ragged yellow heads with a blade he'd lashed to a broom handle. You see the wages of it, rampant all over the face of the earth! She remembers the way his shoulders hunched and his neck emerged from his shirt like the neck of a furious tortoise as he clutched the broom handle with its flashing blade. Every growing season he was the same.

Then one day, deep in summertime, he'd cut down all the plants: her mother's drooping raft of perfumed Albertine roses, the butterfly-sprigged lavender bushes along the path to the washing line, even the bright mint that spilled out of an old china sink. Tirzah and her mother stood at the kitchen window holding hands as he slashed the coloured heads off all the flowers. Let this be a lesson to you womenfolk, he yelled, striding over the mutilated, raspberry-hued London Pride that frothed up against the wall, and banging the window with his filthy knuckles. They could not hear him clearly, but Tirzah recalls the look of his mouth and the sweat on his forehead as he went on about women and their fleshy, indulgent ways. She could feel her mother's hand shaking. They'd stood and watched until the fire he'd built was under way, and all the dying plants were wreathed in smoke. When Tirzah came out later, the smouldering blossoms still smelt sweet.

Tirzah's eyes are closed, her cheek nestled against the fuzzy brown cushion as she thinks now about Biddy's long, thin back garden. She sees the warty old plum trees and the rhododendrons with their collapsed insides that used to make such good dens. Biddy's mother keeps a few chickens down at the far end, and if Tirzah is allowed, she comes round when the chickens put themselves to bed and listens while they settle and croon to each other. She likes to think that the cluck-ing sounds they make are questions: *Whaaat?* they ask with different levels of interest. *Whaaat? Whaaat?* The chickeny smell inside the roosting coop makes you want to sneeze, but it's inviting – dusty and mild, like the chickens themselves. Tirzah suddenly misses the fluty sound of pigeons and all the old plants and flowers that used to grow in her own garden. Biddy still has the tree house they played in when they were little. Tirzah remembers crouching up in the tree, surrounded by ripe plums abuzz with slow-motion bees. Thinking about it now gives her an uncomfortable tightening inside her chest that's both lonely and somehow thwarted. She looks sideways through her lashes at her cousin, wondering if she could explain her thoughts.

Biddy has been watching her. Come on, you, look alive, she says, smiling. First tell me about what's been going on these last ten days. Have you seen Osian? What happened? But Tirzah doesn't want to explain about him or his father, and how Pastor and two of the Horeb elders had come round and squirrelled themselves away in the study at the end of the upstairs hallway. The meeting went on for hours, it seemed to her. Sitting so silently and still in her bedroom, she had begun to feel as if she were solidifying, becoming more and more like the carved figure of a girl, something made of wood, whittled out of a huge lump. When she was called to the study, she could barely stand upright. It was as if she had to creakily unfold and wait for the blood to start flowing in her veins and arteries again before launching herself towards the door. Then she had listened to a talk about chastity, and purity, and how a girl must guard herself against temptation. That's rich, she thought hopelessly. *Osian kissed me. I didn't ask him to.* It wasn't something she could point out, though, so she waited until she could leave the room. An important point, brother, Pastor had said to her father as he left. *Spare the rod and spoil the child* – and this is something never so true as in your situation. He talked over her, as if she were a table. That girl is asking for trouble, going into a boy's house of an evening. She remembers the sound of the men's shoes as they stomped downstairs. She hadn't seen Osian once since then. He hadn't been to any chapel services. Was it horrible? Biddy asks. She squeezes Tirzah's hand. Anyway, Tizzy, never mind all that silly business. You're here now with me, and I've got a corker of an idea. Tirzah watches as Biddy leaps off the sofa and does a little dance on the crescent-shaped rug in front of the empty fireplace. Let's turn the television on.

Biddy's parents have rented a TV for what they have called *a test of faith.* Are you sure, though, Bid? Are you allowed?

Tirzah asks. Bum and celery, who cares? Biddy says, chewing her thumbnail hungrily. What's the point of having a telly if we can't watch the silly thing, I'd like to know. She puts her hands on Tirzah's shoulders and gives her another squeeze. *Robinson Crusoe* will be on, she says coaxingly. You love that book, don't you? Well, now it's a telly programme. Tirzah can't resist the idea of seeing Robinson. If this is a test of our faith, she says, we're the blackest goners. Oh, rubbish, Biddy states. Most people in the world have a telly and watch it until their eyes fall out. How can a book be safe to read, and the pro- gramme based on it be sinful? Your own parents bought you *Robinson Crusoe*, didn't they? Tirzah can see how this seems right. It doesn't make sense otherwise. Biddy switches the TV on, and they wait for it to warm up.

The girls sit side by side and hold hands. Look at the colour of my skin compared to yours, Biddy says, holding up her arm. Tirzah's skin is white, and dotted here and there with small freckles. Biddy's is creamy and without marks. I never noticed that before, Tirzah says. Our hair's the same colour, though. Biddy pulls the elastic from her ponytail and they put their hair together. You can't tell which is which, she says. Except that yours is thick and curly, and mine is soft and wavy. They weave their long hair together. I'm getting mine cut, Biddy states. Oh, please don't, Bid, Tirzah says. I like it that our hair's the same. Biddy contemplates her. I might not then, she answers. Anyway, the programme is starting, so let's concentrate. They settle down again. Tirzah is transfixed. Everything on the screen is almost as she imagined it. The music is dreamy and a little disturbing. They watch as Crusoe swims out to his ship's wreck and dives for supplies. He has difficulty in bringing the huge bundles ashore, and it looks at one point as if he'll drown in the waves, but no, he gets back to the beach and lies there in the shallows, gasping as the ship finally breaks apart and vanishes.

The girls are holding hands tightly, so intent on Robinson's ripped shirt and the way his belly hollows out below his ribs each time he gulps in air that they don't hear the sound of a key turning. They jump when the door bangs, then listen to Biddy's father striding down the hall. They both know it's too late to turn the TV off. Flipping flip, Biddy mutters. Now we're in for it. He stands in front of them, holding a bicycle clip, the other one still clamped round his trouser leg. Duw, Duw. I cannot believe what I am seeing with my own two eyes, he says quietly, pronouncing each word with extreme care. What do you both think you are doing? Running into the Devil's wide-open arms, that is what! Biddy starts to cry extravagantly. But, Dada, she says, sobbing, we wanted to see Robinson Crusoe so much. We love him. Biddy's father turns his attention to Tirzah. Is this gospel? he asks. Tirzah nods and says quietly, Yes, Uncle Maldwyn, but is unwilling to tear her eyes away from the glimpse of Robinson's bare legs climbing a tree. He is wonderfully nimble as he works his way up to the coconuts bunched high above him.

Uncle Maldwyn begins to walk up and down the carpet. Each turn seems to make him sadder. Love him? he asks. Love him? He sounds perplexed. What do you know about such things? He turns away for a moment and briskly strikes his forehead with the hand holding the bicycle clip. Tirzah is surprised by his reaction; he has always been much more easy-going than her own father. What can have happened to make him change? This television is not for little girls, he now declares, whipping round to face them again. Tirzah glances at Biddy. We're not that little, she thinks. I'm going to be seventeen in November. This machine, Uncle Maldwyn says, walking over to the TV and yanking out the plug, is like having the Evil One spewing out filth in the corner of the room. I see that now. The TV sparks and makes a hissing sound as the screen dies. Tirzah tries to look away, but her eyes are locked on the dead, grey rectangle. It is everything that is suggestive and lewd, Uncle Maldwyn says, his voice sinking briefly. His eyes are luminous with righteous anger. The world, the flesh and the Devil! he barks. That's what it represents!

Tirzah decides to make herself invisible. But it's difficult to concentrate on the process with Uncle talking so insistently. His big, pointing finger pins her to the room, making things impossible. Just as her feet start to dissolve he shakes her shoulder and tells her she is on a broad and slippery path. Don't think I haven't heard about your dirty work at Osian's. Such behaviour! In our own family! As if to underline what he's said, he adds that the whole fellowship is most concerned. Tirzah's mind stutters. What do people think I've been doing? she wonders. It's as if icy air were blowing through the room. He stands back and contemplates her. I blame you for persuading Biddy to turn the television on, he says. She is easily led. But Daddy, Biddy says, going to stand close to him, her loose hair swinging. Why can't we watch a nice little thing on the telly if we want to? He puts his finger to her lips. Now, he says, Tirzah, off home with you. It gives me no satisfaction, but I must tell your mam and dad. And Biddy. To your room, naughty, weak girl that you are.

Tirzah grabs her coat and darts out through the front door and around the side of the house to Biddy's garden gate. Once safe, she sinks on to the wet path and cries, remembering how

Biddy tried to stand up for them both, and the way the blank eye of the television stared as if it couldn't believe all the fuss. Raindrops flick her head and run quickly down her scalp. She blindly rises and follows the path until she's at the bottom of the garden. The chicken coop door is wedged shut, but she manages to open it and step inside. Immediately the chickens are alert, and shout *Whaaat? Whaaat?* with scared voices, the sound of flapping and grumbling rising to a crescendo. Tirzah stands amongst the flying dust until finally it is quiet. The simple, sharp smell of feathers and chicken droppings soothes her, and soon she's only hiccupping gently. She doesn't want to go home yet, so she makes a bed out of loose straw and settles down to rest.

When she's comfortable she runs over what happened. I can't seem to stop doing wrong things. Now I've been watching the Devil in the lounge, she thinks, and starts to sneeze. But she can't help remembering Robinson's wild mane. Even though it's a black and white TV, she knows his hair was blond, and his beautiful chest brown. Soon she is back on the island with him, smashing open coconuts for a meal. In the steamy jungle greenly lapping the sand behind them, she can hear tigers roar. His hair, a wheat-coloured halo, and hers, curly and auburn, are wreathed in flames as they sit either side of a blue-tongued fire. The sunset is all the shades of orange that ever were invented. She and Robinson smile at each other in the flickering, coppery light, slurping coconut milk. She can feel the creamy liquid running down her neck. Is that the world, the flesh and the Devil too? she wonders, hardly caring. In the feathery half-light, between sneezes, she hums the programme's theme tune until she is entirely calm.

Consider the Lilies of the Field, How They Grow

(Matthew 6:28)

On Easter Monday the whole family always gather at Tirzah's grandparents' house. This year the get-together falls at the beginning of April. Bampy has a huge garden that runs down the side of the mountain on the furthest outskirts of the village. Many years before, someone had cut large, flat areas for lawns, and made little pathways you could get lost in for hours. Some of the levels are vegetable gardens, some are for fruit. The toilet at her grandparents is outside, up a narrow, winding path behind the house. It has a green, wood-slatted door with a zigzag top edge. Small squares of the *South Wales Argus* are threaded through with a string and hang on a hook for you to use. Upstairs under the beds are fat china pots for weeing in at night. The girls have always loved having holidays with Gran and Bampy; they come at least twice in the long summer holiday. There are always picnics on the top lawn. Gran and Bamps have a curly-legged iron table and chairs up there, thick with paint. Tirzah remembers the tall dahlia beds that form a hedge all around the lawn by late summer, the flower heads like bursting maroon and amber stars. She thinks

23

about Gran's soap-smelling wash-house, and Queenie, the conservatory cat, who sleeps in a segment of sunshine on the ironing board when she can; every time of year is lovely there.

Once, when she was little, and she and Biddy were staying for a holiday, Biddy was practising her handstands on the top lawn. Tirzah had flung herself under the table. She remembers looking up through the curly pattern of the table top, noticing how the shining blue sky had separated itself into tiny scraps. The crushed grass smelt damp and peppery. The knotted blossoms studding the hollyhocks seemed to make the stems droop, and sieved by a breeze, sent drifts of fragrance on to her face. Then there was a crash and she felt something strike her head. When she woke, the garden was a different garden, the sky a different, unkind sort of sky. There was Biddy outstretched beside her, and nearby, the upturned table with its stiff legs splayed.

Tirzah thought she could hear a deep, rumbling growl coming from somewhere near. The tall plants bordering the lawn were scorched and smoking, and from their depths something started to rise, thrashing. Tirzah was unable to move. She lay, picturing her bleeding scalp like a sliced open cherry, and watched as up through the ruined foliage the Devil himself rose. Shaking his craggy, smoking head, he turned eyes like filthy puddles in Tirzah's direction, and she saw his scaly horns were wreathed with dried-up, blackened hollyhock flowers, and realised he was making the sound she had heard. Then, just as he reached for her with a scarlet claw, the growling stopped, Biddy woke and Gran came running. Tirzah clambered to her feet and pulled Biddy upright. Both girls darted across the lawn and crowded into Gran's arms. Handstands, was it? Come on now, up-a-dando, Gran said, eventually letting them go in order to straighten the tumbled furniture. Into the kitchen with you both. Let's bathe your cuts and bruises, and then ice cream is the best medicine.

But these days Tirzah isn't sure any of that Devil stuff really happened. She had been little, when that sort of thing is almost normal. After all, she used to believe her teddy would bite her in the night when she'd been naughty, so who knows? Today is the day of the family get-together, and Tirzah is preparing in her bedroom, only faintly concerned about those old times. She's picked a new outfit to wear from the black bin bag under the stairs; one of her mother's friends always gives them a sack of clothes when she visits, and she has daughters two or three years older than Tirzah. That one will be perfectly nice, her mother had said, busy with her own hair when Tirzah held up some things for approval. Stop being such a fusspot and put something tidy on. Tirzah watched her mother twist a thin hank of hair into a neat lump. Pass me those pins, she'd said, the comb between her lips. No one will be looking at you.

So here she is, pulling on a high-necked, thin, sleeveless jumper the colour of hazelnut shells. It's difficult to see the overall effect in her small mirror, but Tirzah is so amazed at how the fabric moulds itself to her body that a blush rolls up into her hair roots. This looks nice, she tells herself. I'm almost like one of those girls in sixth form. There is a long, narrow skirt with an irregular hem that seems to go with it, so she pulls that on too. The strange way she feels may have to do with the dark clothes they've had to wear leading up to Good Friday. It would have been wrong, she knows, to waltz about in gaudy things when the Saviour was going through his torture. For weeks they'd been singing the sad hymn *Wounded for Me, Wounded for Me*, and Tirzah was sucked into the horror of His pain each time someone started it up.

Now, all that was over for another year. There can't be anything actually sinful about clothes can there? she asks the wonderful Tirzah in the mirror. The outline of her body is startling. But still, there's something uncomfortable about this get-up; it's making her perspire. It's as if she were telling a story about herself, a not quite true one. She almost decides to take it all off, but the pretty, flouncing portions of herself she catches in the mirror stop her. I can just imagine poor old Mam and Dada having forty fits when they see me, she says out loud. Well, blow them. Suddenly feeling bold and grown-up, she decides to keep out of sight until the very moment it's time to go, then slip into the car without being seen. She shivers with excitement. Her outfit is to blame, she finally knows, for her beating heart and wet palms.

Her mother is using the rear-view mirror to peer at Tirzah. Why are you trussed up in that thick coat on such a lovely day, you daft girl? she asks. Tirzah looks out of the window. Answer your mother, her father says, busy manoeuvring the big old car out on to the main street. I'm cold, that's why, she finally manages to tell them, her lips like two slugs that want to go their own way. Are you sickening for something? her mother immediately asks, as Tirzah knew she would. No, Mam, I'm all right. Just a little chilly, she answers. Nesh, that's what you are, her father says with a smile in his voice. The familiar streets go by, but Tirzah's eyes are blurred by tears. She wishes now she'd worn some old, loose thing. These clothes were making her deceitful, and her neck is itching, wrapped around by the tall collar of the knitted top.

I need to get out, she gasps. It is a lovely day, as you said, Mama. So I want to walk. Her father slows the car and makes a big show of finding somewhere to park. You're not going to pander to her, are you, Gwyllim? her mother asks in a sharp voice. Stop the car, start the car. It's ridiculous. She wraps you round her little finger. Tirzah can't believe her ears. The idea of her father being wrapped around anything is a joke. Now, now. The exercise will do her good, he says. Off you go, child. Tirzah almost falls from the car door, she is so eager to get outside. They are gone before she composes herself. The spring sunshine hits her heavily. It's as if someone has brought a heavy book down on her head; she can hardly stand for a moment. The wool coat is smothering her. She takes it off and sinks down on the low wall outside the Co-op. She is torn between the need to get going to her grandparents and the desire to return home and change.

It takes much longer to get there than she remembered it would. All the way she hums the *Wounded* hymn, even though she doesn't want to. Primroses cluster frothily in the verges, and across the fields, where the woods begin, she thinks she can just make out the faintest tinges of green, caught like smoke around the trees' heads. Over the crumbling walls along the lane the catkins shake knobbly inch-long ropes. There are stands of fat pussy willows keeping pace with her, their oval blobs covered with velvety yellow dust. I should be happy, she tells herself, but she has an unshakeable awareness that she will be sorry soon. Her coat is like a sack of coal; she has to shift it from arm to arm. Then, as always, the door appears suddenly in the high garden wall, sooner than you think. There is not even the smallest clue from outside what the garden looks like. Tirzah can hear voices calling, and laughter. The doorknob is stiff, and she has to put her coat down on the road to use both hands. She has difficulty gathering it back up; her arms feel boneless. And then she is inside, looking down the path through the forsythia to where they are all gathered at a long table on the top lawn. Here she is, shouts Biddy, and everyone turns.

The laughter and talk dies, and Tirzah stands transfixed by the pairs of eyes looking at her new clothes. The tightly budded cones of the lilac blossoms are like sickly gas flares behind the double row of seated relatives, and for a moment Tirzah remembers the old Devil she saw amongst the summer hollyhocks. Then a murmur starts, and her grandmother comes rushing towards her like before, but this time with a beaded, half-empty jug of lemonade. Tizzy, my little dwt, she exclaims, smiling. I was getting worried about you. Tirzah's nerves loosen at last, and she runs to hug her gran. She pretends they are alone. Can I give you a hand? she asks, taking the jug. Together they walk into the house, and Tirzah gratefully breathes in the welcoming smell of stored apples and dried lavender. Gran, what do you think of my get-up? she asks, throwing her coat on a chair. Her grandmother turns from the kitchen table, still holding her buttering knife, a large loaf of bread like a sleeping piglet under her arm. Well, she says, her head to one side. I think you look smashing. You've got a lovely little figure on you. But I don't know what the daft old fellowship will say. Horeb indeed. I'd Horeb the lot of them if I had the chance. They smile at each other. Well, I know what Pastor would say, Tirzah says, and Mam and Dada.

To Tirzah, the kitchen momentarily gets smaller and quieter, almost as if it's a little spaceship out on the darkest reaches of the universe. That would be perfect, she thinks. Just me and

Granny hurtling through space in a kitchen. Never you mind, love, Gran says. Come by here and sit down. You look white as a ghost. I'll make you a little mouthful of something. Then you'll feel the ticket. Tirzah sits at the table and watches as her grandmother holds the loaf close, slathers on an even layer of softened butter and deftly saws a thin slice of bread towards her chest with an old bone-handled knife. She then uses the knife's flat side to transfer the slice to a plate. As she quickly does another, she asks Tirzah what she would like inside. I don't mind, Tirzah says, distracted by the sandwich making. Just some lettuce and cucumber. Tirzah realises that the space-kitchen would be no good. No Osian, she thinks. No Biddy, no woods and, especially, no wild and windy mountain. When the sandwich is made, Gran cuts it into four squares and hands the plate to Tirzah. Eat up now, she urges, patting Tirzah on the cheek. This is lovely, Tirzah says between mouthfuls. Are these from your garden? The bread is fresh, and the salad things crispy. Not the cuke, Gran says. It's too early in the year for them. But those lettuces are your bampy's first ones. Very small, mind, but good and juicy. Folk don't realise the nourishment a nice lettuce can give. Tirzah finishes her snack. Just time for a cup of tea for us, I think, Gran says. Then we'll put our coats on and go out to face the music. We're rushing the season this year, having our party in the garden.

Before they have begun their drinks, Tirzah's father appears in the doorway. Now, Gwyllim, Gran says, what's on your mind? It's only natural she wants to look nice, for goodness' sake. This is my business, he says, gesturing for Tirzah to get up. We must have a little talk, I think. He pushes her across the kitchen and into the front room. It's no good you gawping at your grandmother, he goes on, when she cranes her neck to look back. She is an unredeemable heathen. Her gran laughs softly. Still, we love her to bits, and put her on the altar of prayer, he adds, closing the door. He ushers Tirzah to a position in front of the empty fireplace. But there's nothing to be done about your grandmother, and that's the way she likes it, he continues. Tirzah is so aware of the spectacled eyes looking at her troublesome clothes from the old family photographs on the mantelpiece that it seems as if they will catch fire and burn away, leaving her naked. Her father settles himself on the sofa, studying his clasped hands for a moment. Enough about your grandmother, he says. Now. What have you got to say for yourself? He pins her to the rug with a look. Your mother and I are at our wits' end with you. If it's not the television, it's something with a boy. And now look. He makes a gesture with his hands towards her clothes that somehow implies disgust and rejection. He leans forward, making her flinch. I fear for your immortal soul, child, I really do.

Tirzah's lips are stuck together. She stares at the piano behind her father, and tries to read the title of the piece of music on the stand. When she struggles to find words to express her innocence nothing will come out of her mouth but a stupid sound. *Consider the lilies*, her father starts. This is crucial for you to learn. Do you understand me? Tirzah is confused. What have flowers got to do with anything? she wonders, guessing it must be to do with her unsuitable clothes. Solomon in all his glory was not arrayed as one of those flowers, he adds. Tirzah, the Evil One desires your very soul. You do not need to outwardly adorn yourself. And certainly you do not need to show the world the secrets of your fallen body. Cultivate a beauty of the heart, child. An inner, untouched beauty. He struggles up off the sofa as if he'd doubled in weight, and pats her shoulder. That's true about the Devil, Tirzah has to admit, still standing on the rug as he leaves. And she recalls Satan's eyes, dirty yet colourless, utterly devoid of pity, turned on her in the long-ago garden, his claw outstretched. The Devil beckoned me near this very place, she has to admit. Yes, Dada, she calls to the closing door. I will consider more from now on.

So Will the Anger of the Lord
Be Kindled Against Thee

(Deuteronomy 7:4)

The morning after her telling off, Tirzah stuffs the sinful skirt and top back into the bag under the stairs, averting her eyes as she does so. On go her old, pure clothes. Then she goes shopping for her mother. Outside the Co-op, an unfamiliar boy is hanging about with a group of much younger children. She is curious. He looks so much bigger and stronger than any boy she knows; even Osian is small beside him. The way he holds himself is emphatic, but at the same time he is restless, looking around constantly, as if he has to be ready for anything. The name's Brân, he tells her. And these are my Braves. He's carrying a stick, big as a spear. The boys are scruffy, and they seem to think Brân's great. As she rummages for sweets, Tirzah drops her string shopping bag and the little boys run around gathering up scattered potatoes, pushing each other out of the way to get them first. Thank you, Braves, Tirzah says, and the boys snigger, shuffling their feet and darting glances at Brân, who stands well back from the action. Who'd like a sweet? Tirzah asks, and the boys start hopping around, hands jerking up as if on wires, shouting, Me! Me! Me! Brân steps forward. You lot, he yells, frowning and banging the end of his spear on the ground, get your arses into line! The boys all run to surround him. I'll get you hundreds of sweets next time I see you. Now bugger off.

Brân is much taller than Tirzah, and he smells strange, both musky and blackcurrant-sharp. I'm their boss, he says, looking after his gang as they each run for home. Where do you live? Tirzah asks. Who wants to know? he says, shoving his hands in his pockets. Well, I do. Tirzah. That's me, she answers, offering her bag of sweets. He pulls out a clump of honeycomb and chucks it in his mouth, biting furiously and snapping his head back like a dog. Tirzah realises he's starving. Do you want to come to tea? she asks him. Fuck off, he shouts, making her blink. Why should I want to come to your 'ouse? You'm one of them religious nuts. Think you're better than everybody else, don't you? Tirzah doesn't have an answer but almost laughs, it is so far from the way she feels. Anyway, I have to scarper, he says, studying her face, calmer now. See you, Tirzah calls as he jogs down the street in his broken shoes, only now wondering what her mother would have said if she had brought him to tea.

Brân is on Tirzah's mind all week. When she says her prayers, most of them are for him. She remembers his ripped jumper and the way his famished-looking Adam's apple stuck out. He's like nobody's child, she thinks, wondering who his family are. When she asks Biddy, she finds out that he is always running away from home. And he's never in school. His dad's a drinker, she explains. And his mam is always going off somewhere. Tirzah is sure Brân doesn't believe in God. She knows it's her job to tell him he's a sinner, and that the anger of the Lord could fall on his head at any time. Or, she thinks, I should at least get him to chapel. When she next sees him, he's alone, sitting on the Co-op wall, wiping his nose on a ragged sleeve. Tirzah tells him about the Sunday evening service, and how he'd be welcome. Push off, he says. Welcome in chapel? You gorra be joking. But she can tell he's not angry. Anyway, maybe we'll see you, she says, handing him the cheese and potato pasty wrapped in greaseproof her mother had given her for a snack. Tirzah's chest becomes tight and painful, looking at Brân. I have to go now, she says. When she glances back, he has already eaten the pasty and is licking the paper.

On Sunday, Pastor preaches a sermon about biblical curses. Do not be hazy about this, dear brothers and sisters, boys and girls, he says, resting one elbow on the pulpit and leaning forward the better to look each member of the congregation in the eye. The Old Testament is just as relevant to us here in the year of Our Blessed Lord 1972 as it ever was. More so, I would suggest. Everyone starts tuning up: Amen, they say, amen, verily, Lord. Tirzah shrinks down in the pew between her parents. She doesn't like the sound of these curses. One of them is sure to apply to her. She sucks a Polo mint earnestly, looking at her clasped hands. Why does there have to be so much cursing, and being sorry, in everything Pastor preaches? And does the very fact she is daring to question things make her a wicked girl?

I'll confess all my sins, she decides, then I'll be safe. She runs through her secrets, sure God will understand her need for them at present. It can't possibly be wrong to befriend a lost boy and try to help him. After all, she's only doing her duty, following Jesus's words. But you never know. When she finishes praying, Pastor is reading from Deuteronomy, and really getting into the spirit. *Cursed be thou in the city, and cursed be thou in the field*, he booms at the now silent congregation. *If thou will not hearken unto the voice of the Lord thy God, these curses shall come upon thee*. Let us restrain ourselves, dear ones, from wishy-washy thinking, he shouts, waving the massive Bible above his head. Curses! No less. Curses will be upon you. Then he slams the Bible down on the pulpit. Tirzah's body is changing, becoming more and more brittle with fear, and she tries to push her hand through the crook of her mother's arm, but it's rigid. She glances up at her mother's face. Under the brim of her hat she looks terrified too. It's as if no one has a place to hide.

Out in the graveyard, Tirzah takes a gravestone near to the one Osian is perched on. Hello, she says. Are you all right? You haven't been to chapel for a while. Osian smiles without looking at her. Been to my aunty's for a bit, he states. Over by the chapel doors, both their sets of parents are talking to Pastor. Tirzah can sense the space between her and Osian stretching. They are not supposed to talk to each other since the attic episode. Tirzah's shoulders are weighed down by a feeling of precariousness. It's as if, at any moment, God could puncture the fragile blue fabric of the sky and point with a shining finger, cursing her for having a hardened, trespassing heart. She is exposed, but knows that even if a person went to the centre of the earth, the Lord would be able to see them. There is nowhere to run. Tirzah imagines burrowing deep under a huge rock and the Lord hooking her out as if she were a grub. Then, with a jolt, she remembers Brân. His heart must be riddled with sin, she thinks. And he doesn't even understand what a curse is, except for swearing curses.

But how can God blame him if he has never heard the Good News? It doesn't sound fair. She lowers her head so her hair obscures her face and asks Osian if he knows Brân. Be careful with that one, he says, still looking ahead and hardly moving his lips. He's a wrong'un. But, Osian, she says, what shall we do? We're all wrong'uns, aren't we? Osian seems so far away, sat beside her. Dunno, he answers, gazing up at the sky. But that Brân will definitely come to no good.

Tirzah wants to continue talking, but Osian moves quickly to pick a celandine and places it under Tirzah's chin. It behaves like a little golden lamp against her pale throat. More to the point, do you like butter? he asks, studying her serious face. He bounces the celandine gently on both her anxious eyes. What are you doing? she asks, darting a look towards the chapel door. Relax, Osian says. If God made today, He must want us to enjoy it. And anyway, you and I have nothing to be ashamed of. You know I'm talking sense. Stop it, she whispers, glancing over at her parents again. Don't worry, they're deep in some doctrinal discussion, Osian tells her. Or arguing about us. They won't notice a thing. But don't you care about the curses, Osh? Tirzah asks, remembering the Bible's decisive bang. Maybe, he answers, turning his face to the sun again. He doesn't mean it, Lord, Tirzah thinks, sending up an arrow of prayer. She wants to cry, everything is so difficult. And Sunday will roll on, with over-cooked dinner and rice pudding that's either crunchy or solid, then Sunday School, where she teaches a class of tiny girls who won't sit still, and are constantly putting up their hands to go to the toilet. Sometimes she looks into their sweet, inattentive eyes and wonders if they understand a word she says. Then there will be evening service, and later, after-church meeting in the front room of someone's house. They are almost certain to be offered fig rolls. From the gravestone she can see the shape of the forestry spread dark and dense along the side of the mountain. I'd love to be there now, Osian. How about you? she asks, immediately realising she wouldn't want him with her. Osian shades his eyes and gazes at the mountain. More than anything, he answers.

Thou Shalt Not Make Unto Thee
Any Graven Image

(Deuteronomy 5:8)

The following weekend, Biddy and Tirzah are trying to think of something to do. It's late Saturday morning, and they both know that if they're seen looking idle they will be roped in to help with more chores. Biddy has already swept out the chicken coop and cleaned her room. Tirzah flicked a duster over her mother's ornaments and polished all the Sunday shoes. So they hide in Biddy's tree house, both having to struggle now to get through the opening. I don't think this old platform is going to hold out much longer, Tirzah says, deliberately wobbling the wooden floor. Through the glassless windows clumps of just-open plum blossom obscure them from sight. Biddy sniffs deeply. Smell it, she says, shutting her eyes. The girls breathe with concentration. There's pretty, Tirzah says. It's a pink smell, like spicy sweets, that you feel you will never get enough of. Someone is walking under the trees. Shhh, Tirzah whispers, and they crouch, peering down through the gaps in the floorboards to the masses of flowers. Biddy's mother is going to collect eggs from her chickens.

They glimpse the top of her head with its sideways-drifting bun. Then she's gone. Quick you, Tirzah says, pulling Biddy's arm. Let's get going. They swiftly climb down the ladder and dash up the path and out through the garden gate. That was a close one, Biddy says, as they lean briefly against the house. I thought we'd had our chips.

They decide to pick bluebells for everybody. We'll get sandwiches or something from my mam, Tirzah says. She always thinks getting flowers for people is God's work. Tirzah's mother is at the kitchen table when they go in, doing her morning Bible reading. I'm all behind today, she tells them, wiping her eyes with a balled-up hankie. We won't tell, will we, Bid? Tirzah asks. Biddy shakes her head. Well, I really don't know where the morning went, her mother adds, closing her Bible. I only know I have been dancing in the Spirit. Caught up, I was. The girls exchange a look. Can we have some grub, Mam? Tirzah asks. We're going to pick bluebells for everybody. Oh, lovely, her mother answers, pushing her hair back up into the headscarf she wears knotted over her front section of curlers. Bluebells and wood anemones, my favourites. Then she adds: And less of the *grub*, please. Who are we? Heathen? But Tirzah can tell she's in a good mood, her voice is so mild. Mind, she goes on, you'll be lucky. I doubt the bluebells will be out yet. Still, it's unseasonably warm, so you might find some. I loved the bluebell woods when I was a girl, she tells them, moving to the window and staring out at the concrete. I used to go there with my friends, long ago now, it seems. Many happy hours I spent. Mam! Tirzah has to say to get her attention. Hark at me, her mother laughs, looking surprised. Now, where were we? Sandwiches, Mam, Tirzah tells her. Right you are, her mother says briskly. A little something for two growing young ladies.

Quickly she slices cheese and butters bread. I want salad cream in mine, Tirzah tells her. And me, please, Biddy adds. Her mother has finished making their picnic before Tirzah gets back with the greaseproof paper. You are quick, Mam, Tirzah says. Yes, well, I don't hang around, her mother answers, wiping her hands on her apron. And this won't do at all. I must get on with my chores. She disappears into the pantry. Tirzah concentrates on making the sandwiches into firm parcels. Now then, here's a treat, her mother tells them, coming out with the old Quality Street tin. She opens it and they look in. The tin is full of fairy cakes, their sugar-dusted sponge wings perched on dabs of buttercream. The girls sniff the metallic, vanilla-laden smell. The blonde cakes with their weeping crowns of red jam look almost too good to eat. One each, Tirzah's mother says, wrapping them up. Yesterday's, but still nice, I think you'll find. Now off you go, out from under my feet. Tirzah kisses her mother, and then dilutes squash into her dimpled plastic bottle, slinging it over her shoulder from the red strap. Biddy picks up the sandwiches and puts them in her bag. I'll carry the cakes, Tirzah says.

Soon the girls are out of the village and over the low wall that runs along the lane. The bluebell woods are way across the fields. They walk through clumps of thistles tall as they are. In amongst them, sheep bend their necks to the tussocky grass. The sheep droppings look like someone has strewn oversized currants everywhere. The fields go on and on, separated by stony walls they clamber over, but eventually they push through the undergrowth that borders the farthest end, until they can stand on a kind of long, wide ledge where holly and nameless small trees grow. They gaze up at the sun-speckled beech-bud canopy. At first, everything is as it always has been each year they come. There is the stream far below, and the beech trees that seem to be striding down to drink. But all around, the bluebells that they hoped would spread and flow across the hill, lapping the bases of the beech trees and running on in huge lakes of an almost purple colour, are still stiff-tipped and tightly sheathed.

The girls are transfixed for a few moments, adjusting their expectation of dazzling blue. Tirzah remembers her mother's face when she recalled the bluebell woods, and wishes she'd listened instead of rushing her to make the picnic. Come on, dozy, Biddy shouts, and they start to search for the odd, squeaking, blue-crowned stem amongst the glossy leaves. It doesn't take long before they each have a little bunch of blooms, the root tips shining whitely. Let's lay them down and go exploring, Tirzah says. But we'll take our dinner. They decide to visit the stream. As they run through the silent trees they hear sounds of shouting, and stop to listen. Who can that be? Biddy asks, raising her eyebrows and grabbing Tirzah's arm. They wade through the sleeping bluebells and ground ivy towards the sounds, trying to be as quiet as possible. Then they hear a scream, and over it, one voice yelling the same phrase repeatedly.

Look, Tirzah whispers, tugging Biddy's dress. There is a group of small boys kneeling on the bank around a deep pool in the stream. Tirzah can see that Brân is up to his waist in the water and he's bending over, struggling with something that's putting up quite a fight below the surface. The watching little boys are frozen. Brân is shouting, but she doesn't understand what he's saying. His face is contorted, his eyes staring and blank. Tirzah realises with a jolt of fear that the thing struggling beneath the water is a boy. She and Biddy hold each other tight. The beautiful woods have changed; the air seems to move with invisible things; the plants around their shoes coil and uncoil; along each branch mean creatures creep, ready to drop like hanks of rope.

As they watch, Brân pulls the boy up and heaves him on to the bank, where he lies motionless like a heap of wet washing. Brân pokes with his foot, and the heap begins to move. Then another boy comes shakily forward. There is a kind of stone altar on the far bank of the stream, topped by a roughly carved wooden head with what looks like a sharp beak. On a flat slab in front of the head sits a bloody bundle. Tirzah's heart is jumping inside her ribs, and her mouth is drenched with a thin, acidic fluid, but she pulls away from Biddy and moves forward, stumbling, until Brân notices her. She is light-headed and has to force herself to speak. Whatever are you up to, Brân? she calls. Is that a graven image? Brân turns and the boys all move in around him. We are worshippin' the Devil, he shouts, his chest heaving. And havin' a baptism. That's what we're up to. And all the boys join in a wavering cheer. Tirzah is suddenly so cold she will shatter if anyone touches her. As she looks at Brân she sees his soul, like a plastic carrier bag filled with air, escaping from the folds of his bundled-up chest. No! she screams. Stop! And the white bag swiftly collapses, tucking itself away again.

There is a long moment when Brân and Tirzah continue to gaze across the green space between them, and then Brân raises his spear as if to throw it. Tirzah feels as if he has struck her. The sensation in her chest is so intense that for a split second she can't breathe. But then she leaps back and away, and hears Biddy gasp behind her as she drops her bag. They run back up the long bank, weaving through the beech trees, until at last they stumble on to the ledge and fall through the holly bushes, out into the scrubby, sheep-smelling field. Full pelt they still go, weaving through the spiky thistles, scattering the sheep, over the walls, until they arrive back where they began. Only then do they stop, throwing themselves down to rest against the lane's boundary, with its warm, lichened stones. Biddy is still sobbing, but Tirzah is beyond tears; the place where her heart should be is strangely vacant. She can't forget Brân's face as he held the boy under the water, or his altar with the blood-soaked bundle. It is as if the sun-filled, blossom-strewn world she thought was true had split open, and there, wreathed in smoke, grinning at her again over its rim, was the curly-horned, scarlet Devil himself.

Biddy takes the battered package of cake Tirzah has been clutching in her hand all this time. Look, she says, gulping, your mam's nice fairy cakes are crushed. They look at the damaged cakes, amazed to see something so normal and blessed. Then they gather sweet crumbs between their fingers and eat them hungrily, enjoying the melting buttercream and tart jam. It's hard to imagine her mother's kitchen, and ordinary things like fairy cakes and orange squash, being part of the same world as the dark chaos of the scene in the woods. And that's just our village, Tirzah thinks. It makes her wonder about the rows of houses all around her own home. What horrible things might be happening inside them? And what about the wide world? Tirzah dusts her hands off and wipes her mouth. Dammo, Biddy says. After all that, we've gone and left our bluebells behind. Who cares about them?

Tirzah answers. Let's pray for Brân and his gang. And for the whole world. But once she's bowed her head she can't think of a single word to say.

Put Away Thine Abominations out of My Sight

(Jeremiah 4:1)

Pastor has moved on from curses, and is now preaching a series of sermons on God's judgements, and what the consequences of these judgements are. On Sunday morning in Horeb he has been talking about God's judgement on mankind generally. One of the ways God's displeasure manifests itself, he says, is by sickness and mishaps of birth. These are all what the Bible calls *abominations*. Tirzah trips up on the idea of babies; it all sounds wrong. Surely, she thinks in her pew, discreetly plaiting and unplaiting a springy hank of hair, dwty, dribbly, darling babies can't have done anything wrong yet? Why should the sweet things be punished? And how cruel to make them blind or deformed? If God really acts this way, maybe He isn't the God of Love people say He is. Pastor, of course, has the answer: Original sin, beloveds, he repeatedly states. It's as if he wants to bash home this truth to the fellowship. Original sin! he shouts. Original sin!

Tirzah begins to feel headachy, and each time he shouts the phrase a nail of pain jabs her forehead. No one, apart from our Lord Jesus, comes into this sad world pure, dear

45

fallen friends, Pastor sums up, pulling a hankie out to wipe his mouth. Each and every one of us is tainted by the Fall. Eve tempted Adam, and there you have it. We were abominations in our mothers' wombs, and our mothers were fallen. Tirzah's father is agreeing wholeheartedly with what Pastor is saying about everything being women's fault. Amen, he says loudly, nudging his wife. Verily, Pastor concludes, I say unto you: all around we see the abominable, just deserts. Well, it's fine and dandy for Pastor, Tirzah thinks. He can preach about original sin until his head falls off. Surely everyone knows he's holy. The rest of us, though. If we are teeming with sin even before we are born, because of being human, what chance have we got? And if you're a woman, it seems you're even more to blame. Her headache gets worse, just trying to work it out.

Tirzah's parents disagree with these judgements, and have spent Sunday afternoon discussing the issue. Tirzah is not asked for an opinion, but she agrees more with her mother. In the kitchen, she goes back and forth to the dining room, carrying first a plate of bread and butter and then the cut-glass bowl of amber pickled onions. Her mother is boiling the kettle and buttering scones. The caramel-rich smell of a baking tart fills the warm room. Now then, her mother says, vigorously buttering, chwarae teg, Gwyllim. I will not dignify the argument about fallen women by discussing it. But surely our God is a just God. Babies indeed! So it's their own dear fault they may not walk, or see, or speak? And then only some? The rest get off free? That's not my God, I can tell you now. Tirzah's father makes the throaty, growling sound that means they all have to look out, but her mother carries on, waving the butter knife. Think of Mrs Taylor's beautiful babba, with her eyes like forget-me-nots, she says.

I could eat that child in lumps. Just think, Gwyll. Finally, her father loses his temper. Silence, he shouts, red-faced. I am the head of this house. And I say God's ways are above our ways. Enough! Now do your job and turn the gas off under that damned kettle.

The three of them sit down to Sunday afternoon tea. Her father has apologised for cursing, though it's obvious he blames his wife. Out in the street, children are playing football and hop-scotch. Tirzah wishes she were younger and still played games outside. She wishes she were someone else's child, allowed to do such things on a Sunday. She wishes her parents said *damn* more often. And *bloody*, and *sod*. Her mother has been crying, but still briskly eats a tinned half-peach coated in evaporated milk with a tiny spoon, her mouth opening only slightly for each lacquered orange chunk. Now and then she dips a folded piece of bread and butter fussily into the clouded syrup in her bowl and takes a nibble. Tirzah knows exactly what she is expressing by eating a huge and lengthy meal. It is exactly what Tirzah would do: *See how much I care. I am not even put off my food. This is because I am right.* The clock on the dresser ticks unevenly, and her father, peach untouched, sips from a cup too small for his hands, elbows on the table.

There is a thud on the window, and he rushes out to the front door, spilling tea on the white tablecloth. Tirzah can hear him yelling at the children. He's confiscated their ball again. Be off with you! he shouts. Haven't you got homes to go to? This is the Lord's Day! Tirzah and her mother exchange looks. Tirzah knows all the little kids, and pictures their terrified faces. The shouting from the front door continues. Can I have some apple tart, Mam? she asks. It looks delicious. First eat some bread and butter, her mother says, and a nice slice of this tongue. And a couple of Bampy's spring onions. Then, after, it's tart for you, how's that? Tirzah hates tinned tongue, its spongy, cream and maroon speckledness. The smell of death coming from it. Especially its fatty, granular texture. Even the shape of each slice – an oblong with one squashed-in end – is horrible. Who thought up tongue and spring onions? Ugh, she says, involuntarily. No need for rudeness, her mother comments. Never will I allow another slice of tongue into my mouth, Tirzah vows silently, looking down at her clasped hands. A dead creature's tongue being licked by her own tongue, in her own mouth? It's not right.

Picking up the dinky brass prong, she spears a pickled onion and pops it whole into her mouth. Then she crunches, sending a jet of scalding malt vinegar juice down her throat, and starts to cough. You are a silly, cariad, her mother says, now calmly chewing. Have a mouthful of tea. The vinegary fumes of the onion make Tirzah weep. She wipes her eyes with a napkin. It's almost as if she's crying for all the poor deformed babies in the world. Before her father comes back she speaks to her mother. If God cares about every sparrow that falls, Mam, how can He do such things? she whispers, throat burning. Exactly, her mother says, pushing away her empty bowl. But shush, now, and she nods towards the opening door.

In prayer meeting on Tuesday night the brothers and sisters sit in their usual circle. Tirzah calculates how much longer prayer time will go on. There are another four people who might pray. Her father is doing his little hums and coughs. Soon he will tune up. Fifteen minutes, she decides, if only one pair pray. And another twenty if Osian's father starts. She sneaks a look at Osian. He is leaning forward, head in hands. He had smiled at her earlier, when they were listening to

Pastor's talk. Now, to pass the time, she looks at the various footwear people have on. Osian wears his brown lace-ups and looks very neat, but as it's an unusually warm spring evening, several folk are wearing sandals. Oh, never, she thinks, gazing at Mrs White's naked, tortured toes. How can people show them? Don't they realise how disgusting they are? The old weather-beaten twin brothers who always sit side by side are wearing ancient sandals. They are farmers, and mostly silent in meetings. Tirzah is amazed at the length of their toes: each brown foot is a long, wooden hand, the toes like thin, clutching, muscular fingers. Each horny nail is grey and yellow. It's as if someone has thumped them with a hammer.

When she has surveyed the whole group, her eyes finally rest on Pastor's exposed feet. She's amazed he is wearing sandals. It's a rare occurrence. Idly looking at his off-white toes, suddenly she is rigid. He has six on each foot. She counts again, just to be sure. The toes are chubby, and splayed out so that the last-but-one and the pinky toes fall off the side of his sandals. Each big toe isn't big – it's almost the same size as the others. Then she studies his prayerful face, and thinks about last Sunday's sermon. It's like being granted a vision. Everyone is here with their eyes tightly closed. Behold! she wants to declare to them. Don't feel too bad about yourselves. Verily I say unto you, Pastor is an abomination! But what does it mean, she wonders, that he is here, showing himself to the fellowship, and only she can see?

A Brand Plucked out of the Fire

(Zechariah 3:2)

Now that spring has really arrived, the mountainside is interrupted all across its length by fresh growth. In spaces between the huge, battered gorse bushes, ferns emerge like verdant scribbles and push up and out, each frondy arm stretching sideways for room as it climbs higher every day. Osian passed a note to Tirzah in chapel, saying he wanted to see her, and they have slipped secretly away. Ever since the kiss in the attic, Tirzah has been confused about Osian, needing to speak to him, and yet unsure what she would say. They see each other, of course, in all the meetings. But as they're supposed to have no communication, they don't have much chance to talk. Tirzah is nervous on the climb towards the mountain, and not sure why. I know, she realises with a jolt. I'm actually afraid to speak to Osian, that's what it is. Behind this fear is another she doesn't want to admit to herself. I am afraid of myself, she thinks. Of another, unknown version of myself. I didn't know that girl in the attic who, just for a moment, enjoyed the pressure of Osian's lips and the taste of him. She is walking quickly, looking straight ahead. And which Osian is he now? She hates the way things are these days. I never used to worry about Osian or myself before, she thinks, baffled.

They have come up a steep lane, its walls bulging every now and then where ancient yews grow. One yew in particular has always been a stopping point. When they were children, they could climb up behind it, using the trunk's fat warts as footholds, and get right into its crown. They loved perching on the hairy branches, entirely invisible to anyone on the lane below. As they pass today they smile, remembering. Higher, there is a spot that's perfect to sit and have a breather. Behind them, a line of wizened hawthorns wave their tattered blossoms, and beyond the trees the mountain sleepily rests, its top obscured by a long, swelling shoulder of bracken and boulders. The air is warm, and so full of the scent of growing things it feels damp. Osian lies back and rests his head on one folded arm. Come by here, you, he says, and with the other arm pulls Tirzah close to him. She stiffly lays her head on his chest and allows his breathing to rock her slightly. Up above, the smallest clouds meander against the polished blue sky. Everything is as ravishing as it can possibly be, and Tirzah's fears have quietened; now that she can look at Osian and be near him, he seems normal. Are you getting a job soon? she asks, thinking about how Biddy is already doing a paper round. Osian sighs. I've got to help Dad in the shop. Sweeping up and filling shelves. He's found me a bike for making grocery deliveries. What I really want to do is come here every day, he says. We could build ourselves a proper, tidy little place. There's plenty of wood around.

Tirzah sits up. I don't think that would be a good idea, Osian, she says. I do, he answers, his eyes eager and smiling.

We're like two homeless waifs. With nowhere to call our own. Sad, it is. He laughs, and pulls her down again. But we can call each other our own, he adds. You are mine own, Tirzah. Their faces are close, and they look into each other's eyes. Tirzah is turning stiff, as if she were made of cooling glass. How can she stop Osian without shattering herself into sharp pieces that will hurt them both? Now I think we should kiss, he says, and does just that. The kiss is long, and Tirzah's body relaxes despite herself. Soon she is loose and alive like the wind in the beech tops, and wants to wrap her arms and legs around Osian, squeezing him hard until something happens. Opening her eyes she sees the dark hair swept back from his smooth forehead, and the way his eyelids are softly closed, silky and boyish, as if he were asleep, and she pushes him firmly away. Breathless and exhausted, her head completely empty, she only knows she doesn't want to kiss him any more.

She gets up and steps over him, taking in huge mouthfuls of grassy air. I'm sorry, she calls back, moving away. I'm sorry. But all around her lovely things are happening and she is impatient to look at them. Here are the armies of furry, half-grown foxglove spears, with their tight bunches of purple buds, and amongst the bracken, old, scrambling ropes of scarlet pimpernel she can follow. Osian doesn't move, his body flat in the coarse grass. Tirzah wanders to where the cowslips stand sturdily, each flower alone in the turf. She folds her arms across her body, gazing at the oak wood below, and listens to the scream of some small creature unseen in its depths, unsure what to do next. Suddenly it feels as if they should go; imperceptibly the sun has been rolling down the mountainside, kicking up shadows, changing the atmosphere, leaching colour from the sky. Come on, you, she calls, brushing herself down. Home time! Shift your stumps!

Tirzah bends to snap off a few cowslips, even though she knows they will not survive the walk home. I'll take these to press in our Bibles, she decides. Then it isn't so wrong, picking them. She is relieved that Osian doesn't seem upset with her. They take another route home, through the pinewoods, following the man-made road the forestry vehicles use. It is almost completely silent, except for the occasional creaking branch. Once or twice the sound of small scampering feet or the cronk of a crow makes them jump closer. They begin to get the idea they are being watched. This is always the mountain's way, they know; it has its own life, after all, quite apart from people. Something can happen that sends you screaming and running in different directions. This is when you might find you are suddenly alone if you're not careful, and fall, wounding yourself. Tirzah and Osian hold hands, soberly walking. Do you feel as if you daren't turn around? Tirzah asks. Osian squeezes her fingers. Yes, he answers. Let's keep going just the way we are. Everything will be all right. So Tirzah masters the desire to pelt down the tree-stalked road and out into the world of streets and chemists and chip shops, ice-cream vans and women in head squares shopping for veg.

They come towards the long bend in the road. There is a flat area of rough, stone-strewn ground that opens out in a crescent shape where the forestry lorries turn. This ground rises sharply when it reaches the steep, rocky face of the mountainside. The first foxgloves sit in amongst the creases of the rocks, but nothing else. As they walk on, they detect a strange sound ahead. It is so out of place they don't recognise it at first. Osian stops, and looks at Tirzah, but there is really nothing to be done; the forest is to one side, falling steeply away, and the sheer mountain wall to the other. It's too far to go back, he says, moving around so he will be nearest to whatever is going on. As they walk further around the bend they smell petrol smoke and realise there is a fire roaring ahead. Osian grips her hand more firmly.

On the waste ground a car is burning furiously. The air above it quivers, and a high-pitched howling sound comes from the flames. Tirzah and Osian shield their eyes; the heat and noise is shocking. There's Brân! she shouts. Brân and the little boys are dancing round the car. Get away! Osian yells at them. That car could go up any minute! But Brân and the boys can't hear. Suddenly a window explodes and the group around the car scatter. One boy trips and sprawls on the ground, his jumper smouldering. Osian runs forward, his arm over his face, and drags the boy by his leg to safer ground. Tirzah's kneecaps are quivering like upturned saucers. There is a final explosion and parts of the car are flung high in the air. The boys are jumping around on the far side of the wreck, waving burning branches at each other. Tirzah sees Brân striding through the smoke towards Osian, with his flaming torch. Before she can move or scream a warning, he is standing over Osian, who is patting the jumper of the fallen boy and talking to him quietly. Tirzah watches as Brân raises the smouldering branch high and brings it down with force on to Osian's bent back.

As if she has been electrified, Tirzah springs forward and darts towards Brân, flinging herself at him, using her nails to rake his smudged face. Brân throws down his branch and holds her at arm's length. Again Tirzah has the jab in her heart she felt before. Brân's eyes are so light, she wonders if he can actually see properly. They are flecked with grey, and Tirzah can't look away from them. We were havin' our own sort of meetin' until you turned up, he shouts, baring his teeth at her. Why don't you and your boyfriend fuck off where you belong? He shakes her easily, his fingers biting into her flesh. Tirzah spits at him, aiming a wild kick at his stomach. Her foot connects; he lets go of her shoulders, sending her sprawling, and bends double. I belong here just as much as you, she screams. And he's not my boyfriend, she adds, remembering Osian, and glances round to check if he is all right. Osian is curled up next to the little boy. She turns to Brân, hating him. You are going to hell, Brân! she shouts, giving him one final kick in the ribs. The Devil won't save you and I'm glad!

Osian struggles to stand, and the gang gather round the fallen boy and pick him up. You children, go home! Tirzah yells. Leave Brân to his own wicked devices. She watches the boys straggle off down the road, prickling with embarrassment. Devices? she thinks. Why did I say that? I sound like Pastor. She wipes her blurred eyes and rushes to help Osian up. Ducking her head so that his arm can rest across her shoulders, she notices she's no longer holding the cowslips. Dear Osian, she says, and kisses the smoky hand near her cheek. But even as she walks slowly home with him, she is surprised by the way her mind replays the moment when she was close to Brân amongst the flame and smoke. And even though she doesn't want to, there is an unnameable thrill in the pit of her stomach, small and strong as an opening fern, when she remembers how Brân had held her by the shoulders, before throwing her to the ground.

Go Ye Therefore and Teach All Nations

(Matthew 28:19)

New families have moved in to the recently built council housing estate. Some of the young people are in Tirzah's school year.
They have different accents and keep to themselves at break
time, but Tirzah can't see any problems with them, apart from
the fact that they are the lost, like the rest of her classmates.
She is friendly with everybody, just as usual, even though the
newcomers look at her as if she's gone off her rocker when
she talks to them. They don't single her out, though; they act
as if all the village kids are going to give them the plague or
something. But in chapel, everyone is exercised about the
darkness of these new council house tenants' hearts, and the
way they conduct themselves. Tirzah's not sure why; they are
not badly behaved, or poor or dirty or anything. Some of the
families who live there have cars and TVs, and neatly mown
bits of grass, Biddy tells her. Some people she knows who live
in the narrow, terraced streets of the old village haven't got
two pennies to rub together most of the time, and are always
popping round for a cup of sugar or a few potatoes. Not that
being poor or needing sugar and spuds makes you a lost soul,

but some even have the police on their doorsteps most weeks, and certainly would never dream of darkening the door of a place of worship. It all has to do with the fact that these new people are incomers, she decides. The heathen can live amongst us, it seems, as long as their parents and grandparents did too.

Tirzah's next-door neighbours are a family of what her mother calls *work-shy scroungers* who never clean their windows and keep a sad, mangy dog chained up behind the shed. They sit smoking all day on a broken-down sofa in the back garden, bare legs poking out from their bathrobes. The chip pan is forever on the go over there, her mother says. One of the grown-up boys steals bumper tins of Quality Street chocolates from who-knows-where and brings them home to his mother sometimes. She has watched them, squashed on the sofa, chewing, and chucking the coloured wrappers all over the place. Once they threw a handful of sweets over the fence to Tirzah when they saw her peering at them. She remembers now how shot through with delight and horror she'd been at the sight of three purple brazil nut and toffee chocolates rolling along the concrete.

She recalls once being in Mrs Bryn-Davies' kitchen for some reason. The chip fat was smoking and Mrs Bryn-Davies was throwing together sandwiches for her husband's tea. Tirzah recalls how fascinated she'd been, watching Mrs Davies slap a thick slice of cheese on to the bread. Now then, she'd said, and hawking like a man, she'd spat expertly into the centre of the cheese before plonking another piece of bread on top. See 'ow you like tha', you miserable old bugger. She pressed the sandwich together, then winked at Tirzah. 'S'our secret, ennit? she whispered, and Tirzah had nodded. Every afternoon, Mrs Bryn-Davies puts on her headscarf and goes off with her sister to the pictures, even though her younger children have nothing to eat but Jacobs crackers and marg. But none of this makes you one of the lost, or even worthy of being put on the altar, it seems. Only if you live on the new estate must you be evangelised, and everyone is concerned about you. And that doesn't really add up. Of course, I'm not a deacon or an elder, Tirzah allows. What do I know?

So each week now in the prayer meeting, someone chimes up about the burden the Lord has laid on him or her for the souls of the lost on the new estate. Pastor has announced that he understands these deep concerns – indeed, he shares them – but until the Lord speaks to him specifically, he will not make a move. In last night's meeting there were some sharp looks amongst the deacons. Osian's father spoke for them all, he'd said, and the skin around Pastor's tightly pursed lips had gone a light shade of grey. Tirzah felt sorry for him. And she couldn't help noticing that Osian's father was not using a lot of grace or forbearance in the way he addressed poor little Pastor. On he went, getting louder and louder, putting it to Pastor that we didn't have to look thousands of miles away for sinners to make into disciples, when here they were under our very own noses, on our very own doorstep.

Brother, Pastor said in the nasal voice he used for extra authority, recrossing his pinstriped legs, I am warmed by your zeal, but tone it down, please. There was a short, squeezed sort of silence as Osian's father stooped for the Bible he had dropped when he jumped to his feet. As Tirzah looked at him she could hear again the dull thump of an outstretched palm making contact, and see his oily, disarranged hair and rucked-up shirt in the kitchen that night she and Osian had got into trouble. Honestly, she'd thought. How could people be so blind? He should examine himself and his own hard-hearted behaviour before he goes out preaching to the blimmin' lost. And then Pastor had charged them to turn their minds afresh to inland China, and the vast oriental sea of humanity waiting to hear the voice of the Lord. Tirzah had read that these people ate only rice, morning, noon and night. Not that this fact meant anything. But it did make her sorry for them, somehow – never to eat a lovely dollop of mash or a crispy chip. To prayer! To prayer! Pastor had concluded, urging on the unhappy meeting.

Tirzah walks home from school the next day and tries not to dwell on how anxious she is about this interest in the estate. It's not that I'm ashamed, she thinks. But she can picture what they'll look like marching down the road with their banner waving. She knows she will feel an absolute twit, walking into the estate with the fellowship for an outreach meeting. She wishes they weren't all so mad-looking. Oh dear, I am ashamed, she admits. Is this wrong? Or is it perfectly natural? After all, she tells herself, some members of Horeb *are* odd. And then again she realises, her heart slipping down her chest a notch or two, that something perfectly natural usually ends up being wrong; nature is fallen, after all. Her heart does a little wobble. I might as well be ashamed of Jesus, like the hymn says, she realises miserably, and runs around to Biddy's to have a word with her about it all.

Biddy's mam comes to the door, her body so tightly encased in an apron that it looks like a thick bolt of material. She has floury arms, and on her fingers clumps of pastry. Paper round, love, she tells Tirzah, and closes the door carefully with the tips of two white fingers. Thank you, Aunty Ceinwen, Tirzah shouts, already running down the road. From terraced street to terraced street she runs until she sees Biddy in the distance, walking lopsidedly, dragging her newspaper bag along the pavement. When she's caught up, she digs into the bag and helps Biddy push rolled papers through letter boxes. Some doors have what sounds like wild dogs behind them, and at one the paper is snatched by snapping teeth when she pushes it through. Flipping flip, Tirzah says, you need danger money for this job. Biddy grunts as she shoves another paper through a narrow slot. You can say that again, she answers. I'm working for peanuts as it is. Tirzah would love to have a job and earn some pin money for herself; she wouldn't mind if it was peanuts. But her parents don't think it seemly for a young girl to go around to strangers' doors of an evening. When she was younger, Tirzah liked to pretend that she had the wrong parents. Between papers she reminds Biddy. And I have no doubt we were placed in the wrong cradles at birth, she announces, thrusting a paper through a door. Mix-ups like that happen in hospitals all the time.

Oh, that old hairy chestnut, Biddy says, smiling. Here we go again. When she was smaller, Tirzah thought it would be the limit of happiness to have chickens in her garden, and a tree house. Uncle Maldwyn and Aunty Ceinwen could so easily have been her parents, given that Biddy and she were born within days of each other in the same hospital, and they are relatives anyway. It seemed as if God had made a slip-up. They are so much more normal and let Biddy get away with lots of things, although that has changed a bit recently. I am an obedient girl, Biddy, she says now, slapping a rolled newspaper into her palm. I would suit any number of nice, sane parents you'd care to throw at me. I realise that, Biddy says. But not on your blessed nelly would I want yours. They're as mad as a pair of hatters. Tirzah knows this is true, so she nods and struggles with a letter box inconveniently placed at the bottom of a door. But it's not just having a little job that they're strict about, she thinks. It's everything. And that wouldn't suit Biddy at all.

Will you tell me about the new estate? she asks as they turn back towards the paper shop. Yup, Biddy says, dragging her bag along the street behind her. It's really nice in there. Lots of grass and new-planted trees. The playground is great. Tirzah immediately wants to investigate. But what do you think about this plan to do outreach? she asks. I know it's wrong, but I don't want to go. Join the club, Biddy says. I hate outreach full stop. And I don't care about the blinking lost. Tirzah stops walking. But what about being commissioned to go out and make disciples of all men? she says. It's not an option. Jesus commanded us. Biddy looks unimpressed. What if all men don't want to be disciples? I think there are a lot of people who couldn't give a tiddlywink. She takes in Tirzah's nonplussed expression and smiles. Like me, for instance. Put that in your I'm-saving-the-lost pipe and smoke it, holy pants, she says, hoicking the sack on to her shoulder.

Tirzah doesn't have an answer. Then she remembers: Pastor would say it's because all men are deceived, blinded by the Evil One to the danger they are in. She quickly explains this to Biddy. Or there could be other explanations, Biddy says as they arrive at the shop. That's all I'm saying. Wait here, I won't be a mo. Tirzah is feeling as if someone has poked inside her head with a stick and scrambled her brain. She watches Biddy in the shop while she gets her pay from the man who is always barricaded in behind the chocolates. He looks comfy, with the wall of cigarettes and miniature bottles of alcohol behind him, and the rows of sweets in front. Tirzah presses her face to the window. Her parents would say that the shopkeeper is a fallen soul, surrounded by the tokens of his own depraved nature. But he looks happy enough to Tirzah as he counts out coins into Biddy's outspread palm. And so does Biddy. Outreach reminds Tirzah how weird they must be to non-chapel folk. She has always sensed how the people who peer out at them when they go door-to-dooring feel about the Gospel. The way they slam their doors shut is a clue. Who can blame them when her father's favourite pamphlet has *Why You Are Going to Hell* printed in fiery red letters on the front?

On the way home, they eat the Marathon bars Biddy has bought them. What do you mean then, Bid, Tirzah asks, about the point of witnessing to the lost and everything? All I'm saying, Biddy says, chewing thoughtfully, is that people might not want to be saved. Maybe they are quite content being, you know, unsaved. Take that bloke in the shop. We are supposed to believe all sinners are full of gloom and, on top of that, very nasty people. Well, Mr Singh, my boss, he's ever so kind and cheerful. So how do you account for him? Tirzah doesn't want to come out with the thing about how all the lost are hoodwinked by the Devil and kept in a state of happy ignorance regarding the fiery fate that awaits them. Somehow, it sounds a little fantastic, and she can just imagine Biddy rolling her eyes. I do love a Marathon, Biddy says. It's the peanuts and the marshmallow and the toffee, all mixed together. Mmm, Tirzah agrees. Don't forget the chocolate.

She puts her arm through Biddy's and they fall in step along the pavement. What will you do when we're having the open-air meeting? Tirzah asks. How will you get out of it? I'll think of something, Biddy tells her. I always do. Tirzah's chewed peanuts start to become sandy and stick to her teeth, and her breathing speeds up as she thinks about Biddy's soul teetering on the edge of eternal damnation. But on the other hand, she realises, maybe Biddy is right, and all this lost soul and hell stuff is a load of rubbish. She sends up a quick prayer just in case. And if it is all true, then here is someone even closer to home than the housing estate she should be bearing witness to. She has a suspicion that Biddy will be what Pastor would call *a tough nut to crack*.

The Wicked Is Snared by the Work
of His Own Hands

(Psalm 9:16)

On Fridays, all the fellowship teenagers go to Christian Youth Circle. Tirzah doesn't mind CYC; Osian is usually there, and Biddy, and lots of others, some nice, some not so, but she knows everybody and is comfortable with them. The leader of the group is a deacon, Mr Humphries. Come on, you 'orrible lot, he shouts most weeks, when the group are holed up in the cloakroom and CYC should have begun. Come on! Let's get going! He is a big believer in keeping them all busy. You know what the Devil makes work for, don't you, dear folks? he often asks them when they are reluctant to join in. There are plenty of things to make at CYC, and games, and table tennis. Everyone's hands are engaged all the time. Tirzah is accustomed to the idea that the Devil is always lurking, ready to lure a person away on to the wrong path if they are not busy doing good deeds. When she was a child, she often gazed at her hands with a kind of loathing. They seemed so intent on doing nothing. And if I just do nothing, she used to think, I'll soon end up doing the Devil's work. Now she feels sad for her younger self, realising that things are even more complicated than she could ever have imagined back then.

First comes Bible study, and for this everyone has to gather in the vestry. Tirzah decides to drift above the meeting, and take it easy tonight. Osian sits opposite her in the circle, and keeps trying to catch her eye. He has been chosen to read the Bible passage. As he reads, Tirzah thinks how strange it is that these fifteen young people are sitting around in a dusty old room, following the scriptures, when outside another sort of life is going on. Then she starts to think about Brân and wonder what he's up to. Is he cold and hungry? Where is he sleeping? Maybe she should tell Mr Humphries about how Brân seems to be worshipping the Devil, and doing all sorts of dangerous things. But it sounds so far-fetched. The whole episode in the bluebell wood feels like something she dreamt. And the burning car could have been a pure accident. The gang may have been messing about and things got out of hand. She has a sneaking suspicion that Brân would laugh at CYC, or be so bored in chapel that he'd be forced to make something happen.

Tirzah's forehead burns as she thinks about Brân's strong arms and the way he grabbed her. She tingles shamefully at his utter disregard. What is the matter with me? she wonders, trying to concentrate on Osian's voice. Any boy only has to touch me, and I forget everything and want to kiss him to death. But still, the delicious warmth and irresistible sensation of both drowning and drifting is wonderful. And sinful, she supposes, picturing herself tripping gaily down the broad road to destruction. I should hate myself, she thinks, gazing at the way Osian's hands hold his Bible as if offering up a sacrifice.

Suddenly, she remembers a question she wants to ask. When Mr Humphries throws the meeting open for discussion, she puts up her hand. Yes, Tirzah, says Mr Humphries, smiling an encouragement. She tells him about the difficulty she has with original sin. Do you think that all the poor people in the world who have something wrong with them are being punished because of original sin? she asks. And are folk sick because of it?

Mr Humphries invites the other young people to give their opinions, but Tirzah isn't listening. She is imagining people in strange, yet-to-be-discovered places: tiny islands in the middle of immense, clear, glinting seas where it is normal, say, to have six toes on each foot like Pastor, or an ear where you'd expect a nose to be. There could even be a place at the topmost pinnacle of the highest secret mountain in the world where people have the heads of wolves. Maybe these people communicate by howling and barking. She begins to think about what the babies look like. Surely they would be little puppy-faced, sharp-toothed creatures who were cared for by their wolf-headed parents. These are some of the things she has to work out for herself. And fancying boys won't help her find the truth. Dimly, she gets that she is working, by the smallest of steps, towards an understanding. But of what exactly? All she knows is that it's important. For instance, why must what's right or wrong be decided by small groups of nutty people who meet in chapels? She can't help smiling. So does that help, Tirzah? Mr Humphries asks. Yes, thank you, she answers. I understand now.

When everyone is having a drink of squash, Mr Humphries tells them about a weekend away that he's organising for the end of the summer holidays. They will be going to a bed and breakfast at the seaside. He pins a piece of paper to the noticeboard for them to sign up if they are interested, and passes letters around. Give these to your parents, he says. Tell them if they have any questions they can come to me on Sunday. Tirzah is so excited she wants to run around the schoolroom, but she doesn't. A whole weekend far from home. It is difficult to imagine. She looks at Biddy, who's nodding happily at her, and then across to Osian. He's gazing fixedly in her direction in a way that makes her uneasy. Still, she thinks, looking back to Biddy, how wonderful to go to a new place without too many grown-ups to check up on them. But then she realises this is exactly the sort of thing her parents will be anxious about. The idea of CYC going away without her makes her want to scream. She wonders if there is even any point signing up for it. Now then, young Tirzah, Mr Humphries calls, come over by here, please. He hands her a cup of weak squash. Why so tragic? he asks, his crinkly blue eyes behind black-rimmed glasses studying her face. Tirzah relaxes a little; with Mr Humphries things always seem clear. Or, for an instant, as simple as they ought to be. I will speak to your parents, he tells her, biting a chunk from his Butter Osborne biscuit. I take it you would like to come?

Tonight, they are going to have a chip supper. Mr Humphries delegates three boys to go to the chip shop. We're timing you, mind, he tells them. And no running off with the dosh. The boys laugh, very pleased with themselves. Tirzah goes into the cloakroom to get a hankie from her bag. When she turns to leave, Osian is in the doorway. The gloomy cloakroom is not a place Tirzah likes. She backs into a forgotten coat that hangs like the deflated remains of a long-gone member of the congregation. Osian gently pushes Tirzah against it and puts his arms around her. The coat smells of mints and damp wool. Just imagine, Osian whispers, if we could go away on the weekend. He reaches down and plants his lips on hers. Sounds of running feet on floorboards and the clop of table tennis balls echo from the schoolroom. Osian presses himself against Tirzah. Blanking out, she interlaces her hands through the black hair at the nape of his neck. Is this the sort of work the Devil makes? she wonders, pushing the length of her body against him. Even their kneecaps are touching. His lips feel as if they are melded to hers. Everything begins to fall away: the cloakroom, the musty coat, the other members of CYC, Brân on the mountain. All that remains are the bodies of Tirzah and Osian, trying to get inside each other.

Then, like freezing water from a hose, light splashes down on them and they spring apart. There in the doorway is Mr Humphries, his hand still on the light switch. Come on, you two, he says cheerily, your chips are getting soggy. Giving them a final cool look, he leaves. Tirzah is shivering, bereft and ashamed, but above all thankful for Mr Humphries' interruption. She's like a version of her old doll Nanci, who, under her long skirt, had another head where her legs should be. You could turn her up the other way and have a different doll to play with whenever you felt like it. But she'd hated both of Nanci's faces: you didn't know where you were with either of them. And here I am, knowing I only want to be Osian's friend, and then kissing him like a mad person. I might as well have two heads with two separate brains. Osian takes her hand. We'd better go, he says, leading her out to where everyone is unwrapping their newspaper parcels. I don't think old Humphries will tell on us. Tirzah feels as if she doesn't deserve chips, or any treats. And now I've gone and made things worse for Osian and me, she thinks, following him into the hall. If God can see into her heart, will He understand she's two opposite, uncontrollable girls? If He doesn't, then maybe she's not the only stupid one.

Soon the air is laden with the sharp scent of vinegar-soaked newspaper as everyone digs into their chips in the Sunday schoolroom. Part of Tirzah is still in the cloakroom, eagerly holding Osian, breathing him in. She tries to stop thinking about it, but the dying, unfamiliar sensation between her legs won't let her. On the far wall is a painted banner she has hardly taken notice of for years, but now it leaps out and almost punches her in the face. She reads the curling letters that make up the words *Thou God Seest Me*, and blushes so deeply she's sure everyone will be drawn to the glow of her face. But no, all the young people are busy pushing chips into their shining mouths. As the blush fades she begins to shiver. Underneath the chill she detects something else. At the utmost reaches of her hearing she listens to a cry from far away, on the summit of the mountain maybe. At first she does not understand what it means. It's as if the roof of the chapel has lifted off and revealed the sky; clouds race across its darkening surface, and up there, where God has always been, peering down, she sees the stars bursting and the serene mauve moon rising, and, for the first time, nothing else. Then the picture fades, and she's back, a little comforted, in the warm schoolroom, amongst the laughing, greasy-faced crowd under the banner.

Honey and Milk Are Under Thy Tongue

(Song of Solomon 4:11)

Tirzah's tactic for getting her parents' consent to the CYC trip is to maintain a dignified silence. Very cool, I'll be, she decides. If they sniff out the idea she really wants to get away from home, they'll be suspicious and think she's pandering to the flesh. I'm pure as a babe in arms, she pronounces to her tiny bedroom mirror, forgetting about original sin. I can be as prim as the next one, if not primmer. She practises an innocent look, but it's not that believable. She rubs her face smooth with both hands, the better to call up an expression that is above reproach, but the moment she looks at herself in the mirror again, up flashes a picture of Osian with his eyes closed. She can see the way his black eyelashes flare from his eyelids. Even more startling is the way, behind this image, a picture of Brân glows so powerfully that soon Osian is blotted out. She covers her eyes and shakes her hair out. She doesn't want to visit either of them. The truth is, I just can't keep my thoughts in order. They will keep escaping from the corners of my eyes. She finally manages a blank, contented face. There, she thinks, shaken. That's it; butter wouldn't melt. During the announcements in chapel, she'd kept her eyes fixed on her open Bible. When the deacon read out details of the proposed weekend, he made it sound so boring no one in their right mind would want to go anyway.

Well, young lady, her father says at the dinner table. What's all this I hear about you young people gallivanting off to the seaside? Tirzah chews her roast potato. Can I have some more gravy, please? she asks. He is trying to make a little joke, she knows, but it will not do to enter in and start a conversation. It would soon turn into the can-I-go-please-can-I-go game, and before you know it he'd turn nasty. So Tirzah smiles a distant sort of smile and assumes the face she's been practising, while pouring more gravy on her meat. Now then, Gwyll, her mother says, neck starting to blotch up. It would be a lovely treat for Tirzah. She doesn't ever go far. Tirzah's father puts down his cutlery. Doesn't go far? he repeats. Doesn't go far? I've never heard such silliness. Why should she be going far?

Tirzah's heart starts a slow slide. She realises how power-ful her yearning is to escape for a few days. Never before has she wanted to get out of the valley so much. She is sure her parents will never understand; they've lived here all their lives. Anything else is unthinkable to them. Her eyes fill with tears. But her mother, surprisingly, does not give in. Well, Gwyllim, she continues, pointing at him with her knife, I'm only saying it would be a nice thing for her to do. That's all. She gestures with the knife towards Tirzah. That poor child has scarcely been outside this valley all her young life. I do not want her to be like us. Do you? Tirzah stops chewing her potato. This is so strange. Her father is blinking slowly, his mouth opening and closing as he looks at his wife. Tirzah can hear a dog barking in the street, knocking a hole in the silence: *woof, woof, woof.*

71

Three hollow barks. And immediately after the third bark her father picks up his cutlery again and loads his fork. Indeed, he says, if you are that strong about it, then of course Tirzah must go. Let's have an end to this conversation. He pops the food in his mouth and says around it: I have more important things to think about on the Lord's Day.

When her parents go upstairs for their lie-down, Tirzah slips out and walks idly through the streets. She wanders across the school playing fields until she is standing at Osian's back garden gate. He's mowing the lawn with a push-along mower. She tiptoes up behind him and puts her hands over his eyes. He doesn't jump or make a fuss. Tirzah, he says and turns. What are you doing, mowing on the day of rest? she asks. My dad told me to, he says, making his way down the path towards the shed. She's speechless for a moment when he says over his shoulder that his parents don't mind gardening on a Sunday. Osian's father is such a stickler usually. Guess what happened? she demands, recovering, when they are safely behind the tall trellis hung with sprays of rosebuds. What do you and me and Biddy want more than anything? To go on the weekend, he says slowly, reaching to hold her hands. Well, now I can go, Tirzah says, pulling her hands away and jumping up and down. I can go! It's all so funny-peculiar. They just said yes. Mr Humphries is with my parents now, Osian says. Telling them all about it. Maybe he'll persuade them to let me go too.

Tirzah walks back towards the gate, constrained again by the way he is gazing at her. That's nice, Osian, she says. Though you realise nothing is going to happen between us when we're away, don't you? On the weekend and for always. I am sorry about kissing you the way I did. She can hear her voice trailing off. She is ashamed to tell him it was a mistake.

He's still watching her, the sweet, uncertain smile that comes and goes across his mouth jabbing at her heart. Even as she acknowledges how much she loves him, she is also aware of a fleeting, still-obscure idea, small as a twig briskly moving on the surface of a broad river, about her own life and its possibilities. We have our different lives to lead, she says. He shakes his head, and moves quickly to embrace her. The sun is drawing a throaty perfume from the lavender hedge that flows over everything in a wave of spice. There is a taste to Osian's kisses that Tirzah can't help liking, a sweet, creamy taste she finds beguiling. They stand, swaying between the rosebuds and the cushions of purple-tipped stems. Who wouldn't love Osian? she thinks. He is so calm and strong and kind. Then, slicing through the perfumes and sweet-flavoured kisses, comes the realisation she's again saying one thing and doing another. No, she says, pulling away, stunned by how she's let herself be hooked again. Osian, I want to stop. But holding him at arm's length she becomes aware he is not paying attention to her anyway.

Osian gazes over Tirzah's head, and across the seagull-strewn school football pitch that backs on to the houses. He looks wretched. What's wrong? she asks, distracted from her own thoughts. Tell me. Osian shakes his head, his lips set in a serious shape. Old Humphries will do the trick, she tells him. Don't you worry. He'll bang on about Bible study and prayer times, things that your parents will just lap up. Still Osian is silent, and she sees with a prickle of shock that his eyes are tear-filled. Oh no, she says, her own eyes blurring. It doesn't matter really. Who cares about the stupid weekend? If you can't go, then Biddy and I won't. Osian shakes his head again, his arms dropping to his sides. It's not that, he says in a muffled voice. It's all this. And he gestures to include the garden and beyond. Tirzah understands. You mean our parents, and Horeb, and God, and the whole valley, don't you? she asks. He nods. It's everything, he says, and sniffs. Some days I am so squashed.

Tirzah tries to think of the right words to say. But, Osian, she starts, shaking the tears from her eyes, I've been wanting to tell you something about that for so long, and I couldn't. They sit on a couple of big old paint pots, and Tirzah tries to explain the way she saw the chapel schoolroom roof dissolve, and instead of the angry eye of God, there had been a peaceful sky lying like a sparkling blanket over them. She doesn't have the words to express her growing realisation that the tiny world they live in is not the only one, or, indeed, may not even be how they think it is at all. We are each on our own path, she says, trying to express what she doesn't even understand herself. No one else can decide the direction we walk in. Not our parents or Horeb or our friends. I think we are the bosses of ourselves.

Osian listens quietly, without interrupting. It's no good, she says finally. I can't make you understand. I think I get it, he says. But I'm not sure it's true for me. Now you are talking soft, Tirzah says. Not for you? Why not, may I ask? Too special, are we? Osian smiles at her. Calm yourself, girl, he says, stroking her arm. I only mean I'm not strong like you. And my father has big plans for me. I don't think I will ever have the guts to stand up to him. I didn't say it would be easy, Tirzah answers. It will be very hard. But I can't believe you're saying you're not strong. Of course you are. She tries again to tell him all the new thoughts she's been having, but they are still bobbing high above her, like a bunch of escaped balloons.

Dear Osian, she says, squeezing his hands. All I know is that you don't need to be squashed. She decides not to mention her ideas about wolf-headed folk just yet.

Osian seems to perk up, and Tirzah is so relieved she pecks his cheek with her lips. Why is it that when I kiss someone, she thinks, her eyes closed, it's as if every cloud that ever was, and every sky, and all the mountains and valleys, the trees and animals, the rain and sun, everything rushes into one single beautiful thing and becomes simple? She begins to feel floaty. Up I go, she thinks, holding so tight to Osian she can sense herself becoming both part of him and part of the wide world. See, Osian! she cries. We are together, and alone, all at the same time! That is what I was trying to tell you about humans. There is nothing to worry about! The taste of cream and honey drenches her mouth even though she is not kissing Osian now. Hold on! she calls, and Osian strengthens his grip. When she comes down to earth, she's surprised to find they are still sitting on their paint pots behind the shed. Do you understand? she asks. I am getting stronger, and so are you. But Osian shakes his head. All I really want is for us to be a couple, he says. Why can't we be?

The Seed of the Wicked Shall Be Cut Off

(Psalm 37:28)

Tirzah is a new sort of person now, one enveloped in the perfume of lavender, who moves through the Sunday streets without touching the pavement, feet soaked with the verdant scent of fresh-mown grass, trailing leaves and flowers behind her. She has seen a new truth, and is changed. Each waking hour of Monday and Tuesday she dwells on how she spiralled into the sky with her friend Osian. The feeling that she had actually embraced the whole world and was an important part of it is a sort of rapture. It isn't until Tuesday night, in the middle of prayer meeting, that she is yanked back to her ordinary, everyday, non-flowery self. Without warning, she is thrown out of that sun-warmed, bee-hung dream of life and hurled into howling darkness. Something unimaginable happens at prayer meeting and she runs out of the vestry, through the graveyard and up to the mountain without stopping or thinking or looking back. Her throat is raw and her breath rasping. Arriving on the broad shoulder just below the summit, she falls into the whinberry bushes that carpet the mountain, and welcomes the tough plants' bristling support.

Evening is already lowering itself to the grass and creeping up from the ferns. An invisible skylark pours out a song that seems to coax first one, and then another silver pinpoint from beneath the surface of the turquoise sky. Tirzah is blank with sadness. Pressing her hands to her chest, she senses the uncomfortable swelling of her heart, and doesn't know if it will ever stop. But even so, eventually she becomes aware of the benign nothingness in every blade of grass and every squat, embattled tree around her. Through her thin clothes, the whinberry bushes pierce her skin. Beneath the whinberries, pebbles like small, unearthed potatoes rest together companionably, and a fresh, deep-blue breeze plays about her wet face. She is too tired to wonder at the mountain's steady breath, or the way its smell of cooling stones and sheep-rich wool and newly hatched ferns rolls over her as if she were a boulder or a ditch.

She rubs her eyes, repeatedly seeing Osian's wan-lipped, stricken face, and the way he looked at her briefly before standing to face the fellowship at prayer meeting. Each time the tiny snippet of Osian dazedly rising from his chair reruns, she shakes her head. Gradually she calms herself, and deliberately brings to mind all that happened. Every word and action is waiting to be replayed: Pastor had asked, as he always did, if anyone was burdened with a special matter that needed to be brought before the altar, and as usual there was a brief silence. This time Tirzah was aware of a queasy dread growing inside her. Then Osian's father announced he had another's dark and grievous sin to bring into the light. It was almost funny how everyone's eyes had flown open as if controlled by one central pulley. Tirzah could not look away from Osian, although he seemed to be in a private, dreamy world of his own.

There was something in the manner in which Osian's father stood, the set of his shoulders, the way the muscles of his jaw shifted as he clenched his teeth, that seemed to alert Pastor to the possibility of trouble. Now then, dear brother Evans, he said quietly, what are you burdened with this evening? And remember, *with love* is our watchword here. Tirzah began to pray silently, although she could not form any words. Osian's father was barely able to contain himself, that much was obvious; she could see the sheen on his forehead, and the way his trouser hems trembled. When he began to speak, his voice over-filled the small room. Tirzah looked around and saw several people's lips moving, their whispered prayers scurrying insects on a bare floor. Osian's mother was already crying. I want you to pause, brother, Pastor said, nasally now, opening his palms and talking over the rumbling voice. Pause and examine your own heart in this. But Mr Evans went on, walking over Pastor's mild words as if they were no more than weeds on the path he'd chosen to take.

Tirzah slipped her hand into the crook of her mother's shaking arm. I want to go, Mam, she'd said in an undertone. But her mother didn't react. Mr Evans was pulling out a carrier bag from under his chair, and the crackling of the plastic sounded so out of place, Tirzah wanted to put her free hand over her ear. She watched, puzzled, as Mr Evans began to bring a bed sheet out, fist over fist, on and on, until it sat in a gleaming heap on the floor in front of him. Pastor rose, his glasses flashing, and for the first time raised his voice. Mr Evans, he shouted, what is the meaning of this? It is not seemly for you to behave in such a manner in the Lord's house. Mr Evans looked almost gratified by Pastor's words. If you will give me a minute, he said, unruffled, and began to sort the sheet out, billowing it up, straightening it so that it lay lengthways on the floor, lapping the feet of the waiting people like a white expanse of water. I am bringing this matter before you, he said, because I do not know what else to do. The whispered prayers grew silent. Tirzah saw that Osian was now aware of what was happening. Dada! he said, perched on the edge of his seat. What are you doing? I am exposing the filthy, vile sins of your flesh, Mr Evans stated. It is my duty as your father and a deacon of this chapel. Tirzah could not believe what was happening. Only a few days ago, everything had seemed so wonderful.

Pastor's face turned the colour of porridge, his cheekbones poking out sharply. I command you to put away this object, he cried, his voice high and thin. But Mr Evans lifted a hand to silence him. I have God on my side, he said. Behold! And he pointed to a barely visible stain on the sheet. This is a shameful emission, done secretly in the dead of night, in my own home, he went on. At pains to make them see, he traced the shape with his finger. And from my own offspring. Pastor peered short-sightedly, and then recoiled. These are private family matters, he said, and several people murmured in agreement. But Mr Evans was not satisfied. If this young man, he said, pointing now to his son, is so weak, so enslaved by his own lusts that he cannot control himself, then it is the fellowship's place to do it for him.

Tirzah dared not look at Osian. The boys in school made jokes about wet dreams, but she and Biddy had never taken any notice of them. In the stuffy room, everyone was frozen for a moment. She sensed them struggling to understand. The only sounds were the sobs of Osian's mother. With everyone else, Tirzah stared at the silvery ghost of a stain on the bed sheet, her heart shuddering with pity. He has befouled our home with his unclean ways, Mr Evans shouted. I demand judgement from the people. It is my right. At pains to make the fellowship see, he traced the shape again with his finger. Tirzah could not turn her eyes away. Mr Evans was like a conjuror, making the invisible plain. Then he picked up his Bible from where it had been sitting in readiness for this moment, and read, *Woe to them that devise iniquity, and work evil on their beds,* his voice both harsh and thready. The passage was long, and Mr Evans did not stop.

Tirzah couldn't stand it any more. Osian, listen, she called urgently, underneath Mr Evans's forceful reading. Come with me. You don't have to stay here a minute longer. Osian threw her a bewildered glance. Osian, she called again, this time more strongly, across the brilliant expanse of white fabric, knowing that he was powerless to come to her, even if he wanted to. He seemed to flicker on and off like a faulty light bulb before her eyes, and the sheet was a vast lake she could not cross. Still she tried one more time. Come, Osian, she urged, extending her hand. You don't belong in this place. Come with me now. But Osian, his black hair startling against his paper-white face, looked away, distracted by his father. It was then Tirzah had felt herself being carried through the paisley drapes, out of the room.

Now Tirzah becomes aware of strange music all around her. It is a continuous, lilting sigh, a thousand-stringed hum that she understands is the mountain's voice. She is soothed by it, almost held inside it like a small creature would be held in a cocoon. A breeze laden with every living thing touches her temples, and when it moves away it seems to take with it the ragged feelings she has been holding. Cleansed now by the mossy darkness, she gets to her feet. Osian is the best person in the whole village, she knows. She sees again his face with its white bones shining through, and wipes her eyes with the backs of her hands. Poor little Pastor too, she realises. Fair play; he had tried to sort things out in his own way. And most of the funny old brethren and sisters weren't happy with Osian's father: that was as plain as the nose on your face. She does up her cardigan buttons and smooths the wrinkles from her skirt. Something has happened to her; around her body she senses a glow like a force-field. The silly trailing flowers and leaves she'd thought were upholding her have blown away. Within this glow I am untouchable, she thinks, untouchable and strong, and shaking her hair out of her eyes, she runs lightly down to the twinkling lights below.

Have Mercy upon Me, For I Am Desolate

(Psalm 25:16)

The next day, Tirzah goes to school, still light and strong inside her force-field. If the image of a white sheet or pointing finger or wounded look threatens to encroach on her mind's eye, she only has to remember the dusky mountain's breath flowing over her as she lay amongst the thorny bushes, and everything becomes safe again. Nothing can trouble her. As long as she doesn't question the sensation, the layer of light and peace she rests in is impermeable. Deliberately she turns her thoughts away from Osian and what happened at the prayer meeting. He will have to sort his own life out, she decides. I don't think I can help him now. I need all my strength for myself. I am going to pass all my exams, she decides. Who knows what I will do? She sees herself with a case, catching a bus, then maybe a train, and travelling to a new town, her head full of all the things she's learnt. Ignoring how Osian told her it was not the same for him, turning away from his stricken eyes and chalky face, she tells herself that he is surely capable of doing the same.

Not long ago, some of the teachers announced they would be handing out old O-level papers so that everyone can get in extra exam practice before the real things. While they are waiting in the yard for school to start, Tirzah explains to Biddy that she has decided to work hard from now on. I will be busy most evenings, she says. But you can come and revise with me if you like. Biddy shrugs. I'm just going to hope for the best, she announces, chewing a wad of gum. Do you think that's a good idea? Tirzah asks. This is important, you know, for our futures. Got more crucial things to do with my time, Biddy says. The future isn't here yet. Anyway, we've already ploughed through our blinking mocks. Ta ra. This doesn't surprise Tirzah; Biddy always wants to be contrary, and she hates studying.

So Tirzah works carefully through her revision alone, following a timetable she has devised. Every evening she pushes more facts into her brain, slotting them in as though returning a heap of finished books to their places on the shelves of a library. It's as if the more she slots in, the bigger her mental shelves become. For the first time she enjoys the process. Her mocks had gone well, and she hadn't really worked at all. I'm actually quite brainy, she realises with a flare of pleasure, as she goes through her pencil case, sharpening to points the Staedtler Noris pencils her father buys her each year for Christmas. She begins to think about A-levels and suddenly can't wait to learn new things and spend her time in the common room kept only for the sixth formers. She's heard they are allowed to make their own coffee and bring a mug from home. Perhaps she will even be a prefect. On Sunday she persuades her mother she's poorly, and although her father makes a point of giving one of his funny looks when he pops his head around her door, she is allowed to stay home from chapel.

When the first practice exams are given out on Monday, each paper is a serious joy; never has she felt so clever and prepared. The hall with its parquet floor and smeared windows doesn't flatten her. The rows of single desks, the breathings of her hunched classmates and the prowling of the teacher in charge don't make her afraid. When she gets home, she eats with her parents, then goes upstairs and spreads her books on the bed. The evening before the history exam, Biddy appears with dishevelled hair and a pimple at the side of her mouth she's obviously been picking. She slumps on the rug, sighing. What's the matter? Tirzah asks, sitting on her pillow, legs crossed. Then she stiffens. Is something else wrong? Her tongue shrinks from helping her say the name Osian. Is it about the sheet thing? she asks. What's happened? Is he OK? With an arid mouth she waits to know how Osian is and pretends to read her notes. The guilt she's stifled about not going to see him moves like fog to envelop her.

Biddy shrugs. What do you expect? she asks. He's as right as he can be, I s'pose. She bites the side of her thumb. He's trying to concentrate on his schoolwork. He says some of the boys at his school have been crying, they're so worried. Tirzah is groping her way, trying to listen to Biddy, struggling blindly to grasp what the words really say about Osian. He says he can't think straight, Biddy adds. And I know what he means. Tirzah isn't at all satisfied with this report. It's not what she wants to know. Biddy doesn't have a clue, going on about his schoolwork. Why should he worry? He's always in the top class, with all the brainy boys. Tirzah can hardly stand to look at her, sitting there, whingeing and covered in spots. That's all he said? she asks. I suppose he couldn't tell you how he was really feeling, with everyone at chapel around. Actually I spoke to him at the Co-op, Biddy answers. He was shopping for his mother if you must know. Tirzah glares at her. Honestly, you look grotty, she snaps, drawing herself up. You are no oil painting yourself, missus, Biddy says, her voice tear-muffled. Anyway, I just wish I'd revised more. She starts to cry openly. I should have listened to you, Tiz. Tirzah glances at her reluctantly. Well, it's not completely too late, she says. These are only practice exams. Anyway, you usually narrowly sail through without much work, don't you? Biddy nods. So, Tirzah goes on, with your luck you'll be absolutely fine. Why don't you stop snivelling, go home and do some revising? Biddy roughly wipes her eyes. Is that all you can say, Miss Perfect Pants? she shouts, jumping to her feet. You are a nasty old cow! And she slams the door on her way out.

After the history paper, Tirzah manages shakily to recapture her sense of peace. She enjoys the biology exam. It's one of her best subjects. When she turns the completed paper over and looks up, she sees Biddy sprawled in her chair, already finished. They don't speak on the way out. At home, she finds her mother with her legs up on a sofa cushion in the front room. What have you been doing? she asks, patting her hair. Working towards my O-levels, Mam, Tirzah says, dropping her bag in the doorway. Honestly. Have you forgotten I've got exams this year? No, cariad, her mother says, shaking her head. Course not. My clever girl, you are. It is obvious to Tirzah that her parents are content to see her working, but she knows that, as usual, they will be concerned too much emphasis is being placed on the things of this world. So there's no surprise when it starts on Thursday morning. All the learning in the universe won't help you one jot when you stand before the judgement throne at the Last Trump, her father announces over his egg and bacon. It's possible to be too clever. Course, it's all as filthy rags, he adds, rolling the r of *rags* with obvious pleasure while shaking the tomato sauce bottle vigorously. And more toast, if you please, Mair. He tucks his chin in to smother a belch before returning to his theme. Yes, filthy rags, he goes on with satisfaction, waiting with his napkin pushed in the front of his shirt. Tirzah sees, like tiny yellow beads, a perfect string of dribbled egg yolk and a splodge of blood-red sauce dead in the middle of the white linen, and at last she doesn't fight the dimming of the force-field she has been holding on to. It's almost a relief to let it go.

She's further jolted by her mother, who drops the toast to his plate and says that she's had enough talk of rags in this kitchen, filthy or otherwise, thank you. In a shocked and sorrowing voice her father says, Mair, what is wrong with you this morning? Remember your place, please. Oh, I know my place very well, she answers. If you must know, I am grieving over that poor boy. Tirzah suddenly pays attention. Quiet, her father murmurs, glancing at Tirzah. I say this is not the time for that particular discussion. But Tirzah's mother is not to be silenced. She has tears in her eyes, and her neck is blooming with blotches. Have you seen him? she asks Tirzah, who shakes her head, her stomach contracting to ward against an invisible blow. That lovely, innocent boy is being forced to do the rounds of the fellowship, begging forgiveness. Is this right? I ask you, Gwyllim. Is this what our loving Lord would want? Tirzah's mouth is full of cornflakes, but she can't swallow.

Her father jumps to his feet as if he's been stung by a wasp, overturning the kitchen chair, and pulls the napkin free of his shirt. Silence! he shouts, making Tirzah jump. What the Lord would want is contrition, he says. As you know full well. He frowns, and his thick eyebrows meet to form an emphatic line. I am sick to the back teeth of your namby-pamby, female way of looking at things. He is leaning across the table to yell into his wife's face. Wishy-washy, that's what you are, Mair. Tirzah's mother is calm, except for the twisting of her hankie. I will say one more thing, she answers. What I do know full well is this: there are people I could mention, not a million miles away from this spot, who think they are so perfect that humble pie is not on the menu for them. She dabs her eyes. But I say they should cut themselves a big slice and trot around the houses sharing it out.

Tirzah trembles, suddenly so sad she cannot lift a finger, her vision clouded by an image of the soiled bed sheet. Have you finished? her father shouts, thoroughly rattled. There is silence. Good, he says, sending a speck of toast on to the tablecloth. Now I'm off to work for some blessed peace. The blasted noise of that foundry is heaven on earth compared with what I have to listen to down by here.

When he's gone, Tirzah quickly kisses her mother's cheek and runs upstairs, the wet wad of unswallowed cornflakes like a slimy mulch in her mouth. She spits into the toilet and splashes water on her face. Her legs are so weak she has to sit down and breathe deeply. Oh, Osian, she whispers, clenching both hands so that her nails bite into each palm. What sort of friend have I been? Will you forgive me for deserting you? Her heart is heaving miserably in her chest.

The next morning, there is one last practice exam to get through before dinner break, but Tirzah's mind refuses to work. How can she concentrate now, with the picture of Osian continually before her eyes, plodding round, asking forgiveness? She can almost see his flat, dark hair and bowed shoulders. It makes her wince to think of him that way. She can't eat school dinner either, even though it's Russian goulash.

Biddy sits opposite in the canteen. Friends? she asks, her nose shining and her pimple almost gone. Tirzah nods. Of course, Bid. I'm so sorry I was nasty. And I'm sorry I called you a cow, Biddy says. But look, she continues in a Russian accent, enough of this apologising. Can I finish your grub? And she takes Tirzah's plate without waiting for a reply, forking goulash into her mouth. Scrummy, she says. I doubt it has been any closer to Russia than Pontypool, mind, and the peas are a bit stone-like, but still, I love it. She finishes and sighs, leaning closer. So, what's the matter, Tiz? You've been a drip all through break. Is this about Osian? Tirzah looks at Biddy blankly. Why are you talking in that funny voice? she asks. Biddy starts to explain. No, stop, Tirzah says. What do you really know about Osian? If there is something else, why haven't you told me? I asked you the other night, and all you went on about was his exams. Biddy raises her hands to ward off Tirzah's questions, then picks up the laden tray. Answer me, Tirzah demands, visibly shaking. Oh, all right, Biddy says. One, I didn't know the details. I just overheard my parents talking about him having to confess to everybody. And two, we weren't speaking to each other. Also, I didn't want to upset you.

Tirzah stares across the table. How could I have been so selfish? she says in a thin voice. I should have gone to see him. He must think I'm disgusted like all the rest and don't care about him. She hides her face in her hands. Biddy comes around to cuddle her. He won't think that, Tiz, she says, tearful herself now. He knows you love him. You always have. But Tirzah will not be comforted. She is so ashamed of herself it is overwhelming. There is no excuse for my behaviour, she thinks. If I was disgraced, Osian would never abandon me. She recalls his sweet half-smile and can't move; more than a week's worth of tears are waiting to be shed. All the tears she'd turned her back on are falling, here, in the canteen. Now what shall we do? Biddy asks, pulling a tissue from her sleeve and wiping Tirzah's wet face with a clumsy hand. Finally she wipes her own eyes with the tissue. I know, she says. The stupid practice exams are finished. You go home, and find him if you like. I'll say you were poorly.

After Tirzah collects her coat, she starts for her house. It's highly unlikely she will bump into Osian walking the streets, but she sees him so clearly in her mind she can't think straight, and decides to take a shortcut along an unfamiliar alley between the backs of two rows of houses, just in case he's there. Overflowing bins line the lane. There's a bicycle with a single warped wheel, a propped-up old mattress and a stoved-in kettle lying around. Tirzah has to step carefully over a heap of black plastic bags. Overhead, seagulls are fighting each other for a clear way down. It's shocking to see; the village has always been so neat. And you could almost eat out of her own mother's bin. Tirzah stands still, realising she has stumbled on another version of things. This has been here all along, she thinks. Only I was so wrapped up in my own life I didn't know it.

Gradually, she becomes aware of a smell like candied lemons slicing the tainted air. On one side of her, sprawling over the brick wall and stretching ahead to the far end of the lane, some shrub she doesn't know the name of is flourishing. The plant's blooms cluster like speckled, yellow stars, filling the air with a delicious citrus scent. Tirzah watches as greeny-white butterflies open and close their wings, intent on exploring the minuscule golden filaments that burst from the eye of each domed flower head. Maybe things aren't so bad, she thinks, inhaling deeply before swinging her school bag on to the other shoulder. She will find Osian and talk to him, make sure he's coping. Maybe she'll even go with him on his visits around the houses. That might bolster him. On she walks, accompanied by screaming seagulls, past the flower-covered wall, until something catches her eye and she slows down. It's difficult to make out what is propped against the wooden garden gate ahead; it could be a stack of rubbish, but Tirzah instinctively knows it's Osian.

She runs to him and drops her books. He's hunched up, resting his head on his knees. Dust smudges the dark fabric of his school trousers and one shoe is undone. Osian, she says helplessly, and falls to the dirt beside him. He is unresponsive. Tirzah takes his inert hand and presses it to her cheek. She can't think of one thing to say. Instead she kisses his soiled palm, trying to convey through her mute lips what is impossible to explain. After some time, his legs straighten out, and he doesn't seem to care that one trouser leg is working its way up to his knee, or that his bare calf is scratched by stones. Are you poorly, Osian? she manages to ask at last, hating herself for the ridiculousness of the question. He turns his head and looks at her. It's me, Tirzah, she tells him. What are you doing here? Osian searches her eyes with his, but seems incapable of speech. Never mind, she soothes him. Come on, now, up with you. We'll go home. My mam will look after you. Tirzah has to pull with all her strength to get him upright, and drapes his arm across her shoulder to support him. She is gasping with sorrow and love, her throat filled with a choking substance. Beside her, Osian struggles. And so they make their slow way out of the filthy lane.

For Thou Hast Been a Shelter for Me, and a Strong Tower

(Psalm 61:3)

When they finally arrive at the front door of her house, she realises the key isn't attached to the length of string hanging from the inside of the letterbox as usual. Dammo di! she says quietly, still supporting a swaying Osian. She was hoping to get him inside without any doorstep drama and seated in the kitchen before going to tell her mother she'd found him. She has to knock several times before she hears someone running down the stairs. Biddy answers the door and catches Osian as he collapses. Whoa, what's going on? she asks, looking over him to Tirzah and adjusting her hold. Are you in one piece, Tiz? Don't worry about me, Tirzah says, just help get this one inside. What are you doing here, anyway? Waiting for you, Biddy answers. I scarpered straight after I told the secretary you were ill. Your mam's out. They support Osian as he walks down the hall. In the kitchen, they sit him in an easy chair by the fireplace. Biddy puts the kettle on, and Tirzah gets the bread and butter out of the pantry.

Tirzah busies herself with cutting slices of bread, emptying her mind of broken, dusty Osian and the filthy, rubbish-strewn lane. Biddy brings a plate for her to put the slices on and butters the bread expertly. I can do stuff like this, you know, she says, and winks. I'm not completely useless in the kitchen. I'm sure you can, Tirzah answers, pretending not to be surprised. Where did you find his nibs? Biddy adds. Still holding the bread knife, Tirzah starts to cry. That's not going to help anybody, as you so rightly told me not that long ago, Biddy says, shaking her head and taking the sharp knife from Tirzah's hand. Stop grizzling. You're twp, that's what you are. Bringing Osian here. Your mam and dad will be tamping. She gets up to make tea and brings the teapot to the table. Tirzah wipes her eyes and cuts the bread and butter into little squares. She knows her mother won't mind. Osian looks asleep, his head resting on an embroidered antimacassar.

If in doubt, have a cuppa, Biddy says, putting cups ungently on the table. Be careful with the china, Tirzah tells her. You are like a blinking navvy. What we need are biscuits, Biddy states. Tirzah points to a container decorated with roses on the dresser. After she's poured the tea, Biddy puts two sugars in one and stirs it. Sugar's what he needs, she says. Tirzah takes Osian's cup over to him. Wake up, sleepyhead, she croons, bending over. This'll help. He opens his eyes and accepts the cup. Drink it all up, please, she says, and he obediently sips. Then she puts four quarters of buttered bread on a plate and slips it on to his lap. And this, she adds. Again, Osian does as he's told. In silence they eat the fresh bread and butter, sipping their sweet tea between mouthfuls. The bread is so tender and white, and the kitchen so homely that Tirzah can feel herself brightening. That's better, isn't it, Osian? she asks. Biddy takes the biscuit barrel, offering it to him. Ginger nuts, she says. I love 'em. Especially when you dunk 'em. She refills the cups, and they dip their biscuits. Tirzah can't think of what to do next, so she concentrates on the melting, spicy dough in her mouth.

She has begun to wish they could stay in the kitchen eating ginger biscuits for ever, sheltered from all the things that could hurt them, but the sound of a key turning in the front door makes her start. It's Mam, Tirzah says, and jumps up to meet her in the hall. She leads her mother by the hand, trying to explain about Osian. Her mother halts at the kitchen door and takes in the crumb-strewn table and Biddy chewing. Navy blue! she says. I can see you two have made yourselves at home. Why aren't you in school? And what am I running here? A café? Look at the mess on my clean table. Mam, Tirzah says, and tugs her arm. Osian is here, and I don't know what to do with him. Her mother quickly shrugs off her coat and unties her headscarf. Biddy has been helping me, Tirzah adds.

Tirzah's mother makes her way to Osian. She puts her small hand on his forehead. Now, you stay where you are, she tells him as he tries to get up. Let's have a think. Cup of tea, Aunty Mair? Biddy asks, teapot poised. Yes, please, bach, she answers. That would be lovely. We'll have a fresh pot, though, I think. She refills the kettle and sets it to boil. While they wait for the water, Tirzah and her mother look at each other. Oh, Mam, Tirzah finally whispers, glancing at Osian. The poor little dab. Look at him. Yes, but hush now, her mother says, pouring milk into the cups. I need a minute. She sips daintily at her tea and they join her. As Tirzah sticks her nose over the rim of her china cup, the steam plays around her lips and nostrils, and she begins to see there is something wonderfully calming about tea. Now I understand the grown-ups always putting the blimming kettle on, she thinks. The silence is warmly dotted with various small slurps and swallows as the four of them drink together. When they've finished, Osian stands. His colour is more normal, but there is a strained and hungry look to his eyes.

Tirzah helps him on with his coat and gives him his school bag. Where will you go now? she asks. He pushes his hair back from his forehead in a familiar gesture. I have something to say to you before I leave, he announces, and begins, in a clear voice, to name his sin. Tirzah's mother makes a quietening movement with her hands. Now, dear Osian, she says. There is no need for this. I must, he answers. It is my duty as a fallen brother. Fallen brother? Tirzah blurts. I've never heard anything so ridiculous in my life. If we all had to go round the houses every time we did something wrong, no one would ever be in. Me, for instance – I'm the selfishest person around, aren't I, Mam? Shut up, please, her mother says. But Tirzah can't stop. And your own father could do with knocking on some doors, let me tell you. She begins to cry, and is annoyed. I would like an apology from him myself. Osian says nothing. Don't tell me you've forgotten? she demands. Well, I haven't. I remember how he hit you, Osian, she says. I heard him. And you didn't deserve that either.

Osian still waits quietly, and a smile, slight and wavering as a ripple in water, moves his lips while he waits for her to finish. Osian! she repeats. Aren't you angry with him? Admit your father has a lot to answer for. Then she becomes silent for a moment. He has betrayed you, she says. But Osian is unmoved. You told me we are all on our own, walking our own path, didn't you? he asks. Well, this is my sin, he says. And my responsibility. This is my path. No one else's. Tirzah's mother puts her cup carefully in its saucer. But you haven't done anything wrong, dear, she tells him gently. We are only frail humans. You were fast asleep, and your God-given body was just doing what came naturally. Everyone knows that. Even your stiff-necked father.

But Osian continues where he left off. I am deeply convicted by my depraved and lustful actions, he says, as if reciting something he's learnt. I have brought shame on my family and the fellowship. I am striving to be a more worthy disciple, and I'm glad to have the chance to see each one of my brothers and sisters. He walks to the door and gives them a little wave. Please don't go, Tirzah says, wanting to shake him. Stay here with us where it's safe. She would dearly love to build a huge wall around them all, even though that's a stupid idea. I have to go, Osian says. I don't deserve to be with you good people. Tirzah can't bear the thought of him leaving them. I've told you I'm not that good, she says. Will you forgive me for not standing with you when I should have? Osian's lips again make the faintest shape of his old half-smile, but it doesn't last. I have one question to ask, and then I'll leave, he says. Do you forgive me? Tirzah and her mother can only nod. And then he's gone.

If We Confess Our Sins, He Is Faithful
and Just to Forgive

(1 John 1:9)

Tirzah is walking to the manse. Tonight is Pastor's wife's monthly meeting for girls over the age of twelve. The incident with Osian and his father has sunk below the surface of chapel life like a weighted bundle lobbed in a lake, but Tirzah knows that everyone is mindful of it. No matter how heavy and tightly bound, they are aware of the way that sad bundle is wedged between rocks, waiting for a strong current to offer it back to them. We are all to blame, she thinks. We should have done something to protect Osian from his father. But I am the most to blame, first for saying we had to be friends, and then wickedly turning about and kissing him like mad. A new thought stabs her: maybe she got him all stirred up. Maybe the sheet thing is her fault? Worst of all, it seems to her, is the shameful way she abandoned him when he needed her most. She's slowed down, preoccupied with her thoughts. Yesterday at chapel, Osian sat between Mr and Mrs Evans, his head bowed. When any of the brothers and sisters addressed him, he didn't speak; she noticed his father spoke for him. Soon people stopped trying, it being too pitiful and serving to strengthen their feelings of guilt. Her own mother didn't stop, though. She hugged his stiff body and kissed his cold cheek. Through his black hair he shot unfathomable looks. Tirzah, waiting beside her mother, squeezed his hand, and he squeezed back.

She stops walking altogether. Ahead, at the bottom of the tall steps that lead up to the manse, she can hear Biddy and Ffion, a friend of Biddy's from school, talking about the exams. But Tirzah hangs back, seared by the thought of Osian's penitent journey. How did Pastor's wife greet Osian? she wonders. His walk around the fellowship was probably her idea; she's always keen on contrition, forever calling some poor soul out on account of a lapse. Tirzah's mother had been on the sharp end with her a few times. In fact she came home from the Dorcas meeting not long ago looking blotchy and breathless. I told her, she'd said. Mrs Thomas, I said. You may be the wife of a minister, but just you remember the scripture tells us first to sort out the plank in our own eye before we start pointing to the tiny speck in someone else's. Tirzah was impressed. If I did wrong, so be it, her mother had gone on, folding her headsquare into a tiny knot. She always was a judgemental piece, even as a child. Now Tirzah walks on, sure Osian wouldn't have received a scrap of comfort from her. Everyone who goes to the girls' meeting is mesmerised by Mrs Thomas. She is a thin, bow-legged woman who grasps her own throat with nervous fingers while she's talking. Tirzah is amazed by the marks left on her skin when she addresses them each month. On the way home from the meeting they often break into groups and discuss how Mrs Thomas can stand it, throttling herself like that all the time.

Not that long ago, everyone had laughed when Biddy said Mrs Thomas was actually off her onion. Ffion laughed the loudest, her stiff pigtails jerking about. Yeah, she'd said, backing Biddy up, that woman makes everybody cry, just like onions do. Tirzah saw how Ffion would laugh at such a thing; her parents were not chapel-goers, and she only attends when she's bored. Her parents buy her all the latest fashions. That night she was wearing tight denim bell-bottoms that showed off her slender legs, and a striped top that exposed her midriff when she moved. What do you mean? Tirzah had asked her, embarrassed that she didn't understand what *off her onion* meant, starkly aware of her own old-lady skirt and blouse. Mad. Bonkers. Nuts, love, Ffion explained, chewing a fresh oblong of pink Bazooka Joe. Away with the fairies. That's what she is. Tirzah was delighted by the onion idea. It is true, she'd thought. Mrs T is deranged. Some of the girls started to complain, saying it was wrong to talk about the pastor's wife like that. If any of you have got a problem with what I said, Ffion had announced, chewing her gum in an exaggerated way and placing her hands on her hips, let's have it out here and now. Me and Bid are ready. The girls had then drifted off in small clumps, heads together.

Mrs Thomas can't even be kind to herself. Why would a person strangle themselves over and over again? wonders Tirzah as she walks on. Even though she wears high-necked blouses, you can still see the little plum-shaped bruises, some old, some fresh. It's as if she hates herself. She is a scary person, so it's difficult to feel sorry for her. Mrs Thomas has twin boys who hardly ever make a sound. Their coin-flat faces are impassive under two identical coverings of brown hair so thin and shining that they look like child mannequins. Every Sunday they wear miniature tweed replicas of a grown man's suit, with tie and pin, and kneel on the floor either side of their mother's lap in a pew all to themselves. Tirzah sits behind with her parents and she knows the boys are always absorbed with drawing burning aircraft and bodies spurting with blood in their matching lined notebooks. More and more she believes that a sort of fervent, smothered insanity grips the whole congregation. Biddy smiles as Tirzah catches them up at the bottom of the steps. Let's get this over with, she says.

In the crowded room, Tirzah, Biddy and Ffion manage to bag the sofa as usual. Now they are older it's a tight fit, but they are always perfectly good and never fidget. Mrs Thomas would have them down the front in a trice, they know, if she could find a reason for doing so. As they settle, Ffion asks Tirzah how she's done in the exams. Fine, Tirzah says. Come on, tell me, Ffion presses. I s'pect you got all A's. Am I right? Tirzah nods. Ssshh, she adds. The oracle is about to utter. Mrs Thomas is speaking. Now, girls, she says from her place nearest the electric fire, remember, I am the shepherdess tonight, and you are the sheep. That means I lead, and you follow. The girls watch her fingers plucking the fabric of her skirt. You must ask for a prayerful, humble attitude and an open heart. Tirzah is straining to see Mrs Thomas's hands, and nudges Biddy when Mrs Thomas suddenly lunges for her own frilly-collared neck. It's as if the hand belongs to someone else.

Let us pray, Mrs Thomas says, closing her eyes against the terrible sinfulness of the world. And cultivate a blessed state of readiness. Tirzah sits, pinned between Ffion and Biddy, breathing in the smell of Ffion's chewing gum. The three of them always pass a squeeze back and forth each week as Mrs Thomas asks the group to open their hearts. Squeeze, goes Ffion's bony hand in hers. Is anything burdening you, dear ones? Mrs Thomas asks, sighing as she grips either side of her windpipe tightly. There is a long, pressurised sort of silence in the warm room. The electric fire creaks, its two bars glowing like red-hot pokers. Tirzah sends the squeeze on its way, aware of her own burdens. They are like hedgehoggy creatures: tightly curled balls of worry, eager to open out into unhandleable weights, both spiky and floppy. Sometimes even getting out of bed without wakening them is impossible. But one of these burdens is Osian, and truly, she is happy to carry him, if she must.

Behind her glasses, Mrs Thomas has the strangest eyelids, Tirzah realises, scrunching up her own eyes to have a look. Does anyone have such flat eyeballs? Or wet-looking lids? They are meant to be examining their hearts, as Mrs Thomas puts it, but the squeeze has returned, through Biddy, back to Ffion and now Tirzah feels it again and sends it on immediately. Off it goes, through Ffion, then briefly rests in the palm of Biddy's hand, who always returns it in a heartbeat. Tirzah has another look, hoping Mrs T is examining her own heart too, and sees she is on the point of standing up, desperate for someone to crack. Dear girls, we are all fallen creatures, she says, her voice coaxing. But Tirzah can see how tight her hand is and hear her laboured breathing. Waiting makes Mrs Thomas seize up. Tirzah wishes someone would speak.

Soon the questioning will begin, and then the questioning will become a winkling. Eventually she won't shirk her duty: Mrs Thomas will skewer someone. It's a relief when she finally chooses a person; all the other girls can slump back and keep their heads bowed. But still, listening to Mrs Thomas's remorseless questions makes Tirzah blush so thoroughly even her feet are hot. Biddy's long hair completely obscures her face, and Tirzah notices how it quivers like a pair of gauzy nightdresses hanging above a radiator. The squeeze between the girls becomes an elaborate pattern: two short, one long and three quick pulses. Tirzah imagines it's a series of thoughts passing between the three of them. Maybe Biddy or Ffion is trying to dredge up a sin, a trespass, a guilty lapse they can safely offer up to Mrs Thomas before she pounces. It doesn't seem likely with those two, though. But someone should volunteer, Tirzah knows. It's much the best way to do it.

Just as Tirzah begins to feel a bubble of laughter rising almost to her tonsils, she hears Mrs Thomas's voice calling her name. With a thrum of panic between the shoulder blades she stands and puts her palms together, starting to spill words automatically. Mrs Thomas the shepherdess releases her throat and raises a hand for silence. You have many failings, dear child, she says sorrowfully. And one of them is haste. Tirzah looks at her and is confused by the on-off dazzle coming from her lenses when she nods her head. Beware of it, shun it, poor struggling one, Mrs Thomas urges, happy now to have a volunteer. Haste can lead you down some danger-ous paths as a young woman. And while I'm on the subject, shun evil companions. You know who I'm referring to. Girls, she addresses the room. Dear, innocent girls, let Tirzah be a lesson to you.

Lesson? Shun? thinks Tirzah. Which paths? Why danger-ous? The companion is Osian, of course. For a moment, Tirzah wants to whack Mrs Evans with something, knock her glasses off her accusing, stunted little nose. And that goes for Pastor too. Then she realises the horrible woman would have a turn if she knew about Brân. This gives her a brief glow before she dismisses it; that won't help her now. In spite of herself, she

becomes afraid about those dangerous paths and needs to go
to the lav. Come, Mrs Thomas says, confess your sins, dear. You
will be better for it. A whispering breaks out among the girls
in the packed room. Tirzah is casting around for something to
tell Mrs Thomas before she loses patience. There is so much
she could spill out about so many things, but most of it is
unsayable. I have had bad thoughts, she blurts out at last, and
each word is like a bloodied tooth being wrenched from her
jaw. Ah, yes? Mrs Thomas sits forward in her chair. And? No
one will judge you, my child. Out with it. Tirzah suddenly
remembers something. I have harboured wicked thoughts
about you, she says, relieved to have something to say at last.
Mrs Thomas sits back and grips her throat again, paralysing
Tirzah with her flat eyes. Well? she asks. I have been thinking
you'd gone off your onion, Tirzah says, louder now. And for
that I am very sorry.

Mrs Thomas reluctantly lets go of her neck. Above the frill
of her blouse, dark red fingermarks appear. A silence, murky
as canal water, emanates from beneath the chair she sits in,
and Tirzah draws back, reluctant to be touched by it. Thank
you, Mrs Thomas says at last, swallowing with effort while
she looks down at the Bible's open pages. Her shoulders are
more rounded and her hair thinner somehow. The crowded
room waits, the silence teetering now on the edge of laughter.
Tirzah is triumphant, watching Mrs Thomas diminish before
the whole room. But almost immediately, her heart curls up
like a prodded woodlouse, and she prays that no one will laugh.
The red bars of the electric fire blacken at their edges, and the
drawn curtains quiver in a breeze. Everyone is still, and yet the
room feels full of movement. Tirzah is absolutely sure that if
anyone giggles now, Mrs Thomas will be irreparably damaged

in some way. She knows the wild, barely contained part of herself would love that. But suddenly, she doesn't even want strange, cruel Mrs T to suffer. There are more than enough unhappy people in her life already.

Praise Him upon the Loud Cymbals

(Psalm 150:5)

The fellowship is assembled in the chapel schoolroom. This evening they are getting ready for the first open-air meeting of the season on the new estate. Pastor has finally received a word from the Lord that said, Go ye, my people! And so they are going. Pastor has chosen Osian as the pole holder on one side of the banner, and most of the fellowship beam and nod as they take in this kindness; in small ways most people are doing their best to show Osian love. He remotely dips his head Tirzah's way when she waves, his face unreadable as a foreign book these days. She misses the old serene, slightly amused Osian on occasions like this. When she used to catch his eye he made her feel as if they were in on some hilarious, secret joke. But it wouldn't make her feel any better even if he did wink now. There is no hilarious joke; around her, people are buttoning up coats, tucking Bibles under arms, the women tying headscarves firmly under their chins. And they all look as nutty as she knew they would.

Biddy is not amongst the crowd. Tirzah wonders how she has the nerve to construct a believable illness and keep the

104

pretence going, but she obviously does. Her mother always believes the best of her. Maybe that's because she is too clever to do things like accuse Pastor's wife of being off her onion, even though she was the one who thought it. Honestly, Tiz, she'd said on the way home from the girls' meeting the night before, don't show people your hand all the time. Tirzah looked puzzled. Tell 'em what they want to hear, and no more, Biddy explained, irritated by Tirzah's innocence. Anyway, she doesn't have to evangelise today, lucky thing. Pastor is calling the room to order, and Mr Pascoe, the funny man who plays the miniature squeezebox, hasn't heard. The room falls silent, and they listen to him playing a tune, each button clicking when he presses it, until Pastor touches his shoulder and with a start he breaks off mid-note, his bulgy eyes winking rapidly. Brother Pascoe, Pastor says, rubbing his hands and smiling, your eagerness is a lesson to us all. Everyone murmurs an assent. The air escapes from Mr Pascoe's instrument like a dying sigh, and he puts it down on the table so he can wipe his hands with a hankie.

The brethren are in a huddle, praying hard about the out-reach they are going to do. Honestly, Tirzah thinks, anybody would expect we were venturing in through the gates of hell to fight Lucifer himself. She inclines her head and allows her hair to fall forward so she's in a tiny cave with a doorway below her forehead. Slowly she puts her hand in her pocket and roots around. At last she finds what she's groping for and pulls out an old, fuzzy cough sweet. Just as she places it between her lips, her mother leans across and shakes her. Give, she hisses, holding out her hand so that Tirzah has to spit the sweet into it. By the side of Tirzah's chair is the tambourine she is going to play at the meeting. Its coloured ribbons are coiled inside as if asleep. She can hardly take in that she will soon be standing with everybody else on a patch of rough ground somewhere in the new estate, bashing her tambourine on to each hip and elbow as if she were some sort of demented puppet. She can picture the ribbons jerking around in the wind like startled snakes.

Maybe I will be run over by a speeding car, she thinks. It would be worth a broken leg. Or a few ribs. She doubts that will actually happen, though. Then it occurs to her that if the Pentecostal fire they were always asking for fell on the congregation at this very moment, everyone would be so occupied with praising the Lord and dancing and being slain by the Spirit they wouldn't notice the time until it was too late to go out. And surely the flames of the Holy Spirit would engulf the whole village, not just the new estate, and then everyone would be saved. Now the fellowship takes up the hymn her mother has started. *Make a joyful noise unto the Lord*, they all sing. *Praise Him with the cymbals.*

Tirzah decides to absent herself from the rest of the meeting; her body will be there, playing the tambourine and handing out tracts, but the real her will be off somewhere else, lying in the bouncy little whinberry bushes on the summit of the mountain maybe, looking up at the clouds rolling across the grey sky. She is going to make the journey, in her mind, from the chapel schoolroom, all the way to the mountain top, noting every small thing as she travels. This will take ages. Especially if she stops to look at the view or pick berries or make a flower chain. So off she goes with the group, looking at her shoes as they walk to the door, a part of her brain aware that the outreachers are marching forth from the schoolroom. There is Osian and another big boy firmly holding up the banner, and everyone falls in behind. She can hear murmurs as they talk amongst themselves, but by the time they get to the new estate they are silent. With the other part of her brain, Tirzah can sense herself withdrawing, hovering high above the knot of outreachers. As if from far away, Tirzah hears Mr Pascoe ventilating his squeezebox and playing an introductory line. People struggle to find the right note. It's surprising how weak the sound is outdoors, even though they are singing *And Can It Be*, which is a belter. The voices waver up to her like damp campfire smoke, and disappear in the fresh air. Even the bass lines of the deacons can scarcely be heard. In her imagination, Tirzah has reached the long, steep lane she and Osian always used to take to the derelict pub near the boundary of the forest. Today she has so much time she decides to push through the overgrown hedge that surrounds the pub garden and have a look around. It's like being a ghost; she can drift easily from one place to the next, and no one can stop her. The hymn dies away, almost as if the fellowship had forgotten the tune, and Pastor starts to preach. Tirzah can see net curtains moving and a group of children on bicycles coming to listen. This level of interest is surprising; in the old village, all doors stay firmly closed. Even the kids playing in the streets are indifferent when an outreach meeting is on. Tirzah concentrates on the pub garden. Two sheep are grazing the lush, dandelion-studded grass. It's so quiet, she can hear their jaws working, and the juicy scrunch as they chew. Crows are sitting in a dead tree like scruffy ornaments.

Tirzah can make out, over the squawks of the watching birds, the voice of Pastor shouting reedily that all have sinned and come short of something. Hell is real, lost ones! she can hear him yell, his voice almost plaintive. Repent ye! But on the mountainside, sin and punishment, hymns and prayers and Bibles all seem irrelevant. The mountain is ancient and knows other things, she thinks, gazing round at the tall bracken leaning over the hedges. And who's to say they are not true? Its folds and green nooks, the little glades and runs no one sees, are always giving out something she can't quite understand. But she can sense it, smell it even. The open spaces, the short, gnarled hawthorns rooted in the red earth, the old, empty sheep skulls with their wind-fingered jaws, the secret nests of animals, all fill Tirzah with a sense of the limitless, ungraspable splendour of the world. It's as if a new dawn had split the sky, now, towards the end of a ghastly, ordinary day, and she is a glowing, freshly hatched creature. I wish poor Osian could see. This has nothing to do with the God of our chapel.

Tirzah can just make out Pastor summing up his message. God bless you all, dear friends, he's shouting. Remember, God is love. Hell is real! Then Mr Pascoe starts the last hymn. How anyone who is not born into this could swallow these teachings, Tirzah does not know, feeling uncomfortable to countenance such a thought. Now she is being drawn back down into the valley by an invisible thread that is snagged around the chambers of her heart. She wants to hold on to the glow emanating from her body, clutch at the derelict garden, the draggled, peaceful sheep and the crow-hung tree, but they all recede. She can hear a jingly, whacking kind of sound, and with a shock, realises she is playing her tambourine with energy and commitment. *Crash!* go the metal cymbals around its wooden rim. Up and round fly the ribbons. The song winds on and on, and soon they are back at the schoolroom.

Sit down, beloveds, Pastor shouts, sit down all. He has his usual patches of paler skin on each cheekbone. Ladies come out of the kitchen with trays of cake. There is a party atmosphere. I think we all agree who should have the biggest portion of cake and the first cup of tea, he says, walking towards Tirzah. She is confused when he hands her a triangle of Victoria sponge on which the icing sugar sits like untrodden snow. You of all people, dear Tirzah, he tells her, you alone played your humble instrument with grace today. Never have I seen the tambourine played to the glory of God in such a way. Like King David, you were, before the Almighty. Let this be a lesson to us all. The Lord can use even the weakest vessel to do His will. Tirzah looks around at the bright-eyed congregation. You were a conduit today, Pastor says. A conduit for love. Let us pray. Tirzah sits with her cup in one hand and plate in the other, aware of her staring, open-mouthed parents, as Pastor gives thanks for her witness, and imagines she is standing on the mountain top. She sees herself, a doll-like, shining figure, her heart bubbling with joy, walking towards an immense Something with her arms raised, looking at what might be the face of another sort of god.

Any That Pisseth Against the Wall

(1 Samuel 25:22)

The day after Tirzah's tambourine and cake experience, she is finishing breakfast. Dada has left for work, and her mother sits down and says they are going to have someone to stay. Her parents have never volunteered to give a room to one of the needy before; her mother always said their house was too small whenever Pastor made one of his appeals. It would be nice to have a girl, Tirzah says. Not a girl, her mother answers, looking a little shifty. A boy actually. But where will he sleep? Tirzah asks. Your father will explain tonight, her mother says, now busy at the sink. It's the right thing to do, and I thank the Lord for revealing it to me. But, Mam, Tirzah says, carrying things to be washed, you must know more than that. Don't I have a right to know? Her mother turns the hot tap off vigorously. The right, child? she says. What right? I've heard it all now. I'll rights you a smacked bum sandwich if you are not careful. Big as you are. She raises her hand as if to strike Tirzah's cheek. No, count up to ten, Mair, she says under her breath. Tirzah is tickled by her mother and can't help smiling. Go, now! her mother shouts.

Before I really let go. Naughty girl! Rights indeed. I knew your recent blessing wouldn't last.

The girls meet in the tree house to talk. Are you having anybody? Tirzah asks. Nope, Biddy says, nibbling on a biscuit. This is typical, Tirzah thinks. Only my parents will go the extra five hundred miles. It's not fair. Uncle Maldwyn and Aunty Ceinwen don't seem to get bothered by the Lord's revelations. I s'pose he'll be put up in your box room, Biddy says. The box room is tiny. Tirzah wonders if a bed would even fit in it. I hope he's a small boy, Biddy adds, licking her fingers. For his sake. Through a gap in the wooden slats, Tirzah squints at the tiny green plum blobs clustered all over the branches that not long ago were pillowed with blossom. Everything is suddenly irritating; her house will be uncomfortable with a stranger in it. She won't like it. Perhaps he'll be a bit of all right and you'll fall in love with him, Biddy suggests. Don't be so stupid, Tirzah says. I'm going home.

The boy arrives on Saturday. Tirzah and her mother have been hard at work, sorting the box room out. Someone has donated a narrow bed, and the old chair is a bedside table. Tirzah found a copy of *Biggles Learns to Fly*, and an old *Dandy* annual in the attic for the boy to read. She doesn't know if he will be interested, but it's the best she can do. There is no lamp, though – just the ceiling light. Well, says Tirzah's mother, we've never claimed to be the Ritz, but it'll do. Clean and paid for, and better than the street. She is flapping about with a duster, doing a final once-over when there's a knock at the door. They both run downstairs and are just in time to take their places behind Dada in the narrow hall. Through the dimpled glass they can make out a tall, bulky shape. Tirzah suddenly feels an extreme reluctance to see who it is. Dad, she says, pulling her father's sleeve. Don't open it. Her father doesn't reply. Oh, Gwyll, her mother whispers. Are we doing the right thing? Silence, both of you, he says; remember, this is one of the lost, and he flings the door open. Tirzah peers round her father and sees a pockmarked, underfed young man leaning against the doorframe, carrying a duffel bag. O'right? he says, baring his uneven teeth in a grin. This isn't a boy, Tirzah thinks. Her mother sways, and Tirzah has to support her.

Later, the three of them sit around the kitchen table with the door closed. Now then, Tirzah's father says in a loud whisper, exaggeratedly moving his lips, eyebrows rising and falling rapidly. This is a test of our faith. It would be vain to deny it. Derry is not as we expected him to be. The Lord has His mysterious ways. Tirzah can hear the music from Derry's radio tumbling down the stairs and seeping under the door. Never before has this sort of sound been allowed in the house. The beat is keeping time with her heart. But we were told a little boy, Gwyll, her mother says, starting to cry. I was looking forward to a nice little boy. It isn't seemly to have a grown man under our roof. Enough, her father says in his normal voice. Dry up, please. He isn't a grown man. He is nineteen. Still a boy until twenty-one in my eyes. Mind you, what Pastor was thinking, handing something like this our way, I don't know. If I were a lesser man, I would suspect him of having a laugh at our expense. We will have to trust the Lord to protect us. And especially you, Tirzah. You must be on your guard at all times. Why me? Tirzah thinks. I knew it was a bad idea from the beginning. She blushes, thinking of the *Dandy* and *Biggles* she put in his room before they knew he was Derry-the-man.

Her father begins a sermon about the Devil's wiles. Tirzah sits, looking exactly as a good girl should. Just as she expected, her father starts on about stupid old lust, boring old sin and the terrible flesh. Let us pray, he concludes. She and her mother clasp hands and bow their heads. Oh Lord, her father starts, his voice vibrating with emotion, protect us, thy most humble servants. He lays a sweating hand on Tirzah's head. Especially this pure, untouched maiden, dear Father. Tirzah struggles to control the desire to shake his hand off her head and give him a piece of her mind. Amen, they all say. Going up to bed, Tirzah can smell dirty clothes, cigarette smoke and what must be some sort of deodorant spray in the stairwell. On the landing she pauses; the bathroom door is open and she can sense the man is in there.

She decides to walk to her room as if nothing is wrong, but when she passes the bathroom she can't help herself, and looks in. Derry is peeing through the gap in his Y-fronts, his discarded trousers in a heap behind him. The sound is like someone throwing a full bucket of water down the toilet. She can see he is holding his penis in his fist, the arc of urine bursting from its tip a deep yellow. Derry swivels his head to look at her, keeping his chin tucked in, and watches her as she watches until the flow dwindles and finally stops. O'right? he says, giving his penis a small shake, as if to include it in the greeting. Howzit goin'? She can't move for a moment. The scars on his face look like fork marks in uncooked pastry. Well, well, well, he adds, as if speaking to himself, giving her a good, slow, up-and-down inspection. Things in by here are takin' a turn for the better, don' you think? The sight of his grin releases her and she stumbles past to her room.

Tirzah slams the door and leans against it. In the dark, she stills her breathing the better to hear what's happening on the landing. First the toilet flushes, then the light is clicked off. Derry's footsteps move towards the box room, but then she senses him changing direction. For a few paralysed moments she listens to him whistling between his teeth outside her door, and then he walks away. She can't move until she's sure he's in his room. When she's convinced he has gone, she allows herself to slide down and sit on the floor. Tirzah isn't at all sleepy now. It's as if someone has given her a shot of something and now she is more alive than usual. Looking round the room, she searches for something to secure her door with and decides the chair will be perfect, wedging its top bar under the handle. Then she quickly undresses and lies down to ponder on what she saw in the bathroom. So, that's a penis, she thinks. That thing like one of Mr Bayliss the butcher's raw pork sausages? How could I have just stood there and gawped like that? She busies herself with plaiting her hair, trying to think of other things. But when she's drifting off to sleep she thinks about Derry's penis with its helmet-shaped tip. Well, admit it, girl, she sleepily concedes. You are a little bit disappointed.

In her dreams, Tirzah is in a chapel both like, and strangely not like, her own. She realises the walls are the trunks of immensely tall fir trees. Up where the roof should be is a small rectangle of white sky. If Tirzah cranes her neck and squints, she can just make out a bird circling far above. There is a sermon going on, but no one stands in the pulpit. All the congregation are present, still and quiet. When Tirzah studies them, they are like wooden replicas of themselves. There are the little kneeling wooden figures of the Pastor's boys, bending over their notebooks, and sure enough, Pastor's wife sits beside them, strangling herself with a stiff hand. Everyone is in their place, blank faces upturned to the empty pulpit. Tirzah looks at her own hands below the cuffs of her blouse; she is the only one made of flesh and blood.

Then she becomes aware of a slow, lumbery movement at her feet and looks down. Coiling and uncoiling on the floorboards is a short, strong-looking snake. The snake's blunt mouth end has no eyes but seems to know the route. Up it moves, pink scales winking, around and around Tirzah's naked leg, with a firm grip. Tirzah stares, wide-eyed as the snake noses its way under her skirt, and observes the demure smile on its mouth. She squeezes her thighs together, but the snake is too strong. Slowly she relaxes her muscles. I suppose this snake is harmless, she thinks, and rests her head back. The snake is butting his head on the gusset of her pants. She can feel herself melting into the pew, her breathing slow, her legs slack. Then there is a cataclysmic flash and the smell of burning. The moment before she wakes, Tirzah realises that this time, where the sky had been, a huge eye, lashless as a bird's, has appeared and, not unkindly, is examining her.

Flee Also Youthful Lusts

(2 Timothy 2:22)

Derry slips into their lives, with them, but not with them. Tirzah's mother makes his meal and keeps it warm for him in the oven. When he gets home from work around seven o'clock, he takes the dried-out plate of food to his room. In the morning he's up and out before anybody is awake. So apart from encounters on the landing or at the front door, Tirzah hardly ever sees him. Still, the smell of him, his hissy sort of whistling and the sound of his radio remind her there is a stranger in the house. If she comes downstairs in her night-dress, her mother sends her straight back to her room to put a dressing gown on. She can't relax like she used to. He was out all last Sunday, but today he is hanging around.

Earlier, her father had told Derry the times of the services. Derry was out in the back garden, squatting against the empty rockery wall having a smoke. Tirzah watched from the bathroom window as her father, in his dark Sunday suit, came out and theatrically took several sniffs at the thin, early air, pretending to survey the catastrophic garden for a while before addressing Derry. Poor Dada, she thought, looking at

116

the way his Brylcreemed black hair shone, please don't say anything. But he'd issued the invitation to Derry and called him *dear boy*. Tirzah's cheeks flamed as she heard Derry say without emphasis, Isno' gonna 'appen, mate, save your breath. He hadn't even troubled himself to stand when he spoke. Tirzah wanted to cry at the sight of the brave, dipping movement of her father's chin, and the way he stood for a minute, humming, before disappearing back into the house. She'd stayed at the window and breathed in the smoke from Derry's cigarette, watching him cough up phlegm and spit it into the garden's only patch of flowers.

Later, as the congregation stands to sing, Tirzah clutches a hymn book to her coat. Horeb is full this morning, and the men thunder away at the bass line. This usually makes Tirzah shiver with delight, but she is locked into a new way of thinking and can barely hear the singing. The memory of the dream is still with her, and it makes her self-conscious. It's as if the fellowship has only to look at her face and they will guess her shameful, secret thoughts. She feels again the knocking of the dream-snake at the gusset of her pants. Something is happening to Tirzah, and she understands she is becoming a different person. You can never unknow something once you know it, she thinks. And I can't look at any man in the same way now I know what a penis is like. She had never really thought of Osian as having a penis. The idea of him carrying around a little pink thing in his trousers like all the other men in the world makes her dejected and anxious. Anyway, it isn't right, thinking about Osian in this way any more. He certainly would not like her to.

Then another thought darts into her mind. What about Brân? For some reason she imagines that Brân's would be more muscular, more *alive*, for want of a better word, than anybody else's. She can almost feel the wind rushing past her ears as she runs down the Broad Road That Leads to Destruction; this is heaps worse than thinking about bulges, for goodness' sake. I have changed, she thinks, with a judder. Then her mind fills with another picture; this time she is sitting on the stony lip of a well and willingly swinging her legs over the edge. If you're not careful, Tirzah, any minute now you'll jump in and be swallowed up by all this sinful wondering, she thinks. But just as quickly another thought occurs to her: So what if I fell in this well of mine? Maybe it's not even a bottomless well after all. Maybe it's a beautiful pool of clear water. Swimming there would be wonderful, and I'd like it. Maybe, instead of legs and a nose, I actually have a tail and fins, and they are waiting for a dousing in deep water to appear.

Everyone sits, and Tirzah is left standing for a long moment before she realises the hymn has ended. Pastor shoots her a cool look from the pulpit and she blushes, sinking into the pew. Her mother's elbow jabs her side. Whatever's the matter? she hisses. Pull yourself together, for all our sakes. I'm unwell, Tirzah whispers back. I have to get out. Rubbish, her mother answers. There's nothing wrong with you. Sit still and ask the Lord to help you concentrate. She is shredding a tissue into her lap and Tirzah can see her neck beginning to mottle. Her father leans across and places a large hand on Tirzah's leg. *Be still*, he says over-loudly, *and know that I am God.* Listen to Pastor's words, you poor, restless one.

Tirzah goes rigid with fear; maybe her father knows what she's been thinking. When her mind clears, she realises that Pastor is preaching about the sins of the flesh. No one, he shouts, no one in this room is immune to the frailties of these wicked bodies of ours. And when I say frailties, I mean the sins of lust and lasciviousness. Let's call this particular set of spades by their odious name. He pulls out a snow-white handkerchief and wipes his forehead. Everyone is rapt. Everyone is uncomfortable; Tirzah can sense a collective examining of souls. The air positively vibrates with the power of all the examining going on. I'm doubtful anyone even understands what the word lasciviousness means, she thinks, trying to get comfortable in the pew. How can you be a slave to something you don't even know about? It doesn't seem logical. Obviously, it's very sinful, and that's enough for most folk here.

But anyway, can this be true? Tirzah wonders, watching Pastor fold his hankie carefully and slide it back into his trouser pocket. Surely only young people have lusts. Could old, wheelchair-bound Mr Trimble really be a slave to his body? Or Miss Payne the organist, with her snagged hairnet and Parma Violet sweeties? Tirzah has a quick look around. What about old, smelly Mrs Beynon? Tirzah thinks about Mrs Beynon's deformed feet and the little cut-out holes she makes in her Sunday shoes so that her knotted toe joints can poke through unhindered. The little crocheted flowers Mrs Beynon sews to cover things up have always repelled Tirzah. And what about the elders? What about Pastor's wife, with her death-like hands and tight perm? And Mr Porter, the deacon who roots around in his trouser pockets for Murray Mints to hand out and looks after the chapel boiler? I'm probably the one person here who *is* having lascivious thoughts, she realises. Suddenly she is pleased to be almost a grown-up. The back of Osian's head is visible three rows in front. He is half-turned, his elbow resting on the ledge of the pew beside him. Despite everything, the way Osian's lovely fingers twine through his dense hair gives Tirzah the oddest sensation in the pit of her stomach.

The sermon is a long one. Some of the congregation break down and wail. Tirzah's mother is fidgeting. All this talk of the flesh makes her embarrassed, Tirzah knows. It's as if the bodies of the fellowship have heated up, thinking about the sins of the flesh, and the whole room is about to ignite. Her mother's neck is now a solid red column. Pastor has whipped himself into such a righteous frenzy he has blobs of foam in the corners of his mouth. People are moaning, calling on the Lord for forgiveness. Mr Jones, a quiet man who Tirzah doesn't know, stands, visibly trembling, and confesses to having lascivious thoughts about somebody else's wife. Smite me, Lord, he shouts. I am a filthy rag in your presence. This is a signal for people to let everything go. Tirzah sits, cool and collected amidst the sobbing and confessing. She is content to gaze at Osian's head and shoulders, willing him to look round.

Just as her father makes preliminary moves to stand and confess something, Osian turns and darts a look at her. She makes a gesture towards the door, and they both fight their way through the bowed and crying members of the fellowship to the aisle. Osian turns the ornate doorknob and they squeeze through the smallest gap. Out in the churchyard, calm, worldly-looking crows sit on gravestones, and the yew trees squat, keeping guard. What do you want? Osian says. I shouldn't be out here with you. I have to go back. My father will notice I've gone. Behind them, the sounds of shouting and singing seep under the door. What do you mean, what do I want? Tirzah asks. You looked at me first. Anyway, why shouldn't you be out here? Osian kicks the heads off a bunch of dandelion clocks, his head down. You might as well stay with me now, she says, and pulls him away from the path before he can speak. They climb the churchyard wall. There was a time not long ago when you would have been laughing at them with me, she says over her shoulder.

Tirzah and Osian walk in silence all the way up the narrow lane that leads to the deserted pub. Which way? Tirzah asks at the ridge. Shall we go to the top or into the forestry? He doesn't seem to care much. You choose, he says. Tirzah thinks about her dream, and the fir-tree walls of the sort-of chapel she sat in, with its high roofless sky-ceiling. She remembers the examining eye that pinned her to the seat. Forestry, she says, and runs ahead, wondering if there is any point in bringing Osian here. But she still wants to try to find herself and Osian as they used to be. Once they are in through the first thinner ranks of trees, the woody quiet and scented gloom slows them down. Osian hangs back and lets Tirzah pull him along. Soon she finds what she's looking for. Do you remember this place? she asks, tugging him down beside her on to a flat clearing between the roots of a huge tree. If you just rest here and breathe, you might feel better, she tells him. It always worked for us when we were younger.

They lie and look up at the dusty, sparse branches above them. Tirzah can see the way the trees grow; where the branches start to sprout they are small and ragged, and then, higher up, they spring out straight and sinewy, festooned with masses of dark green, needly fingers. It is utterly silent in the forest, and warm. This is my chapel, Tirzah realises, gazing up to the living rafters overhead. Everything worth worshipping is probably here. She wants to tell Osian so much but suddenly is too tired. It's all mixed up: Derry's penis, the friendly snake climbing her leg, the feeling she'd had about the mountain and the forest. The horrible, shameful, drowned bundle of Osian's guilt. Mostly she doesn't think the new, sad Osian would want to listen. We're almost grown-up, you know, she says. Soon we will finish school, and then who knows? You are clever, Osian, and you will be able to do anything you want. She studies his face, but he seems like a stranger.

Tirzah is gripped by a need to make Osian take notice. She thinks hard, her mind darting about, picking up ideas and discarding them; Osian is unreachable. So she empties her mind and waits to see what will happen next. Almost it is as if she were sitting on a branch way above their prone bodies. She sees herself place her hand on the zip of Osian's trousers and rub. Then she is beside him, feeling him change shape and grow firm. Osian grabs her hand and lifts it, pressing her fingers painfully inside his fist. Control yourself, Tirzah, he says, his voice flat. This is a sin. No, Osian, she says, her eyes filling, I only wanted to wake you up. But then she realises she doesn't know what she wanted. Finally she explains it was something to do with trying to make them both into a normal, carefree boy and girl. After a pause she tries again. Won't you talk to me about what happened? I know you have not got over that terrible thing with the bed sheet. He sits up and allows his head to drop between his bent knees. I can't speak about it, he tells her, his voice thickened. Since then my relationship with God has changed. I see what I should do now. Yes, but you don't need to change towards your friends, Tirzah says. He glances at her and seems to soften. For now let's have a cwtch, he says. There's nothing wrong with that. As you keep saying, we are butties. So Tirzah lays her head carefully on his shoulder. Go to sleep, she hears him whisper. I'll keep watch and make sure nothing happens to you. But Tirzah isn't sleepy. No thanks, she says. I think I'm perfectly capable of making sure nothing happens to me myself.

The Love of Money Is the Root of All Evil

(1 Timothy 6:10)

It's difficult to earn any money, Tirzah thinks, gazing at an old, banana-shaped stain on the ceiling, especially when you don't have a job. Her father is perplexed by even the notion of pocket money. But, Dada, she'd screwed herself up to tell him the day after her last birthday, Biddy earns a bit from her newspapers and gets pocket money. Even Osian is paid for working in the shop on Saturdays. Everybody in school gets a little something every week. I don't see why I can't. He ignored the mention of a job. Pocket money? he'd said, eyes big with astonishment. It was as if she'd asked for a pet dragon. What would a good girl want with money, I'd like to know? There is nothing a good girl needs, surely? He was working himself up. And what is this *everybody in school* business? If all your school friends chopped off a hand and fed it to their guinea pigs, would you do the same? He looked at her sharply. What are you doing being friends with these lost souls, may I ask? Tirzah tried to turn him from this last question and soothe him. I might want to get a gift for someone, she'd explained, twisting her fingers behind her back. Or buy a nice book. Nonsense, he said, folding the newspaper with a series of emphatic movements before getting up to go out. Money indeed. I've never heard of such avarice and weakness. And that had been that.

She drapes herself across the bed and tries to imagine ways to save for the CYC weekend deposit, but nothing comes to mind. Does she even want to go now? Biddy isn't madly keen and probably Osian will not be allowed. Still, her mother is squirrelling away little amounts from her grocery shopping allowance, so Tirzah knows she will have to attend. Her mother is very keen on Tirzah's behalf. And no complaining from you, madam, she'd told Tirzah after showing her the old purse the money will go in and where she will hide it. I don't want to hear any of your moaning about sausages for three days on the trot, or any other bits of wisdom, mind, she'd said, smiling. You know your father never notices what he's putting in his mouth, as long as it's hot and on time.

I can do the same with my money for chapel collections, Tirzah decides, feeling a pang at her mother's excitement and jumping up to get her notebook and pencil. Soon she has a little grid drawn out, with all the Sundays and how much she can save. But is this actually stealing from the Lord? she wonders. Her father has decreed that as far as he's concerned, the subject of the holiday is closed. So it's his fault. This is between the two of you women, he'd told them over his plate of liver and onions when Tirzah asked him about the deposit. Her mother had pulled her towards the kitchen, exasperated because Tirzah never knew when to choose her moment. Let me deal with this, please, she'd whispered. I will sort it out. Studying her grid now, Tirzah decides Sunday collection money saving is a start. She must get her schoolbooks out and start to revise. It's no use thinking about anything until the O-levels are over.

Anybody'd think this weekend away was as secret as, say, sanitary towels, Tirzah thinks, hiding her notebook under the mattress and rearranging the bedspread, and opening a geography text book. She recalls her mother's tirade when she'd discovered Tirzah lining all her strange new Dr White's towels in a row on her desk. What in the name of old Roley are you doing? she'd said, glancing over her shoulder towards the landing and the closed study door. The back of the airing cupboard is the place for these. Her cheeks were flushed as she knelt to gather up the scattered towels by their loops. No one wants such things waved under their nose, she'd explained. Tirzah had been infected with her sense of urgency, and rushed around, doing very little, but feeling the need for action. Lying back down now on her bed the wrong way round, her bottom resting on the pillow and her legs against the wall behind the headboard, she remembers how impossible it had been to force those towels back into the bag; they'd mysteriously doubled in size the moment they'd been let out.

Tirzah is on her way home from school when Derry comes alongside her. Hiya, he says, out of puff. You're a fast one. Like a bloody whippet, you are. A stone-deaf whippet. I've been calling you f'rages. Tirzah is surprised; usually no one sees Derry in the daytime. She realises he is a mystery. Where does he go all day? What does he do with himself? Hello, she answers, looking away, not wanting to encourage him to hang around. Let's have a whiff by here, he says, indicating a wall. I could do with a fag. They stop, and Tirzah watches him roll a cigarette and light it. He coughs and spits a blob of ropey-looking mucus not far from her shoes. Tirzah moves away. So, he says, settling his buttocks on the wall and sending a little landslide of shale down, what are you up to? She is so surprised by the question she lets out a tiny laugh. Oh, funny, am I? he asks, taking a deep drag. No, not really, it's just that I'm never up to anything, she says. I'm sorry to seem rude. Then she blushes, realising she is always up to something. He directs a stream of smoke sideways with his lips. Don't get your knickers in a knot, he tells her. Tha' wouldn't do at all.

The idea of her underwear seems to hang in the air, expanding almost, and Tirzah tries to think of something different to say. Where do you work? she asks. Fact'ry, he answers, clearly not interested in talking about his job. So, what type of knickers do a good Christian girl wear? he continues, giving her the once-over. All done up in chains an' locks, I s'pect. Before Tirzah can move, he has slipped a hand under her skirt and slid it around to touch the inside of her bare thigh. Get off! she shouts, a ripple of something like electricity shooting up her leg. She jumps away and drops her school bag. Jesus Jones the First! he exclaims, laughing and coughing. You're a touchy one. Bein' friendly, I was. Tha's all. She stands uncertainly before him. That is blasphemy, she tells him. He spits again. Derry has a job in a factory, she realises. And so he must have money. Her mother had said he was only with them till he got back on his feet. He's contemplating her, and takes another long drag on his cigarette. A scorching, wicked arrow of an idea thwacks Tirzah between the shoulder blades. She takes a step back, distancing herself from Derry's knees, scandalised. How can I even begin to imagine something so wicked? she wonders, looking at the black buttons on his donkey jacket. You're a bit of a stunner, he says quietly, reaching to touch her wind-blown hair. And a real little lady. How do you make them pretty things? Tirzah allows him to twine a springy curl around his index finger. She is looking inward at her own black heart as it smokes and wrinkles, barely registering the almost reverential way he examines the shining ringlet.

Now what's happening? she wonders. I was walking home from school, minding my own business, and look: I'm thinking of charging Derry for a feel. The place on her thigh where he touched her earlier is behaving as if it has just had an extra-sticky plaster ripped off it. This is all wrong, she knows. Derry is one of the lost, and she should shun him. I don't even like him, she tells herself. He's disgusting. She remembers his underfed body. The Lord gave me my hair, she says, pulling herself away again. Get off me. Derry looks crestfallen. Oh, the Lord, is it? he says, grinding his stub out on a stone. Will the Lord mind if you just come and sit by me? And he pats the wall. I promise to be good. So she sits, ready to run if need be. The breeze is cold, and she's hungry, but she doesn't move. Her brain won't stop thinking its thoughts. Really, I could make some money from Derry, she thinks, appalled. It is a bit wrong, but this would be for a good cause. And no one else needs to know.

She is late getting home. And where may I ask have you been? her mother demands cheerfully, tasting from a ladle. I've been waiting ages for you. Look, I've made a steak and kidney pie. With lots of nice gravy. She is dishing out dripping slices. Tirzah throws her cardigan and school bag on the table and runs upstairs, suddenly too ashamed to stay in the kitchen. What on earth is going on? her mother calls, banging down the ladle and quickly following. In the bathroom, Tirzah leans over the toilet. Cariad, her mother calls through the door. Are you poorly? Tirzah is hiccupping now. Oh, Mam, she gulps, between times, I don't know what's wrong, honest I don't. Then she starts to cry at the sight of her mother's rosy, concerned face. Her heart is about to break free from her old gym top. I am such a wicked girl, she sobs. You would hate me if you knew. Now then. Wicked indeed! her mother says, finally coming in. Silly sometimes, maybe. Unwise and all over the place. But this is one of your funny five minutes, that's all. Tirzah goes on hiccupping and sobbing. Nothing happened with Derry, and anyway, she was only going to let him have one touch, she tells herself, but thoughts are as bad as deeds. She leans her head on her mother's bosom, picturing that horrible wall and Derry with his finger in her ringlet, and the root of all evil describing a series of devious shapes energetically around them both.

Foxes Have Holes, and Birds of the Air Have Nests

(Luke 9:58)

After school the next day, Tirzah has the house to herself. She is tidying her room, trying to be a good girl, and thinking about how strange things are now. The only glimpse she's had of Osian, apart from chapel, is of him slowly cycling through the streets, delivering groceries for his father. She tried a wave at first, but he seemed to ignore her, so she gave up. And there has been no sign of Brân for weeks. Tirzah's mind has been snagged on so many spiky, uncomfortable things she has not even thought of him. The musings about his private parts don't count, she tells herself. And it's strange, there was a time when she couldn't help bumping into him; he'd be hanging around outside the Co-op, his followers kicking a half-deflated football, or she'd see them running behind him round the streets, playing some complicated game that usually involved dares of some sort. If a window was smashed, sure enough, Brân would be the one everyone blamed. He was banned from most of the shops on the main street because he'd always nick stuff, passing it to his followers, who'd dart, quick as minnows, out of the shop door and away, stuffing their pockets with sweets or bread rolls or apples, whatever was easy to filch. Maybe they've disbanded, she thinks.

But then how would Brân manage? His little boys are the only thing between him and complete loneliness, she realises, remembering how he'd been, lassoing the boys' attention with the promise of sweets outside the Co-op when she first met him. The little children are still in school, but she hasn't bumped into them outside the shops on the weekend like she used to. Suddenly she recalls seeing him when he was much younger, squatting on the kerb outside a house at the far end of the village. He was with a shabby girl who had a pickled onion in one hand and an Oxo cube in the other. The messy-mouthed girl sat huddled over her snack, wincing happily as she alternately licked the onion and nibbled the brown cube. Just below her knees she had the maroon, angry-looking bands of skin you get from wearing nothing but wellies every day. Brân had been chewing on a piece of bread covered with what looked like dripping. The memory shocks her so much she has to stop folding clothes and close her eyes for a moment. So that was Brân. Never allowed in the house. And that was his little sister.

It seems to Tirzah that Brân is the loneliest of all the people she knows. I should find him, she decides. Maybe I can help him in some way. It's difficult to know how, though. Brân needs a whole new life with a new set of parents and a fresh, pink heart, because she fears his is already beginning to shrivel like a bitter walnut. At chapel they are always being told that Jesus is powerful enough for anything. Certainly He should be able to give some of these things to Brân, but somehow she can't see Brân wanting Jesus to sort him out. Jesus, with his shimmering blue and white robes, his loose waves of strawberry blond hair and outspread, ladylike hands, would be a bit useless trying to befriend Brân. I believe in Him, she thinks, and even I have trouble imagining Jesus would be all that interested in the stupid things I do. I suspect that if Jesus didn't know me from chapel, He'd never give me a second glance. Still, after she's made herself some toast with butter and a smear of Bovril, and is back in her room, she sends an arrow prayer up for Brân, just in case.

The silent house settles around Tirzah. Her mother is leading the afternoon Dorcas meeting and Dada is still at work. Does her father do sums all day? Once, when she was little, she and her mother had popped into the foundry where he was the book-keeper to give him his sandwiches. She recalls the heat and overwhelming, nose-singeing fumes. Her chest had reverberated with the brutal noise of machines. For ages afterwards she'd pictured the foundry as a sort of hell, gobs of molten metal spraying around and tongues of flame lapping the doors of the furnaces. And under it all a deep, persistent, earth-shaking boom that terrified her. Poor Dada, she'd thought. How can he stand it every day? Now, eating her toast she thinks about Derry. He must be at his mysterious factory job too. Lying on her bed, she has to admit something to herself: she would like to see Brân. In her thoughts he is swirled around by tall trees and roaring flames. Each time she pictures him on the mountain, with his hair blown into savage tufts and his rain-hued eyes looking down at her, she's filled with strange thoughts. But honestly, she tells herself, I think Brân is horrible. She remembers him bashing Osian with a burning stick, and how he smelt when she was close to him that day. He needs a good bath. She doesn't even want to think about the state of his underwear.

She gets up, scattering crumbs, and goes down to the kitchen to make herself a drink, glad that Jesus isn't sitting at the table watching her. She tops an inch of orange squash with tap water, aware that He is able to read her innermost thoughts anyway. For the first time in her life she actually wishes that the Son of God would get lost. Brân is a very handsome boy, and that's the truth, she thinks, climbing the stairs again. Am I supposed to pretend he isn't? She picks up her old biology book and thumbs through, but can't stop the brown, lean face of Brân swimming between her eyes and the illustrated pages on asexual reproduction. I'm glad I'm not an amoeba, she thinks, imagining herself touching Brân's narrow waist, and how it would be to rest her cheek against his chest. She hears someone calling her name. For one scared moment she thinks it is Jesus, but then realises her mother's at the foot of the stairs telling her to come down.

At the kitchen table, Tirzah's father rolls out an extra-long prayer as the food gets cold. Tirzah peers through her laced fingers and can tell, even though her eyes are tightly closed, that her mother is impatient for the prayer to end. But her father is carried away. He's finished with thanking the Lord for the blessings laid out before them and is pleading with Him to step in and sort Derry out. Bring him low, Father, he shouts. Crush him. Show him Thy terrible wrath. Turn him from his heathen ways. Tirzah's mother stays quiet. She doesn't want to prolong the prayer by responding in any way. Tirzah looks down at her cooling lamb chop and chips. She would hate to see Derry crushed; he's certainly no saint, but he's not that bad either. And somehow she likes that someone from the normal world is around. Finally, it's over, and they can eat. Now then, her father says, vigorously shaking the bottle of HP sauce, what have you two been up to? Tirzah keeps silent. She's thinking about how her father always seems to be shaking something.

Her mother starts telling him about the knitted squares the ladies are making, and how they will be sewn together and turned into little blankets for the children in Africa. That is good work, Mair, he states, his fork jabbing in her direction. I am moved to prayer again just thinking about you dear women toiling away. Not now, Gwyll, she says, patting the table. Eat up, please. And you? he asks, looking at Tirzah. I was reading, she answers, looking at her chips and stiff little chop. Nothing wrong with a bit of reading, he says. Depending on whether it's edifying or not, of course. Now eat up. She takes hold of her cutlery, but gets no further. I'm not hungry, she says. Can I leave the table? You may be a big girl these days, her father tells her, chewing a large mouthful of his chip butty, but you will sit there until all that plate of good victuals is eaten. He dips a last corner of bread into the HP sauce spread around his plate rim. Think about how blessed you are. They leave Tirzah at the table with her untouched food, and take their cups of tea into the living room.

Tirzah spends time looking for Brân around the village. She does not have so much as a sighting. It's another mystery; where does Brân go all day? Has he really left home to live rough? On Saturday she decides to search the woods where she and Biddy saw him worshipping at his altar. Before she leaves she scans the pantry shelves and snatches a jar of Bovril to take him, pushing it into her pocket. She's pleased with herself; he can always boil stream water and make himself a tasty drink with it. Under a sullen sky the sounds of the village fade quickly as Tirzah crosses the fields. The sheep barely raise their heads when she passes. They look so bored, she thinks. And I don't blame them. Grass all the day long, and maybe a thistle if they're lucky.

Soon the woods rear up and Tirzah picks her way through the brambles, tearing her skirt even though she'd bunched it up in one hand. Inside, the trees drip on to the undergrowth, making small, musical tinkling sounds. Now and then a heavy wet *plonk* lands on Tirzah's head, making her start as if someone's pinched her bottom. She stops to look up through the treetops; it is important she should locate the sky. The light is strange, and the torn scraps she can make out above the trees each time she strains to see are turning from a grubby pink to something more like glowing orange as the afternoon wears on. This isn't a normal sky, she thinks. It's like sunset would be on the last evening of the world. Somehow, this makes her more serious about her search.

Down the broad, steep incline she climbs, trying not to slip, trampling the glossy, sword-like leaves and frilled blossoms of the bluebell carpets. The bulbous jar of Bovril bangs her leg rhythmically. Silence lies on every damp, green surface. Tirzah was planning to call out for Brân, but now it would be unthinkable to make a sound. She is suddenly so nervous her tongue is wedged between her teeth. Invisible threads touch her eyelids as she walks. With each step forward she feels a growing sense that this is a bad idea. Below, near the stream, she sees a dense wigwam of branches and a thin drift of smoke rising. Her heart judders painfully. Is this where Brân is living? she wonders, suddenly struggling to put one foot in front of the other. Tirzah stands, waiting for Brân to appear. She knows the silent minutes are sliding forward all around the world, but in this wood there is the feeling of one immense intake of breath, where nothing moves, nothing happens. Then she hears a prolonged sound of coughing. A pair of crows are disturbed by the noise. Squawking and flapping their tattered wings, they make off, rising through the upper beech canopy. Tirzah stirs, watching them, and when she looks back towards the wigwam, there is Brân, knee deep in the undergrowth, a tall crown of iridescent feathers and ferns on his head, and daubs of something dark on his face. Tirzah begins to walk shakily forward; he is beckoning to her.

I Will Kindle a Fire in the Forest Thereof

(Jeremiah 21:14)

It's difficult for Tirzah to understand, but slowly she realises that a whole night has passed and another day begun since she was last in her bed. Someone's tucked her in so tightly she can't raise her shoulders. She looks around. The room is just the same. All her things are in place. On her desk are piles of revision notes and a rusty apple core; in the wardrobe she knows her row of clothes hang, waiting for her to give them shape; her empty shoes stand side by side under the chair. But I don't feel the same, she thinks, struggling to free her arms and hold them up. And I don't know why. Her nightdress sleeves fall back and she sees cuts and bruises on her skin, but can't remember how she came by them. There are crescent moons of dirt under her fingernails. She lets her arms fall to the plump coverlet. Why doesn't someone come to check on me? she wonders, suddenly hit by a longing for her mother. She closes her eyes, soon fast asleep again.

When she wakes it is dark, and a feeble light from the bulb on the landing shines in through the glass panel above her door. She hears footsteps climbing the stairs. Recognising her mother's step, Tirzah covers her head with the bedclothes. Now she is afraid to see anybody. The door opens and she listens as her mother moves around, closing the curtains and straightening things, finally coming to sit on the side of the bed, squashing Tirzah's thigh. Slowly she pulls the bedclothes away from Tirzah's face. They look at each other. Tirzah can see her mother's trembling lower lip and tear-filled eyes. She has a balled-up lace hankie in one fist. What's wrong, Mam? Tirzah asks, shocked. How can you ask me that? her mother says, moving slightly away from Tirzah. I've heard it all now. You are going to hell in a handcart, and you don't even seem to care.

But, Tirzah stammers, sitting up, what is happening then? I'm frightened, Mam. So you should be, her mother answers, her expression softening for a moment. You will be the death of us, child. She strokes Tirzah's hair away from her face. Don't you know where you've been? Coming home as black as the road. A whole night away. A whole night! What were you doing? Stumbling in like a ghost on Sunday morning. Us up all night worrying. Out searching, your father was. All on his own. He's been in his study since the early hours, interceding for you. Not even a wink of sleep. Tirzah tries to think, but all she can bring to mind are her feet slipping on the bluebells' shining leaf-blades and the sound of crows spiralling up to a bronze sky. She can't separate her dreams from her memories.

Honestly, Mama, she says, I don't know what came over me to stay out like that. Her mother stands and makes a shrugging movement with her shoulders, lifting her palms as if to receive a large parcel. Well, well, I never thought I'd see the day a member of my own family would behave like any old person, she announces. Tirzah frowns at her. You're right,

Mama, she says, half to herself. I must have done something bad to be gone so long. I wish someone would tell me. Her mother sniffs into her damp hankie. Wishing never did anybody any good, she replies. As I know full well. She moves to the door. It's best I leave you to ponder, she adds, hand on the doorknob. You have brought shame on us all. Tomorrow, after dinner, you are called before the elders. We had to tell Pastor in the end, of course. She closes the door gently.

Alone, Tirzah puts her head in her hands and forces herself to remember. Her brain is beating loud and painful in her ears, working hard to think. She is so weak even sitting up in bed is asking too much. For a while it is impossible to organise her thoughts. She feels small and irrelevant as a lost shoe. A mist swims before her eyes and she can't shift it. Gradually, she can make out flashes of sharp little scenes, but before she can understand what they mean, mist covers them again. Concentrate, Tirzah, she tells herself, knocking her temple with a fist. Suddenly Brân's feathered headdress and painted face loom out at her. It's to do with Brân, she thinks. I bet all this is to do with him. Then, as if this thought has tripped a switch, she begins to recall what happened from the moment she saw Brân across the stream.

Brân had beckoned her to come to him, and she'd jumped across the brook, weightless as one airy filament of a dandelion clock. Next she was outside his wooden den, and he was pointing to the crows perched like sharp-eyed guards high up in the trees. The rasping sound of his voice calling them fills her quiet bedroom. She can almost smell the smoky fire and broken ferns. Brân's cry is a sound so full of something beyond any noise she has ever heard in the village that she cannot grasp its real meaning, but there, in those woods, the crows understood and swooped down to settle nearer, cawing an answer. Brân paced the beaten earth, raising and lowering his arms, lifting his voice to the coppery sky while the crows croaked.

Tirzah had trouble filling her lungs and emptying them; it was all so sad and strange. Brân! she called, and her voice sounded sharp enough to rip a hole in the leafy world around them. Brân, I've been searching everywhere for you this past week. He turned, and looked surprised to see her again. Brân, she repeated and went close to him, shaking his naked arm. Don't you know me? He made a quieting movement with his dirty hand and then raised it to point again, this time to the apex of his wigwam. Tirzah looked and saw a bold bird, dark as a sloe berry, its wings outspread like ink-dipped, tattered banners. He is my prince now, Brân said, eyes hectic with excitement. In their shifting grey depths Tirzah could see herself and Brân, and nothing else.

Then she was inside the wooden hut. Ferns were deep and damp on the floor, and old feathers filled the gaps between the branches. He is an old devil, really, Brân told her. He's the boyo who rules the wood and the valley and the country hereabouts. This place is even named after him. He squints at her, head to one side. I have been given this knowledge. But you can only know these things if you have eyes to see, he whispered, scaring her. Tirzah squatted and filled her lungs with the smell of everything. No, Brân, a bird can't be a king, she'd said, unsure if this was true. How can you believe that? And no one should worship the Devil, like you said you were. She felt desperate to make herself clear. He can't love you, Brân, she'd said. He is the Great Deceiver. Satan wants your downfall, and that's the truth. But Brân was not listening. I have fallen, he states calmly. And I don't want to get back up. But anyway, out by here there are as many gods as you want. Piles of 'em. You just have to pick one for yourself.

As he talked, Brân was fiddling with something in his lap. Tirzah shuffled nearer and saw a creature, maybe a vole, struggling in his hands. Please let it go, Brân, she said, her voice wobbling. But Brân had snapped the squeaking thing's neck. She crawled outside after him and watched as he lifted the animal up to the dark bird on the roof, then threw it down. Tirzah heard a feathered rush and saw the bird plunge, grab the vole in its scaly claws and, labouring to gain height, slowly disappear. Now everything will be fine and dandy tonight, Brân said. It'll be tidy, just you see. Tirzah looked at the trees standing in patient ranks around her and the bulky canopy above. The sky was a dusky violet streaked with crimson and, higher up, all pricked over with silver pinpoints. I have to go, she'd said. My mam and dad will be worried. But already it was too dark, and Brân was back inside his hut, feeding the fire.

And now here she is, in serious trouble, hungry and chilly under her coverlet. A pang of guilt empties her chest when she thinks about her terrified parents, and she is forced to gulp in air. How could she have thought for one moment that it was a good idea to sleep out in the woods? She remembers waking up in Brân's wigwam and running home in the thinnest, earliest part of the dawn. Really, she hadn't been away so many hours. But the picture of Dada searching the streets, not wanting to let anyone know, and her mother, praying alone in the kitchen, makes her sob silently into her pillow until she falls asleep.

Blessed Are the Pure in Heart

(Matthew 5:8)

In the morning Tirzah wakes to the sound of heavy rain at the bedroom window. Oh, flipping misery, she thinks, why do you always make that noise? Getting up is going to take a huge effort; her bedclothes are a dead weight. It's as if they have been rained on all night. She bends her legs, pushes the covers down and gets out, stiffly inching her way upright. Then she remembers everything, and her heart swells with misery. She can't go to school because she has to see the elders. Her bedroom clock says seven o'clock. What will she do all morning? She is surprised that Derry is still in the bathroom, splashing and whistling. Tirzah huddles on the top stair. Derry doesn't care about any of us, Tirzah realises. He's his own boss. He's part of a different world and isn't interested in the smallest thing to do with ours. This thought makes her bolder somehow, and she knocks the door eventually. He opens it wide. What? he asks. Can't a bloke even do his bleedin' ablutions on his day off in this house without being 'arrassed by somebody?

Tirzah catches a glimpse of the small tufts of hair sprouting like eyelashes above each barely visible nipple, and can't help looking down at the fuzz climbing from his pyjama waistband towards his belly button. I'm so sorry, she stammers, pink with awkwardness. It's just that I have to get ready. She inhales deodorant and another, more embarrassing smell. Yeah, Derry says, looping his towel around his shoulders, I just done a dump. He grins and makes her squeeze past him in the doorway. And where were you the other night? he asks, nudging her with his naked elbow. Anybody would have thought the sun had fallen out of the sky, the commotion around here. Tirzah's face is burning, and she wants to slam the door on him, but he won't move. I even had a stroll around myself, looking for you. Tirzah gives him a bleak look. Oh, really? she asks. Seriously, he continues, blushing slightly. I was dead worried. Then he seems to recover himself and gives her one of his thorough looking-overs, the tip of his tongue poking out. She can only stand and continue to look into his eyes, remembering her terrible money-earning plan. And here he is, she thinks, with not a penny to be seen. Deary, deary me, he continues as he turns away, shaking his head. What you need is someone to look after you, an' tha's the truth.

Tirzah locks the bathroom door and immediately opens the window wide. She gags, noticing two crinkly hairs on the toilet seat. Derry is such a funny mixture, she thinks. Why can't people be one thing or the other? Trying to understand them is like balancing on a long, drooping elastic band held between two mountains. In the bathroom cabinet mirror she looks at her reflection: the tip of her nose is red, and her eyes are watering. There is a red, two-inch graze on her cheek, crooked and angry. She turns away and runs a bath. The water never gets comfortably hot, but when there is enough to cover her feet and ankles she climbs in and tries to get a lather going in her sponge.

Sitting in the cool water, she wishes she could really run away. No one believes me, she whispers into the echoey bathroom. But really, I don't think I've ever done anything wrong, apart from making Mam and Dada worry. She is so unhappy she can't rouse herself to get out of the bath and wee, and watches as the cloud of urine, warmer than the bath water, quivers out from between her thighs. Poor me, she thinks, examining her damaged legs and innocent-looking toes; here I am, sitting in my own wee, and nobody cares. Her stomach is empty and growling. Her head is so heavy she has to concentrate to keep it in place. She hauls herself out and rewraps her dressing gown tightly. Even though she is starving she forces herself to stay in her room until twelve, taking as much time as she can to get dressed and dry her hair.

In the kitchen her mother is standing at the stove. There you are, she says, sounding businesslike, and throws a towel over her shoulder. She lifts a slotted spoon out of a small pan and slides two ragged, domed eggs on to a plate, and says over her shoulder, I've made you a nice little something. Poached eggs on toast are good and digestible. Now then! I want you to eat them both, and no jawing about it. Tirzah sinks into a chair. Her mother stands with the laden plate. But, Tirzah starts to say, and her mother lifts a hand to stop her. Tirzah, she says, setting the plate down and now tucking the hand towel into the waistband of her apron as she turns back to the stove. For once in your sorry life, do as you are told.

Tirzah starts to nibble her toast, and suddenly she can't eat her breakfast quickly enough. The soft egg yolks taste so creamy, almost like molten cheese; it's as if she has never eaten them before. She is struck by how easy it is to eat and bathe, things like that, when she has done something so wrong. Her mother comes to the table, bringing two cups of tea with her. There you are, she says, nodding towards Tirzah's scraped-clean plate. They sit together. Rain drums on the sloping roof of the kitchen, and it's so dark they need the light on. Tirzah's mother tells her she has taken breakfast up to Dada earlier, but he didn't eat it. He's been in that old study of his all night and all morning, she says, holding her cup in front of her mouth with two hands. Not a morsel has passed that man's lips for over twenty-four hours. And he hasn't gone in to work. Tirzah swallows the lump in her throat. Mam, she says, so low her mother has to lean forward. I am sorry to have made you and Dada so worried. I got lost in the woods and made a nest to sleep in, that's all. That's all? her mother says. That sounds like an awful lot to me, madam.

Tirzah sends her mind to the mountain, and the hiding place in the forest. She curls up in the roots of the tree she and Osian lay under, and inhales the pines and the cold earth's unhurried breath. For an illuminated, blessed moment she glimpses again that the whole world is out there and indifferent to all the fuss down in these narrow streets. All the straight-backed pews and mildewed hymnals, ham sandwiches and kettles in the chapel kitchen, the Bible stickers the juniors collect so eagerly each week: they are only fragments of the wonderful world. It's a vision so fleeting, like a lone picture glimpsed in a fanned-through book, that she almost misses it. She is left with only the effect the picture made.

Tirzah begins to feel calm, happy even. She is surprised, but the mood is so engrossing she isn't concerned by her lack of nerves. She gazes with a new-found love at her rattled mother. What do you think the elders will say to me? she asks idly. Her mother puts her cup down and examines Tirzah with narrowed eyes, placing her hand on Tirzah's forehead. Of course, you are not the ticket today, she says almost to herself. Are you poorly? No, Mama. I am absolutely, completely all right, Tirzah answers. Her mother folds both lips in on themselves. Navy blue! she blurts, immediately covering her mouth with a reddened hand. Now look what you've made me say. Swearing it is; doesn't matter what the actual words are. God knows the intent. Tirzah can't help smiling. And take that look off your face, her mother says. Or I'll wipe it off for you. Of course I worry. She pulls a sharply ironed hankie out of an apron pocket and dabs her eyes. And you should too. Silly, silly girl. I can hardly stand to look at you.

Tirzah can only lean across the crumb-strewn table and pat her mother's hand. I'm sorry, Mam, she whispers. Please don't be angry with me. Her mother searches her face with wet eyes. You seem to be unaware I was once a girl just like you, cariad, she says, almost shyly, stroking Tirzah's cheek. I do know how you feel sometimes. But, Mam, Tirzah says, jerking her hand away. I haven't done anything really wrong. I'm sure of it now. She refuses to think about her mother as a young girl anything like herself. Her mother shakes her head and pushes the hankie against her mouth, silently weeping. Don't let your father hear that sort of hardened talk, she says. It will break his heart. Tirzah comes around to kiss the top of her mother's head. She can't explain. It's as if she were living amongst a group of people to whom she looks identical, but she's another species entirely. Still, she thinks, putting her coat and shoes on, this business is most unpleasant, even if I am an alien of some sort. Slipping her hand in her pocket, she finds the forgotten jar of Bovril and slips it into the hall glove drawer.

In the narrow passage lined with scripture texts in ornate frames, Tirzah pauses, looking up the stairs. Derry comes out of his room and she watches his loose-limbed descent. Hiya, he says, brushing against her coat as he goes past. But at the front door he stops and looks back. Good luck, you. He gives her a smiling nod. Don't let the buggers grind you down. The slam of the door behind him bounces along the tiled floor, making Tirzah's armpits tingle. In the hall he leaves a breath of cigarette smoke and mint chewing gum. The front-room clock keeps up its usual uneven *tick-tock*, and Tirzah listens to it fighting – fast, then slow, fast, then slow – always the same, and to the faint noise of her mother washing the kitchen floor. When she's ready she goes up, trying not to make a sound, and stands outside her father's study. Dada, she calls quietly, knocking the door. Dada, it's me. From inside the room there is a silence so profound that it seems to press like deep water on her eardrums. Can I come in, Dada? she asks, tapping with her fingertips, pressing her straining ear to the door. Won't you talk to me for a minute? Dada? She waits a few seconds, then taps again. I'm going now, Dada, she says, her lips against the wood. Goodbye. Someone is moving in the room, but nothing else happens.

Tirzah's umbrella is red. Along the street, in every netted front-room window she passes, the scarlet flower of her umbrella blooms for a moment. The smells of Monday fry-up drift out through windows. Soon her shoes are dark with water, and her feet freezing, even though it's now June. Osian is waiting in his doorway. She stops to look at him, realising he's lost weight. Tirzah, he calls, and comes out into the rain to hold her free hand, tiptoeing because he's only wearing slippers on his feet. Her eyes rest upon his dear face. She stands under her umbrella and waits for him to speak. Osian keeps checking up and down the street. What is it, Osian? she asks, looking at him warily. It's as if someone has taken a cloth and wiped their friendship away. Hastily he says he knows she is a good girl deep down. But, Tirzah, he goes on, squeezing her shoulder so tightly it hurts, our hearts are desperately wicked.

Tirzah looks at her hand grasping the umbrella, wondering at the way it looks pinker than usual. Like a doll's, or even a false hand, she thinks, a little scared. But no, it's all right: it's just the reflection of the red umbrella fabric on her skin. She can't believe what Osian is saying. It's still difficult to get used to the idea that someone has swapped this fidgety person with the real Osian she loved. The rain is wetting his new fringe, separating it into strands. You've had all your lovely hair cut off, she says, and raises her free hand to touch it. He shies away, and she sees a white strip of skin on his forehead where the sun couldn't reach until now. Have you got anything to be ashamed of? he says. Confess. Let me help you find your way back to the fold. No, I don't need to confess, she tells him, smitten by his question, his unsureness. And I'm able to find my own way back to the fold, if that's what I want to do. Anyway, why don't you fry your own fish? You have your own troubles, she adds. But he's looking back into the dark hallway, not listening. I have to go now, he says, and dashes through his front door without saying goodbye. Everyone is shutting their door on me today, Tirzah thinks.

On she climbs to the manse, and now she remembers Brân with his painted face, and the way he gave her a tin cup of something meaty he had killed and cooked. He was pleased to do it, she could tell. They'd sat in his leafy, feathery wigwam wreathed in smoke, while he told her how he'd built it and what life was like in the woods. Tirzah watched his glowing grey eyes and sharp teeth catching the firelight each time he grinned. This was the good Brân, but she knew there were other versions, and some of them were very different. Probably everybody has different versions of themselves, all layered up inside. She recalls how she spat out brittle, needle-like bones when he was busy tending the flames, not wanting to hurt his feelings. Outside, the trees sighed and rustled through the night, but she and Brân, wrapped in odds and ends, had slept either side of the fire. As she nears the bigger houses higher up the valley, she tells herself there is nothing surprising about the fact that Brân is good and bad in parts. Everyone's a funny mixture.

The manse's steep front garden is overgrown with a sprawling, waxy-leaved shrub that looks as if someone has thrown splotches of yellow paint at it. Tall steps climb to the front door. It's a long hike, and Tirzah is gasping when she gets there. She has to put down her brolly and use both hands to lift the lion-faced brass knocker. There are four empty milk bottles beside the door, one with a sodden note for the milkman in its neck. Flecks of rain like sprinkled rice pellets are still falling into the puddles beyond the porch as she waits, looking down on the village. Far below is the roof of her own house, and just under that roof she knows there is a book-filled room, smelling of paraffin and the Fisherman's Friend sweets her father likes to crunch when he's reading Spurgeon or some old Puritan.

Poor Dada, she thinks. Doesn't he know none of this is really that important? He acts as if God was his jailer and had to be sucked up to, or there would be no privileges. She pictures him kneeling by his desk, telling God all about the disappointment a father like himself has in a daughter like Tirzah. He's probably apologising for me, she thinks. Telling God it's not His servant's fault, how he's done his best, to no avail. What must it be like always to expect the worst of people? Even your own daughter? She's nonplussed for a moment when the door opens, and Pastor stands there, his wispy hair in three separate bands across his scalp, his grey cardigan buttoned up, and his tie tightly knotted. Tirzah looks at his serious black shoes gleaming and the way his twelve toes pull them out of shape. Come you inside, Tirzah, he says, clasping his hands. This is indeed a sad day.

Thy Elders and Thy Judges Shall Come Forth

(Deuteronomy 21:2)

No one asks Tirzah to take off her wet coat, no one invites her to sit down, so she stands in Pastor's study and drips on to the carpet. Empty cups and a crumb-pocked plate with one curling sandwich at its edge sit on the big desk. Arranged in a line are the four elders, sitting on tall-backed chairs. To Tirzah they are unknown, and yet familiar; these are the men who sit on the platform below the pulpit on a Sunday and thunder out the hymns. They don't need hymn books; they know everything there is to know. Even though she watches them every week as they stalk out before Pastor from the vestry, they are strangers to her, just columns of black fabric topped with grey or white hair. She supposes they are holy. Now they sit, each holding an open Bible. One is blowing his nose, and after holding his hankie up so he can examine its contents, spends some time wiping and rewiping. Pastor, who has a chair behind his desk, doesn't sit at all. He wanders around the big, book-gloomy room, his forehead corrugated and his lips a narrow line.

There is a chair facing the elders for Tirzah. Finally, when the silence in the room becomes so ponderous she thinks she will fall to the floor under the weight of it, Pastor stops pacing around in front of his bookshelves and gestures for her to be seated. Brethren, he says, let us pray and ask the Lord's guidance in this matter. The rain-soaked material of Tirzah's coat is seeping through her skirt and into her knickers. It's a ticklish sensation. One of the elders begins to pray, but to Tirzah his words are lost from the moment they leave his mouth and emerge into the room. Like moths rising from a dusty old drawer, the words flutter down to the worn rug, then up to the rows of books and back again. With each change in direction they mean less and less. How strange, she thinks, that I am in this room, listening to these people. With an effort she remembers why. It's so silly. I know I shouldn't have been away a whole night, but all I did was sleep in a tent of feathers and twigs in the woods, she thinks. And now look what's happened.

Soon there is silence in the room again, and with a start Tirzah realises someone has asked her a question. The elders are waiting, but it is impossible for her to answer. Now then, Tirzah, Pastor says briskly, these are the facts: you left the bosom of your family and went heaven knows where. You were not seen again till the following day. What are you ashamed of? There is another silence. Come, come, Pastor says, talking as if she were backward. You will feel better when you tell us what you were doing. But Tirzah suddenly knows this is not true. For a start, these men will not believe her, and more importantly, for now, nobody is aware of Brân and his home in the woods. She remembers how happy he seemed, talking about his little tent, content with his crows. She can imagine how a bunch of do-gooders would troop through the trees, trampling the plants, sending the birds screaming, and root him out. He would know she had betrayed him. Brân is not hurting anyone, she thinks, deliberately forgetting some things and picturing his glinting eyes and lean brown cheeks grinning in the firelight. And neither am I. She wants to hold this secret close.

Pastor is starting to get a little uncomfortable. I've known you all your life, he says, his voice sounding as if he might cry. Let us deal with this and put it on the altar of contrition. The Lord is compassionate. Tirzah is aware that her damp dress and underclothes are thoroughly stuck to her thighs now. Even so, it's as if a warm flame is burning in her chest. Dear Pastor, she says. There is nothing to tell. I haven't done anything to be ashamed of. Unless getting lost and falling asleep is a sin now? One of the elders slaps both hands down on his knees. All the rest start talking over each other. Tirzah can sense they are at once thrilled and disappointed. I was lost, and decided to sleep in the woods, that's all, she says again, loudly, looking from one bearded, sceptical face to another. Wayward girls used to be chased up the mountainside by good, chapel-going people brandishing Bibles. A couple of the elders look so old they might well have been around in those days. But it's funny to think that if the mountain were to be her punishment, she wouldn't mind one little bit.

Pastor falls to his knees and loudly prays for Tirzah's soul. Have mercy on this poor, hard-hearted girl, he says, raising an arm and clenching thin air spasmodically. She is a smoking flax. Tirzah watches the activity in the room, lost in a warm trance, willing to wait and see what happens next. She thinks about Osian, his suspicious gaze under her red umbrella, how he took her hand and said he thought she was a good girl but that we are all deceivers, of ourselves and others; she thinks of her parents, keeping themselves busy at home while they wait for a judgement. The flame that softly glows in her chest spreads to fill her body. She looks at Pastor's screwed-up eyes and the anguished men pleading fervently, and sees how fearful they are for her. She wants to assure them that everything's all right. But it's no use.

Pastor finishes his prayer and with an effort regains his seat. Tirzah, on her damp chair, looks intently at him. He gazes across the desk at her. There is an odd look to him. Then Tirzah realises he has taken off the fine, wire-framed glasses he always wears. Without them his eyes bulge slightly and look unguarded. For a few long moments he allows the shouting men to carry on unchecked. Poor little Pastor, Tirzah thinks, seeing how slack his lips are and how his neck droops. Finally, he straightens up, repositioning his glasses on his nose, carefully fingering the curved arms to fit behind his ears. He coughs, and the men all stop talking immediately and swivel to attend to him. My dear elect ones, he says in his usual mild voice, this is a test of our wisdom, make no mistake. To arms! To arms! They look at each other before finally turning their attention to Tirzah. This young girl is in the grip of the enemy, and she doesn't even recognise him, he announces, making a swooping movement with his arm in Tirzah's direction so big it belongs outdoors. Such are his wiles, we well know. And such is her blindness. The men all nod. Amen, says the one who slapped his knees.

Pastor goes on to tell the elders that they should pray again for guidance before making a judgement. We must not flinch, he urges them. Principalities and powers, that's what we are up against here, brothers. This is a spiritual battle. Tirzah goes on waiting while they murmur together. The warm glow that has enlivened her is cooling from the feet up. Just as it reaches her knees, Pastor instructs her to go into the room the girls use for their meetings. I will come for you, child, he tells her, already bowing his head. Tirzah sees some of the elders creakily preparing to kneel as she gets up from her chair. Her damp dress and coat don't behave in the way they usually do, and stay in a kind of bunched-up pouch that balloons out around her bottom. She tries, while walking out, to pull them down, and manages a funny little hobbled dance to the door.

Outside in the hall, she deliberately unhunches her shoulders, only now realising she must have been holding her breath for some time. The hall looks watery. Drowned light caused by rivulets of rain wavers through the big dimpled windows either side of the front door. The air smells like the breath of a pond. There are three doors, and Tirzah can't remember which one she should go in. Her middle is chilly now; soon the cold will reach her heart. And then what? She opens the nearest door and immediately knows it's the wrong one. The door is heavy, and swings wide, revealing Pastor's wife, stockinged feet up on a pouffe, eating a cream cake. On her lap she balances a cup of milky coffee. Tirzah is not pleased to see the tops of Mrs Thomas's wiry legs where her skirt has worked its way up. Excuse me, she says, backing out. Mrs Thomas is still poised, hand holding the cake with its shining rosette of scarlet jam halfway to her open mouth, seemingly transfixed by the sight of Tirzah at the door. Before she can make a move, Tirzah has retreated and slipped into the next room.

Tirzah walks to the window and with her fingertip begins to follow the endless raindrops as they trickle downwards, hardly knowing what she is doing. The sight of Mrs Thomas cwtched up in her cosy room, stuffing cake, has jolted her thoughts. Still tracing raindrops she goes over the scene: the half-eaten cake, the squashed shape of the pouffe, the blipping sound of the gas fire, and most of all, skinny Mrs Thomas's sugar-rimmed mouth shaping up for another sweet bite. Why am I waiting for these people to tell me what to do? she wonders with a lonely sort of clarity, experiencing a freezing, hollow pain in her throat. But this soon gives way to something else so new that at first she doesn't recognise it. She starts to tremble and painfully nips her tongue.

Another, buzzing kind of heat passes through her body; never before has she felt so angry. I am an ordinary girl, and always trying to do what's right. Then she thinks about Osian, the way he is now smaller somehow. Osian has been felled by these people. That's how she sees it; he has been lopped at the knees. Well, I'm not going to be felled, she thinks, and without hesitation she walks out of the room, down the drowned hallway and out through the manse door. The rain has stopped and the sky is rinsed clear of colour. She stands to watch tiny birds soar and loop through the immense, glowing nothingness above the valley. Never, she thinks. Never again will she allow these old fuddy-duddies to boss her around. The air out here smells vital and bracing. Clutching the edges of her raincoat beneath her chin with one hand, Tirzah runs down the steep steps holding her scarlet umbrella, while below her the village windows and roofs wink in the wavering sunlight. She can see a red oblong, small as a toy, appearing and disappearing between the houses. I could jump on that bus, she realises. I could just leave all these people behind and go to the city. Why don't I? But even as she thinks this, another idea flashes across her mind, brilliant as a comet, and she knows what to do next.

All the Beasts of the Forest Do Creep Forth

(Psalm 104:20)

Tirzah makes her way quickly through the deserted village streets to Mr Singh's shop, trying to conjure up a picture of the little camp in the clearing, but all she can see are dense, waiting trees. The village is closing in on her and she is impatient to be gone. There is the familiar oily smell of drying pavements rising to her nose as she rushes along. It's as if everyone's heard about her meeting with the elders and is shunning her. Out of the tail of her eye she imagines the whisk of a coat or the turn of a shoulder as people slip indoors. For a moment, when she gets to the shop and stands across the street, she thinks it's closed, but a man comes out with a carrier bag, and the bell jingles. She pushes the door open and is greeted by the singed haze from the heater that Mr Singh has on all year round, and punctuating Mr Singh's cigarette smoke, the tang of smoky bacon crisps. These smells are so ordinary and comforting that Tirzah fills her lungs several times while she looks around.

Mr Singh gives her a nod. He is busy eating a loosely made cheese sandwich while he reads the paper. Tirzah can tell from the crunching sounds that he has put some crisps from the open packet on the counter into it. She stands by the magazines and hears the faintest of taps as flakes of grated cheese fall from the sandwich to the plate, her mouth watering. In a glass cabinet on the counter, shiny pasties and pies are kept warm by two fiercely burning light bulbs, and her stomach growls. It feels like weeks since she ate the poached eggs her mother made. Eventually she roots deep in the lining of her coat and scrapes enough money together to buy a Curly Wurly and a packet of Quavers. A group of kids from school comes in, and Tirzah hides behind the bleach and cleaning items. The children are younger than Tirzah, and remind her of how she and Biddy used to be, jostling for ages around the comics, taking their time choosing sweets. Tirzah stands behind the Omo and Brillo pads, feeling like a leper, until it's safe to slip out.

Leaving the village and its shrinking puddles behind, Tirzah puts the Curly Wurly in the pocket of her dress for later, even though she is already famished. Once she is over the stone wall, she opens the Quavers and eats them quickly, striding out for the open fields and the woods. It's warm work. She shrugs her shoulders and lets both her raincoat and umbrella drop into the damp grass, but then hesitates and goes back to roll them up together. She hides the neat parcel under the broad, pimply leaves of a burdock plant and goes on. Swifts dart through the middle air, dividing and redividing the immaculate sky. The light is that mean, after-rain sort of light that usually makes her feel unhappy. She walks amongst the swaying stands of thistles, and their tough stems graze her bare arms. She can hear bees singing on each purple tassel. Tirzah is going to find Brân. She needs to see him, in his wild wigwam, with his attendant birds. This is all she can think of: Brân in his headdress, Brân in the firelight, Brân's smooth, dark chest and eyes the colour of a shallow brook. Nothing else will do.

Brân is not by the stream. His wigwam leans skew-whiff, and when she jumps the clear, busy water to have a closer look she sees it's half-destroyed. Strings fringed with little furred pelts and feathers flutter from the encircling branches, and the remains of his fire are still there, but the ashes and thin bones are cold. The place already has an abandoned feel. Even the stained altar is empty. Tirzah flops down to the matted undergrowth. The living weight of the forest presses upon her shoulders and unprotected neck. She is too lonely to cry, or get up and leave. Maybe I can rebuild the den, she thinks, and live here myself. But she is a home-bird, used to her little bedroom and her coverlet. She would eventually miss the bleachy-clean bathroom and her mother's warm kitchen. She doesn't know what to do next and can't even force her mind to wonder where Brân is now. So she sits and waits, and soon becomes aware of the little stones huddled together in amongst the bright sorrel leaves and nameless creeping plants. Who put them there? she wonders, looking at the way they seem to nestle together. Do they know each other? She is engrossed, watching tiny insects darting amongst them, intent on their tasks. That they don't know or care about her is bracing.

The afternoon begins to feel stretched, and the light, without diminishing, changes, withdrawing into the brambles. She is still sitting, stiff and chilled, in a sort of dusk that seems thickest near the ground. There is a small commotion behind her, and when she looks round she sees Brân striding through the tall ferns. He is carrying a spear and has acquired a little dog. When he sees her, he stops dead still, raising the spear to his shoulder. She watches, and he comes nearer cautiously. Then he lowers his spear. Brân, she says. He scowls, as if he is trying to remember who she is, with his stiff hair fanning around his shoulders. She is calm, waiting for what Brân will do. The dog runs to her knees and sniffs her skin and hair, wiffling excitedly. Heel, shouts Brân, stamping the base of the spear on the ground. Immediately the dog wheels round and runs to stand close to him. Tirzah doesn't move. Then she remembers the Curly Wurly and offers it. The dog barks abruptly, the sound like a series of dull explosions in the woods, and runs in circles, its scarlet tongue escaping. Brân comes close and snatches the chocolate, slipping it into a pack he's carrying across his body. Up you get, he says, his voice gruff, and pulls her by both hands. I knew you'd turn up again. How could you know that? Tirzah asks.

Brân leads the way, walking quickly, deeper into the woods. Soon Tirzah has the impression that these woods are in a different country, where the trees are strange, the plants and flowers only distant cousins of the plants she knows. Birds blunder through the canopy, their wings making sounds like fists punching through newspaper, but she can't see them. Still she follows Brân and his excited dog, who vanishes and at intervals reappears ahead of them, his long ears flying up and down. When Tirzah flags, Brân stops and grasps her hand, urging her on. Eventually she is so tired that he carries her, piggy-back. Tirzah rests her head on his neck, aware of the animal smell of his hair, and falls into a trance, his angular collarbones pushing into her forearms. The woods slide past, and the glancing slaps of the head-high ferns are part of her dream.

When she wakes she can see out through an arched, leafy doorway to where a small fire is crackling, and her ears are filled with its pops and hisses. The tickle of grassy bedding is under her. Lying in Brân's cabin, she sees it is made of bent, freshly cut saplings. Brân has staked them to the ground in a circle and tied them together above in a bunch. She is impressed by the way he has woven thinner branches horizontally to make everything secure. This place seems much better than his first den. Sitting up, she can see Brân squatting over the flames, his features sharply leaping as he feeds twigs to the fitful yellow tongues lapping his hands. For the first time she notices how bony his knees are. His arms are too slender for his hands now; she is shocked by how thin he looks. After stumbling out to wee behind the shelter, she joins him near the fire.

Brân divides the Curly Wurly and gives her half. Is there anything else to eat? she asks, her mouth full of the insubstantial toffee. Brân shakes his head and offers her a glass pop bottle full of water from the brook. She drinks and can taste the forest's mulchy and plentiful heart in it. They sit, palms up, absorbing the warmth. This is a version of my Robinson Crusoe dream, Tirzah realises, wishing they had some coconuts to chew on. But we're in Wales, where you're lucky to get a cherry. She tells Brân how much she likes his new shelter, but she can tell he is waiting for something, his whole body tense, and soon she is waiting too. A ragged cawing, far away, snags on the silence. Brân lifts his head expectantly towards the sound. Is that your crow? Tirzah asks. Brân steps over the fire, and for an instant his eyes and mouth are blacker shapes in the softly shadowed dusk. Then he is swallowed whole and disappears.

Tirzah crouches, licked by wavering light, and listens to a muffled flurry of huge wings and the unbearable raw squawk of the bird calling to Brân. Then there are no sounds, and their absence makes her strain to hear. But she is not worried; Brân will return, she knows. For now, it is wonderful to have

escaped the village for a while. Through the treetops she can
make out fragments of bright sky; it looks as if the sun is still
shining, while down here they sit in a kind of gloaming. Just
when the fire starts to blur and her eyelids are drooping, he
is back, the crow with its spurred claws clutching his ragged
shoulder. He talks, and the bird swivels, peering around at his
face, its curved beak inches from Brân's eye, as if listening.
Tirzah is close enough to see the grey, bristly feathers that
neatly cover the bird's nostrils. These two understand each
other in some way, she realises. The bird makes a series of
short, broody sounds, looking into Brân's face, then across
at her, then back. What is he saying? Tirzah asks Brân. Now,
that'd be tellin', he answers.

When the fire has almost died, the crow hops to the
ground and waddles away. Brân gestures for her to come with
him and leads her back into the shelter. They lie together on
his bed space. The living, sweet-smelling branches enclose
them. Brân rests his head on one elbow, and lifting Tirzah's
dress, strokes her thigh with his free hand. Soon she can
make out his face in the twilight and touch the hair falling
around her head like coarse grass. In a daze, she asks if the
Prince of Crows told him to do this. So what if he did? he
answers. The shadowed hollows of his eyes look empty, his
face a mask. Tirzah pulls him down so that he crushes her
breasts. The smell of him fills her throat. She feels his hand
pushing inside her pants, sliding his fingers through her
pubic hair, tugging it. Then his weight is along the length
of her and she opens her legs; a famished need to be filled
up by Brân blossoms there. He grabs her face and presses
his teeth to her forehead, pushing his penis inside her. They
are locked together.

Tirzah's body is acting in new ways; it's as if an entirely strange person has taken her place. Instinctively she moves with Brân, loving the taut and urgent way he pushes into her, his laboured breathing. She lifts her knees and struggles to get closer, hugging him with her legs. With her hand she reaches down and fingers the place where his penis enters her like a root, thrilled by the way he stretches her as he moves. Then she falls back and relaxes, taking great care to notice all these new sensations. If the God of chapel has organised sex to be like this she will have to look at Him again, she realises, trying to reconcile the rude, earthbound struggle she and Brân are locked in with the way her mind is expanding to embrace the world. Soon she is thinking of the trillions of icy stars suspended behind the late afternoon sky, then about the homeward-flying birds calling to each other above these woods, and how the swaying trees around her lift their pliant arms to greet them. She thinks of the loamy earth beneath Brân's den and imagines the worms and blind creatures squirming upward.

Finally her thoughts come to rest with Brân's crow on the roof, who listens, hearing everything, his head cocked to one side. Invisible threads connect us to the world, she thinks, her mind sparking with joy as she flies from the pressure of Brân's stringy, labouring body and the taste of his lips, to the nest they are lying in, and on out to the shining god she saw on the mountain the day of the outreach meeting. Smoothly, laughing, she soars again from that summit to the wheeling birds in the skies, and then swoops to the countless ranks of trees that cover the earth. Tirzah is still wondering at the multitudes of people in all the countries she will never know when her mind snaps back to Brân, who is silently getting to his feet and leaving. She listens, her bare legs trembling as they are licked by cold air, missing the weight of his body. Brân is talking outside. The mystifying Tirzah she glimpsed when she and Brân were together slips neatly back inside her, as if she had never existed. Then there is a silence broken only by the sound of restless claws clutching and hopping on the roof branches.

The Devil … Walketh About, Seeking Whom He Might Devour

(1 Peter 5:8)

After Tirzah leaves Brân's deserted camp deep in the tree-filled valley, she is not sure which path to take. But the land, even here, rises up in much the same way it did at his first campsite in the familiar woods, near the stream. She can hear the sound of flowing water lower down to her left and guesses it must run all the way through the wood. She decides she must only be four or five miles from home, and sniffs the evening air, her eyes widening to let in the failing light. She is in pain, and weak with hunger, the skin on her back scratched by the bedding in Brân's hut, the muscles in her thighs twitching. Fluid is slowly running down between her legs. She stops to look, shocked to see blood and something else, viscous and thick, dirtying her legs. She wants to hunker down and pee, but is too jumpy, so quickly wipes her legs with a handful of ferns, aware that a fresh blurt of liquid is dripping even before she's finished. Fighting a desire to run wildly, she makes herself wait, taking careful stock of her surroundings. Then, even though the territory is strange, she decides to climb and does not stop scrambling until the trees start to thin out.

That shivery, uncovered feeling she gets when walking up a darkened stairwell is with her, that sense of threatening things keeping pace on tiptoe. The joy she was flooded with earlier has evaporated, and something hollow takes its place. I am a lost girl in a forgotten forest, she tells herself. No one would mind if I disappeared for good. If I fell and couldn't get up, who would care? What would Osian think if he could see her, filthy and wild, scrabbling about in the woods? He would be disgusted and hate her. What about her parents? And Biddy? But she instantly puts aside such thoughts. Again she forces herself to stand and think sensibly: these shady, crouching shapes are only the brambles and ferns she loves in the daylight. She has picked blackberries in places like this with Biddy and Osian many times. There is nothing to be afraid of. But still, behind her, peering out from the undergrowth and mirroring her every movement and pause, she cannot shake the feeling that something is eager to catch her. Something vile and ravenous. Off she goes again, weaving between the crowds of twilit tree trunks. Suddenly, as if the woods have given her a shove, she is flung out on to flat, open ground.

Sure enough, the thistly fields are recognisable. The withdrawing light settles like peace around her, and she waits for her breathing to return to normal. The dripping between her legs has slowed. With the looming trees behind, she now walks over greying, dewy grass, calmly climbing the stone boundary walls when they block her way, until she knows where she is. Each stone her palms touch is slightly warm, the lichen-covered surfaces comforting. Here I am, she tells herself. Here I am in one piece, and everything is all right.

She conjures up the image of her little bedroom, and her bed with its puffy eiderdown. Under the pillow her flannelette nightgown is folded, waiting to drop over her head. Out here, Tirzah is like a tiny speck caught on the immense patchwork spread of a hundred fields. Finally, she runs, and doesn't once look back, not even when she gets in amongst the narrow, glowing windows of the village.

Her breath is loud in her ears when she reaches Mr Singh's shop. She can hardly believe her eyes, but there he is, pulling his shutter down and padlocking the shop. It must only be eight o'clock. The sky is a celestial, dying blue as Tirzah walks the rest of the way home and lets herself in quietly. Standing in the hall she remembers her mac and umbrella, and how she stashed them in the field. Dammo, she thinks. I'll be in trouble for that as well. Somehow, though, if you set a coat and brolly against what she has done today, it's hardly worth getting yourself in a knot about. The dining-room clock is still snipping up the seconds, and the dire old verses in their frames go on doing their best to frighten her to death. Silently, head down, she concentrates on locating her parents.

There is a scuffling sound from upstairs, and a clearing of the throat that can only be her father. So he's still in his study. She tiptoes down the hall to the closed kitchen door and puts her hand on the wooden knob. Pressing her ear to the paintwork for a moment, she slowly turns the handle and inches it open. Without stepping into the room she twists her head around the door and has a quick look. There, in the easy chair by the fire, is her mother, sleeping, Bible open on her lap. Tirzah can see from the way her cheeks are tight and shiny she has been crying. Oh, poor little Mam, she thinks, a lump expanding in her throat. Then she shuts the door and makes for her bedroom.

Tirzah takes her clothes off. The stained knickers she was wearing need to be washed out immediately. She sniffs the sticky gusset and detects, like mushrooms and old leaves, the earthy, sour smell of Brân's semen, and mixed with it, the tang of her own blood. What's done is done, she thinks. And turning from Brân's famished face and wiry fingers, decides to banish all thoughts of what happened from her mind. She daren't have a bath; the roaring of the boiler would wake everyone up, so in the bathroom she washes with cold water. Rivulets course down her goose-bumped skin, and the sponge refuses to froth, no matter how much soap she rubs on it. Between her legs feels like a slippery, hot bruise; it's painful in an entirely new way. Carefully she pats herself clean. Back in the room, her flesh burns it's so chilled. Putting the soft nightie on, she is comforted by the warm folds draping around her body. This is lovely, she thinks, burrowing down between the crackling sheets. It's luxurious, noting her aches and pains now she's safe in bed. Just when she is about to slip over smooth, shining rocks into the deep pool of sleep, her mother opens the bedroom door and turns the light on.

Tirzah struggles to sit, pulling the eiderdown to her shoulders. Well, I'll go to the foot of our stairs! her mother exclaims, plonking her fists on her hips. Where did you spring from? I was getting worried about you. Tirzah doesn't speak. How long have you been here? her mother asks again. I'm not sure, Tirzah says, trying to be as truthful as possible. She wonders if her parents have heard about her walking out of the manse. Mam, she calls, and lifts her arms for an embrace. Come to me, her mother says in a thickened voice, and rushes to kneel by the bed. Enclosing Tirzah with fierce arms, she plants firm kisses along her forehead and pushes the strong curls back. Tirzah snuggles in, her mind blank as a bowl of milk. Now then, I think the best thing would be to forget this whole business with the elders, her mother says when she has sat back on her heels. Don't you, cariad? Yes, Mama, Tirzah, says. I would like that. I'll speak to his nibs, her mother adds, getting to her feet. There's enough trouble in this old world without us adding to it. I'm sure the Lord agrees with me. She wipes her eyes with a hankie fished from the pocket of her apron. Do you want a bowl of soup? You must be famished.

Tirzah lies against her pillows when her mother leaves, and wonders at the way things are turning out. She can't help smiling. Is it really going to be this easy to explain her absence? Her room has never felt so enveloping and safe. But then, like an unexpected wave filled with pebbles and ropes of weed, another feeling dumps itself on her. What she has done is so wicked no one in the fellowship will ever get over it. Surely she is a fallen, impure girl now. In a way, chapel doesn't matter, but it's not right to lie to my mother, she tells herself. And it's not safe. To act the way I've acted is not safe. Inside her empty heart she experiences something worse than the sharpest hunger.

Reluctantly she turns her mind to Brân. He hadn't spoken to her. Did he even care who she was? He's probably completely mad, she realises; no one can talk to a crow. He is a wild, stinking, dangerous thing. How could I have lain down with him and opened my legs that way? She clenches her fists until the nails hurt her palms, thinking of the soiled pants drying in their miserable little knot under the bed. She begins to fear that the real, inner Tirzah is not there any more, not that mysterious girl who jumped out in Brân's hut, but the soft, holy part of her she has always sensed happily inhabiting her skull and extending down past her throat like a mollusc in a complicated shell. Maybe it has gone. And she is the one who lost it. Then another thought falls on her. Maybe the very Devil has yanked her soul out and devoured it in one gulp. And she, Tirzah, handed it to him on a plate.

The Widow … Shall Come,
and Shall Eat and Be Satisfied

(Deuteronomy 14:29)

In the days that follow, Tirzah lives in a kind of featureless stupor. Her parents have ructions at the manse with Pastor about her running away from the elders, but she is only dimly aware of the upset. Later, in the kitchen, her father announces that he's told Pastor this is a private matter, and he will deal with it as he sees fit. And the way he deals with it is to ignore Tirzah, which suits her just fine. Her exams are about to start, and will go on for nearly a month. She is trying to lasso her mind, make it attend to history and English and maths. In her room, surrounded by papers, she sits at the desk and stares at nothing. After the first biology paper, she can't remember one thing about the questions or how she answered them. Her mind is wearing a groove around other things, but she forces herself to keep working, and eventually starts to feel more alive. One evening, she realises Derry is spending most of his time out of the house these days. Not that he ever hung around a lot, but still, now he seems to slip in so late his food is welded to its hot plate; her mother grumbles every morning as she scrubs the dried-on leftovers in the sink, threatening to stop cooking for him. And he's off to work before even her father gets up, almost as if he's avoiding them all. She doesn't blame him for making himself scarce. Even though he's a peculiar article, she misses having another human being around the house. The smell of his deodorant and cigarettes are the only clues he's here at all. She thinks about the way he winks at her when they pass on the stairs, and decides to peep into his room.

The bed is tightly made, and the cold, lino-floored room has an unlived-in feel. Hospital corners and then some more, Tirzah thinks, venturing to sit on the taut coverlet. How did Derry learn to make a bed that way? Where are his parents? She knows he was not brought up in this valley. His accent is slightly more guttural than everybody here. She's used to it now, but still when he speaks there are some words he squashes, and others he opens out in a different way, and she has to think twice to understand him. Maybe he grew up in a children's home. She should ask him more about himself. When I can, I'll have a chat and get him to open up, she decides. I'll ask him more about his job and his parents. Somehow she knows Derry's on her side, even though he thinks, as he once told her, that she's not all there.

There are no photos in frames on the chair that serves as his bedside table. His few spare clothes are neatly stacked on the single shelf of the closet. She knocks the empty wire hangers and they send out a mournful tinkle; he doesn't seem to like hanging anything up. Feeling twitchy, she quickly pushes her hands in between the mattress and bed frame and pulls something out. This is the first time she has seen a dirty magazine. Some of the women are lying down with their legs spread, and she can hardly stand to look at the way they hold the lips of their private parts open with sharp, red fingernails, as if inviting someone in. Their pink, juicy insides are raw-looking. Tirzah is mesmerised by what appears to be an endless display of fresh wounds. Is this what she looked like to Brân?

Do men like looking at such sights? They must do. Some of the women are kneeling, bottoms presented to the camera, tousled heads twisted to slyly glance over their shoulders from under turquoise eyelids. Tirzah is weak and her ears burn. She has never seen an anus before, not even her own. Usually, she would turn her eyes away from a cat's pale bottom if she could help it. Ych-y-fi, she says under her breath. There's rude. Why would anybody want to inspect that? Do women do things like this for their husbands? Do the women enjoy it? A wriggle of laughter tries to escape from her chest. Dirty, that's what it is. A dark and fascinating doorway has swung open, and Tirzah is poised on the threshold. She wants to step through, but hesitates, held rigid by a mixture of fear and curiosity. What about the people she knows? Imagine Pastor's wife squatting like that. It can't be true. Then an image of her parents pops into her head. She rams the magazine back under the mattress and rushes to the bathroom. Never in this world have I seen anything like it, she thinks, looking at her flushed face in the mirror. Lord, protect me from lewd thoughts, she breathes, trying to swallow spurts of laughter as she pats her cheeks with a towel.

Back in her room, she sits at the desk and opens a book. It all looks like double Dutch; the words keep scrambling about on the page. Right, she thinks, fidgeting in the seat and feeling grubby, if I can't revise, I will make myself read *Little Women* through to the end. Then, when that's finished, I'll go back and have a final look at geography, ready for tomorrow. But before the first few pages are finished, she's imagining Meg, Jo and Amy doing what the women in the magazine were doing. Not Beth, though. Or Marmee. That would be the absolute limit. Jo would be most sexy, with her cropped hair and spirit of adventure, but such a thought is wicked. Jo is so wonderful. And Meg so shiningly good. That vain, silly Amy with the stupid nose is the most likely one. Tirzah shakes her head to clear it. Closing the book, she kicks off her shoes and falls on the bed.

What about Derry? Does looking at those women make Derry a sinner through and through? Poor Derry, she thinks. He can't help it. And she remembers him twining one of her curls around his finger, and the way her answer had shut off his eyes' sweet, awakened expression. In the real world, he probably wouldn't ask a girlfriend to do the things those women do. But who knows? Maybe Derry would actually like to see Tirzah bent over, giving him the old glad eye with her bottom in the air? I could never do something like that, she thinks. But *judge not that ye be not judged*, she remembers, blushing to own that she had contemplated charging Derry for what the kids in school called *a grope*. I've done nothing I'd be proud to write home about, and that's the truth, she tells herself.

The exam goes smoothly, she thinks. If finding it easy is a good sign, then she's done well. At teatime, her parents still haven't asked how things are going. I sat an exam today, she announces, and they both look at her, waiting for what she will say next. I'm not going to tell them anything else, she thinks, irritated by their raised eyebrows. Instead, she asks where Derry is these days. Her mother's nose is shining as she dishes out fried fish. Derry is leaving us soon, she says. But why? Tirzah asks. Shouldn't we be caring for him? Why is he going from us? Her mother shoots her a look. That is none of your business, she answers, pouring parsley-flecked white sauce over the sizzling slices of fish. How many potatoes? Tirzah thinks of Derry's cold bedroom, and his magazine. I'm not hungry, she says. Her mother looks more closely at her. Now then, she says, ignoring what Tirzah has said and ladling two potatoes on to her plate. Eat up, there's a good girl. Derry was only ever going to be here for a short time, just until he got his own place. And your father says our work with him is finished. She sits down and puts her hands together. He is a very lost, hardened soul, and has turned his face from the Lord. She looks across at Tirzah. Besides, she adds, it's not as if he was a friend of yours, is it? Her father comes into the kitchen and sits. Throughout grace, Tirzah wants to howl, thinking of how alone she will be in the house without Derry's presence. Her father tucks in, mashing his potatoes into the parsley sauce. Lovely meal, Mair, he says. Very nice. Tirzah's mother flushes. Thank you, Gwyll, she says, popping a morsel of fish into her smiling mouth.

Tirzah hates this dinner. She doesn't understand the point of fish. And why smother it in white sauce? She watches her parents eating contentedly. I'm sorry, she tells them. I cannot eat. She gets up to leave the table. And where do you think you're off to? her father asks. I don't remember giving you permission. Sit down. Tirzah stops a tear sliding down her face with a finger, her throat full of something like feathers. She gazes at her mother. Oh, Gwyll, her mother says. She's upset about Derry going. You know what she's like about the strangest people. Her father sniffs. I've never heard such nonsense, he says. Derry's had his chance. He has turned his back on the Lord. And the Lord will not be mocked. Tirzah would like to say something, but it's no use. The trouble with her parents is they can only think of people as souls, saved souls and unsaved souls. That's all they care about. She is suddenly plunged into a grey world, crowded with millions of unloved souls drifting around like patches of smog. In amongst them is Derry. Who will look after Derry now?

Her father puts down his cutlery. You may leave the table, he tells her, but first, an announcement. Tirzah and her mother stare at him. Widows and orphans and suchlike, he says abruptly. That is where we should be labouring. Mair, he continues, very interested in the tablecloth, we have a Mrs Rowland and her daughter Muriel coming this Friday. A sad tale, but I feel an assurance that we can spread God's love and show them the error of their ways. Amen. Now, off you go. He picks his fork back up and heaps it with food. Then, without looking at either of them, he opens his mouth wide and shoves the forkful in. Gwyllim! Tirzah's mother says. For shame! Now I understand why you complimented my cooking. I thought at the time it was odd. There's devious you are. Trying to butter me up like that. Just to foist some strange new people on me. Now, Mair, her father starts, and then fizzles out. Tirzah is so fed up with both of them that she leaves silently. Running upstairs, she quickly ducks into Derry's room and takes his magazine. Then she rests against her closed door, trying to think of a good hiding place, and finally squeezes it behind her wardrobe.

When Tirzah gets home from school the next day, her mother is cleaning Derry's room. Later he arrives to get his things and lingers to talk to Tirzah in the hall. She has been waiting for him, her coat buttoned up against the cold she feels inside, but cannot think of anything to say now he's here. She looks at him properly, for one last time. Don' get yourself all 'et up, he tells her. Maybe I'll drop you a note to tell you where I am? Tirzah nods and tries to shape her lips into a smile. Then if you're ever, you know, in another jam, he goes on, you can just write me a letter. They stand in the gloomy hallway. Come 'ere, he says, to Tirzah's surprise, and embraces her quickly, fumbling to get his arms around her bulky coat before her mother comes downstairs with his old duffel bag. Tirzah is glad she was able to stash the magazine under his few clothes, unbeknownst to her mother. Thank you, missus, he says, when she hands it over to him. Thank you for 'aving me. There we are then, Tirzah's mother answers. All the best to you, Derry. Tirzah reaches and touches his hand. He smells of coal dust and cigarette smoke. Goodbye, Derry, she says, before running upstairs.

Mrs Rowland and Muriel are due to arrive at seven on Friday evening. Everything is ready. Tirzah's mother has found a picture of a rose-smothered cottage in the attic and hung it. She has even bought a bunch of white carnations from the market for the bedside chair. I'm doing this for the Lord and the Lord only, she says, arranging the dry-looking buds in a jug. Throwing money down the drain, I call it, buying flowers. I know, Mam, Tirzah says. They look at each other across the bed. Mrs Rowland and Muriel are going to have to sleep top to tail in the bed that was barely big enough for Derry. Tirzah hopes they are small. She and her mother have been exercised about this sleeping arrangement. Let's have a go, her mother says, and they lie on the bed together. Tirzah has her head on a pillow at the bottom of the bed, and beside her are her mother's small, stockinged feet. Half of her body is resting in thin air. I don't think I can hold on much longer, Mam, she says, and falls to the floor. Oh dear, her mother giggles, peering down at her. This is going to be a tall order for them. Still, it's better than nothing, I suppose.

At half past six they are summoned to the front room. Tirzah, you sit there, please, her father says, indicating the sofa. And, Mair, you there. They sink down, and Tirzah wonders what he is going to tell them that can merit a visit to the front room. Tirzah looks at the silver bowl on the sideboard and the sculpture of a sailor's head on the wall. All her mother's best things are in here where she rarely gets to see them. Tirzah waits for her father to speak. He is quiet for so long that Tirzah's mother asks him if he's feeling all right. You're frightening me, Gwyllim, she says, getting her hankie out. He seems to snap to attention. First we will pray, he says, and starts by asking for wisdom and grace. Tirzah opens one eye slightly to look at her mother, but quickly closes it again when she sees her mother is not praying at all, but looking boldly at her husband. Amen, he finally says. Amen, echoes Tirzah.

This is a delicate matter, he tells them, running a finger round inside the collar of his work shirt. And one that requires the utmost discretion from both of you. Well? her mother asks, not at all meekly. Cough it up, man. He shoots her a look from under his brows, and says, all in one breath: Mrs Rowland is what you would call *a fallen woman*, and poor Muriel is the fruit of one of her illicit relationships. He puffs out his cheeks and lets them deflate slowly. These are the sorts of people we are supposed to be helping, he adds, patting the air with both hands in a hushing gesture towards his wife. He who is without sin, Mair, cast the first stone. That is what the Son of God said. Just as Tirzah's mother opens her mouth to speak, there is a knock on the front door. That will be them now, he states, jumping up. And may the Lord help us.

But the Righteous Are Bold As a Lion

(Proverbs 28:1)

When Tirzah eventually gets to bed, she cannot rest. The past few hours have been so strange that, when she recalls each scene, it flashes on and off in a series of unlikely shades. She is reminded of the Quality Street wrappers she loved in Christmases past, and the way you could look through the little coloured squares and see the front room and all its usual things bathed in blue or red, or the one she loved best, topaz. She thinks about the moments in the hall before her father had answered Mrs Rowland's knock. Here they were again, she and her parents together, leaning forward to look through the front door's misty panel at the strangers outside. This time, in place of the dread they had felt on seeing Derry's unexpectedly tall shape, Tirzah was perplexed at how small Mrs Rowland's outline was. The girl Muriel must be minuscule, she'd thought, unable to make her out at all.

There had been a sense of inevitability about everything: her father pulling the door open, her mother's uneven breathing, the faces of Mrs Rowland and her daughter floating like two dulled hand mirrors in the porch. For a moment it was

179

as if time had snagged, and no one could move or say a word. Tirzah, standing behind her mother, who in turn was peering out from around her father, tried to focus on the figures outside. Mrs Rowland was the size of a girl, and Muriel barely came to her shoulder. Neither of them smiled. Mrs Rowland's painted mouth did not appear to be the sort of mouth that ever smiled. Muriel had on a bedraggled green party dress and a tiara. On her feet were wellington boots she'd decorated with stickers. Mrs Rowland's blouse exposed her fallen-in, almost mauve-coloured chest flesh. Tirzah had never seen such tight trousers or such high, toy-sized shoes as the ones worn by Mrs Rowland on her bare feet. Somehow, none of this was a surprise. Then her father sprang into action. Welcome, welcome, he shouted, making a series of flapping movements, as if trying to waft them in. Her mother was silent, but Tirzah could sense her extreme queasiness about the idea of Mrs Rowland and Muriel setting foot inside her home. Now, as Tirzah turns to try to find a cool spot on the pillow, she recalls the scene. Everybody's skin looked bloodless. It was as if Mrs Rowland had sucked the life out of them all with her purplish lips.

Muriel and Mrs Rowland stepped over the threshold simultaneously and soundlessly, making Tirzah jump. Pick up our guests' bags, please, her father said, already leading the way. He disappeared into the front room with them, leaving Tirzah and her mother in the hall. They stared at each other, and Tirzah could see her mother's two front teeth biting into her bottom lip. Never mind, Mammy, she remembers saying. You go on, I'll sort these bags out. Indeed you will not, her mother answered, her voice rising. Tirzah could see two points of blood glinting on her bitten lip. She'd plunged forward to grab the various packages left on the doorstep. No child of mine is playing skivvy to the likes of those two, she'd gone on in a kind of stifled scream, swinging the bags into the hall and letting go. They both watched the bags slide to a halt on the polished hall tiles. Well, it's pointless us standing here like two statues, she went on, her voice now faded to a quiver. I suppose I will put the blessed kettle on, as usual. You go and ask them if they take sugar.

Tirzah couldn't help thinking that she should knock the front-room door, but then decided that was ridiculous. This is my home, she'd thought. I don't need permission to go where I like. She opened the door and stood waiting for the three of them to look up. They were huddled together with their heads almost touching, her father on the edge of his chair, Mrs Rowland and Muriel on the settee, pointed knees inclined towards each other, hardly taking up any space. They all swivelled to look at her. Well, I never did, her father said, sending her an over-emphasised frown. We were right in the middle of praying. Oh, really? Tirzah said. Sorry. Would anyone like a cup of tea? Mammy wants to know. I don't allow Muriel to drink tea, Mrs Rowland announced in a deep, catarrhal voice. Tirzah had felt her eyes widening; how could such a hollow, reverberating voice come out of that narrow throat? I'm sure we can find her something, Tirzah's father said. Mrs Rowland ignored him. I will have a strong cup with three heaped spoonfuls, and a glass of fresh milk for Muriel. Tirzah looked at her father. You heard, her father said. Three sugars. Strong. Off you go.

In the kitchen, Tirzah's mother sat like a dropped bundle of washing. The kettle was beginning to hiss. Tirzah bustled about, trying to chat while she set the tray. She splashed milk into a glass for Muriel, and shook out some biscuits from the barrel. Finally, she hunkered down before her mother. Now, Mama, what's the matter? she coaxed, giving her mother's clasped hands a squeeze. But her mother hadn't said a word. You'll be better after a sit down, Tirzah said, and poured her a cup of tea. I'll just take this to that lot in there. She was about to leave when she realised her mother was struggling for breath. Almost dropping the tray on to the table, she darted back. It's all right, it's all right, her mother said between long gasps. I'm just so angry I can hardly breathe. And this is righteous anger, mind. Why, Mam? Tirzah asked, fanning her flushed cheeks with a place mat. Her mother's breathing calmed. In a few moments she was her normal self again, but the look in her eyes was new to Tirzah. I do not like being tricked into something. I will have it out with his majesty, she answered evenly, nodding her head towards the door. Once and for all.

Tirzah tries to close her eyes tightly so she can sleep, but it's no good, they just keep springing open. Looking around, she is struck anew by the room she is in, how utterly dismal it is. Poor Derry, how did he manage to sleep in this hammocky contraption? He was much bigger than me, she thinks, and I barely fit. The street lamp beams through the curtains, and a cold breeze, rising from the lino, seems to be active under the bed. A faint memory of the absent white carnations pervades the air. Up the stairs comes an unfamiliar sound: her parents are having a proper, yelling argument. Tirzah strains to hear, and after a few minutes realises that her father has stopped shouting and is silent. Now the only voice is her mother's. Earlier, he'd announced that Mrs Rowland and Muriel could not possibly be expected to sleep in the box room. Tirzah knew he was speaking, but the words made no sense. Finally, she'd understood she was to give up her own bed for them. She opened her mouth to object, but snapped it shut when her mother gripped her arm. Shush. Don't say a word, bach, she'd whispered into Tirzah's hair. Go to Derry's room now, and tomorrow night you will be back in your own bed, I promise.

Now, in spite of the collapsed mattress, Tirzah begins to feel sleepy. Before her eyes close she sees Mrs Rowland and Muriel in the front room, their dark eyes patient and watchful over the rims of their cups while the discussion about room changes goes on. She remembers her father struggling up the stairs with all the bags behind the pair of them, and her mother's stiff walk down the hallway to the kitchen. Maybe tomorrow she will pop to Biddy's and tell her all about Mrs R and her daughter. She smiles, thinking how Biddy will kill herself laughing. By then, Tirzah will be able to join in, and the whole sorry incident can be folded away. Suddenly she is fully awake, remembering the way her mother had slammed the kitchen door; this was something that had never happened before. Then she half gets out of bed, shaken by a realisation that her mother's anger is not just for her own self, but for Tirzah too.

She can't help suppressing a small throb of sympathy for her father. He is always trying to do the right thing, but he so often gets them all in a mess. He is a good person, she knows, seeing in a flash that she is very much like him in some ways. And now he's in for it from dear Mam, she thinks, her throat full. She recalls her mother's trip to the market to buy the bunch of flowers, and the way she'd tried to make the room a bit pretty for the then unknown Mrs Rowland. Perched on what feels like a metal bar, she hears again the ripple of her mother's giggle and recalls her pink face when she'd peered over the mattress edge to see Tirzah on the floor. Finally, she remembers the entirely unfamiliar topaz glints in her mother's usually soft brown eyes, and the way her mouth looked as she said she was going to *have it out with his majesty*. Tirzah allows herself to lie back down, aware of a blanket of warmth lowering itself gently over her in spite of everything.

When Thou Doest Thine Alms,
Do Not Sound a Trumpet

(Matthew 6:2)

Tirzah is confused for a moment when she wakes; the cheerless room is so unfamiliar to her. She pulls the eiderdown up to just below her eyes and decides to pretend to be asleep for as long as possible. The day stretches out before her, an expanse of rocky terrain she is compelled to cross. She can sense herself shrinking away from her own life. It's as if the will to go about doing normal things is being whittled away in barely noticed strips. One day soon she will be incapable of standing upright, so thin will she have been shaved. But the truth is that her normal life is not what other girls would call normal. It makes her tired, thinking about the way things are now. Everybody I love, or even like, is leaving me, she thinks. Derry's gone, just when we had started to be friends; Osian is as good as gone too. Brân is a locked box with a thrown-away key. School will be changing, and in sixth form, people will already have their established friends. Apart from Biddy and Ffion, there are lots of people she could have been friends with, but that was never allowed.

So even might-be friends have always been lost to her. I am lonely these days, she thinks.

The house is quiet. Maybe her father has already gone to work. She concentrates on listening. Usually, she wakes to the sound of her mother bustling in the kitchen. She loves to hear the chime of spoons and the other kitchen noises from her bed. But today there is not a peep from anyone or anything. A startling idea pops into her mind: maybe the Rapture has occurred and only sinful Tirzah is left behind. Everyone worthy has been caught up to heaven. Life could be so much simpler without the fellowship and all the rules that went with being saved. And most of the village would just go on its lost way. Gran and Bampy would still be here, and people like Mr Singh in the shop. Lovely, Tirzah thinks, imagining the way her new life as one of the lost could expand. She's often watched the other kids in school and been amazed at how easy everything is for them. They never appear to be chastised, or searching their souls. If they want to, say, have a new bike or a pet, no one interrogates them about their avarice and worldliness. If they're naughty, they get a clip round the ear and all is forgiven. She is checked as her thoughts dance about: Mrs Rowland and Muriel would still be around, unfortunately.

Tirzah pauses on the landing. No sounds from anywhere. The door to her own bedroom is ajar. Are Mrs Rowland and Muriel still asleep? It doesn't seem that early. Tirzah feels as if she is being willed towards her bedroom, and walks to the door, avoiding the creaky floorboards. She can't resist putting her eye to the gap. The sliver of room she can make out is empty. Without further thought, she steps in and surveys the made-up bed. The small bowl of carnations sits on the bedside table but none of their visitors' things are visible. Sure enough, her room is its dim and peaceful self, waiting for her to come back to it. She climbs on the bed and lies down. It's almost like being embraced, lying here. But when she snuggles her head into the pillow there is a long, dark red hair, very much like the colour of her own, stark as a vein against the white cotton. The only way she can tell the hair is not hers is that it's straight. Reluctant to even bring herself to pick it up and throw it away, she leaps to her feet, thinking about the doll-like, unmuscled limbs of Mrs Rowland and Muriel lying together, their waxy hair flung on her pillows.

There is a noise downstairs that pulls her back to the landing. Her mother has come in through the front door and is in the hallway, shoving bits of clothing into Mrs Rowland's holdall. Tirzah watches as she zips the bag when it is full and gives it a kick with her small foot before turning away and walking out of sight to the kitchen. Tirzah runs down to find out what's gone on. Her mother is at the stove, humming a hymn tune. Mam, Tirzah calls, walking forward to tug the trim bow of her mother's apron, where are Mrs Rowland and Muriel? What have you done with them? Her mother turns, smiling, and kisses her on the forehead. They've flown away, she answers, fluttering her fingers. Really? Tirzah asks. And where have they flown to? Sit down, her mother says, and I will make you a special little breakfast to celebrate. Tirzah waits for her bacon butty. Would you like HP sauce? her mother asks. She is behaving as if nothing has happened. Tirzah keeps studying her face for signs of upset, but there are none.

When the bacon sandwich is ready, Tirzah takes a salty mouthful, then puts it down on the plate. Now, Mama, you must explain. Must I? her mother says. Tirzah's breakfast is delicious, but she folds her arms and will not eat another bite unless the beans are spilled. There's naughty you are, cariad, her mother says, still smiling. Aren't you hungry? She leans to take the sandwich away, and Tirzah grabs the plate, capturing her mother's hand. Come on, Mama, she says. Tell me, please. Well then, her mother answers, squeezing Tirzah's fingers before letting go. All I will say on the subject is that I have sorted the whole sorry mess out, and Mrs Rowland and Muriel are gone from this house for good. Tirzah's tongue is stuck to the roof of her mouth. What about her father? She can just imagine his fury at being thwarted. Is Dada all right? she manages to ask, picking up her sandwich again and taking a huge bite. And where have the two of them gone? Your father will get over it in time, her mother says. I have my limits, and they were reached when I set eyes on that lewd woman and her child. Mind, she adds, not that I blame little Muriel. But she must go where her mother goes. So I took the pair of them up to the manse and left them on the doorstep. See how Pastor and his missus like that. Tirzah's ears stretch, she is so shocked.

After breakfast, they go upstairs to give the bedroom a good clean again. Look, Mam, Tirzah says, pointing to the long hair on the pillow. Her mother takes a look, squinting. Dammo di, she says under her breath and doesn't apologise. There's nasty. She picks up the hair and opens the window. Out you go, she says, and good riddance. They strip the bed and open both windows. Mama, Tirzah says. I feel sorry about Mrs Rowland's having nowhere to live, don't you? Her mother doesn't answer. These wretched flowers can go too, she says, grasping the flowers by their necks and plonking them in the wastebasket. The sight of carnations will always remind me of this business. Tirzah doesn't want to chuck the flowers away; they had just begun to shake out their frilly, ice-white hearts, releasing a peppery scent. Can't I keep them? she asks, already disentangling the stalks from the bin. If you like, cariad, her mother says, her arms full of bedclothes. I'm off to put these in the twin-tub; you get on with putting the hoover around. Later I'll take Mrs R's bags around to the manse.

Alone in her room, Tirzah snaps each carnation at a slightly higher joint and rearranges them in the bowl. As she puts her nose to their cold faces, she thinks about Mrs Rowland and Muriel, now at the mercy of Pastor and his wife, and feels a twang of sadness. What will happen to them? They have no home to go to obviously. It must have been wrong to throw them out. But then she's forced to admit that her mother's action has saved the family months of who-knows-what, and that's the simple truth. As she turns away from the flowers, she sees her old coat hanging on the back of the door and notices something like a thin tube sticking up from the pocket. Pulling it out, she is puzzled to find it is a tight roll of money. She sits on the bare bed and teases it open, counting out four five-pound notes. For a moment she stares at them. Wait a minute, she thinks. When did I last wear this? And then she remembers: she had been so cold and unhappy on the day Derry left, she'd put it on while she was waiting to say goodbye to him. Her mother must have taken it from Derry's room and put it back on its hook here.

Tirzah thinks back to Derry in the hall and the way he had fumbled the hug he'd given her. She'd thought it was because he was rushing and didn't want her mother to see him, but now she realises he was putting this money in her pocket. She can almost hear a pinging sound in her chest as a bulb of joy bursts alight. The thought of Derry in his donkey jacket going off to work every day and secretly giving her some of his hard-earned wage is sweet. In the middle of the roll she notices a scrap of paper. Her fingers are trembling as she smooths it out, still scarcely believing so much money is for her, but on the note Derry has written her name. She looks out of the window at the roofs of the houses opposite. Now she will be able to go on the CYC weekend if she wants to. Or maybe she should save the money, keep it somewhere safe until she knows what to do with it. Just as she's looking around for a good hiding place, a picture of Mrs Rowland's battered old bag in the hall swims before her eyes. Swiftly she runs down and slips ten pounds into the side pocket, then pulls the hoover out of the cupboard and drags it up to her room.

The Angel of the Lord Descended from Heaven

(Matthew 28:2)

The exams pass Tirzah in a haze: up and out to school, a few hours sitting in the stuffy hall in her row, writing, writing. Then home, then back. On and on, until, suddenly they are over. Tirzah has been on automatic. It's just as well I did so much preparation, she realises. I almost didn't have to think. Now that the summer holidays are well under way, Tirzah is fed up with having the freedom to do whatever she likes. Even last year, she and Biddy and Osian would meet every day, after chores, and play. What were we doing? she wonders, puzzled by how busy they'd been. The lovely sun-filled days slid by unconsciously, full of now-mysterious pastimes. This summer, the serious, heat-darkened trees stand expectantly at the edges of fields; cows raise their heavy heads to scan each other with wet, fly-pocked eyes; the ice-cream van dribbles its tune uninterrupted around the streets. In Biddy's garden, the ruffled cheeks of the sprawling, flesh-coloured roses deepen and give off a ghostly smell of woodsmoke when she presses her nose and lips into them, but Biddy is caught up with Ffion, and Tirzah can't summon the energy to talk to her anyway. Everything is waiting, waiting. All Tirzah can do is lie like an old pancake on her cool bed, with the bedroom curtains closed and billowing, and wait too.

She wonders why Derry has not written when he said he would, how Brân is surviving and especially where the real Osian has gone. The new Osian does not have any free time; his father is keeping his nose to the grindstone in the shop. She even thinks about Mrs Rowland and Muriel, and whether they found the money she gave them. She wasn't surprised that Pastor said nothing on the subject of those two when he shook hands in the chapel porch the Sunday after her mother had plonked them on his doorstep. As far as she knows, he hasn't mentioned her meeting with the elders since her father went to see him at the manse. Life is so very strange these days; familiar things are showing secret sides of themselves to her. The street is full of dust and the boredom of small children shooed outside to play, and inside her home the air is thick with questions that unravel like dropped stitches from a knitting needle when she tries to make sense of them.

Her mother came to the room earlier, put a hand to Tirzah's forehead and asked what she was doing sinfully hiding in the darkness on such a beautiful day. Tirzah stared at her brisk mother in the gloom. I don't know, Mama, she'd said. If it's those old exam results you're worried about, her mother went on, put your mind at rest. You're a pretty one; only have to snap your fingers, you will, and a perfect husband will appear. Tirzah pressed her lips together. A nice little shop job will do until you get married, her mother went on. Don't worry about silly old A-levels. But I like studying, Tirzah muttered. The idea of a shop and getting married made her even more burdened. Why are you looking as if you've gone soft in the brain? her mother had asked, shaking her head. What is wrong with you these days? When Tirzah said nothing more, she'd whispered that she was going to make them a treat and bent to kiss the tip of Tirzah's nose. Some nice lemonade will buck you up. Now Tirzah listens to the busy sounds from below. Dear Mama, she thinks. I can't see how a piece of cake will help. She is drifting towards sleep when her mother calls. Waking up, she feels snakelike for a bewildered moment, without bones or the power to walk. When she finally stands, she sways and clutches the desk to steady herself.

In the kitchen, the back door is open and a gusty breeze messes with the pages of the missionary calendar pinned to the side of the dresser. This wind is getting on my nerves, her mother says, pushing a floppy clump of hair back from her hot forehead with a bent wrist. She seems transfixed by the Chinese faces on each month of the calendar. Why do Orientals all look the same? And all have such funny names? she asks, trying to decipher the foreign words beneath each picture. Mam, honestly, Tirzah says, sinking down on to the doorstep. You must stop saying things like that. Oh, go on with you. It's not that I'm judging, her mother explains. We're all going to be treated the same come the Last Trump. Doesn't matter to the Lord which way your eyes slant. In reply, the pages lift and fall. What we need is a good hum-dinger of a storm to wash all this sticky air away, she goes on. Like walking through treacle, it is. She wafts her skirt hem around. Even my knees are perspiring, she adds, and takes off her wrap-around apron. I've had enough of you, for starters, she says, throwing it on a chair. Maybe that's what all this waiting is about, Tirzah thinks, her jaw relaxing as she rests her head against the doorframe. Maybe it's just a weather thing, nothing else. Suddenly she wishes it would rain for days and days. I'm going twp, she thinks. Wishing for rain now, of all things.

Her mother brings a cut-glass jug from the pantry. Lemonade, she announces, looking pleased. Tirzah turns round and her mother indicates the table with a sideways nod. I thought I'd push the boat out a bit. This is our secret, mind. A cloth embroidered around its edges with ladies in crinolines and baskets of pink and purple flowers has been laid over the scrubbed wooden surface. In the middle sits a plate of plump scones, and on either side, two bowls. One is full of scarlet jam and the other, lumpy, luscious-looking cream. A single rose from Biddy's garden droops over the lip of a fat-bellied vase. Ooh, says Tirzah, sitting. Her mother pours the cloudy lemonade. Tirzah can see translucent moons of fruit falling into the glasses. The scones are weightless, and she lifts one to her nose, breaking it open. This is heavenly, she says, taking a deep breath. Then she darts a look at her mother, but there is no reprimand for her flippancy; her mother only nods, kicking off her indoor shoes and slicing her own scone in half. May the Lord preserve me from the sin of pride, but these are not bad, she says. Even if I say so myself as shouldn't.

Tirzah piles her scone with jam, and then balances a clot of thick cream on top. Her mother is already eating. Mama, Tirzah says. How did you get to be so good at cakes and things? Her mother laughs softly. Practice, love, she says. Many years of it. I can't cook a thing, Tirzah says, eyeing her scone. Almost it's too perfect to eat. When did you start cooking? Her mother sits back in her chair. Let me see, she murmurs, thinking. It would have been when I was about twelve. Tirzah is surprised. Of course, I did a bit before that. Just for the fun of it. But I had to learn quick at twelve. Why? Tirzah asks. Wasn't your mother doing the cooking? My mam died, cariad, her mother says. Haven't you wondered why you only have one granny? Tirzah's eyes blur, and her beautiful scone wavers on its plate. Oh no, she says. There's sad for you. Yes, it was, is all her mother will say. What about your dad? Tirzah adds, struck by how much she has never asked about her mother. Good question, her mother says, chewing. He turned to drink, if the truth be told, and an early grave. Now eat up your nice treat. Tirzah is looking at her neat, dark-haired mother with fresh eyes. To have no parents, she cannot imagine it. I love you to bits, she says. And I love you, her mother answers, sniffing. Tirzah has difficulty swallowing when she thinks for the first time about her mother as a motherless little girl.

She can only just bring herself to drink the tart lemonade, her tongue puckering each time she sips. What do you say to me packing this up and taking it out with me? she asks. I would like to walk up the lane to the mountain. You do that, her mother says, and goes to the pantry for a plastic box. Or I might go to the woods, Tirzah adds, though as soon as she's said it she knows she doesn't want to go there. You love the woods and that old mountain, don't you? her mother says, smiling. Just the way I used to. She hands Tirzah the box. Be careful out there, though. Anything can happen, I always say. Tirzah nods. Her mother unties the ribbon holding Tirzah's hair and regathers it. But I think you already know that, don't you, cariad? Tirzah is reluctant to meet her mother's eyes. Let me plait this for you, her mother suggests, already splitting Tirzah's hair into three thick sections. That way your neck will be a bit cooler. She quickly weaves the strands together and ties the end with the ribbon. Anyway, she adds. Aunty Ceinwen is coming round for a chat, and you would be bored. So off you go.

Tirzah pictures the narrow, yew-flanked lane nosing its way up the mountain. It will be deep amongst the foxglove spears now, the banks smothered with red campion and meadow-sweet; she can almost smell the vanilla-scented breath of the flowers. She remembers how small birds twitter invisibly in the still tunnel of the lane as you toil up. It's too much like hard work, that climb, she decides. But then she thinks about the thistly fields lying open to the hot sky, and the crumbling stone walls she will have to scramble over if she goes towards the woods. There will be no shelter in the fields. Maybe I'll walk out past chapel, where there's farmland, and find a cool place to lie down, she thinks. It's an area she hasn't explored. She and Biddy and Osian never went that way. She sets off through the streets; it's funny, walking to chapel but not going to a meeting.

The chapel looks comfortable when she first glimpses it through the graveyard. There it rests, nearly part of the earth it sits on; up the walls creepers spread, inching their way to the roof. Birds have made their home in the eaves. Who would guess the things that have gone on inside? All the countless hours of repentance and crying, pleading and confessing. She skirts around to the back, past the crooked, mossy headstones, through the drone of insects, swishing her legs against the pollen-laden early summer grasses. In the shade of the chapel wall she rests a moment but is soon driven on by the coolness of the air. There is an overgrown door in the high hedge, and she pushes its flaking green wood. No one has been this way for a long time. It's like a door in a story she half-remembers. Stepping through, Tirzah feels as if she is entering another country.

She crunches over dried-out snail shells and empty hazel-nut casings and follows the lane until she finds a stile. The countryside stretches out like a promised land, washed with sunlight, dotted with small boundary trees, all new to her. This is just what I wanted, she realises, sitting on the top bar of the stile. Here is somewhere strange and yet welcoming. Somewhere beautiful and different from the high places she knows and the dark, wooded places she has come to dread. She climbs down from the stile to the gently sloping field and runs into the sunshine. The smell of baking earth and sap-filled plants rising makes her giddy. She falls back into the springy meadow, just the way she always did on the mountainside amongst the whinberry bushes. When she reaches the ground, there is a sigh as the grasses flatten, and out into the gold-and-blue breeze fly crimson butterflies no bigger than her smallest fingernail. A skylark is labouring musically high above.

Tirzah makes a nest for herself and opens the plastic box her mother gave her. The scone tastes better here than it ever could have in a kitchen. After she has eaten and wiped her fingers in the grass, she lies back. Soon the warm lick of the sun and the soft shoves of the breeze send her to sleep. The long afternoon rolls over her. When she wakes it is evening and cooler. Her clothes are damp from the grass and her hand is numb. She sits up and shakes it awake. It's as if she has been sleeping for weeks, she is so alive and buzzing. The quiet, dewy fields are changing colour. The trees look lilac and the sky is lined with bronze just where it meets the horizon. She can see a farm and outbuildings in a fold she hadn't noticed before. Tirzah is content to go on waiting now she senses that soon something will happen. I just have to be patient for a little longer, she thinks, pulling her dress down to cover her bare legs. And whatever it is will show itself to me.

Even though she has been looking intently, she is surprised when she sees winking stars; the summer sky is still light, though the sun has gone down. She can't remember, as soon as she's noticed them, just when they first appeared. Scanning the luminous, untroubled sky, it seems that each time she looks away another star has switched on. Then, as the first chilly breaths of evening creep around her ankles, Tirzah sees something white emerging from the far trees. Silently and speedily it glides towards her, long wings stretched wide and scarcely moving. In its peaceful wake the evening deepens. She watches as its heart-shaped white face becomes clearer. With a weightless rush and the sound of wind-blown blossom falling, it lands on a heap of stones not far from where she sits. There is nothing for Tirzah to say. The thing she has been waiting for has happened, and she is enfolded for a few moments in the hushed embrace of feathers. At last she dares to look, and as she does, the creature's huge black eyes turn to contemplate her for a hundred heartbeats. Then off it launches, pure and silent, and merges with the shining dusk.

Thy Visitation Cometh;
Now Shall Be Their Perplexity

(Micah 7:4)

When Tirzah gets home, her parents are out, thankfully. She pulls herself up the stairs, using the banister like a rope. In her room, she shrugs off her summer dress and lets her pants drop around her ankles. Her bra is constricting, and under her breasts there is an inflamed-looking line. She rubs it with her fingers. It must be this heat making me come over all funny, she thinks, looking at her reflection in the semi-dark. The air of the bedroom is muffled. Struggling to breathe, she throws the window open, panicking slightly. She splashes water from a glass on the bedside table on to her body and tries to calm down by thinking of her time in the countryside. She remembers the huge white bird moving towards her like an unfurling flower, and how it gazed at her in the twilight. I am discovering more about the world all the time, she realises, unplaiting her hair. And I believe there is nothing to be afraid of. Her long hair is cool as milk against her naked back. Without washing or cleaning her teeth she falls asleep.

In the morning she lies on her bed trying to remember a dream. All she can picture are shining wings and the perfume of sun-baked leaves. Through the slit in the curtains a hard slice of sunlight comes and goes. In the bottom drawer of her chest she finds half-familiar things to put on. The hot weather has come so suddenly there has been little chance to prepare. She climbs into last year's shorts and struggles to do them up. Over the top she wears a roomy but too-short shirt. By the desk her mother has left a battered suitcase for her to fill. Today, she remembers, with a little jolt of joy, she and Biddy are going for a two-week holiday to their grandparents. And the grown-ups are going away too. Quickly she stuffs things in her case and rushes downstairs. In the kitchen her mother has left a glass of orange juice and half a grapefruit. She gulps down the juice and runs out.

When she comes round the corner into Biddy's garden, there she is, lying on a lounger. Well, well, at last, Biddy says calmly, without opening her eyes. The Queen of blinking Sheba has arrived. It's almost dinner time. Tirzah sits on the end of the lounger and it tips them both off. Biddy lies on the grass with her legs hooked over the chair and doesn't move. Already the day is hot. Tirzah struggles to get up. Are you packed? she asks. Dunno, Biddy says. Let's ask my mam. Tirzah remembers her own unfinished case and dashes home. Her mother is checking its contents. And where, may I enquire, are your undies? she asks. Are you planning to run around with no knickers? And where is your nightdress? Tirzah shrugs. Honestly, her mother says. You haven't got a clue, have you? No, I haven't, Tirzah agrees. That's why I need my little mam to sort me out, see? Look at this case, her mother orders, and tell me what is missing. Tirzah looks and looks. Something to read? she suggests at last. Something to wash with, you soft girl, her mother says. Go and get your sponge bag. I have enough to do, getting myself and his nibs ready.

While the girls stay at their grandparents', Tirzah and Biddy's parents are going on their yearly fortnight to a Bible conference at the seaside with members of the fellowship. They will be staying in empty university suites, and like to go without the girls. That way they can sit through as many meetings and after-meetings as they like, without being distracted. Hundreds of Christians will be there. Uncle Maldwyn and Aunty Ceinwen go away much more often than her own parents, to hotels and bed-and-breakfast places. My brother Maldwyn has always been a bit lax – over-indulgent, really, her father likes to say when Aunty Ceinwen has a new dress or hat for chapel. Tirzah is intrigued by the look that comes over her mother's face when he talks about Aunty Ceinwen having new things. It's a constricted smile, battling with itself. Tirzah knows this is because her mother would love to have a new dress, or a husband who allowed her a new hat when she fancied one, and is wrestling with jealousy. Leave her alone, she'd say. Nothing wrong with a treat now and again. Not that I would know, of course. When Tirzah comes down to the kitchen, boxes of food and tins of cake are waiting to be packed in Dada's big car. He does not see why anyone would want to eat in a restaurant, throwing their good money at strangers.

After the kissing and goodbyes, Tirzah and Biddy walk along the lane carrying their cases, out past the edge of the village. The little trees that waved with catkins not long ago are letting down frondy branches thick with leaves now. Thank flip we are not going on a Christian holiday, Biddy says, overtaking Tirzah. I have quite enough of Jesus as I can take in an ordinary week, thank you very much. That's why I might not go on the CYC weekend. Tirzah nods, remembering how, at Easter, primroses shone sweetly along the base of the stone wall. In their place, buttercups clump today. How could so much happen in such a short time? Then her mind jumps to the recurring dream she had when she was younger, about the Devil appearing from amongst her bampy's dahlias, all smoking and scaly. She hasn't thought about the Devil for ages. Is that a bad thing? Has he lulled her into a false sense of security, as Pastor always warns? Tirzah is about to remind Biddy of their old ideas about the Devil lurking behind every bush, but decides against it. Biddy would think that was so childish.

Come on, you slug, Biddy shouts over her shoulder. Gran will have a nice little bite waiting for us, and I'm starving. Step on it. Tirzah can't walk any faster. You go on, she calls. I need a breather. The heat seems to be pulling every shred of strength from her muscles. She sits in the verge, resting against the warm stones of the wall, and looks at the uncountable, glossy green circles of pennywort trailing from the cracks. I love walls like this, with all their strange things growing away, she thinks. There is another sprawling plant that she especially likes, covered with tiny, trumpet-shaped purple flowers and veined, ivy-like leaves. It is wonderful to her that something so pretty and strong can grow with so little encouragement. Up close, the wall is noisy with the buzz and drone of insects. Tirzah lays her ear against the gap between two lichened stones and listens intently to the music inside. Over and through everything, a gently rising and falling hum spreads: it is the breeze from the fields. Tirzah can detect an oily smell of sheep wool and the stringent breath of crushed dandelions. It seems like years ago she used to play the game of flying out from herself and squeezing into some small, secret place. I'm too old for that game now, she realises. Reluctantly she clambers to her feet and picks up the case.

The garden door appears sooner than she expects it, as usual. She leaves the case in the conservatory and goes to look for Bampy. He is always doing something in his green-houses, so she takes the narrow, curving path through the blackcurrant bushes and the netted gooseberries, and as she walks she begins to liven up. Bamps! she calls. It's me! Where are you? She can smell cigarette smoke, and smiles. Is that my other favourite girl? her bampy shouts. I'm in with my toms. Tirzah sees him, curved and thin, his old cardigan with its stuffed pockets stretched down at the front. As always, the last half-a-thumb of a cigarette is stuck in the middle of his lower lip. Come and give me a cwtch, he calls, stretching an arm to catch her. Tirzah runs and wraps her arms around his narrow chest. Oh, Bampy, I've missed you, she says against his cardigan. He squeezes her with one arm. In the other he is nursing a hairy stem heavy with green tomatoes. I'm giving these a good talking to, he tells her. They need a bit of love, just like everything else.

They pull a few tender balls of lettuce and handfuls of thin spring onions. Your gran will be tamping, I've been so long, he says, shaking earth off the lettuce roots. In the kitchen, it is so dark that for an instant Tirzah is blinded. She stiffens, suddenly unsure of her footing, and then the sound of Biddy's laughter lightens the room. Tirzah finds her gran in the tiny back scullery where the sink and cooker are. Nice to see you, love, she says, opening her arms for Tirzah to come to her. The room is rich with the smell of baking pastry and spring onions. Then her gran stands back. Let me get a good look, she says, smiling. Tirzah does a twirl. What do you think? she asks. Her gran inspects her, but then narrows her eyes, her intake of breath a little hiss. What's wrong with me? Tirzah asks, alarmed. But her gran turns to the oven. You go and sit down next to Biddy, my love, she says, bending to take out a golden, onion-flecked flan. It's time to eat.

Tirzah steals looks across the table. When her granny catches her eye she smiles, but to Tirzah the smile looks odd. Eat up, little ones, she urges them, slipping seconds of quiche on to their plates. Bampy is salting his radishes and crunching them into the silence. Biddy keeps on eating long after everyone else has finished. Are you stuffing yourself just to annoy me? Tirzah whispers. Take your time, why don't you? Biddy pokes her tongue out at Tirzah. Thank you, Gran, she says, getting up. I enjoyed that. Then she disappears with Bampy to the shops. I'll make us a cup of tea, Gran says. Tirzah rests her head on the wing of one of the fireside chairs, content to do nothing. When the tea is ready, they sit opposite each other. Now, child, her grandmother says, have you got anything you want to tell me? Anything at all you are concerned about? I don't think so, Tirzah answers, worried again. Why? Her gran is silent for a moment. Have you been sick in the mornings? she asks, leaning to take Tirzah's hand. Or experienced anything strange lately? Have you missed your visitor? Tirzah feels an extreme reluctance to answer. Her cheeks start to burn, which scares her even more. I have been tired, she says slowly, without looking up. And the other things you mentioned. Uninvited, an image of dark woods and a ferny den flash before her.

Gran puts her cup down. Now, dear, she says, try not to be upset by what I'm going to say. She takes a deep breath. I might be wrong, but I seldom am about these things. Call it the second sight. Tirzah raises her eyes. I don't understand, she says. But then, as if the knowledge had been dammed up and has now broken through, she is flooded with a realisation. She stares at her gran, waiting for her to speak. Brace up, my love, she says, enclosing Tirzah's small hands in hers. The reason you are off colour and not yourself is because you are going to have a baby. Am I right? Could you be with child? Tirzah sees her grandmother's strong, brown face and tear-filled eyes and knows the words she says are true, but while the brass clock with its face of navy stars ticks on the mantel and the browny-black cat stalks in from the garden she can feel herself backing away. Her heartbeats sound slow and hollow in her ears, and her gran's seated figure recedes until she is a tiny stick woman at the end of a long corridor.

For what seems like hours, there is nothing. But then rough, warm hands are patting her cheek. Tirzah is ice-cold, shivering in the chair near the fireplace, and even with a blanket over her knees she can't get warm. It's as if she has turned to stone. Scenes, like shreds of torn paper blown in the wind, drift past her face: the stream, the bent saplings in the woods, the knowing old crows and Brân crouching in the firelight, but she cannot hold on to any of them. Under the blanket she rests her hands on her stomach, trying to pull her thoughts together. Gran brings her another hot drink. Here, she coaxes, holding the cup to Tirzah's chilled lips. I know you won't believe me, my beauty, but this is not the end of the world, she says. After the rumpus has died down, and your mammy and daddy see things clearly, you will all be right as rain. Tirzah turns her face away and stares into the bunch of dried flowers in the firebasket. Now then, her gran goes on, standing over Tirzah. Everyone will want to know who the young man is. But Tirzah shakes her head and keeps her eyes closed, watching, stricken, as all her certainties fly away like hastily pegged laundry on a windy day.

In Sin Did My Mother Conceive Me

(Psalm 51.5)

Tirzah has been so mute and shivery, Gran helps her upstairs to the double bed the girls always share when they are staying. After tucking her in, Gran kneels down and makes a fire in the little tiled grate; Tirzah cannot warm up, even though she can see the afternoon sun through the window and knows it's hot outside. Gran looks over her shoulder from where she kneels, holding some pages of the newspaper above the fire to make it draw. I don't want you to worry about a thing this afternoon, she says. Rest is what you need, and quiet. Your mam and dad will be here shortly. Tirzah stiffens in the bed; her parents are away, so how will they come? Gran knocks the paper back into the fireplace as it ignites. Who'd have thought it? she goes on, almost to herself. Tirzah can't imagine seeing her parents. The idea that she has a real, growing baby inside her is so unexpected, so horrible, so impossible she can't stop sobbing. But deep down, there is another quite calm part of her, she realises. A part that maybe already knew. There, look at you, her grandmother says, manoeuvring into a position where she can pull herself upright using the bedpost. She sits on the bed and pushes Tirzah's hair away from her forehead. You're all over the place. Oh, my little dumpling, she croons, gathering Tirzah's stiff body into her arms, don't fret. I'm here by you.

When Gran's gone downstairs, Tirzah can still feel tears sliding into her hair. Soon the pillow is wet. She burrows under the eiderdown, allowing her body to sink into the mattress. The small fire sounds like a bubbling pot of water. Tirzah looks at the faded photo on the mantelpiece: old-fashioned people stand outside a chapel. The weather is gloomy if the shadows are anything to go by. There is a bride, and the groom looks as if he's wearing someone else's clothes. All the other men have round spectacles and shoulders that are out of proportion with their thin, dark-suited frames. The women wear tiny, scone-like hats, except the bride. Her head is swathed in flowers. Tirzah knows this photograph well. But now she gazes at the bride, and wonders if she was happy. Did she marry her true love? She slips down from the high mattress and tiptoes across to pick the photo up and takes it back to bed. Did you have a baby? she asks the smiling, flower-wreathed bride. Was there a secret you kept from everyone? These people are dead now. And everything they cared about, everybody they knew, is gone too. She wipes her drying cheeks.

The bed Tirzah lies in is so high that when she was little, Bampy made a wooden step to climb on. Its springs made a wheezing sound when you turned over. She moves her legs, and sure enough, the bed sways and sings for a moment. Deliberately, she switches her mind to think about the times she and Biddy have shared this bed. When they stayed over in winter, they always loved to watch the firelight judder across the ceiling. Nothing bad could ever happen. They were safe, even if outside a storm roared. They could look at the door left open just an inch, and as they drifted off to sleep, listen to the grown-ups talking and their bampy playing the piano downstairs. But now Tirzah sees that the small window deeply set in the wall, the multi-coloured rag rug by the bed, the huge, dark chest of drawers with its brass keyholes, will all be gone someday. Strangers will live here and bring their own furniture. Everything will change. It was changing already. Soon this new baby will be in the world, and like it or not, everyone in Horeb and the family will have to budge up to make room for it. Lulled by the old, comfy bed, Tirzah falls asleep.

When she wakes up, the light has a summer evening look. Tirzah is swamped by heavy waves of fear and starts to panic just as Biddy appears. What are you doing? she asks, taking in Tirzah's rigid body and the way her hands are clutching and unclutching the bedclothes. Are you cracking up? Tirzah turns to face her and lifts the bedclothes. When Biddy has lain down, they hold hands under the covers. Biddy rests her head on Tirzah's shoulder. What are you going to do now, Tizzy? she asks in a whisper. Who have you been seeing? Tell me. But Tirzah can't answer. The enormity of her situation is too much to think about. Her eyes sting again, and soon she and Biddy are both crying. I can't lie here snivelling, she thinks after a while. I have to get up and face my parents. Come on, she says, gently pushing Biddy. Let's go downstairs. Anyway, Gran says this is not the end of the world. It's a rumpus that will die down. Biddy makes a little sound in her throat. Dear Gran doesn't understand anything about anything, she says. On the landing, Tirzah stops to listen. She can tell by the way the conservatory door has squeaked that people have come into the kitchen. The girls sit on the top stair, leaning into each other's shoulders, and wait.

Biddy is restless, picking the fringe of her sun top and sighing. Whatever's the matter with you? Tirzah asks. I'm the one who should be fussing. Biddy doesn't respond. She stares into Tirzah's eyes until Tirzah gives her a jab with her elbow. Stop it, she snaps. What? Biddy takes her hand. Can I ask you a question, Tizzy? she says. Don't be angry, though, promise? Go on, for goodness' sake, just say it, Tirzah answers. Honestly. Sometimes you get on my toot. Right, I will go on, Biddy says. She speaks in a quiet voice. Is the father of your baby Osian? Tirzah senses a hedge full of thorns growing up around her. How could she have been so thick? Of course people will blame Osian. This is what everyone will think. Osian won't be able to bear it. Some people believe he is the Devil's plaything as it is. She drops her head into her hands. Oh, heck, Biddy says. I'm so sorry. Me and my big cakehole. She puts her arms around Tirzah and rocks her. It's none of my business anyway, she goes on. Tirzah is struck by a new sense of danger. How will Osian manage when this gets around? She must think of how to convince everyone he is innocent.

Her mind empties out, but eventually the rise and fall of voices below drags her back to the landing and the top step. She wipes her eyes and straightens her clothes. Even though she strains to distinguish who the voices belong to, it's impossible to be sure through the closed door. You don't think it's the elders, do you? Biddy asks. Tirzah shakes her head. Gradually she distinguishes her father's voice amongst the others, and when her mother appears at the bottom of the stairs she is almost relieved. Come, her mother calls, beckoning. When Tirzah stands close she can see the stricken look

210

in her eyes. We phoned from our lodgings to tell your granny we'd arrived safely, she hears her mother say, and she said we should come home. She places her hand on Tirzah's back. Your dada, Uncle Maldwyn and Aunty Ceinwen are going to wait in the kitchen. Oh, cariad, her mother whispers, shaking her head. What have you done? Tirzah goes before her into the front room. Everything is the same but not the same. The piano, the fruit bowl, the lumpy sofa: they all look shabby now, diminished in some way connected with what has happened. She sits on the edge of the sofa, ashamed to look again into her mother's injured eyes.

Tirzah tries to understand, but the words come to her as if spoken underwater. She stares at her mother's mouth and sees it moving. Her mother's hands wring a hankie, and her neck is mottled. I'm sorry, Mama, she says. I can't hear you. Again, her heart is thumping slowly and loudly. She detects dishes clinking in the kitchen and the normal sound of a kettle boiling, but they don't apply to her. Her mother comes across to sit beside her on the sofa. I don't want to see Dada and Aunty and Uncle, Tirzah says. But will you tell them Osian is not the father? Her mother nods. What will happen to me now? Will you send me away, Mama? She hears her mother say her name. We will look after you, child, she whispers. What did you think? Then she grabs Tirzah fiercely to her. Oh, cariad, she says again, rocking Tirzah, this isn't what I wanted for you. When did it happen? Who with? Tirzah cannot say; her throat has closed on the words. She looks into her mother's eyes. Are you and Dada angry with me? she manages to ask.

Her mother shrugs. You leave your dada to me, she says. His bark is much worse than his bite. And we of all people are in no position to be angry. How could we be angry, when I was

211

in the same boat as you seventeen years ago? Well, almost the same boat. Dada was my steady boyfriend, of course. Whereas nobody knows who on earth the father of this little waif is. What? Tirzah asks, trying to take this in. Were you expecting a baby without being married? She is without the strength to sit up any more, and nestles her head into her mother's lap to listen to what she has to say. Her head is fizzing with the knowledge that she herself was that baby. When her mother has finished telling her how she and Dada loved each other and wanted her so much, even though they were young, Tirzah thinks again of the faded people in the old photo upstairs, and how they are unknowable to her; she can never hope to understand long-ago strangers when even the here-and-now people she thought she knew are full of secrets. She pictures her parents, both so young, and the cloud of disapproval that swirled around them years ago. Everything has changed again. The image of her parents grows sharper. They are no longer the fuzzy, chapel-bound figures she thought they were. They are bigger, more colourful, nigh-on wonderful to her now.

Wash Me and I Shall Be Whiter Than Snow

(Psalm 51:7)

It is decided that Tirzah and Biddy will stay and have their summer holiday as usual. We don't need to tell the whole valley our business yet, her mother had said, unsmilingly, when she kissed Tirzah goodbye. They will know soon enough. And we will go back to the conference. She set her mouth into a quivering smile. It's important to keep up a show of normality, at least. Tirzah stays in the front room, waiting for them to leave. The thought of seeing her father, or her aunt and uncle, is unbearable. As soon as they're gone, her heart lifts, light as a bubble. Every day when she and Biddy wake up, the sun is lying in a golden block on the bedclothes and the sky through the little square window is a fresh, wind-blown blue. The girls chase each other downstairs in their nighties and eat breakfast with Gran and Bampy. Bacon and egg today, Gran announces one morning. Then I want you both to pack a bag. I hope you brought your swimming cossies? The girls nod; they love to sunbathe on the top lawn here. It's so private, like a flowery outdoor room, and only the birds can see them sprawled on their blanket. Although for the past few

213

years Tirzah has sunbathed in the shade. Once she burnt to a crimson crisp, and still remembers the pain as the skin lifted off her shoulders like tissue paper.

Gran goes on breaking eggs into the frying pan. Where are we going? Biddy asks. Can't you give us a clue? Oh, sorry, Gran says, squinting at the spitting eggs. Didn't I say? We are going on an outing. Tirzah and Biddy look at each other across the white tablecloth. Do you know about this, Bamps? Tirzah asks. But he lifts his hands and laughs. Don't ask me, he says. I never get told anything. Tirzah is lost in a dream of being a little girl again. Nothing can shake her from it. Gran puts before her a familiar, thick, cream-coloured plate. Around its border, under the glaze, is a cunning little trailing garland of fruit and flowers. Tirzah looks at her plump egg, the yolk like an orange eyeball gazing at her, and the still-sizzling rashers of bacon, and is hit with nausea. Off to the bathroom with you quick, her granny says, picking the plate up to put in the oven.

Tirzah retches, but can only produce a scummy yellow fluid. Is this all that's inside me? she thinks. Am I full of nothing but sour water? She waits until the heaving stops, trying not to think about the baby lying like a grub in an apple somewhere beneath her heart, and then washes her face and cleans her teeth. In the mirror, she can see her wet eyes and wild hair. Who am I fooling? she wonders. I am not a child any more, even if I am living like one. I am almost grown up. I am going to be a mother soon. But it's too improbable for Tirzah to hold on to. She decides that for a couple of weeks she will go on being Tirzah the girl who is staying at her grandmother's, and nothing else. She will not make any decisions or worry about anyone. I will play in the garden with Biddy, she thinks, and cook and read and help Bampy with his greenhouses. Later, I will think things through. Not now. Quickly she gathers her hair into a loose ponytail and runs back to the kitchen. Bampy is standing up, finishing his toast. I'm frying you a fresh egg, her grandmother says. Then we will have to be organised.

The three of them, each carrying a bag, walk across the broad common, strewn with sheep currants and dandelions, towards the loop in the road where the buses turn. Swallows throw themselves elegantly around the sky, and the houses they pass have gardens hectic with flowers. Step on it, girls, Gran says, panting. We mustn't be late. Tirzah can see faces looking their way from the windows of a bus. But where are we going? Biddy asks again. The seaside, Gran announces. The girls stand still and look at her. We're going to the sea, she repeats, smiling at their response. Tirzah is so excited she can only stare at Biddy. I managed to get us seats on the Hope Baptist Women's Guild outing, Gran says as she pushes them up the steps of the bus. And it wasn't easy, I can tell you.

Biddy and Tirzah sit at the back, Tirzah next to the window. You can have the window on the way home, she tells Biddy. It's only fair. But Biddy doesn't mind. When they have been travelling for about an hour, Gran lurches up the aisle and gives them each a Thermos cup of cocoa and a square of gingerbread. The girls talk about the seaside as they nibble their cake. Biddy stayed at a bed-and-breakfast place once in Barry Island with her parents. She tells Tirzah how, when they were eating their evening meal, the landlady would trip past the window in high heels, hair tied in a chiffon head square and her lips painted red, on her way to the bingo hall. Tirzah tries to imagine that. No one she knows wears lipstick, except Mrs

Rowland. No one even knows how to play bingo. And guess what? Biddy adds. Our landlady's hair was dyed yellow. What did your parents say? Tirzah asks. My dad got worked up, Biddy answers. Every time she went past, he would start on about how disgusting it was, wasting honest people's hard-earned money on gambling and strong drink. Might as well throw it straight down the drain, he said. Then Mam would start about how a landlady should be able to spend her own hard-earned money any way she chose, and that there was no evidence of anyone being a drinker. Their landlady kept a very tidy house, and the bathroom was exemplary, and so on. It was unbelievably boring listening to the pair of them go on and on and on, Biddy says, finishing her cake. Tirzah can just imagine Aunty Ceinwen and Uncle Mal, and poor Biddy stuck in the middle.

There are a few small children on the bus, and every now and again one of them needs attention. Ladies mill around the child, handing each other things, while thin wails rise. Soon the air is warm and acrid with the smell of bodies and snacks and vomit. Tirzah is surprised she hasn't felt ill yet; usually on a bus she is nauseous almost immediately and has to stand by the driver, who opens the door for her. She recalls the way she used to grab the pole, nearly swooning while she dragged great lungfuls of cold air in. She remembers the many times she wasn't quick enough, and the wonderful relief of retching. She remembers the sight of her spoilt shoes. Poor Mama, she thinks. Having to put up with me all these years. It was a well-known fact that Tirzah was a very sick-prone child. Today, anyway, she is well, and enjoys the gingerbread and cocoa without the slightest problem.

Soon someone shouts. The sea is visible for the first time. But it's always ages before you actually get there, Biddy says.

Tirzah looks out of the window at the bungalows on the beach road. They are painted ice-cream colours, utterly unlike the red-brick terraces at home. Nobody has much growing in the front garden here, just yuccas and battered-looking palms. Gulls hang in the air like sea spirits. She looks hard but there is not one crow to be seen. The side of the road is studded with shops selling buckets and spades, chips and ice cream. Tirzah is restless. She longs to throw her tight clothes off, run across the wide, corrugated sands and feel the sea breeze raking her hair. Even when the bus finally stops, it's a lifetime before they can get off. Stop pushing me, you big bully, Biddy says, shoving Tirzah. I can't go anywhere yet. The Women's Guild seem to be crawling out of the bus. It's enough to make Tirzah scream. She forces herself to wait, resting her head on a plush seatback.

When they are all on the pavement, the chief Women's Guild lady makes some announcements. She has a head square tied tightly under her chin, and a little shiny sausage curl in the middle of her forehead. Tirzah is amazed by the way her bosom pushes the front of her cotton dress out in a sort of ridge. She cannot imagine ever looking like that. The lady holds up a green flag on a tall pole. This will be stuck in the sand so everyone knows how to find us, she announces. They are all going to get deckchairs and sit in a circle on the beach. That way the children will be safe and can play where they can be kept an eye on. She gives Tirzah and Biddy a look. Their grandmother says, Don't worry about this pair. They are very sensible. The woman locks eyes with Gran for a moment. Well, it's up to you, of course, Bronwen, she says, and Gran says, Yes, it is, Brenda. Biddy smiles, trying to look sensible, but Tirzah is gazing out to the distant hint of sea.

The air at the seaside gets inside Tirzah's lungs, clearing them out. It's like drinking a cup of the most crystalline water in the world. Come on, girls, Gran says. Let's get our bags and deckchairs in position. Then you can go off and explore. Soon everything is sorted out. Gran settles in a deckchair with a cardigan around her shoulders and her sandals off. This is the life, she says, putting on sunglasses with big winglike shapes at the outer edges. Off you go now. Tirzah slips her panties down under her skirt and feels the sea breeze floating up her naked legs. She pulls the costume to her waist, wriggles her arms inside her T-shirt and undoes her bra. Then she pulls the costume over her breasts, treads out of her skirt and flings her top away. Put this old thing of mine on over your costume, love, her grandmother says, handing her a faded shirt. Just in case. Tirzah doesn't want to wear the shirt. I'm still almost flat as a pancake, she says, kicking sand into little heaps. We don't want to upset the Hope ladies, lovey, Gran says quietly. They have eyes like hawks and can sniff out a secret in a trice. Tirzah blushes as she puts on the soft shirt and does it up, all the time keeping her eyes trained on the sea. Then she takes off over the soft sand, not waiting for anyone.

When she gets to the sea she doesn't stop, even though the cold water forces a scream from her mouth. In she strides, eager to dive under the waves. It's a long way to the breakers, but she keeps going, loving the way that the sea encroaches with cold hands towards her waist, and then over her breasts. Everything is shimmering and slapping, salty and pure. There is a tall, frothy-topped wave rolling in, and at the perfect moment she fearlessly dives into its green wall, unaware of any danger. A roar fills her head and pebbles bounce off her skin. Down she goes, with her eyes closed, sea-green legs paddling, her hair a wet flame streaking out above her. She rolls around on the seabed, never wanting to come up. But too soon her lungs empty and she rises. As she breaks through the surface, lifted by the power of the water, she is a new, better version of herself.

Here on the vast beach she has changed from being just a child, a girl of the misty, tree-crowded valleys and the whinberry-topped mountains, to a creature of the sea and the lively air and towering clouds. I belong to the whole world, she thinks, a feeling of bliss rising from her throat. Inside, the tiny bud of a baby sleeps, folding in on itself as it grows and changes too. Then, as she wades into the shallows and shields her eyes, she picks out, amongst all the other people on the beach, the ring of deckchairs with its green flag flapping. Little children are milling around it. No, wait, she thinks. I'm just stupid me. I am only Tirzah, and very ordinary. She starts to shiver violently, her soaking hair like a hank of weed down her back, and her grandmother's shirt gripping wetly. Suddenly, she longs to be kneeling in the dry sand at her gran's feet, wrapped in a rough towel, waiting with Biddy for a stick of celery stuffed along its juicy groove with cream cheese. She can see Biddy's tiny figure standing at the edge of the group, shielding her eyes, searching the sea for her. After our picnic, she thinks, it would be nice to go with Biddy and search out those red-armed anemones that wave in the rock pools. She's only ever seen them in a book. But for now Tirzah is too exhausted even to run up the beach.

He That Is Without Sin Among You, Let Him First Cast a Stone

(John 8:7)

The holiday is over too quickly. Tirzah is now a lightly baked biscuit colour, her hair coppery at the ends, and her freckles have multiplied. She can detect her belly expanding almost by the hour. The girls walk back home through the lanes on a day so hot the tarmac is molten in patches and exhausted leaves droop like sleeping bats on the branches. Silence lies over the village, only broken at intervals by the hollow *rrooh-rrooh* of unseen pigeons. Tirzah is wishing she was anywhere but here, going anywhere but home. Biddy is scuffing her sandals, blowing fragile, misshapen bubbles with her chewing gum. This case weighs a blimmin' ton, she gasps, pausing to sit in the shade of the hawthorn trees not far from the Co-op. Tirzah drops down beside her and looks at the branches above. Already there are sprays of berries forming. Surely it was only days ago the tree was weighed down with May blossom thick as rice pudding?

Wait there, she says, and gets up. In the Co-op, the electric fly-catcher crackles, and the cheese counter gives off a sharp smell. Tirzah walks past the bacon and ham displays and makes straight for the freezer. A gust of icy air shoots up her nose when she slides open the cover to get at the things inside. She picks out two strawberry-flavoured milk lollies. In the queue waiting to pay she can feel them softening in their paper packets. Someone in front is having luncheon meat sliced and chats to the assistant who slices it. The steely hiss of the blade makes Tirzah shrink inside. When she is finally served, the assistant nods towards the lollies. Change those for two frozen ones, lovey, she says. They won't be worth a lick by the time you get them home. Thank you, Mrs Ellis-Jones, Tirzah says.

Biddy is dozing when Tirzah gets back. She lays the icy lolly on her bare neck. Ouch, says Biddy. Ooh, yummy. They sit and bite into the creamy pink ice cream. Tirzah thinks for the first time about the village, and how everyone will behave once they know her news. How will people like nice Mrs Ellis-Jones react? It's a lonely thought. Soon her lolly is finished, and she reads the joke on the wooden stick, but it's not funny. So what do you think your dada is going to say? Biddy asks, sucking a dropped blob of ice cream from her arm. How do I know? Tirzah answers, frowning. I can't read minds. Back in the village, it suddenly seems to Tirzah that all her troubles have flown home to roost like noisy birds. Pardon me for breathing, Biddy says, licking her fingers clean. I'm sorry, Bid. Tirzah tucks her arm through Biddy's. It's just that I'm so scared. The girls sit in silence, watching the comings and goings at the Co-op. I wonder where that Brân is, Biddy says after a while. You know, the scruffy boy who used to hang around here all the time with those little kids. Tirzah's palms prickle. I used to think he was quite dishy, she adds. I fancied him. Do you know what I mean? No, I do not, Tirzah answers, getting up. Come on, we might as well get going.

At home, the hall is so dark Tirzah blinks to clear her eyes. Her parents' cases are piled at the foot of the stairs. Sounds are coming from the kitchen, so she puts her case down and calls. There is no answer, but the sounds stop. Mama? she calls again as she opens the kitchen door. Is that you? Her parents are sitting opposite each other at the table. Tirzah is not sure what to do. Her father does not look at her; he is staring at his clasped hands. Come in, don't hover, child, her mother says quietly. Sit down by here. Tirzah forces herself to walk to the table and sit. Her head is buzzing and there is a sharp lump like a dry crust in her throat. No one speaks. Because she can't stand another moment waiting, Tirzah decides to say something. Even as she is opening her mouth, she has no idea what will come out. Both her parents are listening, neither looking at the other. I think I should go away from the valley, Tirzah hears herself saying. Right away, to somewhere no one knows me, or you. I think that's what I should do.

There is another silence. Tirzah's eyes rest on the plates and jugs on the dresser, and the kettle sitting on the hob. She looks at the two easy chairs either side of the empty fireplace, with their old flat cushions and antimacassars, then back to her parents. Dada? she says. Will you ever forgive me? Her father rests his elbow on the table and covers his eyes with one hand. He is swallowing, unable to speak. Gwyllim, Tirzah's mother says, answer her, please. His shoulders move, and he makes a noise in his throat. Tirzah feels as if someone has slapped her face; the sight of her father weeping is too much to bear. I'm so sorry, Dada dear, she says. Truly, truly, I am. She is crying without a sound, her nose running unchecked. You have shamed yourself, he says at last. And our hearts are broken in pieces for you. And even now, you won't come clean. Tirzah's mother struggles to stand. I'll put the kettle on, she says, wiping her eyes. We will have tea and try to sort something out. Gwyllim, you get the cups and saucers.

Tirzah watches her parents preparing tea. Neatly they step around each other, each exactly knowing what the other will do. Her father's face is so strange, she is afraid for him. There is a stooped look to his shoulders and an empty look to his eyes. Poor Dada, she thinks, her chest burning. Her mother stirs the tea in the pot and then pours it. They all sit together and drink. When her father finishes, he sets his cup down and clears his throat. Many nights have I wrestled with the Lord in prayer, he tells them. Many dark nights. And this I will say: no one is going from this house. No one is running away from this village. Tirzah's mother reaches across the table to hold his hand. Now then, her father continues, his voice more normal. This is going to be a difficult time. We will be burnt in the fires, and no mistake. Tirzah wonders what he means. You, he says, nodding at her. You have shown yourself to be a wicked, loose girl. You have been a silly, wayward girl all your life. But this really takes the cake. Never did I think you would do such a secretive, wicked thing as this. Never in all my born days. He raises a finger, just getting going. Her mother starts to talk, but he raises his hand. Excuse me, Mair, he says. Know your place.

Tirzah's mother bangs the table with her palm. Remember all the things we discussed when we were away, and don't give me all this preachifying, Gwyllim, she says. I've heard it too many times. Know my place? I know many things, thank you very much. You may be the head of this house, but you are also a man, and a fallen man, just as I am a fallen woman. Tirzah looks from one to the other. Yes, Tirzah has been weak and foolish and deceitful, her mother goes on. Yes, we are ashamed. But – and now she raises her finger in the air – we have nothing to write home about on that score. Mair! Dada shouts. Don't Mair me, either, Tirzah's mother says, cutting him off. Let us be honest, as we are commanded to be. What's done is done. You, Tirzah, will stop talking about going away. I have never heard such nonsense. Where, pray, would you go for a start? And you, Gwyllim, will come down from your holy mountain top and start behaving like a human being. There is another silence. I think that's all for now, she adds, her voice flat. But we have questions for you, Tirzah. And we will require answers. For now, off you go.

Tirzah cannot stay in the stuffy house. Relief that her first meeting with her father is over makes her both calmer and more jittery. And there's so much to sort out, I don't know what to do first, she thinks, not noticing where she is walking. Should I go and see Osian? Should I go and speak to Pastor? What about sixth form? When will my O-level results be through? She shakes her head to free herself from all the questions flying around. Soon the walk takes her to the fields and towards the woods. I need to find Brân, she thinks, suddenly sure. I should try and talk to him. Across the fields, the late afternoon sun is coating each blade of grass with orange stripes, illuminating the tiny gnats that rise in puffs before her. She tries to work out what to say, but cannot imagine telling Brân he is going to be a father. It would be like telling a boulder or a hillside, somehow. I will just go looking for him and see what happens, she decides.

Suddenly fuzzy with exhaustion, her legs are unsure on the tussocky ground. Stepping into the summer woods is like walking into a huge, verdant room. The smell of ripe vegetation is a delirious mixture of lemon and vanilla, cinnamon and something almost chocolatey. Nothing moves. The trees breathe out and out, giving up their healing perfumes. Tirzah is dazzled by the countless greens. Even the light is leafy, softly focused and dappling. Further in she walks, swishing through the undergrowth, warding off thin branches. Then she hears the sound of someone walking boldly up ahead, swiftly coming her way, and freezes. Her ears are tuned for any clue; her eyes strain to see in the half-light. Gradually a figure breaks through.

Tirzah is struggling to breathe evenly. Brân, she calls, Brân! He steps into the clearing and looks blindly at her. Columns of sunshine tower around him. His hair is bushy, like a long, ragged mane around his shoulders now. Brân, it's me, Tirzah, she says again. But Brân is stooping, and when he stands upright again he is holding a stone, big as his fist. He raises it and takes aim. No, Brân, Tirzah calls, holding out her hand. Don't. Brân is alert, still holding the stone. She sees he is wearing tattered shorts tied with string at the waist, and broken black shoes. His skin is dark brown and his face bony. She licks her dry lips, but before she can say another word, Brân leans his shoulder back and expertly hurls the stone. It hits Tirzah heavily in the middle of the forehead and she drops to the earth, eaten by the dark.

And I Will Bind Up That Which Was Broken

(Ezekiel 34:16)

Tirzah wakes and realises she is being carried by someone. She tries to remember where she is, vaguely recalling Brân surrounded by bolts of sunlight. Her eyelids are coated with something sticky, the lashes caked together so she cannot open them properly. For minutes she droops in what must be Brân's arms, her head hanging heavily like a turnip in a string bag. He is going downhill towards the stream, almost running, his arms trembling with the effort of supporting her. When they are near the water, he tries to lower her to the ground and falls to his knees. Tirzah lies motionless, surrounded by his smell. She senses she is alone for a moment and sits up, rubbing her crusted eyes. Then he is back, holding in his cupped, dirty hands a few drops of stream water and a bunch of some weed. His chest is still heaving as he leans forward and tries to clean her eyes. Tirzah pushes him away and struggles to stand. Take me to the stream, she says. And Brân helps her through the undergrowth.

She sits at the stream's edge where the rough grasses grow and dabbles her hands and cleans her eyes. The clear water, lively with minnows, refreshes her a little. Brân drops to the ground beside her. He is doing something to her skirt. Get your paws off me, she cries, pushing him away. I hate you. He snatches his hands back as if she has burnt him, and she realises he had been trying to smooth down her clothes so that they cover her thighs. She has a tissue in her pocket and she wets it. The bunch of weeds lies in her lap, and he points to it, and then to her bleeding face. The scent of cut celery rises from the torn stems. Tirzah grabs the bunch and hurls it into the stream. Investigating her forehead with her fingertips, she feels a swollen lump forming. In the middle of the lump she can detect a spongy wound. Pain radiates from it. Brân is still silent, and she studies his averted face. He looks nothing like the boy she knew only a few months back; his eye sockets are deep and bruised, his cheeks collapsed. Bones seem to be about to break through his skin, they are so sharp. His body is covered in scratches and scabs, some old, some fresh.

The throbbing of Tirzah's wound intensifies when she tries to stand, making her stumble. I'm going now, she tells Brân. So don't try to stop me. I will never set foot in these woods again. He keeps his eyes lowered and seems utterly spent. Looking at the blood-soaked ball of wet tissue in her hand, sadness for him congests her chest. What is going to happen to you? she asks. You are a wicked, wicked boy to throw that stone at me. Brân is still silent, but when he lifts his eyes to hers briefly, she can see immediately how unsure he is. His ankles are ingrained with dirt, and one big toe, its nail long and jagged, pokes through the open flap of his shoe. Where are your crow friends now? she asks. And as if she has conjured them, high above, the hoarse cawing of birds saws the green air. Brân gazes up to the treetops, an expression of dread in his eyes. Tirzah is afraid. I must never tell him about the baby, she thinks. Now, you go away, back where you belong, she tells him. He makes a move as if to touch her hair, but she shrugs him off. Then, in an instant, he has vanished.

When Tirzah arrives home, her mother raises her hands to her cheeks. Whatever's happened to you now? she asks, shooing Tirzah into the kitchen. Every day it's something. I don't think my heart can take much more. She reaches up for the first-aid box from the top of the dresser and gets out antiseptic cream and plasters. Tirzah sits at the table, her head aching, and watches her mother rush around. Into an enamel bowl she puts a few drops of TCP and some warm water, and brings it to the table. The clean, medical smell of the antiseptic rises in a vapour and bathes Tirzah's face. She hardly makes a sound as her mother washes the cut. When a big, square plaster is in place her mother clears away and puts the kettle on. Now, she says, coming to sit beside Tirzah. What happened this time? Tirzah is silent. I'm going to get cross with you in a minute, her mother says. Come on, tell me everything. But Tirzah will not say a word, even when her mother begins to cry. I don't understand why you won't talk to me, she says, tears slipping across her flushed cheeks. I promise not to be angry. Tirzah leans to put her arms around her mother's shoulders. I had a little accident, that's all. I'm sorry, Mama, she whispers, and gives her a long kiss on the forehead. Then she leaves her mother hunched at the table and goes to her room to rest.

Gazing at the ceiling, Tirzah thinks about Brân. There is the lump again in her throat, and she knows it is made up of all the secrets she is keeping. She can't imagine how life will be in the future, and as for Brân, she senses something terrible will happen to him before long. I suppose what he needs is the Lord, she thinks. Only He has the power to change people. But even as she thinks this, she is doubtful. God is irrelevant to Brân. He is a worshipper of other powers, and Tirzah isn't sure what they are. She wonders if what Brân says about the gods of the valley is true; after all, the world is stranger than she ever realised. She remembers her visitation in the twilit field, her sense of the presence of something that was both part of the evening and the woods. The huge, white-winged owl which sat with her briefly, sharing the dusk. Who had that been? She tries to imagine Brân coming to chapel. Pastor is always telling the fellowship stories about hardened sinners repenting and changing. Why couldn't this happen to Brân? It would be a miracle. She tries to picture a neat, clean-haired Brân sitting in a pew with his Bible open. Please help Brân, she prays, just in case God is listening. You say you care about the outcast and the lost, but where is the evidence? Amen. Then she is asleep.

Tirzah's mother has arranged visits from the district nurse. Betty Palfrey and I were in school together, she tells them one evening later in the week as they eat. You remember her, don't you, Gwyll? Good as gold, she is. I'm sure you will like her, Tirzah. But Tirzah doesn't want to listen. I'm not poorly, she says, putting her cutlery down and folding her arms. Why do I need to see a nurse? I will not dignify that with an answer, her mother says. Eat your nice food. Tirzah looks at her father. Dada, I don't want to see the nurse, she says. I don't have to if I don't want to, do I? Her father frowns over his cup. Enough, child, he says. Your mother and I don't want to do many things. And some of them are as a result of your actions. Grow up, now. Exactly, her mother adds, pointing with her potato-laden fork. Your father didn't want to inform

Pastor of your situation, but he did. There can be no hiding from this, you know, not any more. She pops the potato in her mouth and goes on: You have to think for two these days, my girl. At least have some meat, before it gets cold. Tirzah picks up her cutlery and starts to eat again. Everything is becoming more and more vexing. She knows her parents are dreading chapel on Sunday. That's something else they have to face. The fellowship will be sure to have heard the news by now. Pastor always tells his wife everything, and that's as good as telling the *Western Mail*. Tirzah looks at her parents as they chew. Poor little dabs, she thinks.

On Sunday morning, Tirzah's mother briskly rips the plaster off her forehead. Ouch, Mam! Tirzah exclaims. You did that on purpose. Oh, deary me, her mother says under her breath, biting her bottom lip as she inspects the bump. There's a sight. Like a prizefighter, you are. Tirzah looks in the bathroom mirror. The bruise has flowered all the way down to her eyebrows and up into her hairline. At its centre there sits a vivid, puckered rosette. I can't go out like this, Mam, she says, flushing. I look hideous. Nonsense, her mother says, don't be so vain. Get dressed and come downstairs. Life goes on. In her room, Tirzah tries to arrange her hair so that you can't see the marks, but it's no good. Even with a side parting the scab looks like a squinting red eye in the middle of her discoloured forehead. Bugger and bloody, she says out loud. How do these things keep happening to me? Now I look ugly on top of everything else. And I'm cursing like a navvy. Already, most of her clothes don't fit the way they used to, even though her belly is only showing a little. It's as if her shape has redistributed itself embarrassingly. She decides on a smock dress, but her breasts are looking for a way out. It's a little shorter than she remembers it. Dada won't like the way her knees are on display.

Her parents are waiting in their Sunday best. They both turn to look as she stands at the bottom of the stairs. A blush moves up from her chest to the top of her head. There is a brief silence. Pity it's August and not November, her mother says eventually, surveying her. Then you could at least wear a coat and cover up. I always say a good coat hides a multitude of sins. Now, Mair, I've heard you say some silly things, and that is up there with the silliest, her father says, trying to remain calm. And, as such, hardly worth wasting breath over. He points to Tirzah's exposed knees. I would mention something about those, he adds, but Tirzah has bigger fish to fry than her legs. They watch as Tirzah nervously flexes and unflexes her knees so that they do a little dance. Surely now is not the time for such levity? her mother says. Stop that at once.

For a moment they all stand looking at each other, reluctant to go outside. Her father nods. You are right, Mair, he says. Thank you. Dignity in all things. He turns to Tirzah. This is not the time for horsing about. Remember that, facetious child. Tirzah's mother rummages in her Sunday handbag and brings out a packet of Polos. They all take one. Come along, Dada says, sighing a minty sigh. He squares his shoulders and declares in the words of the hymn: *Forward be our watchword, steps and voices joined.* They file down the hall. At the front door, he stops and they gather round him. Tirzah has begun to dread this little area and its bristly mat. She's hovered on the threshold of too many nasty surprises here already. Now then, mind what I say, he says, opening the front door to the silent, sun-filled morning. Heads up, and off we go into the lion's den, so to speak.

Let Not Wickedness Dwell in Thy Tabernacles

(Job 11:14)

By the time Tirzah has walked up the hill to chapel, her
forehead burns and the wound feels as if it is pouring fresh
blood. Mam, she gasps when they get to the graveyard, I
don't think I can go any further. People skirt around them,
and no one greets them with a Good Sabbath, brother, or
Good morning, sisters, as they pass. Familiar splotches of
purple surface high up on Tirzah's mother's neck. She bustles
back to where Tirzah is sitting under a mossy angel, her best
handbag banging against her thigh. Well, charming, she says.
I can't say I'm surprised. Whited sepulchres, the lot of them.
And they don't fool me. Her father stands by Tirzah's side.
Mair, he says, shut up now, please. Tend to your daughter.
He fans Tirzah with his Bible. Pastor's wife is coming up
the path, shooing the twins in front of her as if they were
two little geese. Quick, quick, Tirzah can hear her urging
the boys. But they stop to have a look. Good morning, boys,
Tirzah says. They stare at her with unblinking eyes. Boo! she
shouts, and turning in perfect formation, they run up the
path to the big, half-open door.

Now, that was most uncalled for, Pastor's wife says, tucking her chin in. And, I might add, unladylike. Though why should that surprise me? Really! Tirzah feels a surge of nausea forcing its way up into her mouth. Just as her father starts to apologise on her behalf, she is sick, the sound of splattering magnified on the chapel path by the still, hot air trapped amongst the gravestones. Pastor's wife makes a quick hopping movement but is not in time to prevent a few blobs hitting the buckles of her black patent shoes. Tirzah watches her mother get a lace-edged hankie from her bag and stoop to wipe them. Leave it, if you please, says Pastor's wife, backing away. For shame. She walks briskly towards the chapel door. That girl should not be out amongst decent people, she adds over her shoulder. Tirzah is unmoved by the things Mrs Thomas said; in her head, as silently and imperceptibly as far-off planets in the night sky, the old ideas about sin and guilt have been moving into new positions. Then the three of them are alone amongst the birdsong and the washed-blue butterflies and the motionless, dark-hearted yew trees. Tirzah's mother is pale now. Mair, her father soothes, pray for strength. Put them on the altar and leave them there. He pats his wife on the back as if she were a troubled pony. That is not helping, Gwyll, her mother says, twitching away from his hand. What I am experiencing is righteous anger.

Tirzah's strength is returning; she's better in some ways, and much worse in others. She looks from her father to her mother. Even with her fresh insights, it's still daunting to face the whole of the congregation. We don't have to go in there, do we? she asks in a trembling voice. The fluty sound of the organ drifts out. I would much rather go home. Look at the state of me. What do you think, Gwyll? her mother asks.

Her father's lips are drawn up mirthlessly at the corners, and between his eyebrows there is a new frown mark. He drops down to where Tirzah is sitting beneath the angel, and she pushes her hand under his elbow. Oh, Dada, she says, blushing. I am responsible for your difficulties today. This is all my fault. He seems to wake up. Yes, you are, he answers. But never mind that now. I told you this was going to be difficult. It will be a test of us all. We will see if the hundreds of fine words we hear each Sunday are actually true. Gwyllim, dear, her mother says, taking off her jacket and folding it neatly. I will not give that lot the satisfaction. In we go, surely? Certainly, he says. Gird your loins.

They wait for her mother to blow her nose. Now, remember, she says, wiping Tirzah's cheeks. All sins are the same before God. He is merciful. And I believe you are truly repentant. She gives out another round of mints and settles her hat. Then they walk towards the chapel door, her parents hand in hand. The first hymn is under way as they get to their pew. Ahead, Tirzah can see Osian standing between his parents. She doesn't think he will look round, but he does, an unreadable expression on his face as he briefly meets her eye. She has difficulty finding the hymn, and when she does, her voice comes out in a bleat. The service rolls on: scripture reading, short prayer, children's Bible verses, announcements, collection, long prayer. Tirzah barely notices the usual Sunday morning pattern. She wishes she was at home, lying on her bed, smelling the scent of roasting meat rising from the kitchen. But even pretending to be at home in her imaginary room, she would know that the eyes of the fellowship were swivelling to look at her.

Soon the sermon starts. Tirzah cannot understand a word Pastor is saying. He looks like a little puppet up there in his wooden box, and she is struggling to hold on to her seat. The pew is so hard and slippery she has to brace her feet against the rungs of the pew in front. Surely I didn't always have trouble sitting in chapel, she thinks, wondering if this is another sign she is not welcome any more. In spite of her dazed state she becomes aware of a disturbance outside. People begin to look round. Tirzah thinks she can hear pop music, but that is so unlikely she dismisses it. Her mother nudges her. What's going on? she mouths. Tirzah shrugs, although she thinks she can guess. Someone is kicking the chapel door now, and there is a havoc of shouting and scuffling outside. Pastor is ignoring the situation, or maybe he is too caught up in the Spirit. Dread settles on Tirzah like fine dust.

Suddenly, the big chapel door is flung open, and the unmistakeable sound of a pop song tumbles into the shocked room. Tirzah forces herself to look round. There, in front of a depleted group of his boys, Brân stands. On his shoulder he is carrying a blaring cassette player. He wears a headdress of ferns and feathers, and his face and bony bare chest are streaked with mud. The boys cluster round him, laughing and pushing each other. A dog is jumping, its barks like gunshots. Brân steps forward and for a moment Tirzah thinks she feels a blast of air laden with dead leaves and something else she can't quite make out. Could those be crows sweeping into chapel, skimming people's heads? She thinks she can hear, over the music, their squawking laughter. She is cold and shaking. It is as if Brân is the living proof of all her secret wrongdoing. She hides against her mother's side and covers her eyes, afraid he will see her and shout out that she is a slut and a hypocrite. This is her own fault: she's gone on, nagging him about coming to chapel enough times.

Brân stalks down the aisle, the music throbbing. Behind him, the boys dance and squabble. Pastor still doesn't seem to have noticed what is happening. Where is God, dear ones? he is shouting from the pulpit, his glasses glinting as he waves the big Bible above his head. I ask you, brothers and sisters, where is He? Brân has reached the area where the four elders sit on tall chairs. God is up my arse! he shouts, wiggling his backside and turning the volume on the cassette machine to maximum. Tirzah looks over to where old Mrs Hughes-Edwards usually sits, and sees her pitch forward, hat lifting as she faints and drops into the space between the pews. Pastor's twin sons are standing to get a better look. After a few frozen seconds people start to jump up. Someone wails and is hushed. Pastor finally has grasped what's happening. Dear boy, he shouts over the barking dog and the beat of the music, stretching out an arm, you are troubled. Let us help you.

Brân steps over the chains that edge the elders' seating area. He is dancing to the music, whooping and waving his free hand in the air. Fuck off, you religious nutter, he yells, his eyes scanning the rows of people. Tirzah is sure he is looking for her. She crouches, still watching everything, but it is too fantastical to take in. She is fighting down an urge to scream with terrified laughter. Soon he will spot her and try to do something. Oh, Mama, she whispers, shaking her mother's elbow, someone must stop that boy. Gwyllim, her mother says, shift yourself, for the love of God. Tirzah's father stands and walks quickly to the front of the chapel, and on his way, other men join him. Tirzah doesn't want to see, but her eyes are locked on the scene. The elders have scattered, and Brân is dodging her father, but not for long. He is grabbed, and her father switches the cassette player off. Sudden silence, like a huge white cloud, fills the room. Then they manhandle Brân out into the vestry. The dog follows, snapping at their heels. His boys are left to sit uncertainly on the long front seat. The slamming door cuts off the sound of Brân's curses. Those in the congregation who are standing drop back into their pews.

Everyone is looking towards the pulpit, but Pastor is not to be seen. Tirzah positions herself so she can see him kneeling in prayer. There is a struggle across the room as people try to pick Mrs Hughes-Edwards up from the gap between the pews. Tirzah has to cover her mouth in case a blurt of laughter again tries to escape. What is wrong with me? she wonders. Laughing at someone else's misfortune, when all this is happening? Two men are hauling up the heavy old lady, their hands under her armpits. As she rises and falls back again, someone repeatedly positions her straw hat. Tirzah has to bend over her Bible, stifling giggles again. Don't upset yourself, her mother says. It's all over now. Finally, Pastor appears behind the pulpit. Peace, he calls. Let us have peace in the sanctuary. Brân's followers are sitting in the front row, very quiet now. And that applies to you little lot too, Pastor adds, studying them. I know a few of your parents, he says, and some are tidy people who will be shocked at your behaviour today. One boy starts to cry. Now then, Pastor goes on. Hush. Let us call upon the Lord, because we all need Him in our various ways today. Tirzah bows her head and prays fervently, asking for mercy for herself, for Brân, and as Pastor said, for everyone.

Glad Tidings of Good Things

(Isaiah 52:7)

Tirzah can smell the burnt Sunday roast four doors away from their house when they finally make it home from chapel. It's hard to believe what happened this morning. After Brân was removed, Pastor did not resume his interrupted sermon. He left in charge the elder who had blown his nose and examined his wet hankie the day she'd been called to the manse, and went to join Brân and the men in the vestry. The fellowship swayed and murmured like a field of wheat through Mr Brynmor-Evans's talk. They did not join in with any gusto to the hymns he announced. His baritone trundled over them like a huge rolling boulder, and people's voices were mere shovelled gravel in comparison. They were straining to hear what was going on behind the vestry door. In the end Mr Brynmor-Evans said, with barely suppressed scorn, that it didn't take much opposition for some folk to lose their way. Narrow is the path, and the weak are easily drawn from it, he told them. After a hasty final hymn, he closed the interminable meeting, shaking his head at everyone. Tirzah and her mother filed out silently. All the way home, not one word passed between them.

Now Tirzah is feeling scared and exposed. Surely it is obvious I am connected with Brân, she thinks. Or am I just feeling so guilty I can't think straight? She takes off her cardigan and hangs it up on the back of the door. This roast has had it, her mother says, holding the smoking pan at arm's length. We'll have to think of something else. Tirzah's father finally arrives, and sits in the easy chair, his head resting back on the antimacassar. Never have I seen such a desperate case, he says at last, when Tirzah's mother returns from throwing the meat on to the compost heap. Why? she asks, wiping her hands. Whatever went on, Gwyll? Tirzah goes to sit next to her father. Did he say anything about anyone, I wonder? she asks, convinced now that he came to see her, then reddens at the way her parents look at her. What a funny question, her mother says, frowning. Funny-peculiar, I mean. She turns her attention back to her husband. It was like having a wild animal in there, he continues. I can't explain. Poor thing, her mother says. With no one to look after him, I'm not surprised. Tirzah is surprised though: her mother has changed her tune. Not all that long ago she had been very keen to rid them of Mrs Rowland and her daughter. He landed me one on the jaw, mind, her father adds, rubbing his chin. Oh, Dada, Tirzah says, how awful. Didn't hurt, actually, he tells them. That boy is as weak as a kitten, I would say. Tirzah listens, feeling as if someone has jabbed her heart with a penknife.

Her mother decides while she's frying up some bacon that it wouldn't be right to have this makeshift meal in the dining room, it being Sunday. Tirzah puts the cutlery out on the kitchen table and fills a jug with water. More cosy in here anyway, her mother goes on, putting plates of bacon and bubble and squeak in front of them. Anyone for some baked beans? she asks, holding up a pan and a large spoon. Her soft, dark curls have flopped over her forehead, and her cheeks are flushed. Pile it on, Mair, there's a good girl, her father says, buttering himself some bread. Famished, I am. Tirzah looks from one to the other of them and shakes her head. How could grown-ups behave this way? Nothing – it didn't matter how upsetting – seemed to put them off their food. Maybe you get used to things when you become an adult. Her own throat clenched up when she first heard Brân outside the chapel door, and it hasn't unclenched yet.

Her father tells them how Brân ran, swearing, round and round the vestry, jumping from chair to chair, shadowed by his dog. She pictures Brân scattering feathers and ferns as he looked for a way out. How would the stuffy little room with its high window have seemed to him? He hadn't been inside a building for months. The airy green woods were his home. What happened in the end? her mother asks, eyes fluid with tears. Pastor said to let him go, so I opened the side door, her father says, and he bolted. Gone, he was. Just like that. Pastor was very troubled. Tirzah pushes her plate away. Mam, she says, I'm going to lie down, but her parents barely notice. They are clearing the table so that they can kneel, resting their clasped hands on the seats of the kitchen chairs, and pray for Brân.

On her bed, Tirzah thinks of Brân running back alone to the woods. She is too sad to cry, too dense with misery even to shift position; again, the thought of Brân weak as a kitten smites her for some reason. She recalls how thin and weak he had been, struggling to carry her to the stream. At the time she hadn't cared how he was, but now she can see he was failing. This is all my fault. I should have stood up and gone to him, she realises. Maybe he was asking for help in his own mad way. Everything is such a terrible old mess. I can't help anyone, not even myself. She is drifting off to sleep when there is a rumbling commotion inside her. Laying her hands on her belly, she imagines it to be the first stirrings of her tiny child. Or, she concedes, it could just be that she's hungry. At least my baby is safe, tucked away under my heart, she thinks, picturing a smiling, potato-shaped blob with little white sprouting arms and legs somersaulting in the dark. I can do that one thing right, I should hope.

When she goes down to breakfast in the morning there is an envelope on the mat by the front door. Picking it up she sees it has her name on it. The kitchen is empty; the kettle is still hot and her mother has left some bread for her to toast. She fires up the grill and slices herself two pieces. Then she pours a glass of milk. It's not until she sits down and reaches for the butter that she pulls the envelope from her dressing-gown pocket and props it against the milk jug. Tirzah studies the writing on it; she knows who it is from. She places it back against the jug, realising her toast is burning. Flipping flip, she says, scraping the charred top layer from each slice into the sink. While she eats the spoilt toast she stares at the envelope. A reluctance to find out what's inside is slowly paralysing her. When she's finished eating, the thought of lifting her arm and doing things with her fingers seems out of the question, but when her mother comes in through the back door with the laundry basket, Tirzah snatches the envelope and dashes upstairs to dress.

Later, rushing along the warm, windy street, Tirzah is pelted with a sudden squall. The raindrops are blood-heat, and she doesn't mind her dress and hair getting wet. The sun is uneasy, jumping out from behind coffee-coloured, shining-edged clouds, blasting the street with harsh, dazzling light, then shutting down, deadening the puddles and car bonnets. With the envelope in her sleeve, Tirzah makes for the mountain lane and doesn't stop. Her shoes are heavy with moisture and keep making farting noises as they flex. On and on she runs, gasping, flanked by drying foxglove spears that rattle in the gusts of wind, past the old yew tree that used to be her friend. When she reaches the derelict pub she slows down, clambers through the tall ferns to the low forestry wall and leans against it. From here she can look up to the familiar, gently curving summit. In amongst its carpet of whinberry bushes and stunted hawthorns, the eternal sheep chew. Now and then, one will bleat and another answer. Tirzah wonders what they are saying to each other. What could sheep possibly have to say that they had not already said, here on the mountain?

The stones of the wall are patterned with discs of rough, sulphur-hued lichen. The purple-flowered creeping plants she loves sprout from the dry cracks. Above the mountain's sage-green breast, a sparrowhawk is making its sharp and hungry call as it twirls in the wind-bothered sky. Tirzah begins to relax, her body unkinking as she breathes the wild air. Even though she is warm from her walk, deep inside she feels icy somehow. She climbs over the wall, slips under the arms of the pine trees and is instantly anointed with resin and old, warm, woody smells. The sounds of the mountain are muffled, and when she has gone no more than ten paces they fall silent. The only sound is the perpetual sighing of the treetops. Tirzah knows how to find the gnarled tree stump she and Osian always lay in. Soon she is there and squeezes into a narrow opening between two exposed roots. This tree must be ancient, she thinks; it had lived and died before the forestry was even planted. Now it is my shelter. In amongst the dusty roots, Tirzah's damp yellow dress gleams. She stretches out her bare legs and kicks off her soaked shoes. Finally, she is ready to open the letter from Osian.

At first she doesn't understand. Why would he be talking about the Christian Youth Circle's trip now? All that is ancient history, surely? No one is going to allow Tirzah to go anyway. As soon as her pregnancy is officially known, she will have a job to get someone to stand next to her at the bus stop, let alone allow a child of theirs to go on holiday with her. She throws the letter down. Has Osian gone soft in the head? After a few moments she picks the letter back up. Osian is saying that if they were to go on the weekend away, they could talk properly. He doesn't mention her pregnancy, she notices, but maybe he doesn't like to. Her chilly heart is suddenly warm. He writes that he has something important to say. Tirzah is unsure what he could mean, but she is so happy Osian wants to see her that she laughs out loud in the silent wood. The way they have been with each other – the way he has been since the horrible sheet incident – maybe they can sort it out.

Tirzah stands and brushes herself down. She will go to Biddy's and write a reply to Osian, inviting him to meet up so they can talk about it. Now she has something to do she feels entirely different. Yes, it will be tricky getting permission to go away, but she and her mother have the saved money tucked by. Not to mention Derry's ten pounds. And between them they can handle Dada. She falters for a moment. Poor Dada. He has had some nasty shocks recently. She remembers the unfamiliar way his eyes look these days: it's as if someone had taken a threaded needle and tacked the skin around them, then pulled. She walks on, shaking her hair out of her eyes and deliberately turning her thoughts away. Thank goodness Mr Humphries the CYC deacon is nice, not so deacony as the others. He likes them both, she can tell. He will be on their side. Anyway, some things are much easier than you imagine they will be. She knows that now. On the other hand, of course, some things are much harder. She slows her pace. Already she is approaching the village.

I Will Clothe Thee with Change of Raiment

(Zechariah 3:4)

A tiny click from the bedroom door wakes Tirzah. Swinging her legs on to the carpet, she sees a brown envelope propped up on the side table and realises this must be her exam results. It's odd, she thinks, reading the typewritten address. Usually the only things she gets in the post are birthday cards, and here is her second letter in a week. After holding it in her lap for a while, she opens it, dry-eyed and calm, and reads the long row of A's. Then she stuffs the letter and envelope under her mattress and gets ready to go out. Tirzah's mother has decided they will visit the city to buy maternity clothes. On the way to the train station, Tirzah contemplates taking off, running away, showing a neat pair of heels, but she feels too burdened to run these days. It's hard to believe she was, not long ago, the girl who could sprint all the way to the summit of the mountain without stopping. In the train she looks at the dirty window, pretending to enjoy the view, but imprinted on her burning eyes is the neat row of A's on their sheet of white paper. Even when she closes her eyelids, the list is there, irrelevant to her now as a dead language on a stone tablet.

She ignores her mother's suggestion they move to the shaded side of the carriage. Why did we have to come all the way down here to go shopping? Tirzah asks, as they wait to get off. Having sat in full sunshine, her head is now so hot her hair seems to be coiling tightly away from her scalp all by itself. Her mother gives her a squinty look. Well, I'm only asking, Tirzah says, lifting the collar of her dress and flapping it. It just seems a bit over the top to me. The only other time she's been to the city was on a bus trip with her grandparents and Biddy to see the Christmas panto. She remembers the blood-red velvet theatre and the heart-stopping glow that seemed to surround the baddie every time he appeared. It was dull whenever he was offstage. She realises her mother is standing on the platform with her eyes looking skywards, lips moving as she counts up to ten. Tirzah waits, thinking how in the frosted, twinkly dark of Christmas the city seemed like the panto's backdrop. Now the city is too noisy and full of rushing people. Boy's bach! her mother exclaims, grabbing her arm and shaking it. You, madam, are a naughty girl. Ungrateful and cheeky. Tirzah tries not to squirm. If you were a year or two younger I would cheerfully give you a smacked bottom. Do you want to get straight back on the train? For a start, no one knows us here, so I can be less ashamed. Her bottom lip is doing a little jiggle and her eyes are brimming. She is hurting Tirzah. Ouch, Mammy, Tirzah says, fighting the urge to snatch her arm away. I'm sorry. I am naughty and don't deserve to have anything or go anywhere. Her mother manages a smile, loosening her grip. Let's forget about this small upset, she says, tucking her arm through Tirzah's. She takes a deep breath. I thought we could have a gander at the castle if we've got time later.

Tirzah trails along, trying not to hate the sight of her mother's neat behind jostling under her floral skirt. Honestly, she thinks, I would be quite content to wear a sack if I could get away with it. In a department store they buy two maternity smocks, bras and some big pants. Her mother had to manhandle her into the dresses and jerk her into the bras. Shape up, child, she'd said, panting. I know you don't want maternity clothes, but you'll need them soon enough, believe me. Tirzah looked at herself in the mirror with one of the dresses flapping around her, and teetered between crying and laughing. It was airless and uncomfortable in the cubicle with her mother prodding her from all angles. Yes, Mama, she'd said, pulling the dress off without waiting for her mother to undo her. Let's get out of here, quick. By the time they stop for a bite to eat, Tirzah is wispy with heat and the buffetings from crowded pavements. Come on, her mother says finally, let's have a meal in the market. Tirzah follows her mother to a stall with a few tables on a wooden platform. You guard our places, her mother says, putting her bags on the table. I will go and order. Tirzah sits carefully on a rickety chair. It's funny, but while most of her is ready to evaporate, her feet and hands are so heavy they weigh her down. The smell of fish and spoiling vegetables from the surrounding stalls forces itself into her throat. She starts dreaming of a glass of clear water clinking with ice cubes.

I ordered us faggots and peas, her mother says, appearing with cutlery. I know you like them. Tirzah tries to smile. Lovely, Mam, she says. The idea of gravy flooded with claggy pea water is daunting. She could maybe nibble a small sandwich without crusts. But when the faggots come, their rich, brown smell suddenly makes her hungry. Tirzah drinks her warm juice while her mother says a prayer. People are staring over at them, she can see. Amen. Now let's eat up, her mother says, showering her own bowl with vinegar. When Tirzah puts a tiny blob of faggot in her mouth she is relieved to find it delicious. There you are, her mother goes on, pepper in hand. What you need is a nice dinner inside you. They both eat every scrap, even the bread that comes as part of the meal. Now I'd love an ice cream, Tirzah says with her hands on her belly, leaning back. All through the meal, neither of them mentions the brown envelope, and Tirzah is glad.

After they have eaten a bowl of ice cream and her mother has paid, they find the toilets. Around the walls, brass pipework shines. The air is laden with bleach. Squares of carefully ripped cardboard for walking on dot the damp floor. That's what I like, Tirzah's mother says, tidying her hair at the mirror over the single sink, a nice, clean lav. She licks her two middle fingertips and shapes her eyebrows into arches. Tirzah remembers her mother's idea about visiting the castle and decides to say she is too tired. Mam, she whispers, leaning against the toilet door, I want to go home now. Poor little dwt, her mother murmurs, stroking Tirzah's cheek. So you shall. When they've spruced themselves up, they walk slowly back to the station. Do you mind about the castle, Mam? Tirzah asks, feeling a pang of guilt. The castle has been there for hundreds of years, her mother answers, it can wait a bit longer. Soon they are on the train, and this time it is quiet and cool. Have a little snooze, her mother says. Lie down and rest your head in my lap.

When she is settled, Tirzah tells her mother about the O-level results. I'm not a bit surprised, is all her mother says. You are a clever one. Of course, she goes on, looking out of the window, you won't be going back to school this September.

There is no point. And it would be most unseemly. Maybe next year you will be able to pick things up again, if you still want to. Tirzah feels as if all the bones in her body have been extracted, and she slumps further into her mother's lap, then makes an effort to sit up. Yes, Mama. I do want to go back to school, she answers, if you will look after the baby for me. You do? her mother says, squeezing her hand. Then of course I will. Tirzah returns the squeeze, relaxing a little, and listens to the rhythm of the train on the tracks. *Clever one, clever one, you are a clever one*, it seems to sing as she falls asleep, head against her mother's shoulder.

The next morning, Tirzah walks in through Biddy's open back door. Her aunty nods hello from where she is kneeling in the hallway. It's too hot to be polishing tiles, Tirzah says. Her aunt goes on rhythmically wiping with a cloth. Someone's got to do it, she answers, not looking up again. Not everybody can swan around all day sunbathing like some I could mention. Tirzah blushes and stumbles up the stairs to find Biddy. They wait in her bedroom until Biddy's mother has left for her job at the village butcher's. As soon as she's out of the way, the girls lay a tray with three glasses of squash and a plate of digestives. Then they go out to the garden and sit on the loungers, listening to the bumblebees manoeuvring themselves in amongst the roses. Dead on time, Osian knocks the garden door and Biddy lets him in. Tirzah watches as he walks towards her. He has changed, but it is difficult to say in what way. You sit down there, Biddy tells him, indicating the empty lounger. I won't be a minute. From the bottom of the garden there is a disturbance in the chicken run, and the chickens take a while to settle again. They sense a stranger is here, Tirzah says. But I am not a stranger, Osian answers, looking at her expressionlessly from under his dark fringe. She remembers to ask if he is happy with his exam results. What? he asks, as if she'd said something strange. Your results, she repeats. How did you do? Oh, not bad, he answers. She is squashed by a certainty of the wrongness of everything; her small mound of a belly and fattening waist are mysteries to her. All the words she wanted to say scatter. They wait until Biddy comes back with the tray. I'll have that, Biddy, Osian says, springing up and taking the tray out of her hands as she walks carefully towards them.

In the garden, Tirzah senses all the plants leaning in to listen, and her unhappiness rises like a cake in a hot oven. Osian is so unlike himself she begins to suspect this grave person sitting upright on the lounger is an impostor. Where is the boy who created a miniature world in his attic and put a girl with a ponytail and a basket in the centre, like a queen? Where is the easy, lanky boy she loved? She studies his mouth. Where is his lopsided smile now? Biddy kneels and hands out the squash. Osian drinks in one go, his throat convulsing with each gulp. Tirzah holds a biscuit in her hot hand. So, Osian, Biddy says, what is it you want to say to Tirzah? His eyes switch back and forth between the girls. Tirzah bites her biscuit, but it has a gritty texture in her mouth. I want Biddy to stay here with me, she tells him. Of course, he says, and clears his throat in a way she does not recognise.

He tells her that he thinks they should both go on the CYC weekend. I know, Tirzah says. You said that in your letter. He ignores her and goes on to explain that his plan is to talk to Deacon Humphries first. Let's see what he thinks, he says. Tirzah waits for a few seconds, searching his face. You do know I am having a baby, don't you? she blurts at last, hoping to make him say something about it. Osian nods slightly, not meeting her eye. It will be a chance for us to get away from all this, he continues, making a gesture with his arm, both stunted and impassioned. Then, as if someone had switched him off, he stops talking. Tirzah is defeated. Well, Biddy says, after the seconds have lengthened hopelessly. You do what you just said, Osian. Talk to Mr Humphries and see if he can think of a plan of action. Then we'll see. She looks at Tirzah for approval, and Tirzah nods again. Osian says goodbye, and for a moment it looks as if he will shake their hands like a minister. Biddy walks with him to the garden door, but Tirzah can't imagine she will ever move again.

Uncovered, Yea, Thy Shame Shall Be Seen

(Isaiah 47:3)

For a while after Osian leaves the garden, Tirzah continues to lie on the lounger. Something is lodged in her throat, bitter as a crab apple. All she wants to do now is hide in bed with the curtains closed and the door shut. Before you ask, Biddy says, I will come with you on the blimming weekend away, if you are allowed. They contemplate the gentle curve of Tirzah's stomach. Flip, Biddy, she says. I don't think I have the power to even get home. Biddy stands over her. Shall I get your mam? she asks, biting her bottom lip. You do look a funny colour. Tirzah grabs her arm. No, she says. I'll just sit up for a bit. Biddy pours some more squash. Maybe you should eat another biscuit? Tirzah nods. I'll join you, Biddy says. They sit on the lounger together, the hot, scented garden glittering black and green around them. What do you think about Osian now? Biddy asks, crunching. Tirzah shrugs. I thought he was acting as if he wasn't all there, if you know what I mean, Biddy adds. Tirzah nods; she is remembering his odd new way of clearing his throat, and those jerky gestures.

When Tirzah finally stands, it is as if she has wads of cotton wool under her feet, and her joints are stiff. Biddy links arms and helps keep her upright. When they get to Tirzah's house, Biddy yells, Yoo hoo! Aunty Mair! and pushes the back door open with her knee. Is anybody home? Tirzah's mother appears. Tut, she says, ducking her head under Tirzah's limp arm. Between them they support her up the stairs. Just when I think I've prayed enough, up pops something else to lay on the altar, she goes on, almost to herself. Now what jinks have you girls been up to? What has happened? Her bosom rises and falls as she looks down at Tirzah, now prone on the bed. Nothing, honest, Biddy says. Just chatting in the garden, we were. They help Tirzah out of her clothes. She's boiling, Biddy says, shall I get a cold flannel? When she has gone, Tirzah opens her eyes. I don't know what's the matter with me, Mam, she says. Tears trickle into her hair. Hush, bach, her mother says, coming to perch beside her. All you need is a rest. Overdone it, you have. Biddy brings the damp flannel and her mother wipes Tirzah's flushed face, pushing the thick hair away where it is stuck to her cheeks. There we are, she whispers. Mammy will look after you. Soon Tirzah is half-asleep, but part of her feels as if it is hovering over the bed, seeing how ridiculous she looks lying there in her underwear with her swollen tummy. As the cover her mother is throwing over her floats down, Tirzah snaps back to herself in the bed. No, Mama, she says. I won't lie here like an invalid, and she stands unsteadily, wrapping herself in the sheet. She stares at them both for a long moment, then her mother turns abruptly, and Biddy follows. Tirzah trails behind, her feet tangling in the sheet as she negotiates the stairs.

In the kitchen, Tirzah's mother turns to Biddy and takes her hand. Will you do something for me, cariad? she asks.

Biddy nods. Run to the doctor's and see if Mrs Palfrey is on duty, would you? If she's there, ask her to come round as soon as she can. I think that would be the best thing. If not, leave a message. There's a good girl you are. She kisses Biddy on the forehead. No, Mam. Stop, Tirzah shouts. I'm not ill. But her mother pretends she is not there. Would you like a little cake to take with you? she asks Biddy. When the old Quality Street tin is offered her, Biddy selects a chocolate fairy cake, and is already eating it before she gets to the door. Don't rush, mind, in this heat, Tirzah's mother tells her. I'll be all right, Aunty Mair, Biddy says. I won't be a tick. She stops briefly. Bye, Tizzy, she calls, and is gone.

Defeated, Tirzah returns to bed, where she falls into a light slumber. Gradually, she becomes aware of voices, and drifts up through white, weightless films of nothing. The voices echo, oddly doubled, and she is being hauled towards them. She tries to dive beneath the surface again; it was lovely, that place where she was light and delicate as a meringue, but already her room is taking shape around her, and the sensation of heaviness returns. Now the voices are getting louder; her mother and somebody else are coming to the room. Tirzah shrinks under the sheet, like a creature yanked from its shell. Her mother's head appears around the door. She's awake, she tells the stranger who is waiting outside. Are you decent? she asks. Tirzah scrabbles to sit up and pull the flimsy cover to her chin.

Mrs Palfrey steps in carrying a medical bag. Tirzah gives her mother a narrow-eyed look. Don't look at me sideways like that, madam, her mother says cheerfully. I told you Mrs Palfrey would be calling soon. Tirzah is frozen, aware of how naked she is under the sheet. Mrs Palfrey comes to the bed and takes Tirzah's hand. Now, there's nothing for you to worry about. We're all women here. Firstly, please call me Betty. Her mother nods brightly at Tirzah. This is what we'll do today, she goes on, taking things out of her bag. Tirzah listens, blushing. How can her body suddenly be something strangers can look at and examine? The thought of Mrs Palfrey handling her is unthinkable, but she is helpless to prevent it. The world of adults is unspeakably vile, she decides, as she lies down and does as she's told. Mrs Palfrey's hands are cool. They touch her without really touching. Tirzah closes her eyes and tries not to feel anything, but still the cool fingers flutter over her until she thinks she will scream. Finally Mrs Palfrey gently rocks Tirzah's small bump, spreading her hands around it. Tirzah studies her face, without meeting her eyes, waiting for a worrying pronouncement, but Mrs Palfrey smiles and winks. Nearly three months, I would say, she announces. More or less. She gives Tirzah a questioning look, and Tirzah gives the smallest of nods.

When Mrs Palfrey has gone to the bathroom to wash her hands, Tirzah's mother sits on the bed. Now, that wasn't so bad, was it? she asks. But Tirzah is too upset to answer. Things will never be the same. Again, everything she thought she knew has ratcheted around, and she will have to change position with it. Her body, which she has always hugged to herself, is now something anyone can prod and poke. Her mother tucks her in, and Tirzah deliberately will not look at her. She senses her mother has changed too, become someone who is not to be trusted. I suppose this is what it's like to grow up, she thinks, a sensation of extreme loneliness gathering like fog around her. Her mother takes her hands. Listen, she says. I know you believe I've betrayed you, getting Betty here, but

that is a silly thing to think. I have to look after you. There
are rules and regulations surrounding a pregnant girl of your
age, you know. Sooner or later, arrangements have to be made
with the authorities. Things you don't give a thought to. I
have to arrange them. When a person is pregnant, they don't
just waltz around and then pop out to have their baby under
the nearest tree. They have to book a bed in the maternity
ward. They have a midwife. She gently shakes Tirzah's hands,
forcing her to look up. It doesn't all just fall into place, you
daft thing.

Tirzah sees her mother's brown, spiky-lashed eyes and pink
cheeks. Here is her curly hair caught up in its thin bun. Best
of all are her mother's small, freckled hands, like two homely
birds. Suddenly Tirzah sighs, and when she breathes out, most
of the furrowed, barbed thoughts she's had flow out with it.
Oh, Mam, she whispers. Thank you. But, there's embarrassing it all is. Her mother smiles. That's not the half of it, love,
she says. You wait. Mrs Palfrey comes back in. Not the half of
what? she asks. The embarrassment, Tirzah's mother says. The
two women laugh quietly, and even though she doesn't want
to, Tirzah can't help smiling with them.

Later, Tirzah wakes from another sleep and is hungry. So
all the usual things still go on, even when you believe the end
of the world has come, she thinks, sitting on the toilet. She
shakes her head, remembering Mrs Palfrey's cold hands, like
two instruments, examining her. Still, I've done that now, I
know what it's like, she tells herself, realising she is making small
steps towards something, even though part of her would rather
not. But anyway, this is all my own doing. No one forced me
to go with Brân. I will just have to get on with it. The smell
of frying sausages wafts up the stairs, and she quickly dabbles

her fingers under the tap and rushes down. She can see her parents have been talking by the way they turn bland-eyed faces towards her when she appears in the doorway.

Just in time, her mother says. I have made bangers tonight. With onion gravy and mash. Thank the Lord for small mercies, her father says, rubbing his hands. I could eat a maggoty horse between two bread vans I am so famished. And I am surprised at your flippant attitude, Tirzah's mother announces, ladling onion-strewn gravy on to her father's plate. As if the Lord would bother Himself with a couple of sausages. Now, now, Mair, her father says, it was only a little joke. I apologise. Half-listening, Tirzah contemplates the pillow of creamy potato cradling the slightly burnt sausages, and the way they sit in their pond of gravy. It all acts like a kind of balm to her. She eats, flanked by her gently bickering parents. When she has finished, and is waiting for pudding, all the swirling fear and loneliness she felt in the bedroom has gone, for the time being.

Awake Thou That Sleepest, and Arise

(Ephesians 5:14)

There is a grubby flatness to each day now. The grass in Biddy's garden is singed, and when Tirzah steps on it with bare feet, the dry blades are like the bristles of a scrubbing brush. The street drains give out a murky, rotten breath, making her gag when she walks to the shops for her mother. The rows of houses are utterly silent, their curtains motionless as carved marble, their front doors peeling. Patches of tarmac melt by midday, splitting to reveal glittering black seams, and the roads are aflap with mysterious bits of paper that turn over slowly when the occasional car drives past. Tirzah's eyes are drawn to the exhausted sky hovering over the valley. Several days crawl by without a single cloud to break them up. Sitting on the shady kitchen doorstep with her knees bent, the egg of her pregnant belly pushes against her thighs. The concrete her father laid years ago is breaking apart, and sturdy plants have crept out of the cracks. Stretching her legs, she traces the outline of her belly button, but then stops; thinking about what's happening below the surface makes her queasy. Even though she doesn't think it's true, she imagines the red root, knotted with veins, burrowing all the way inwards to where it is attached to the hungry stranger she will have to push out come winter.

Instead she tries to remember the way the gutters spurt water when it rains, and the pounding on the roof when a storm visits the valley at night. She rests her head against the doorpost, hungry for the commotion of gurgling, splashing water. Up in the forestry, the firs' desiccated arms must be reaching up to the unkind sky. Surely even the poor sheep are panting under the hawthorns. It's as if she's only ever read in ancient books that the horizons used to frown with clouds. Could it be true that cool water fell in dashes and darts on to the waiting earth once upon a time? I can hardly believe it, Tirzah thinks, watching a swirling devil of dust career across the crumbling garden.

She can't be bothered to go and pour herself a drink, even though she would love one. The house is empty, each room full of stuffy odours. Her father is at work, her mother out. Biddy has roped Ffion into one of her many schemes for making a bit of extra money. People are doing: earning money, working for a living. Osian's serving in his father's shop. Somewhere, Derry is hard at work in his factory. Probably everyone in the fellowship is beavering away at something. She is the only person in the whole valley who has absolutely nothing to do. Even her Sunday school class has been taken from her. Now she doesn't teach them any more, the little girls who used to drive her mad are very dear. For a few days last week she'd busied herself making six pretty hairclips as goodbye gifts for them. She looks at her hot, idle hands. The Devil is probably stymied; he can't shake himself to conjure up even the smallest act of naughtiness for her. Anyway, he's done a fine job already.

She gets up from the step and supports herself by holding the doorknob, less and less sure if the Devil even exists. I don't need much prodding by anyone to do the wrong thing, she thinks. And neither do some other people I could mention.

Tirzah runs the kitchen tap and immerses her wrists in the flow for as long as she can stand it. The cold water seems to dawdle up her arms and over her shoulders, settling under her shoulder blades, cooling her body. Drying with the rough kitchen towel she finally decides to start organising her case for the CYC holiday at the weekend. Osian had pushed a note through the door a few days after their meeting in the garden to say everything was settled with Mr Humphries. She told her father while he sat in the easy chair by the empty fireplace. I am doubtful about the wisdom of this, he'd announced, shaking his open newspaper into order. I will have a word with Brother Humphries myself. Please don't do that, Dada, she'd said. I don't want you to. Everything has been settled. As she left the room, her father was saying he detected a shamelessness about Tirzah these days that he did not like. Tirzah waited behind the partially closed door and listened, sure her mother would stand up for her, but there had been silence.

Tirzah packs a maternity smock, some big panties and her spare, robust flesh-coloured bra. One nightdress should be enough, she decides, stuffing it in. Gathering her iron tablets and toiletries together, she remembers how, not that long ago, she'd forgotten to pack undies and a sponge bag, so excited had she been to be going to stay with her gran. That girl was an entirely different person to the girl I am now, she thinks. For a start, I was not pregnant then. I was light and happy. But she knows this is not true. I was pregnant, she tells herself. I just didn't know it yet. Already, secretly, the baby she and Brân had made was growing faster than a weed. She pities that blind, silly girl. But shutting her case, she also acknowledges how the girl she used to be exasperates her now – and scares her too. She doesn't want to think about the young people she will soon see. How will they behave towards her? Not one of them has called round recently. Osian said in his note that everyone was happy she had decided to come.

All Friday morning, Tirzah ricochets between a sense that the weekend is going to be wonderful and a swooping dread. By the afternoon she is exhausted. I have to lie down, Mama, she says, leaving her oily cheese on toast uneaten. In the bathroom, she leans over the toilet and allows thick, stringy saliva to spool out of her mouth. Her mother knocks the door and comes in. Now, what is the matter? she asks. Tirzah straightens up and inspects herself in the mirror. There are pockmarks around her lips and her hair stands out like the broken spokes of a wheel. In the middle of her forehead is the scar from Brân's stone. She examines the white, puckered area and decides it looks as if someone has tried to gouge her brain out in a hurry. I can't go, she says tremulously to her mother's reflection. Daddy was right. It would be shameless, don't you think? It's a bit late for such thoughts, her mother answers, gazing back at her. Your father's got the blessed car out of the garage, and you know how much of a song and dance he makes about that. Come on. She smiles. You are stronger than you think. Am I? Tirzah asks.

Biddy is going to travel with them. Tirzah's mother waits in the doorway to wave them off, and her father is running the engine, his click-on sunglasses crookedly attached to his specs. Tirzah tries not to look at him in the rear-view mirror. He tuts, peering out of the window, and toots the horn. Where is that benighted girl? he mutters, rummaging in his tin of car sweets. Biddy scrambles in at last. Here, she says, and gives Tirzah a posy of forget-me-nots. Raising them to her nose, Tirzah can detect a whiff of something like waterweed quivering briefly above the car's heated leather. She closes her eyes as a lightning-sharp image of Brân and the stream in the woods flashes through her head. So piercing is the memory she gasps, and forces her eyes open to look at the flower clusters; they are already dying, but each tiny floret still has an orange, three-pronged eye. Are you all right? Biddy asks, and Tirzah tries to smile.

Her father tells them the journey will take an hour and a half and there's to be no stopping. I don't want to think about the petrol we will consume, he adds. Why you two couldn't go on the bus with everyone else, I will never know. Biddy and Tirzah look at each other. Not good enough for your ladyships, was it? he says, his double-lensed eyes glaring at them from the mirror. But, Uncle Gwyll, Biddy says, I have been looking forward to a ride in your posh car for ages. Thank you very much for letting me come with you. She leans forward and kisses his cheek. Well now, Tirzah's father says. Who would like a little car sweet? The girls both take an icing-sugar-drenched cube and then they are off. When they turn the corner at the end of the road, Tirzah is smitten with the realisation that she forgot to wave. She sits thinking about her mother's cheerful face as she stood in the doorway, and trembles with sadness. Biddy slips her arm through Tirzah's. Now what's up, Tizzy? she whispers. I will miss my mam, Tirzah says, wiping her eyes with the backs of her hands. You are a funny one, Biddy says. I've been counting the seconds till I could leave mine behind.

Biddy dozes, but Tirzah keeps her eyes on the road rushing past; she doesn't want to miss the new bridge across the estuary when they get to it. She has only seen pictures of its white, soaring wings and the wide, sullen water beneath. Everyone says how wonderful it is. Suddenly, her father is waking them up. Have we arrived? she asks, shocked that she could have fallen asleep. Her father is already emptying the boot. But I didn't see the bridge, she tells Biddy, gathering her tattered flowers and struggling out. You don't mean the Severn Bridge, surely? Biddy says. We haven't gone to England, you dimwit. We are still in Wales. Tirzah can sense, even though she has never been here before, that they are in the middle of that empty, nothing time in a seaside town when afternoon is over and there is a pause, like the long space between one slow breath and the next, before evening arrives. She shivers, sniffing rain and decaying seaweed, afraid to ask where they are in case Biddy gives her another disbelieving look. This place has a very different atmosphere to the beach they went to with Gran and the Hope Baptist Women's Guild.

Gulls scream over the long row of B & Bs. Opposite is the deserted promenade, with the grey line of the sea above it. On the breeze comes a burst of iodine and frying chips. Her father carries their bags to the front door and then gets back in the car. Without waiting to hear their goodbyes, he nods and drives off. Tirzah and Biddy stand outside the garden railings. The garden is small and covered with crazy paving, and inside there is a pretend well sitting on a manhole cover. From the middle of a pile of old tyres, red-hot pokers erupt on long stems, and flaking gnomes peer out from pots of begonias. A *No Vacancies* sign rucks up a net at the window. Tirzah allows Biddy to grab her hand and pull her towards the front door. Wake up, Tizzy, she says. We are in Porthcawl. You've heard of that, haven't you? Now, listen hard, she says, leaning her head to one side. Tirzah listens, and gradually, from far across the bay, she hears screaming and woozy, discordant music. That's the funfair, Biddy tells her. I am dying to go, aren't you? I love that music. Tirzah fights the urge to cover her ears; the deep, far-off beat seems to be affecting her pulse rate, and she doesn't like it.

As a Wandering Bird Cast Out of the Nest

(Isaiah 16:2)

After ringing the bell, they wait. Tirzah is about to give up when, through the etched ferns on the frosted glass, they detect a figure approaching. Half a female face appears in the gap of the opened door. We're with the CYC group, Biddy says. A woman they presume to be the landlady answers. Her eye doesn't move, and the portion of mouth they can see barely opens. You'd better come in, she says, and allows them to squeeze past her into the hall. Tirzah bangs her case on pieces of furniture trying to get through. The woman raises both hands to adjust her hair. Welcome to Glan-y-Mor, she says, examining herself in the mirror behind them, and making a pouting gesture with her lips. I'm Mrs Partridge. She leans over and sniffs them as if she suspects they have gone off. You're early, she adds. I wasn't expecting anybody for a good hour. She straightens, looking from Tirzah to Biddy and then back again. A silence that the radio in a back room cannot fill blooms as she gives Tirzah's smock a hard survey. Aren't you lot chapel people? she asks, putting her hands on her hips. I'm very particular, you know. I don't

have just any old Tom, Dick or Harry in my establishment.
It's not a policy of mine.

Tirzah pulls her cardigan across her body. Oh, we are
certainly chapel, she says, blushing. Mrs Partridge ignores her.
Your Mr Humphries never mentioned anything out of the
ordinary, she goes on, sniffing again, this time in a way that
lifts her top lip. And I'll tell you something straight. I would
have said no. I run a respectable house, for tidy people. Before
Tirzah can speak, Biddy moves to stand in front of her. Well,
we're here now, she answers the woman loudly, and I'm telling
you something straight back: we have never been treated so
rudely in our lives. Mrs Partridge blinks. An icy few seconds
are filled by faint sounds of music from a room at the back
of the house. That's my Roy Castle programme starting, Mrs
Partridge tells them, veering round. First left at the top of the
stairs, she calls, walking away. In a louder voice she shouts,
Cooked dinner when the main party arrives! and then slams
the door behind her. Biddy and Tirzah are left standing with
their cases in the hall.

They climb the stairs and, when the door of their bedroom
closes, stare at each other. Tirzah turns away first. Well, at least
that's over with, she says in a quivery voice. Biddy falls on to
one of the narrow beds. Oof, she says, her arms behind her
head, what a nasty cow that one is. Quiet, Biddy! Tirzah says.
I felt so ashamed. Did you see the way her X-ray eyes bored
through my dress? Biddy blows a raspberry. Rubbish, she
says. For a start, there's nothing to see. That woman is just a
suspicious old boot. Oh, I don't know, Tirzah says, dropping
on to a spindly chair. Can you blame the poor thing? I mean,
look at the state of me. Yes, I can blame her, Biddy answers.
You look perfectly lovely. I've seen her sort before. Holier

than thou so-and-so. Biddy! Tirzah repeats, now in a stronger voice. Will you stop it? But she can't keep her face straight. Oh, stop it yourself, Biddy answers. You are far too soft. It's one of your few faults, Tiz. She wriggles, moving so she can check the bed sheets under the candlewick cover. Typical, she says. Blinking nylon. And if I'm not mistaken, someone's been in here squirting air freshener around. Mrs P, I expect. She doesn't strike me as the type who'd do any actual cleaning.

They prowl the room, opening drawers and checking inside the rickety wardrobe. There is a large, knobbly package wrapped in tightly bound plastic on one of the shelves. What do you think is in there? Tirzah asks, poking it with her finger. Probably a previous visitor who didn't fit with madam's policy, Biddy answers. I know, Tirzah says, let's make a picnic of the bits and pieces we've got. They pile the items on her bed. One Club biscuit, a Marathon, half a packet of Polos, some iced gems and a crushed bag of salt and vinegar crisps. Not bad, Biddy says. Tirzah is hungry but can't decide what to eat. Finally, she has a few iced gems. She walks over to the window. I didn't want to have a sea view anyway, she says, looking out at a wall. She sucks her iced gem and feels the tiny turban of stiff icing atop the stale morsel of biscuit collapse on her tongue. Down below there is a line of bins and what looks like a one-wheeled motorbike and sidecar, partially covered with a tarpaulin. Tirzah rests her forehead on the window and decides not to think any more. I'm going to have a rest, she says, and lies on the other bed, watching Biddy work her way through the food. You can't eat crisps and Polos at the same time, she mumbles, before falling asleep.

They are woken by a clanging bell. Where are we? Tirzah asks, expecting to see her bedroom at home. Don't ask me,

Biddy says. This is s'posed to be a holiday. That bell sounds like junior school assembly. They smooth their clothes and hair and walk down the stairs. Warm air greets them, laden with the moist smell of boiling broad beans and some sort of roasting meat. I think everyone's in the dining room, Biddy says, jumping the last few stairs. Through the door the sound of chattering and scraping cutlery can be heard. You go first, Tirzah says. Before she can stop her, Biddy throws the door open. Surprise! she shouts. Guess who I've got here? The sounds in the room die, and all the young people gaze at Biddy. Mr Humphries is standing at one of the tables, dishing meat to each plate, and he looks up, a floppy slice of meat ready on his fork. Tirzah has to step in, so she does, lips trying to form a smile. It feels cold where she stands. Almost as if a sea wind were bowling through the hall, trying to knock her down.

No one moves. No one makes a sound. Tirzah seeks out Osian's face, and when she sees him looking through his black fringe at her, she knows he has not told anyone about her coming. No one has given permission. She looks at Mr Humphries. He is trying to say something, still holding the meat-pronged fork. Someone lets out a bleat of laughter, and then the room is suddenly boiling with the noise of raised voices. Tirzah can't leave the doorway or walk any further into the room. Biddy tries to pull her by the hand. Let go of me, Tirzah says, in an appalled whisper. She's like an upturned jigsaw; all the small fragments of herself she has been holding together for so long are losing their grip on each other and falling away. Then a girl she barely recognises shouts something. Pardon me, Tirzah stutters, stepping forward. What did you say? The girl shouts again, this time louder. What are you doing here? she calls clearly across the room. Tirzah looks in turn at each face around the tables, trying to understand what the girl means. It's not difficult, you scrubber, the girl shouts, red now and bolder. My mam and dad would never have let me come if they'd known you were going to be here. Get lost, why don't you?

Biddy rushes in a zigzag through the seated people, yelling, Shut your gob, girlo! Skidding to a stop, she promptly grabs the ponytail of the now silent girl and with two fists yanks forcefully. The girl and Biddy fall to the floor amidst the chairs, and Mr Humphries finally drops his serving fork to lunge after them. As Tirzah turns to leave, she can see Osian trying to get across the room. He has kicked his chair away and is pushing through the crowd, but she doesn't wait. Flying like an injured bird, she flits through the front door and out on to the crazy paving. Rain is falling in graceful curtains all along the promenade. Tirzah hesitates on the kerb; from across the bay she can smell frying burgers. The air is odd here, and the sounds are incomprehensible. The colours are not colours she's used to. She allows herself to drift across the gritty road and down the stone steps on to the compacted sand.

I should get lost, she thinks, feeling the strange girl's words slap her afresh, and begins to race towards the shoreline. It is difficult to run over the wet, sculpted beach; her body is like lead and her feet are awkward on the bumpy surface. Splashes of just-warm water sting her legs. Sheets of falling rain soak her face and bare forearms. The sea's long, curved margin moves forward and back, tearing and mending itself incessantly. Tirzah scans the flat horizon. A band of glowing light keeps it in place. Hundreds of seagulls flock above her, shrieking to each other. She is running fast now, so fast that at last she trips and falls heavily, belly-first, unable to save herself. The force of the fall knocks the breath from her body. Spreadeagled, she feels the sea wind lick the whorls of her ears; her long hair is spread out and coiled in salt water. Sand grinds her cheek and closed eyelid. She pushes with her arms, rising slowly to her knees.

Through gulps, she hears someone shouting her name but cannot turn. She is thinking of her tiny, jolted baby holding on in the warm dark. She shudders at the thought of how he must be feeling and massages her tummy with soaking hands. There, there, my little bud, she whispers. Go to sleep again. Mama is here. She is panting, her stomach tense, throbbing with the shock of the fall. She wipes her eyes and plants one foot on the ground. Then, using both hands, she presses on her bent knee until she is upright. At the water's edge, she watches a saturated crow struggling, its wing trailing like part of a mangled umbrella in the foam. What are you doing here? she calls. This isn't your place, or mine. Everything that happened earlier in the dining room has been wiped from her mind. She's untethered, rising easily away from the horrible ruckus in the B & B, freed from the fear that has piggybacked on her for the past weeks. Squawking, yellow-beaked seagulls flock around the injured crow, their pristine grey wings like weapons. Tirzah turns away. She thinks about the long rows of secretive houses at home, and the thistle-strewn fields. She remembers the places where the scarlet blobs of wild strawberries swell in the summer. Even the beech woods and the little brown stream she vowed she would never go near again are beloved. How could she have ever wanted to leave all that? She pictures her parents settling down in the kitchen to eat their tea and imagines her empty place at the table, and her heart thumps with longing.

Behold, Thou Art Fair, My Beloved

(Song of Songs 1:16)

Tirzah becomes aware of the salty rain slanting across her body, then the sand rising over her sandals, and her stinging face. Finally, she realises she is still standing on the beach. The sodden hem of her dress is wrapped around her knees, and she bends to squeeze out the water. At her feet sit small shells like glossy bumps. Tirzah stoops to get a closer look. The hinged, cream-and-brown shells look like the folded, shrunken wings of petrified angels. Some have fallen into separate halves. Every upturned half is a minuscule ridged bowl brimming with water. Every other is a convex nail that could have fallen from the tips of some sea creature's fingers. The beach is embossed with millions of them, all the same, all different. She can hear the faintest of clicks and holds her breath to listen better. The sounds are coming from countless holes in the compacted sand. How lovely this is, she realises. How perfectly belonging to itself. She brushes her hands, but the wet sand is stuck to her skin. Suddenly she is wary.

Not far off, Osian is standing silently, waiting for her to see him. Everything that happened earlier in the dining room falls on Tirzah again, like a pile of dirty washing thrown down the stairs. She waits for her thoughts to settle. Further up the beach, over Osian's shoulder, a line of three donkeys plod to their warm stables. She can hear the donkey man shout, Hup, hup, hup, and suddenly lighter, she smiles. Osian, she shouts, dragging her eyes back to his face, you shouldn't have lied to me. He makes the briefest movement with his head. Tirzah is transfixed by his spray of black hair and the beautiful, stark face beneath. Oh, Osian, she says. What has happened to you? He makes another helpless gesture, with his hands this time. All her old love for him billows like smoke across her heart. He steps towards her, holding out his arms stiffly. There are tears on his cheeks, and his lashes are clumped together. He is trying to say sorry, but she stops him with a kiss on his cheek. It's all right, she says, as the gulls soar over them, laughing. Everything will work out in the end, you'll see.

Tirzah wraps him in her arms. He is breathing raggedly, and his whole body trembles. Enough, she says. Quiet, now. Tirzah gazes up the beach again; she is sick of the curded shoreline behind her, and the crow turning over and over in the shallows. She is thinking about ways to get home. I'm not meant to be a girl with wet clothes and salty hair, she thinks. I need to go back to the mountain and the valley. The flicker of warmth she felt when she saw the sweet donkeys bursts into a blaze. Up in the sky, beyond the white birds and the rain clouds, she senses the sun glowing. Or maybe it is something else, she thinks, remembering the glittering presence she saw months ago on the summit of the mountain, and then in the evening fields. Now she is impatient to be gone. It's as if she is standing on a familiar, deserted platform, waiting for the train to transport her to the next bit of her life. Osian is part of this long, sorry day, and it's already finished. Come on, she says to him. Time to leave.

Tirzah tries to walk past Osian, but he blocks her path. She sees Biddy waving from the promenade, her long hair racing out to one side in the sea breeze, and can just make out their two cases on the pavement. She waves back. I'm going home, she tells Osian, as he grabs her arm. Let go of me. She shakes his hand off and is about to walk away when she becomes aware he is trying to speak. Wait, he mumbles. I need to tell you something. He is grey under his tan, his mouth leached of colour. Tirzah frowns; she wants to help him but doesn't know how. I love you, she tells him. You know it was wrong, making me believe I would be welcome here, don't you? I don't understand why you did it. He doesn't respond. Come on, say something, she goes on, her voice breaking. I hope we will always be friends, she says. The times we kissed, the times I kissed you, I shouldn't have. That was my mistake, and I'm sorry if it made you hope for something more. She can't think of another word to say, but he is inexpressibly dear to her, standing there, struggling to find words. He is shaking his head, as if to clear it. Then he starts to talk, and it gushes out like rainwater from a pipe. Slow down, Osian, she says. I can't understand you. And I can't hang around here in these wet clothes for much longer.

The rain has cleared and people are starting to appear on the beach after their evening meals in the hotels and bed and breakfast places along the front. I will state it plain then, Osian says, mastering his jagged voice. I think we should get married. There. That's what I'm trying to say. Tirzah stares. I am declaring God's truth, he goes on quickly. I've prayed a lot about what the Lord requires of me. And I am willing to submit. This way I can put myself right with the Almighty.

And you can too. Tirzah starts to walk away, stumbling in her water-logged sandals. Who will look after you and the baby? Osian says more boldly, following her. You need someone like me to sort you out. Have you lost your marbles? she asks, walking as swiftly as she can. By her side, Osian keeps up easily. It's the Lord's will, Tirzah, he says, grabbing her arm again. There's no point in arguing.

By now, Tirzah has arrived at the bottom of the promenade steps. Biddy is waiting above. She climbs a few steps and turns. Leave me alone, she tells Osian. I don't want to marry you, or anybody, thank you. I want to be Tirzah. Just me. Not part of a pair. Is that plain enough for you? And I couldn't care less what the Lord has told you. She can't help laughing. And why do you think He hasn't mentioned His plan to me? I call that a bit rude, she adds, before running up the last few steps to meet Biddy. She's out of breath. Let's go, she says, trying to contain her wet hair. Biddy glances at Osian and then shows her a dress and some other things she has in a carrier bag. We can go to the public conveniences for you to change, she says. Tirzah looks back at Osian standing in the sand. Honestly, love, she calls, you mean well, but I think you're nuts. Then she and Biddy walk away, towards town.

They make for the bus station. Tirzah is so exhausted she has to lean on Biddy. After she has changed out of her wet clothes, they empty their purses on to a bench and count up. Where did you get all this dosh from? Tirzah asks. Never you mind, Biddy answers. I was looking forward to a fine old time at the fair, so I've been saving, if you must know. It's expensive, the fair. I'm sorry, Bid, Tirzah says. I've spoilt your holiday. Don't matter, Biddy says, rummaging in her bag. Who cares about the blimmin' CYC? I'm in the doghouse for nearly scalping that mouthy piece. Tirzah suddenly remembers Biddy running over to the girl who shouted at her. Anyway, look what I've got, Biddy says, waving two shocking-pink sticks of rock. They unwrap the cellophane and start to suck. I could do with a bag of chips, Tirzah says. With lots of salt and vinegar. Biddy looks at her watch. We've got plenty of time before the bus, she says. I'll go and find us some. She gets up and sucks her rock. We're rolling in money, she goes on, jingling the coins in her purse. Even after the bus fare we still have enough for a minced beef pie between us.

After Biddy leaves, Tirzah thinks about Osian. She recalls his eyes earlier, and how their whites glittered like faulty bulbs from out of the darkness of his face. Has he actually been driven mad? She remembers his trembling lips and the way he'd flinched from his father's shouted accusations at the meeting, and how she'd tried to call to him. At that very moment, he was changing, right before her eyes; in those breathless, punchy moments when everyone looked at the stained sheet as it billowed across the floor, Osian was disappearing from her. Now, in the bus station, a breeze blows an empty can around musically. Tirzah watches a thin dog pull a soiled wrapper from a broken rubbish bin. The way the dog steadies the dirty scrap with one paw before stooping to lick it clean presses on her heart. Here you are, she calls, waving the stick of rock. The dog slinks near as she smashes the rock on the floor. I know this isn't good for you, she tells it. But beggars can't expect a pork chop. The dog snatches up white and pink fragments, crunching energetically. Something about the way the hungry dog eats reminds her of Brân. Suddenly she brims with a searing sadness. Her mind can't get any further than that, so she waits for Biddy with the dog warming her side.

By the time Biddy returns, she is scared by the bruised feeling of her bump; the skin is tightly pulled and tender. You have that, Bid, she says, looking at the collapsed pie. I'll just have a few chips. They take it in turns to sip from a can of Fanta. The hot, clumped-together chips are soft, and Tirzah is soon oily-lipped and full. She shares some with the dog. Nothing like a nice bag of chips, she says, when they finish. They wait in the darkening station for the bus to come, and when it does, Tirzah struggles up the steps, lugging her case. The dog stands and watches, his plumy tail beating. You poor thing, she says, with no one to love you. The dog has followed them to the bus steps and sits looking up at her. Goodbye, doggy, she calls as the door shuts.

They sit at the back, and Tirzah tries to catch a last glimpse of the dog before the bus drives out of the station. It seems like the saddest thing: an old, famished dog who lives in the terminus. I wish I'd brought that poor little feller in the bus with me, she says. I could have looked after him. I always wanted a pet. Don't be daft, Tiz, Biddy answers, busying herself with their stuff. He's bound to have fleas and scabs and things. Your mother would have a fit. You lie down across the seats and rest now, she goes on, tucking her cardigan around Tirzah. I will wake you. Tirzah closes her eyes. Thank goodness for Biddy, she realises. She always knows what to do. I don't deserve her. But soon her thoughts skim away; behind her lids she is playing through the time since her father drove off. Each scene is garish and far-fetched. Osian's blank brown eyes whizz past and merge with the eyes of the lost dog she has left behind. The scenes slip by, faster and faster, until at last they blur into a ribbon of clashing shades she cannot separate.

For These Things I Weep ... Mine Eye Runneth

(Lamentations 1:16)

Tirzah's father gets slowly to his feet when she comes into the kitchen, dragging her case. After a brief silence in which he rubs his forehead with the side of his hand and glances back to his wife, he tells Tirzah to get out of his sight. But, Dada, why? Tirzah begins, feeling as if someone has thrown a cup of icy water over her head. Why aren't you at the blessed weekend you nagged us to let you go on? Your poor mother and I haven't had a minute's peace for I don't know how many months, he goes on. And just when we are about to have a breather, something else happens. He gives her a hard look. Lo and behold, here you are, bouncing back again like a bad penny. Tirzah looks at the scene; her parents were about to settle down with the radio before going to bed. The teapot wears its knitted cosy half on, half off, and a plate of chocolate biscuits waits. Confused, she glances from her father to the silent figure of her mother behind him.

But, Mama, she says, trying again, taking a step nearer and putting her case down quietly. I couldn't stay with the CYC. Honest, I couldn't. Her mother lies just where she is, head resting back on the embroidered chair-back, her unslippered feet on a stool, and looks at Tirzah coolly. I was just dying to come home to you and Dada, Tirzah says, heat crawling up from her neck to her cheeks. I was homesick. Her excuse sounds so obviously untruthful, she tries again. Well, anyway. Something terrible happened. The words die on her tongue: they don't seem to care. Her mother indicates the biscuits with the merest nod. Take some of these, she says, and get yourself a cup. Then do as your father tells you. Tirzah flinches as if she has been slapped. I can see I'm not wanted here, she shouts. And I don't want your stupid tea. It would choke me. She fumbles for the handle and slams the door behind her.

Fully clothed, Tirzah climbs carefully on to her bed and arranges herself as comfortably as she can. Her joints ache unfamiliarly, and she wishes her pregnant stomach was detachable. With an arm over her eyes she wonders about everything. Never before have her parents behaved this way. Am I a bad penny? she wonders, remembering her father's words and her mother's stillness. Probably she was. But what else has happened to make her mother so silent? She still can't believe the way things have turned out. Her ears buzz as she reruns how her mother hadn't even lifted her head from the chair when she appeared at the door. Tirzah recalls the way her mother's half-curled fingers rested on her flowered skirt, and how her delicate crossed ankles looked. Mama usually has such busy hands and feet, she thinks, suddenly crying fiercely and longing for her mother to come and cwtch her. But later, when she is cold and hungry, the only sounds are footsteps going in and out of the bathroom and the click of a bedroom door.

Tirzah wakes some time in the early morning. No one has come and put a blanket over her in the night, and her limbs are chilled and stiff. When she takes off her clothes she discovers dry sand in her bra, and for a sweet moment cannot understand why it should be there. Under the pillow is a clean nightdress, and dropping it over her head, she hears the soft slither as it falls around her ankles. In the mean, pearly light she looks at all the familiar things on the desk and shelves, but they do not help. She must work out something difficult and doesn't know how. Wrapped in the blanket, she gets back on the bed and tries to think. It's a new idea: that she is not welcome in her own home. Is it really true? Reluctantly, she relives the last months, leaving nothing out. But this time she thinks about her parents, all the times she has disappeared. All the times she has reappeared, bleeding and silent. All the unanswered, tearful questions. Then the meetings with Pastor and the elders on her behalf. All the worry and shame. It's as if a covering has been yanked away to reveal an ugly mess, full of sadness. And she has been the cause of most of it.

She gazes around the bedroom; the wardrobe door is open, and inside, her too-small clothes wait patiently for someone who can wear them. Her empty school bag gapes from the back of the chair. These are the belongings of the girl she used to be. That simple life has vanished as quickly and silently as mist descends to hide the mountains when rain is coming. Her thoughts are so electrifying she can't keep still and creeps downstairs with the trailing blanket still wrapped around her shoulders. In the kitchen, the sight of two cups and saucers and the empty biscuit plate waiting to be washed makes her sniff again. But there is no use grizzling, she sees that now. Grizzling never changed a thing. No one is going to come and say, There, there, to her. And why should they? Something new is growing inside. Something hardier. She fills the kettle and puts it on the flame. Then, shedding the warm cover, makes up a tray and cuts bread for toast. The clock on the dresser is wanting five minutes to seven o'clock. When the slices under the flaring grill are a perfect golden brown she grabs them and spreads butter. Snatching the kettle up the second it starts to sing, she makes tea.

Soon everything is ready, and she surveys the tray before climbing the stairs. This is the first time she has ever made her parents breakfast in bed. Quickly she wipes her eyes again. Climbing the stairs, she is just in time to hear the alarm clock shrilling in their room. Without making a sound, she takes their tray in. Good morning, both, she says to the two mounds under the covers, and lays the tray on an area of the bed that is flat. The room smells of pent-up air and warm bodies. On the dressing table her mother's open Bible lies amidst some bottles of scent and face cream. On the floor, by her father's side of the bed, there are some balled-up tissues. Tirzah turns without saying another word and dashes out, shutting the door quietly.

She waits in her room until they are both washed and dressed and downstairs, then runs herself a bath. Into the water she throws one of the old, cut-off stocking feet her mother fills with oats and ties with ribbon, watching as clouds of oaty fluid escape from it. Soon the water is milky. She trims her toenails and shapes them with the rusty nail file kept in the cabinet. The tangled nest of her hair is crispy and caked with sand. Pulling it away from her face, she tries to imagine what she would look like with it short. That is something I will never do to my mama, she thinks, shaking it out to feel the ends brush the tops of her buttocks. She loves my hair. In the bath, she lies full length. Even now, she is not too long for the bath. Creamy water laps her belly, covering her legs and arms, soothing all the small cuts and bruises she has acquired in the past few days. With one hand she palms water and drips it into her belly button. A skein of sand travels down the smooth, curved skin.

Poor old Osian, she thinks. Did he really believe she would marry him? How much praying and fasting had he done to come up with that? She was to be the sacrifice he would make to appease the Lord. Well, stuff that. And what his parents would have made of the idea is no mystery. Tirzah is the whore of Babylon to his father, at least, she's sure. Love him, though, for wanting to save her. What he doesn't know is that I don't need saving, she thinks, looking at her feet emerging from the cloudy water. I can save myself eventually. It's as if she is crawling forward; each time something happens, she is a little nearer her goal. Even though she doesn't know what her goal is yet. She thinks about last night in the kitchen. The next thing to do is talk to Mama and Dada. She can't imagine they would have been overjoyed if she had decided to marry Osian, even if it did make her respectable. She will tell them about her new resolution to be a grown-up. She will truly apologise for all the things that have hurt them and ask their forgiveness. Quickly she dresses and goes downstairs.

In the empty kitchen, her breakfast is laid out. She sits and picks up the glass of orange juice. There is a folded note on her plate. Tirzah feels her heart beginning to drum. The orange juice in her mouth tastes acidic, burning her throat as it goes down. Quickly she unfolds the paper, and reads. The writing is her mother's. They have been called to a special meeting at chapel this morning. She is not to worry. They don't know when they will be back. At the end, her mother says Tirzah's midday snack is in the pantry. Sure enough, there on the slate shelf is a neat greaseproof paper packet. Tirzah lets out a squeaky sob. Oh, Mama, she thinks. What's happening now? Why a meeting on a Saturday morning, of all things? The thought of Mam carefully preparing her dinner before she and Dada went to the meeting is too much. Past crying, she sits back at the table to wait, rests her head on folded arms and forces herself to breathe slowly.

Who Hath Woe? ... Who Hath Contentions?

(Proverbs 23:29)

Tirzah decides to do some housework; the morning is sliding forward so excruciatingly, and she must do something other than blub and wipe her nose on her sleeve. Pulling out the vacuum cleaner's wilful tentacle, she knocks her ankle on the understairs cupboard door. Bloody, bloody, bloody, she mutters, bending to have a look. The graze has minute red dots all along its length. She wets her finger and brushes them off, then watches as they spring out of the injured skin again. The bloom of pain gives her an odd hum of satisfaction. She clatters around, vigorously swishing the brush head, wrestling with rugs and yanking the heavy body of the cleaner so that it bangs the skirting boards and furniture legs. When that's finished and the horrible contraption has been put away, she gets out the Mansion polish and sets to work on the sideboard in the front room. As she rushes around picking up her mother's ornaments and sweeping the cloth under them, she is trying to outdistance her anxieties about the emergency meeting. There are moments when she forgets, but with a vicious squeeze, the meeting always drops back into her mind, and her nerves quiver like one of those hundred-armed sea anemones she and Biddy saw in a rock pool on that summer outing with the Women's Guild.

All her energy evaporates, and she leaves the polishing rag and Mansion tin on the coffee table. What do people do when they are waiting? she wonders, and decides to make a drink. Back in the kitchen, she gets her snack from the pantry and opens it on to a plate. She makes herself some squash and perches at the table to eat. Her sandwiches are ham and tomato. Biting into one, her tongue touches the juice-sodden bread and recoils. I can't eat tomato-soaked bread, she thinks, slapping the neat little square down. What was Mama thinking? She gets up to find a biscuit. Crunching a custard cream, she stops mid-chew. There I go again, she thinks. Behaving like a spoilt child. It's going to be a long job, this one. You can't just will yourself to be more mature. Maybe it creeps up on you when you aren't looking, like time. She eats all the squashy sandwiches quickly. She is grubby from the earlier housework, so she goes up to the bathroom. After washing her face and hands in cool water, she uses her mother's talc, lifting her smock to dust her small white bump and the hot places under her breasts. After gathering her hair in a ribbon, she decides to go to Biddy's.

At Biddy's back door she hesitates. Aunty Ceinwen wasn't that friendly last time. She tiptoes along the path to have a look through the living-room window. There is Biddy, lying on the sofa, eating an apple. Tirzah gently taps the window and watches as Biddy sits up and smiles, gesturing for her to come in. Hiya, ducky, Biddy says, opening the kitchen door. Mam and Dad are at the dreaded meeting. Tirzah steps in and Biddy tosses her an apple from the bowl on the table. What's the matter? she asks. Are you worried about the fellowship and what's going on? Of course I am, you stupid thing, Tirzah answers. Biddy raises her eyebrows. Touchy, aren't we? she says. Well, it's blimmin' obvious, isn't it? Tirzah answers. They sit on the sofa, crunching their apples. After a few minutes, Tirzah waggles Biddy's foot. I'm sorry, she says. I am so nasty, and you are always so nice to me. Biddy drops her bottom lip and pushes it forward. Don't worry, she answers in a drippy, guttural voice. I am a stupid thing sometimes. Mam and Da are always going on to me about it. Well, I think you are lovely, Tirzah tells her. And that's an end to it. So stop making that horrible face.

Biddy has been watching television. How come you have a television again? Tirzah asks. What about *the devil-in-the-living-room*, and all that? Biddy doesn't look away from the screen. I worked on the pair of them, she says. Ground 'em down. You know. And it turns out Mam really loves that *New Faces* programme. Tirzah doesn't know about grinding anyone down, or at least, doesn't think she does, so she tries to concentrate on the cartoon. An outsized dog lopes down a dark passageway with a scrawny, tousle-haired boy. Something monstrous is running after them, roaring. What is this? she asks, a little nervous for the pair on the screen. Biddy tells her the programme is called *Scooby Doo*. I love it, she says. It's hysterical. I watch it every Saturday. Tirzah is dying to ask Biddy about the meeting but doesn't want to interrupt. The cartoon is long, but finally, two sensible-looking girls are reunited with the other, nutty pair, and the monster is revealed as an old man they all know well.

I didn't expect that, Biddy sighs, getting up to switch the television off. He seemed like such a nice old gentleman to me. Just goes to show. She throws herself back on the sofa. And now I have to get through a whole week until the next one. Tirzah stares at her, vexed by how she can spend so much time thinking about a stupid cartoon. Listen, she says. This is serious. Do you know what the meeting is about? Biddy gives her a look. I thought you of all people would already know, she answers. Tirzah is silent as everything becomes obvious to her. The meeting is about you, Biddy says, moving to sit close. Didn't you realise? What do you mean? Tirzah asks, her voice weak. Well, Biddy goes on, trying to find the best words. There is a disagreement about whether you should be allowed to come to meetings now. Some folk think you should be cast out, some want you to stay.

Tirzah's heart is slowing down. Each muffled beat sounds like the footstep of a monster in a dark tunnel. She gasps for air. At this very moment her parents are facing the fellowship on her behalf: the row of elders in their tall seats, the congregation shouting at each other, Pastor in the pulpit. She understands now why her parents were so strange last night, poor little Mam lying with her feet up, Dada rubbing his forehead and calling her a bad penny. She can sense Biddy looking at her. Tirzah, she is calling, her voice making Tirzah jump. Then everything snaps back and she is herself again. I must go to them, she says, struggling to get up. This is to do with me, after all. Biddy grabs her hands. That's not a good idea, she says. Your parents wouldn't want you to. Tirzah stares at her. How do you know? she asks. Because if they had wanted you there, they'd have taken you with them, Biddy answers. You should try and be a bit more like me, she continues. Your trouble is you care too much about chapel and God.

Tirzah lets Biddy persuade her to lie down while she goes to get her a drink. She closes her eyes, knowing Biddy is right. But then Biddy would never get herself into any of the predicaments Tirzah has stumbled into. She wonders if Pastor will speak for her, and thinks about the times she has been to the manse because of her wrongdoings. Pastor's wife will not be on her side, that's for sure. She remembers the splodges on her black patent shoes. Osian's father will be strongly against. What about Aunty Ceinwen and Uncle Maldwyn? Are people going to be ripped away from each other because of what she's done? The funny old chapel she has known since she was a baby broken apart? All those powdery ancient ladies who used to slip her a Murray Mint or a fruit pastille and pat her cheek? And what will her punishment be? Mr Humphries probably rang Pastor last night and told him about the CYC fiasco. She sees now what an outsider would see: trouble follows her around. Things are disrupted wherever she goes, and she doesn't even know how it happens. But underneath all these things she is not wicked. If God can see my heart, He will know, she thinks, a fraction calmer.

Soon Biddy is back with a drink. What's this? Tirzah asks, sipping obediently, and pleasantly shocked by the cold prickle of tiny bubbles bursting on its surface. It's cola. I did a bit of grinding to get my mother to buy it for me, Biddy says, looking at her over her own glass and burping. This is a right to-do, she continues. Now will you tell me who the father is? There is no father, Tirzah answers. Into her mind leaps the sharp, brindled face of Brân. But after the first moments his image begins to dissolve like a freshly painted picture splashed with water. In a moment or two she can no longer remember what he looks like. There never has been, she adds. Have you gone completely round the twist? Biddy asks. You're not the blimmin' Virgin Mary, you know. She is staring at Tirzah with her mouth open. Heavens to blinking Betsy, she goes on. Are you actually saying you never went with a man? Tirzah gives Biddy a kiss on the forehead. Putting her empty glass in the washing up bowl, she leaves without saying another word. At the bottom of Biddy's garden the chickens make their little chuckling queries, and the swags of streaky, apricot-coloured roses lolling over the path sway in a breeze. Tirzah presses her nose into an overblown flower and sniffs. Brilliant petals drop until she is left holding nothing but a hairy-tongued heart.

All she can do now is go home and wait. In the hall the clock ticks unevenly. The house is empty and without comfort. She walks from room to room, touching the familiar objects. She is trying to say goodbye to it all, just in case. Outside her parents' room she pauses, but does not open the door, understanding now that the room is their sanctuary. The sound she has been painfully listening for finally arrives. Her parents are not speaking, but she hears the sound of the tap running in the kitchen and realises one of them is putting the kettle on the flame. If things were really that bad, would they be thinking of making tea? She dismisses that thought immediately. Of course they would. It doesn't matter what occurs, people always make tea. Mama? she calls from the landing. Dada? Her father appears at the foot of the stairs. You'd better come down, child, he says.

Strong Drink Shall Be Bitter to Them That Drink It

(Isaiah 24:9)

Tirzah joins her parents at the table. I don't know about you, Gwyll, her mother states as the kettle starts its heating-up song, but a cup of char will not cut the mustard with me at a time such as this. Her father doesn't seem to hear. I'm getting the brandy out, that's what I'm doing. She heads for the pantry, and once inside, starts clinking and banging. Now, where is that bottle? she asks, her voice muffled. Tirzah knows that the unopened bottle is at the back of the sideboard in the front room and goes to fetch it. Returning to the table, she puts it down and then gets three glasses. What is this? her father says, startled back to life. Spirits? And in the middle of the day? He looks as if he's going to start ranting. Tirzah's mother gives her a slant-eyed look. I won't ask how you knew where the bottle was, madam, she says, struggling with the stopper. Tirzah's father opens his mouth to speak. Hush, please, her flushed-faced mother tells him, raising a small hand. I need something to bolster me. The Lord will understand. Tirzah's father folds his lips in on each other. His face is claylike and damp, and his hair has slipped from its usual sharp shape. Strands spring forward, giving him a rough air that Tirzah has never seen before. I don't want any argy-bargy, her mother goes on briskly. Everyone is having a little tot.

They sit with their glasses in front of them. The smell of the brandy is like spicy toffee. God forgive us, her mother says and swallows hers in one go. Tirzah does the same. She and her mother both have a fit of coughing and start to laugh. Come on, Gwyll, Tirzah's mother says, gasping and wiping her mouth with the back of her hand. Down the hatch with it. Never did I think I would see this day, he starts. Oh, shush, Gwyllim, it's for the shock, Tirzah's mother tells him. Tirzah thinks she can already feel the liquor running like a small, hot train through her veins. Her father's hand is shaking as he lifts the glass. He swallows the brandy down. I took the pledge when I was twelve, he announces, licking his lips, bemused. And now, on this day of all days, I have broken it. There is a small silence in which they sit and wait. Tirzah can't stop a little snort of laughter escaping. Her mother pours them each another generous measure. Well, if the blessed pledge is broken, one more won't make much difference, will it? she says, suddenly animated. They drink again. Your face, Gwyll, her mother giggles, pointing with a wandering finger. It's like a slapped dap. Tirzah's head is a wind-filled pillowcase, blowing on the line. Whee! she shouts, watching her father's mouth twitch. Together, they all yelp with laughter.

Just as suddenly, the swell of laughter falters. Tirzah is uncertain: has she been howling with sorrow? Her parents are wiping their eyes; all three of them are shaken. Very bitter, her father says, out of nowhere. People were very bitter today. He gives his eyes a final dab and folds his hankie. Tirzah's mother weaves her way to the stove. I will make tea now, I think, she says carefully. Go on, Gwyll. Tell her. Her father goes on in a flat voice. It seems that as soon as everyone was more or less present, Pastor had tried to remind them they were children of God, urging them to love one another, but Osian's dad strode to the front, shouting him down. People were arguing across the pews, brother to brother. There was no order at all, her father says, shaking his head. I felt sorry for poor old Pastor. Unseemly, it was. Tirzah is staring at her father, but he appears reluctant to proceed. What happened next? she asks. Then Osian's father pointed with his Bible, her mother says. Foghorning, he was, as is his way, and he denounced us before God and man. He said you were a bad influence on the young people, and we were weak parents. Did Osian's father say anything more about me? Tirzah asks. Her head is deflated now, and she has no inclination to laugh. Her parents both look at her. Tirzah's body prickles with needles of heat. She jumps as the kettle starts to scream. Never mind what else he spouted, her mother says. Your father was very calm, credit to him. Eventually, though, he got up, marched to the front and punched the sorry man right in the mouth. Knocked him down in front of the pulpit.

Tirzah's vision is suddenly obscured. She rubs her eyes. That her father would strike another brother, even if it was Osian's horrible father, is outside her understanding. That the fellowship has fallen apart over so small a thing as a baby is shocking. When her sight clears she turns her father's hand over and sees it is cut across the knuckles and swollen. Every word she wants to say shrivels in her mouth even before she has begun to form it. She goes to the sink and splashes her face with water, and then turns to her parents. I am sorry, she manages to tell them. In her womb, the baby feels like a dead weight, and her legs give way. Mama, she cries. Her mother rises as Tirzah crumples to the floor, but is hampered by her chair. Tirzah comes round almost immediately, but she cannot move. If I could just lie here on the cool tiles for ever, she thinks, I would be content. She keeps her eyes closed, listening to her parents struggling to help her, and knows for their sake she must look lively. I'm not hurt, she whispers. Let me lie by here for a bit. Her parents sit close to her on the floor, stroking her as if she were a sick pet.

When Tirzah is in bed, her mother sits with her. I am so ashamed of all that drinking we did, she says. I am to blame. It was my idea. Tirzah tries to think of something to say. Brandy, of all things, her mother goes on. I don't even like the stuff. Her lips are ashen, not their usual sweet, pink colour. The Devil has swooped in by here, through the chink we gave him. Tirzah pushes her hand inside her mother's so that it is held like a small bird. I don't know what to do next, cariad, her mother sighs. Your dada has gone to the manse to officially resign from the deaconship. Uncle Maldwyn is stepping out with him. Even if we are to stay, Dada says it is only right. It will be a blow for him. She shifts to lie with Tirzah on the bed, and Tirzah moves to make room. A breeze wraps itself around her, even as she snuggles into her mother's shoulder. Their hair mingles as they rest their heads on the propped-up pillows. We have an appointment at the hospital clinic on Monday, she hears her mother say. Try to rest. Tirzah is staring at the ceiling. I am going to lay this family on the Almighty's merciful altar, and leave us to Him, her mother adds. Tirzah stretches out her tense legs until they tremble, listening to her mother praying for them all.

They are woken by the front door banging. I must have dropped off, her mother says. Dada's back. She tidies herself at Tirzah's mirror and leaves the room. Tirzah forces herself to join them. Her mother is busy again in the kitchen. We will have a bite to eat, she says, rushing to the pantry. Her father is sitting in his easy chair. Tirzah tries to read his profile, but he looks like a stranger to her. She barely has the strength to make it to a chair at the table, and once there, she rests her head on her folded arms. Soon there is a plate of corned beef sandwiches and some buttered Welsh cakes laid out. Spit spot, you two, her mother says. You will both feel better after a little something. Dad? Tirzah prompts. What happened at the manse? But her father doesn't answer. He is making his way through a sandwich, stopping at intervals to take gulps of tea. He could be chewing leather from the look of him, Tirzah thinks. His eyelids are reddened and his mouth set oddly. Don't bother your father now, her mother says, stealing a look at him. Without a word to either of them, he leaves the kitchen and goes out into the garden. They both get up and peer round the net curtain. What's he doing? Tirzah asks. Her father is standing on the cemented-over lawn, hands on his hips. He is gazing around as if the garden is a strange, new sight. Tirzah's heart jounces unpleasantly in her chest. Is Dada going funny in the head? she whispers. Don't talk so soft, her mother says, and gives her a sharp jab in the chest with her elbow. Who could blame him if he did? Go to your room, for goodness' sake.

Instead, Tirzah decides to have another look at him from behind the curtains in the bathroom. Her mother is out in the garden now, and from this angle, they look stunted, their heads overlarge. She carefully opens the window to listen. Her father is squatting on the edge of the empty china sink. I'm going to plant this up again with some nice mint, Mair, he's saying. Are you, Gwyll? her mother answers. And all this, he gestures with his arm to the expanse of cement. All this is going to be broken up. I'll have plenty of time now I'm not one of the brethren any more. Tirzah eyes blur and she clutches the curtain, watching as her mother stands close and puts her arms around him. There is silence for a while, and Tirzah begins to feel guilty for spying. She is about to leave when her father starts speaking again. The babby will need somewhere nice to play, see, Mair, he says. Come next summer it will be crawling, and this surface will hurt its soft knees. Her mother nods. We can't have that, he adds. Grass is what a little one needs. Somewhere to toddle around. Then they are silent again. Tirzah gazes at the way her father's head rests on her mother's breast, her tears unchecked and her nose running, then tiptoes away.

He Shall Appear to Your Joy

(Isaiah 66:5)

Tirzah is trying to aim her wee into a jug while her mother gives instructions from outside the bathroom door. I can't do it, Tirzah says. I can't go. Her mother pushes the door open. Stop being so childish and squeeze a few drops out this minute, she says. Then give the wretched jug to me. She slams the door behind her. Tirzah manages to produce an eggcup of urine at last. We're going to be late, her mother shouts. Tirzah carries the jug down and puts it on the kitchen table. Thank you, and about time, her mother says, pouring the scant contents into an empty tablet bottle. Now we must go. Tirzah has a hectic churning in her stomach. As they walk to the bus stop she wants to explain how nervous she is, but her mother is rushing, nose pointed in a way that Tirzah knows means she is not happy to talk. Keep up, child, she says, without looking round. Waiting for the bus, Tirzah can't stop herself. Tugging her mother's sleeve and talking quietly so the ladies in the queue can't hear, she explains that she doesn't want to go to the hospital. Her mother is peering up the road. I'm perfectly well now, Tirzah adds, so no need, see? Shush, her mother says.

I don't want to listen to you any more today. If we miss this appointment I will be cross.

Down the valley they go on the snaking road, the bus racketing over potholes. They hold on to the seatbacks in front. I will put pen to paper and complain about this driver, the woman opposite says to anyone who will listen. We could all be killed. Her mother checks that Tirzah is all right. Have a mint, she says. Not long now. They sit and suck, shoulders bumping as the bus swerves and rattles. Next stop, please! her mother calls, blushing, and the bus, sounding like a stirred-up box of cutlery, churns to a halt. Her mother walks past the driver and down the steps, announcing she is going to report him to his betters. Then they are on the narrow pavement, their dress hems flaring as the bus drives off. Walking down the road to the hospital, Tirzah's legs are as frail as two long blades of jointed grass, but she keeps following, and soon they are through the tall pillars that stand either side of the hospital gates. Her mother asks the way to the antenatal department from a face that appears through a gap in the window of a kiosk.

The department they need is in a row of single-storey corrugated iron structures shaped like tunnels. What are these? Tirzah asks. She doesn't want to go inside. Old buildings left over from the war, her mother tells her. Still, they've made an effort, painting them white, and the curtains are pretty. Around the borders of the buildings, scarlet flowers crowd. If Tirzah squints, they look like smeared clots of blood on big rolls of bandages. She puts her sweating hand into her mother's. Oh, her mother says, stopping at last. Are you frightened? Tirzah can only nod. There is nothing to it, she goes on. Millions of women are pregnant every day, and they all survive a little check-up. She is trying to get Tirzah to smile. And after, we'll go into town and have a treat. In the waiting room, every other seat is taken by a pregnant woman, and in between sits the non-pregnant person who has come with them. Two places are free, so they take them. Tirzah looks around. She feels as if she doesn't belong, but here she is, with her bump like a mushroom pushing her smock out.

The dark-skinned girl sitting opposite her is even younger than Tirzah. She is cradling a family-sized pop bottle of amber liquid in her arms. Tirzah nudges her mother, who is looking for something in her bag. Here it is, she says, bringing out the tablet bottle of wee. You hold it. The girl looks at Tirzah's sample and stops swinging her legs. She has elongated, solid-looking ringlets, and her top does not cover her stretched belly. Tirzah is shocked by the way the girl's navel sticks out like a knuckle. With her is a tiny, sun-seamed old lady, whose oiled iron-grey hair is plaited tightly around her small head. The girl and the old lady are holding hands and sharing something crunchy from a paper bag. Tirzah realises that the enormous bottle is full of the girl's urine. She starts to blush for her. Gypsies, her mother whispers over-loudly. I can spot them a mile off. Tirzah is almost relieved when a nurse calls her name.

The examination room smells medicinal, icy somehow, and she holds her mother's hand, deliberately unfocusing her eyes; there are too many dishes and metal instruments glinting. When the nurse comes towards her with a gleaming contraption in her hands, she is frozen. Her mother says to lie back on the tissue-covered bed and relax. Tirzah's body obeys, but her head is detaching itself. Like a long, cold finger the thing slides in between her legs and seems to burn her shrinking insides. Finally, the nurse washes her hands and says they can go. Out in the open air again, Tirzah can't stop talking. Her mother listens, smiling now and then. Tirzah is already turning her back on the way her secret, private places have been investigated. She walks quickly back to the bus stop, shaking the hair from her hot forehead, and sees the buddleia drooping over the hospital walls. A continuous, throat-catching perfume billows from them. Their nodding, rusty-purple snouts are thronged with black butterflies whose scalloped, white-spotted wings never stop vibrating. Tirzah halts. It is as if someone has called her name. A rushing sensation swirls around her. Everything seems burnished; the dusty cars, the drain covers, even the bins outside the terraced houses, all seem to be held in a sparkling net. Oh, Mam, she calls, her throat clogged, isn't everything wonderful? Her mother looks back. Come on, you daft article, she laughs. First you are terrified, then you are ecstatic about some old, weedy flowers. It's relief you're feeling. They carry on, arm in arm. Do you understand me, though? Tirzah asks. She can't find words for the way the world has renewed itself. I think I do, her mother says.

They get off the bus outside the town hall. We could go to the park first, her mother says, examining Tirzah's face. I think you're flagging, though. Tirzah loves the park with its bandstand and avenue of sweet chestnuts, but she needs to sit down. Her mother takes her to a café and orders hot sausage rolls for them both. Tirzah has a cup of milky coffee from the shining machine on the counter. There is a particular cake sitting amongst the others in the display cabinet that she loves. Her mother follows her gaze. Would you like one of those? she asks. Tirzah is still dreamy from the buddleias. Thank you, Mam, she says. They eat the sausage rolls with blobs of ketchup, using knives and forks. This is nice, her mother comments, gathering up the curled flakes left on her plate with a licked finger. Speaking as a cook myself. When Tirzah's cake arrives she turns the plate round to get a good look; in a pleated silver cupcake case lined with fragile pastry, there is an uneven mound of coffee icing crowned with a half-walnut. I would never choose a custard tart, she says, eyeing her mother's choice. Each to their own, madam, her mother answers, and pats her cheek.

Tirzah sits on a bench watching the crowds walk past while her mother goes into Woolworth's. I am a rock in a boisterous stream, she thinks. Soon her mind turns to the broken fellowship and what will happen next. Her earlier mood deflates like a piece of punched bread dough as she remembers her father's damaged knuckles and the way he had sat with his hair mussed up, dutifully eating a sandwich. She is puzzled now by how happy she felt coming out of the hospital, smitten by her own selfishness again. Then, looking up, she sees Derry walking towards her, his strong eyebrows raised in recognition.

It's such a long time since she saw him. Dear Derry, she says, feeling a flare of warmth as he comes to sit by her side, and then cannot think of another thing to say. 'Ello, stranger, he says, you look beautiful, and he reaches to curl a coil of her hair around his finger. Remembering the other time he tried that, she doesn't stop him. He appears less famished now somehow, and his hair is cut in a different way. You look tidy, she tells him. She is aware of her growing bump under her maternity smock, and a blush billows up from her chest. Derry holds his cigarette away from her. How's it goin'? he asks, looking briefly at her tummy. I 'eard about you on the grapevine. Tha' must've set the cat amongst the pigeons. He is smiling, showing his irregular teeth, and she can't help smiling too. Then he coughs, hunching his shoulders. Shoppers still walk past, but Tirzah does not see them.

After a silence, he blurts out that he's sorry he didn't write like he promised. I couldn't find the proper words, see? he says. Looking away for a moment, he drops his fag and steps on the stub. I'm no' much of a writer. And I got it into my 'ead you didn't wanna 'ave nothing to do with me. I was a bit of a pig. Wasn't I? He gazes at her, his Adam's apple bobbing. Yes, you were a bit, especially at first, Tirzah says, smiling. But later I saw through all that. I did wait for your letter, and I thought maybe you were fed up with us and had changed your mind. Not that I blamed you, she adds. No, Derry says, his hand slicing the air emphatically, I should never have touched you up, stuff like that. So stop sayin' otherwise. I feel bad. A bit fresh, I was, to say the least. She looks steadily back at him. Never mind that now, she says. I would have liked to at least thank you for the money you gave me. He listens intently, jutting his jaw, the two deep lines between his eyebrows noticeable. Tirzah is suddenly distracted: from a distance she can just see her mother coming towards them through the crowds. You have to go now, she tells him. He looks around. Can we meet? he asks quickly. It's important, like. All right, Tirzah says, surprised. But not in the village. It'll have to be here. Derry nods and says he has a few days off work soon. They hurriedly make arrangements and Tirzah is alone again on the bench. Who were you gassing to? her mother asks when she arrives. She is laden with bags and puffing a little. Only I thought I saw someone sat beside you. Tirzah shakes her head. On the bus, she thinks about Derry. She believed he had forgotten her. But now she sees that isn't true.

That Which Hath Wings Shall Tell the Matter

(Ecclesiastes 10:20)

Tirzah's mother has her sleeves rolled up and is using a pair of large wooden tongs to transfer dripping laundry to the spinning compartment of her twin-tub. Out you go, she says, you are under my feet. Tirzah slowly leaves the soapy kitchen. The throb of the twin-tub has been getting on her nerves, but even so, she wanted to hang around. Fresh air, her mother shouts over the spin cycle, it's good for you. Without giving much thought, Tirzah wanders round to Biddy's. Aunty Ceinwen is also washing. Through a patch of clear glass in the misted-up kitchen window, Tirzah sees her hot face passing back and forth, tied around with a headscarf like a pudding ready for steaming, and decides not to enter. Her uncle and aunty have stuck by them and left Horeb, but she knows they are upset with her, so she drifts down to the chicken coop. Purple-leaved mint has seeded itself all along the paths, giving up a clean, clear smell as Tirzah's ankles brush past. Two dusty chickens are pecking in the sparse grass, so she sits on the edge of an old log to watch them. One of the chickens jerks towards her. Helloooo, Tirzah croons. What's happening in chicken world today? The bird stares fiercely out of one eye, then jabs her big toenail with its beak. Oi, Tirzah exclaims. That hurt. The chicken makes off, back to the grass.

Someone is coming down the garden path, and for a moment Tirzah thinks it might be her aunty, but Biddy appears with a bowl of bits for the chickens. Hiya, she says, stopping abruptly. What are you doing all on your tod? Well, it's washing day, isn't it? Tirzah answers, looking at the chickens. I've been chucked out of the house. I see, Biddy says, and gives a series of low whistles as she strews peelings on the grass. Here you are, ladies, she calls. A little treat because you've been so good. We've been up to our eyes in eggs, she tells Tirzah. I've been allowed to sell some and keep the money. The chickens run to the food, shifting their light bodies from side to side, tiny heads motionless, their scarlet combs wobbling. Biddy contemplates Tirzah. What do you want to do? she asks. I know. Shall I show you my new dress?

Leaning against the wall in Biddy's room, Tirzah's hands are squashed behind her back, but she doesn't move. The same not-belonging mood she felt in the hospital waiting room is on her. Biddy poses in a new maxi dress. What d'you think? she asks, fishing in the top to align her breasts. This is called shirring, she explains, pulling the bodice to show Tirzah how the little elasticated seams stretch. The effect is a nice, close fit. Tirzah, with an effort, steps forward to have a better look. You are a sight for sore eyes, she says. But where will you wear it? Biddy drops on to the bed, the tiered skirt riffling all around her. Through her dishevelled hair, she says something about a beginning of term sixth form disco. What? Tirzah asks. You never said anything about sixth form. Then she understands: Biddy didn't want to mention her new school plans for fear of upsetting her. Oh, she says. I see. That sounds nice. It'll probably be boring, Biddy says, you know what these school things are like. I managed to get a smattering of B's and scraped a place, goodness knows how. Dunno if I'll stick it out, mind. She's chattering, her face pink, but she can't help playing with the lovely, swishy fabric of her dress. You will be the prettiest girl there, Tirzah tells her. She can see herself, distended and lumpy, in Biddy's mirror.

Biddy takes the dress off and puts it away. Anyway, she says, from inside her T-shirt, let's stop talking about stupid me. How are you about, you know, being denounced? Her face appears in the small neck hole. It looks strange, devoid of all her hair. Tirzah gives her a look. Poor little Osian, though, Biddy adds, squeezing her whole head through. Tirzah's ears prick up like a pony's. What do you mean? Has something else happened? she asks. Biddy's blush intensifies. Snatching up her hairbrush, she turns to the mirror. I thought you would know, she says, settling herself at the dressing table. You always think I'll know, but I don't, so tell me, Tirzah presses. She is looking into the blue eyes of Biddy's reflection, suddenly chilled. Biddy sighs. I don't want to say anything to upset you, Tizzy, she explains. Don't ask me. But Tirzah must know. She grabs Biddy's shoulders and squeezes. Quick, she says. Spit it out. You've already shoved being denounced in my face, so I think I'll survive anything else you have to say.

So Biddy tells how, after Osian's father had denounced Tirzah and her parents, he turned on Osian. This is the man, he had shouted. He is her despoiler! We all know him and his lustful ways of old. Tirzah's knees won't hold her upright, and Biddy helps her to sit on the bed. Oh no, Tirzah says, her hands covering her mouth. Then what happened? Osian stood up and stared at his father for a moment, Biddy goes on, her eyes growing big with unshed tears. White, he was. Even his lips. Everyone thought he was going to give his father what for at last. But, instead, he swore before God he was not the father of your baby, and then ran out of chapel. Oh, she adds, then Pastor announced that the fellowship believed him, so that was good. Where is he now? Tirzah asks, her voice choking. No one has heard, Biddy says. He's disappeared. Osian, run away? Tirzah cannot believe it. So now two people she knows have gone. Even if she has been told there is no such thing, she must be very bad luck. I am a terrible influence, she thinks. And without saying goodbye, she leaves Biddy. Unable to see clearly, she stumbles going downstairs and stops briefly, realising she must take care.

In her room, she closes the curtains and lies down. Her mind vacillates between worry for Osian and thinking about Biddy in sixth form now. Biddy doing A-levels is a shock. Tirzah was always the clever one, and Biddy came to her for help. She pulls the list of results out of the drawer and has another look, smoothing out the crumpled paper. What's the use? she thinks, tracing down the row of A's with her finger. All that stuff is over for me. Over and dead. Next year might as well be next century. The joke is that Biddy never wanted to stay on after O-levels. She boasted she was going to scarper to the city as soon as possible and get a job in a boutique. I want to blimmin' live a bit, have a laugh, she always said. And I worked really hard, Tirzah thinks, and did well, and now look. She ignores the fact that she will be caring for a baby. The thought of waiting another whole year before going back to school seems unbearable. And then there's Osian, with his feet firmly mired in the valley, never really wanting to leave. And he is the one who has flown away. But where to? He always talked about doing A-levels. Why would he give up on all that?

She wishes she was the one making plans to go back for the autumn term. I would love to have a new pencil case and bag, she thinks, imagining the walk to school on one of those high-sky, thin mornings when the trees are spreading their flames all across the woods and mountain. In the past, she would meet Biddy and walk to school with her. She clenches her fists and shuts her eyes tightly. What she wouldn't give for things to be as they used to be. She'd never complain about wearing sensible shoes and a long skirt again if she could be one of those girls now. For the first time, she properly thinks about the fact that she can't go back to school with everyone else this September, and how much she is taking for granted that her mother will babysit next year for her. She winces, remembering how upset her mother had been when she and Dada came back from the meeting with Tirzah's headmaster and someone from social services. I don't want to speak of it, she'd said, flopping on to a chair. Never have I felt so ashamed in all my born days. Her father had gone up to his study without saying a word. Tirzah barely took any notice of them at the time. I must have a proper talk with my mother, she decides. Like a proper adult. And now, on top of all these things, she must find out where Osian has gone. Soon she is so burdened and hopeless the only thing to do is sleep.

For a moment, when she wakes, it's as if the room is frantic with ragged black wings, and her ears echo with harsh, spiralling cries. She tries to breathe slowly and evenly, and gradually, the familiar outlines firm up, and she becomes calmer. The room is dim, and what light there is seems to come and go. There is a furious tapping at the window, and for a second she is terrified again. It's probably only rain, she tells herself. There is nothing to be afraid of. It seems unlikely, though, after the incessant sun, so she goes to the window to check. Finally, without warning, the hot weather has broken, and she is glad, watching rivulets of water worming their way down the glass. Soon, the grey dust that has settled over everything will be washed away, and the valley will gleam again. Back on the bed, she recalls the dream, and her heartbeats quicken. She had been in a twilit place, hemmed in by saw-toothed plants, the air so hot and laden with vegetable smells she could barely draw it in. The more she'd struggled, the more lost she became, and underfoot were all sorts of creatures waiting to take hold if she didn't keep moving. Soon she was hungry, her eyes wild from trying to see the way. She'd looked up through the undergrowth, straining for a glimpse of the sky.

Tirzah doesn't want to think about the dream any more. Downstairs, she can hear her mother moving about in the kitchen. But she needs to remember the dream before it fades, so she closes her eyes and sees her torn clothes and bleeding feet. The branches pressing in on her were alive, and scored her skin as she blundered around. Just as she was about to sink down and give herself up to the nameless creatures waiting for her, a huge black bird swooped, grasped her with its claws and carried her high above the terrible forest. Then, after a long journey, it let her down in a grassy place. She recognised the stream and the beech trees flanked around the smooth, open area. The crow that had rescued her opened its beak and spoke in its own language, then flew away, filling the air with the sound of beating wings. Tirzah had called after it. Now she realises the sounds coming from her own throat were in that unknown language too.

Tirzah shivers, and with her bare feet searches for her slippers on the floor. Then she puts on her old woollen dressing gown, wrapping it tightly. In the mirror, her eyes look strange; the irises are a glittering, artificial blue, the pupils shrunk to tiny black dots, and she turns away appalled. Mam, she shouts, Mama? and dashes downstairs, stumbling off the last three steps. What on earth is the matter? her mother says, running from the kitchen. Tirzah throws herself into her mother's arms. Now, now, her mother whispers. Did the storm scare you? Come into the kitchen. I know I usually make this in the spring, but there was some nice meat in the butcher's today. Tirzah allows herself to be led, loving her mother's neat back ahead of her, and the big bow of her apron tied in the middle. Lamb stew is simmering in a saucepan on the stove, and soon Tirzah is sitting at the table with a broad bowlful. The liquid is fragrant and clear, with tiny discs of oil on its surface. As always, there are bright green rings of leek and chunks of carrot floating alongside the peas and nuggets of sweet lamb. On her side plate is a fat, floury bread roll. Tuck in, her mother says. Can I dunk my bread just this once, Mama? Tirzah asks, tearing the bread. Of course you can, my sweetheart, her mother answers. It's only you and me in by here.

Outside, the rain slaps the concrete and pings off the windows. Tirzah puts a brothy piece of bread in her mouth and thinks about the chickens. They will all be huddled in the dry now, like sensible birds. The purple mint leaves clustering the pathways will bob stiffly with the weight of water. She is happy to be safe with her mother in such a storm. She remembers the talking crow in her dream, and her own strange replies, but already cannot recall what they had said to each other. She must think hard; surely the crow was telling her something important. She wants it to be about Osian. Everything all right, cariad? her mother is asking. She searches Tirzah's face with a yearning look. You're not eating your cawl. I made it specially for you. Tirzah looks down into her bowl. It's lovely, Mama, she manages to say. I'm just having a breather. Now her tongue is coated with lamb fat and she is worrying at a scrap of gristle that won't yield to her teeth. She squints around to check the dim corners of the room, fearful she can detect a kerfuffle of flapping wings.

Take Knowledge of All the Lurking
Places Where He Hideth

(1 Samuel 23:23)

A couple of weeks into the new term, Tirzah wakes early and at last allows herself to peer through the gap in her curtains. Biddy appears, running down the street, school coat half-trailing, bag brimming with new books. Ffion is waiting for her to catch up. Tirzah watches, craning her neck, as they walk out of sight, talking and laughing. Soon all the children are gone and the street is empty again. Summer is over. Already, swags of rain-washed blackberries shine like jet brooches in the hedges. There is a smell of ripening apples and drying grass, warm and sharp, lying over the hazy valley. The cream meadowsweet that brimmed frothily along the edges of the road to her grandparents' is now spoilt. Chilly little breezes rush down from the mountain, bringing with them the smoky perfume of bracken. For Tirzah, it is as if the world has rolled on, huge and indifferent. What do I matter? she thinks, getting back into bed and putting an arm over her eyes. The bedclothes are tight across her belly. Why should anything slow down and wait for me? It's calming, this idea of being small as a stone in a forgotten gully. Nothing matters really, she thinks drowsily.

Later, when she wakes again, she still has the cold, desolate feeling around her shoulders that seeing Biddy gave her. The things in her room don't apply to her any more. She can't run in her gym shoes. Her excellent O-level results are not important. But still, I am me, not some stone in a ditch. And I matter to myself, she reflects. I always will. The difference now is that the thought brings no comfort. Caring is a burden; if you don't care, then of course nothing matters. You need never be sad or lonely or worried. She lies still, even though she needs to use the toilet, and sends her mind to the top of the mountain, above the forestry, way above the woods, and searches for that glowing, joyful presence she once ran towards. Was that real? It's as if the encounter on the mountain top on the day of the outreach meeting happened to someone else. But the more she thinks about it now, the more convinced she becomes that she was the girl who raised her arms and embraced such golden, unknown glory. Getting up, she sits on the toilet and enjoys the sound of urine splashing into the pan. Her heart expands, and the memory of that day revisits her as she puts her clothes on, lingering like the aftertaste of something delicious in her mouth.

The house is empty, her breakfast laid out as usual, iron tablets by the side of her plate. On the dresser is her mother's knitting basket, and inside, skewered with thin wooden nee-dles, is a lacy, nearly finished white baby jacket. Tirzah pulls the knitting out and carefully lays it in an airy pile on the table. Here are the tiny, unattached sleeves, here is the back, not much bigger than her hand, and the two front panels, all waiting to be connected. Tirzah cannot believe that her baby will be born in the new year. Surely this jacket would only fit a doll. She stuffs the garment back in the basket and thinks about breakfast instead. Eating cornflakes, she recalls the crow-dream she had during the storm and decides on a plan: she will try to find out what's happened to Osian. That's not an impossible task. Then, with a small, uncomfortable thrill that straightens her back, she is forced to admit that her dream had been about Brân, not Osian at all, no matter how much she's been worrying about him. She'd known all along, but had deliberately ignored the truth. Brân is the one who is the Prince of Crows. Or so he always said. She remembers how he'd cringed from the birds the last time she had seen him in the woods. Some prince he turned out to be, she thinks, swilling her bowl and cup.

Tirzah walks up the quiet street with her mother's shopping bag. When she gets to the Co-op, she sits on the wall for a moment, remembering Brân's little boys scrabbling for sweeties all those months ago. She will find one of the boys and talk to him. But it's term time now, and everyone's at school. In the shop she stands in line at the bacon counter and watches Mrs Ellis-Jones come from the storeroom to help. When she sees Tirzah, she mutters something to the other shop assistant. Well? she says through thin lips when it's Tirzah's turn. What do you want? Tirzah hands over her mother's note and looks unblinkingly over the pre-packed bricks of cheese. Mrs Ellis-Jones goes a deep, painful colour and scans the list. Some people have no shame, she says, averting her eyes and clumsily trying to nip a pile of bacon from the tray in the chiller with her metal tongs. Not that bacon, thank you, Tirzah says. My mother would like fresh-cut. She waits while Mrs Ellis-Jones cuts her eight new slices. When she pays, the woman makes a big show of not touching her hand. Tirzah remembers how Mrs Ellis-Jones had told her to change her melting lollies for icy ones early in the summer. Swap those, lovey, she'd said, winking. You'd have to pour 'em out by the time you got home. Tirzah glances at Mrs Ellis-Jones's stony face. Thank you, she says again. Goodbye now. The bag isn't heavy, but her legs tremble as she opens the door. The clang of the bell makes her armpits tingle.

There is a ball being kicked against a wall, and Tirzah traces the sound to the alley down the side of the Co-op. She drops her bag and straightens, hands pressed to the small of her back. One of Brân's boys is half-heartedly dribbling the ball about. Hiya, she says, stepping near him. The boy stops, his foot on the ball, and gives her a blank-eyed stare. Aren't you a butty of Brân's? she asks. He busies himself with stuffing his T-shirt into his shorts. Do you remember me? she goes on, and the boy gives a nod. Now he is closer, she is sure he was the one Brân baptised in the stream. Didn't I see you with Brân down by the stream in the woods that day? He picks up the ball. Nuh, he says, I gotta be off, and tries to push past. My mam is waiting. You're mooching off school, so I don't think that's true, Tirzah says, holding his arm lightly. I just want to know how Brân is. Do you see him now? The boy shakes her hand off and runs out of the alley. Get lost! he shouts back, and spits in her direction. None of us goes to those stupid woods no more. He boots his ball ahead of him up the street and runs after it.

Tirzah re-enters the shop and buys a few more items, then walks home as quickly as she can. In her room she wraps the things she bought – a pork pie, some Cadbury's Fruit & Nut chocolate and four apples – in an old tablecloth. Her hands are shaking, and the apples keep escaping. Then she remembers Derry's money, and from the tin in the back of her wardrobe takes out the remaining notes, pushing them into the chocolate wrapper with just their ends showing. All the time she's been busy, she's kept her mind blank. Now she sits on the floor next to the food and silently weeps for Brân. How must he be managing, abandoned by his boys? She pictures him, tattered and filthy, stumbling around in the ferns, his broken-down shoes falling off. A picture of him snaffling the cheese and onion pasty she gave him outside the Co-op comes to her, and she gulps as she remembers how he had licked the oily wrapping when he thought no one was looking. Down in the pantry she grabs some Oxo cubes. When she opens her mother's Quality Street tin, a homely waft of fruit and spice catches in her nostrils, and she takes out the nub of bara brith. Lastly, under the stairs she finds a shrunken jumper of her father's. Then the parcel is complete, and returning to her room, she ties the cloth's four corners together round the provisions to make a lumpy bundle.

Her mother's Yoo hoo! reaches up the stairs and Tirzah makes her way to the kitchen. There's one good thing about being denounced, her mother says from the pantry, a person has a lot more time to do things. Tirzah stands in the doorway, hoping she won't look in the cake tin. I've just been to see your granny and bamps, she goes on. They would love to see you. Tirzah has the bundle behind her back. I'll pop up soon, she says, hovering. You look like frightened Ike, all pale and staring, child, her mother observes, distracted by a bluebottle. Whatever's the matter? Then she starts flapping with a duster. Buzz off! she shouts. Dirty creature! Tirzah backs out of the kitchen, leaving the house by the front door, and walks away from the village. At the long stone wall enclosing the first of the fields she is halted for a moment, but soon finds the gate and pushes through. The stubbly fields stretch on and on, and Tirzah begins to feel like a tiny speck on the surface of the world, scarcely visible, inching along, liable to be crushed at any moment. She has forgotten to eat and is light-headed, but nothing matters to her more than getting this parcel to Brân. When she's done that, she can think about something else.

The sheep ignore her as she walks past them across the grass. In a daze, she struggles to climb the walls, scraping her shins, but doesn't stop. Without warning, the woods rear up, and bending to enter under the low branches and arching brambles, she trips and slides down the bluebell bank, coming to rest not far from the stream and Brân's first den. Invisible birds agitate the canopy, and old man's beard is lying like garlands of soap suds over the undergrowth. She balances carefully on two large stones in the stream and crosses, dodging the nettles. On the bare earth, the scorch marks from Brân's long-dead fire can be seen. Tirzah clears her throat, preparing to call out, but the thought of tearing the greenish, listening air trapped under the trees feels wrong. She sits on the edge of the trampled earth and hears the stream singing incessantly to itself. Suddenly she is thirsty, and leaving the bundle out in the open, she makes for the water, but the stinging nettles throng more luxuriantly where the water is easiest to scoop up.

She looks back at the bundle. From a distance, the checked tablecloth looks so out of place, and its contents are so inadequate, she wonders if Brân will even see it, and if he did, would he want it? She decides to call a few times, just in case he is near, and then make a run for home. Cupping her hands, she lets out a cry that seems to die as it leaves her lips. She tries again, but it's as if the trees hungrily snatch the sound from her. There is nothing for it but to leave. Making her way laboriously back up the long bank, she thinks she can detect a leafy kind of commotion happening behind her, as if the undergrowth were being thrashed aside by someone striking out with a stick. Once upon a time, she would have imagined the Devil was after her. Now, using the very last shreds of her energy, she rushes, bent double, up and out into the daylight.

Know and Consider What Thou Wilt Do

(1 Samuel 25:17)

From her bed, Tirzah can hear a visitor arrive. A familiar male voice is raised in answer to her father's greeting. She sits up and listens, frowning, as the voices recede down the hall. So, it's the front room for them. She lies against the pillows, the muscles of her lower back radiating a dull ache. Since her secret visit to the woods, she has not been feeling right. Mrs Betty Palfrey has been coming to do blood pressure readings and urine tests. Tirzah is bed-bound for a week, even though, for the past four days, all her results are healthy. She has tried to reread some favourite childhood books, but boredom floors her every time, and she lets each book slip from her fingers, incapable of holding on to her thoughts for more than a page or two. She is eaten up by how this baby is preventing her from doing what she has to do. It's difficult to be calm, with her mind so full of things. Everyone is telling her to relax. We don't want to be carted off to the hospital at this stage, do we? asks Mrs Palfrey, squeezing her little black bladder of air in her fist on one of these daily blood pressure check-ups. No, we don't, Mrs P, Tirzah says, trying to take unhurried breaths.

Now the voice downstairs is bothering her, and she closes her eyes, the better to listen. Of course, it's Pastor, she says to her room, conjuring up his narrow, indoor-pale face and winking steel-rimmed glasses. Why is Pastor calling all these weeks after the whole family have been thrown out of chapel? Except for Biddy, who is overjoyed about not going to services, they have been the strangest, saddest weeks she can ever remember. Her father spends all his spare time out in the garden, smashing up concrete with a pickaxe. The reverberating, muffled *thump, thump, thump* is almost normal now. Tirzah and her mother watch him through the kitchen window. He raises the swinging pickaxe, his body bending backward at an unlikely angle. Then he sends it crashing down. There's something too extreme about the effort he is putting in. It reminds Tirzah of the time, years ago, when she and her mother watched him scythe their lovely garden flat. Now he's on the rampage again, to restore it. Everything seems wrong in the house. Without the meetings to hang their days on, time has no proper shape. There are holes appearing, and they try to fill them in their own ways.

When Tirzah and her mother bump into members of Horeb around the village, it's all glances and blushes, hemming and hawing, or righteous stares and the twitching of garment hems. Though, as her mother says, to be fair, this is not true of everybody. But there was one day when her mother came in from grocery shopping and sat in the kitchen like a bag of old charity clothes. What's happened? Tirzah asked, kneeling to hold her balled-up hands. I believe Pastor's wife just shook my dust off her robe, so to speak, her mother mumbled, voice distorted by tears. Tirzah looked puzzled. Well, her mother had said, warming up, what I mean is, the very fact I stood near her in the butcher's might have contaminated her, and she brushed me off like this. And she re-enacted someone flicking something nasty off themselves. Oh, she did, did she? Tirzah had said, her temperature rising. I would like to do a bit of shaking myself. But her mother had chided her, and asked her to think what Jesus would have done. Tirzah was silent. Anyway, I'm happy that I was sick on her best shoes, she'd said at last, remembering Pastor's wife's black patent affairs all splatted. So am I, her mother answered, reviving enough to attend to her flattened, unpinned bun. May the Lord forgive me.

Now Tirzah sits and waits for what will happen next downstairs. I always seem to be skulking on the landing, and I'm fed up with it, she thinks, glad about her meeting with Derry tomorrow. At least that's something different to look forward to. She wonders again why he said it was important they meet, but is distracted by her mother bustling out of the front room to the kitchen. The conversation escaping through the open door is lively. When the tea is made, her mother takes a tray in and shuts the door again. Tirzah sits on in the dimness. If the weekdays have felt strange, then Sundays have been so long and empty, with her father locked away in his study. The sound of her mother singing from the hymnal while she has a meeting on her own in the front room sends Tirzah into a black mood that only sleep can save her from. She can't pray these days and doesn't even care, she realises now. As always, she wonders how this has happened. If it wasn't for all her worries, she would be as happy as Biddy never to go to chapel again.

Wrapping the dressing gown around her bump, she thinks about Biddy's last visit. It's all Ffion this, Ffion that and Ffion the other with her now. When Tirzah gazed at Biddy from her bed, trying to look interested in a story about some sixth form boys, she thought her face would freeze and fall off in one piece. I'm relieved when she leaves, she thinks. There is always a brief, airless gap when Tirzah is solitary again and she can examine her loneliness. It's as if she and Biddy are on opposite banks of a river, each walking along in the same direction but unable to hear each other over the sound of the water. She would dearly love to know what Biddy is studying for A-level, but will not ask. She jumps a little on the step when the front-room door opens, sending a block of light into the hallway. Pastor is shaking hands with her parents before he leaves. She waits for the sound of the door closing, then goes down to them. Her mother's eyes are red, and her father's grim expression has something else bubbling behind it she can't read.

Come into the front room, he says. We have good tidings of great joy. Tirzah sits beside her mother on the hard sofa and holds her hand. Let us pray, her father says, as if he were a deacon again. Tirzah looks at her mother questioningly and gets a wet-eyed nod back. The prayer rambles on until her mother coughs. Tirzah gathers that they are all welcomed back into the fold. Her father has thanked the Lord for softening the hard, judgemental hearts of the brethren and sisters, and convicting them of their erroneous ways. Amen, Lord, he ends sonorously. So be it, and amen. Tirzah and her mother echo him in whispers. Then he leaps to his feet, and grasping his hands around the hilt of an imaginary sword, makes swishing movements above their heads. I beseeched that the Lord would take His righteous sword in hand and slay them all, he shouts, eyes shining, and my prayer was answered. Calm down now, Gwyll, her mother says, ducking and looking uneasy.

The fellowship is all over the place, and that's nothing to be triumphant about in my book.

Tirzah starts to ask questions, but her father will not be rushed. Of course, I knew it was only a matter of time before they begged me to come back, he goes on, settling into his chair. Didn't I say so, Mair? No, you did not, Gwyllim, she answers. And that's God's honest truth. She turns to Tirzah. The fellowship has split into two, she explains. Pastor and some of the fellowship want us back, and Osian's father and his faction don't, so they've left. She starts to cry, fumbling for her hankie. I have never felt so guilty in my life. Hooray, thinks Tirzah. Good riddance to them. Well, Mam, she says, you must admit, some of them were very nasty to us. Her mother is crying into her hankie. We will be in Horeb, the house of the Lord, and apparently they will meet in the room above the surgery, her father tells her. And that zealot will lead the poor articles. See how they like that. He's rubbing his hands and smiling broadly. I don't know why you're snivelling, Mair, he adds. This is a victory. But her mother shakes her head, covering her mouth. Tirzah sits silently. If Mama feels guilty and she hasn't actually done anything wrong, then how much more should I feel, she thinks, patting her mother's shoulder. Everyone to bed, her father announces. Sufficient unto the day is the evil thereof, I think.

In the morning, when Mrs Palfrey comes, Tirzah is up and dressed. You're looking perky, she comments. That's what I like to see. I told her to stay in bed, her mother says, but she is a naughty, wilful girl who knows best. Mrs Palfrey laughs. Don't you fret, Mair, she says. Tirzah's as strong as a little horse. Later, when her mother is busy polishing the hall tiles, Tirzah tiptoes down the stairs and out through the back door. She has to rush but manages to catch the bus to town. When she gets to the park it's early, so she sits on a bench and looks up into the linden trees. A breeze is lifting the skirts of the yellowing leaves so they show their silvery underthings. Most leaves have a bunch of fuzzy sage-green berries hanging with them. Their smell of candied fruit is all around her. Golden sunlight lies over the silent bandstand and the barely swaying swings. Tirzah is content to wait. Soon she is half-asleep. Then a shadow falls on her face and she wakes. Derry is looking down at her. Sleepin' Beauty, he says, and sits by her side.

The warmth and drowsiness of the empty park have sent Tirzah into a peaceful, distant sort of mood. So, Derry, she says, smiling. You needed to speak to me about something? The effort of turning her head to look at him is huge somehow. He talks quickly and emphatically, and Tirzah makes an effort to listen. Incredulously, she hears him say he loves her. I wan' us to get 'itched, he finishes, running out of steam. Well? he asks, nudging her when she doesn't answer immediately. Wha's your answer? I'm sorry, Derry, Tirzah manages to say, I can't. He drops down on to one knee and opens a tiny box. But have a gander at this, he says. Tidy, tha' is. Tirzah's bag falls off her lap. Derry is holding up the box with its sparkling ring for her to look at. Put that away, she says, unsure of what to do next. Get up, dear Derry, she adds at last. You are so sweet, and I know you want to help me. However, I won't marry you. Derry wipes his nose on his sleeve and shoves the box back in his pocket. I knew you'd say tha', he continues, getting to his feet and sitting beside her. But I always loved you, see? From the first time I clapped eyes on you, I knew I'd love you for ever, and tha's the truth.

His face is young and entirely unguarded, his eyes magnified by tears. You sure? he asks after a moment, his Adam's apple jigging up and down. Yes, she says, her own eyes watering. You should have a pretty girl who is mad about you, not some nutty, pregnant mess like me. He shakes his head. It's only you I do want, he says, his lips quivering. The thing is, I don't have to even think about it, Tirzah tells him, forcing the words out. I won't marry anybody. It's not just you. She links arms with him. I'm so sorry to make you sad, though. The wind in the trees sounds like distant applause. They sit side by side on the bench. So, it was love, was it, when you went and shoved your hand up my skirt? All those times you gave me the eye? Tirzah asks, nudging him. Smutty, that was, he says. Didn't know no better then, see? The gilded quiet is all around them, and here and there coppery leaves twirl to the ground. Anyway. Let's just sit by 'ere for a bit. I need a fag.

I Saw in the Night Visions

(Daniel 7:13)

On Sunday, they are all up early for chapel. Tirzah's mother makes a special breakfast to mark the occasion. Drop scones and jam, she calls excitedly, waving her spatula. Tirzah's smock dress is starting to fill out, and her lips and toes are oddly swollen and unpliable every day when she wakes. I'm not quite the ticket, Mam, she says, slipping into her chair. Shush, please, her mother says from the stove. I don't want to hear talk like that this morning. Look lively. Dada will be down in a minute. She slides some golden, lacy-edged drop scones on to a warmed plate and brings them to the table. Have some of your gran's goosegog jam, she urges. Do you good. Tirzah's father appears at the kitchen door. Oh, Gwyll, there's handsome you look, her mother says, hands on hips. Doesn't he look handsome, Tiz? He turns one way, and then the other, wearing the suit he always wears on Sundays. I'm glad to see you in your nice suit again, Tirzah mumbles, averting her eyes. He sits and helps himself to scones.

Thank you, both, he says, chewing. While I set no store by earthly appearances, I understand these things are important to you women. Tirzah can see her mother's back stiffen, but she continues to turn the scones smoothly on the bakestone. There, she says, finally joining them. Eat up, and I will tell you my vision. Tirzah's father halts the progress of his laden fork midway to his mouth. What's this, Mair? he asks. Has the Lord made Himself known to you? He puts the fork down. Tirzah gazes at her mother's blotchy neck and wobbly lips. Last night, Gwyll, she tells him. It was wonderful. Steady on, he says. Just tell us what you saw, please. We don't need the dramatics. Tirzah gazes out through the open back door to the heaps of broken concrete. Well, in my vision, her mother says, I was at the stove, cooking. Stop right there, her father commands, raising a finger. How do you know what you were doing? You could have been boiling washrags. Her mother shakes her head impatiently. Gwyllim, take care. As usual, you are trying to quench the Spirit, she says.

Tirzah swallows a bite of warm scone, and it clogs her throat like a lump of uncooked dough. Go on, Mama, she says, after taking a sip of tea. Her mother stands up and walks away from them. Where are you off to now? her father asks, his lips pursed. I was standing right here, cooking, she goes on, indicating the spot and giving her husband a look. Cottage pie, it was. When something turned me round. Wait, he says again. What turned you round? Tirzah's mother's face is transfigured. Something turned me round, she repeats. And here, on this old mat, was the Son of God; sort of hovering He was, all billowy and white. They wait for her to continue. Get a move on, Mair, her father says finally, picking his fork back up. Then what? Then, she continues, the Lord called my name. Mair, Mair, He said. Yes, Lord, I answered. Tirzah's father makes a tiny clicking noise in the back of his throat.

Her mother goes on: Then He said, Mair, lift up your apron. So I did.

Tirzah's eyes are stretching, her fingers clenched. Lift up your what, Mama? she whispers, balanced on the edge between screaming and laughing. Her mother's eyes leak tears and her smile's intensity is disfiguring. My apron, cariad. She lifts her apron as if she were about to curtsy. The Lord told me that He would fill my apron to overflowing with blessings. And then He dissolved before my very eyes. Tirzah's father scrapes back his chair. You have been under a great strain these past weeks, he says, clearing his throat. He nods towards Tirzah. And for that I blame you, child. And while we are on the subject, I do not like this talk of the Son of God *dissolving*. What is He? An Alka Seltzer? I'll say no more. You are always too familiar with the Lord for my liking. Tirzah's mother sits down and wipes her eyes. Do not mock what you don't understand, brother, she tells him calmly, and he folds his lips in on themselves and leaves the room. Tirzah is so tired of this old argument between her parents. A yearning to run and run and never stop settles on her. Everything about home is so samey and stifling. But she helps clear the table in silence. Her mother tidies up, sounding like a radio with a faulty signal as she sings little snatches of various hymns. When everything is in order, she takes Tirzah's face in her hands and plants a passionate, moist kiss on her forehead. You understand me, I know, she says. Ignore your dad.

They call for Uncle Maldwyn and Aunty Ceinwen. Biddy isn't ready, so everyone waits on the pavement. Aunty Ceinwen gives Tirzah a long hug. There now, she says, flustered. Tirzah is pleased and waits for something else, but her aunty has turned to see where Biddy is. Walking into chapel, Tirzah scoots down the aisle, inhaling the smell of holy dust and damp hymn books; her belly seems to be leading the way. She keeps her head down, so as not to show the star-shaped scar on her forehead; it pulses painfully, as if annoyed. Her parents stop to shake hands and kiss people. In their usual seats, Tirzah slumps and looks around. There are many gaps in the congregation: no Osian and his family, no Mr and Mrs Dainton, no old Mrs Elias. Hardly anyone from CYC. But from across the way, Biddy is smiling at her. In the row in front, Pastor's wife and the twins sit. The boys swivel to have a nose, identical eyes level with the pew back. Tirzah holds out two Polo mints, and their small fists palm them as they turn to face the front. Pastor walks from the vestry alone and Tirzah realises that all the deacons and elders have deserted him. Dear Pastor, she thinks, her eyes prickling. The service proceeds as always, though the singing is weedy without Osian's father's powerful bass and the others who have left. Tirzah sings her hardest, trying to make up for the lack. Her mother is transported for the whole meeting, whispering words to Jesus, catching her breath sometimes when He answers back, Tirzah supposes. Pastor finally says a word of welcome. Praise the Lord, someone shouts, and the fellowship sound the amen.

In the graveyard, autumn lies over every monument and headstone. Barrelling mountain breezes bring with them the tang of sheep droppings and drying grasses. Tirzah and Biddy sit under the angel and wait for their parents. Tirzah's hair is moving as if the mountain's fingers were rearranging her curls. No one has spoken to her yet, but still she feels at home. These are the faithful people who have known her since she was a tiny child. Several of them smile as they pass on the way home to dinner. Tirzah closes her eyes and lifts her face to the flickering, late September sun. Soon she becomes aware of a shadow. Pastor's wife is standing before her, handbag looped over her elbow. Tirzah says nothing. Mrs Thomas keeps darting glances over to the group outside the chapel door. I just want to get one thing straight, young lady, she says, enunciating each word quickly and precisely. Butter wouldn't melt, but you don't fool me. Tirzah gets up unhurriedly. And I could say exactly the same about you, she answers, leaving Mrs Thomas gaping. Da iawn, Biddy says, clapping. What a nasty piece of work she is.

The grown-ups talk all the way home, and the girls stroll ahead, arm in arm. Ta ra, Biddy calls, disappearing down the street after her parents. Tirzah waits for the front door to be unlocked and then tells her mother she is going for a little walk, rushing away before she is forbidden. The smells of roasting meat and boiling cabbage drift from doorways as she meanders along the quiet streets. Up ahead of her a lone woman walks. Tirzah catches up, realising it is Osian's mother. Hello, Aunty Margiad, she says as they come abreast. Mrs Evans gives her a vague look, her coat undone and hanging unevenly, and puts a hand to her forehead. They are standing in the road, and Tirzah realises they are nowhere near Osian's house. She wants to tell Mrs Evans that Osian is not to blame for anything, but can't find the words. Are you coming from the meeting, Aunty Margiad? she asks instead. Mrs Evans is even thinner now, and Tirzah sees her girlish, muscular legs are bare. The T-shirt under her Sunday coat is one of Osian's.

Shall I walk you home? Tirzah asks, gently leading Mrs Evans back down the road. Come now, you need a rest, I think. Mrs Evans stops abruptly and clutches Tirzah's arm. Her lips are dark red, as if she has been chewing them. My boy has gone, she says. His father threw him out. Tirzah feels the nerves sparking up her spine. Gone to my sister's, he has. And started a new school. I packed his bag and threw it to him out the bedroom window. He'll be safe now. Tirzah is so elated to know where Osian is she barely listens to his mother for a moment. Mrs Evans is speaking in a monotone, but each sentence is punctuated by a dry sob. He was hiding in the garden, waiting for me, she says. Tirzah can hear her own heartbeats echoing in the chambers of her ears. Helplessly, she begins to cry, thinking of Osian, alone, hiding behind the shed. There, there, little one, Mrs Evans soothes, gazing up the street as if looking for someone. He's going to Bible college after his A-levels, to be a minister, she adds. Shhh, though. It's a secret.

Tirzah sits on the kerb and Mrs Evans wanders away, retracing the steps they took together. Tirzah is powerless to stop her. She rests, and recalls her mother's apron of blessings. It's a long time since I was blessed, she thinks. Poor Mama, perhaps she's going off her onion as well. It's all so sad. The Osian she once knew would not have thought for one minute of becoming a minister. He was always telling her she worried about God too much. The only good thing is he's far away from his father now. Blodwen meanders up and rubs against Tirzah's knees, purring loudly. What are you doing so far from home? Tirzah asks, picking her up and stroking the dense, dappled fur. There's a naughty girl you are, Blod. And she tries to empty her mind of everything spiky and painful. The patched-up congregation, Pastor's wife, Mrs Evans, Brân and his crows – she sends them all on their way, but round and round her head they go like chipped horses on an unhappy merry-go-round. In the houses on either side, people sit down to beef and roasties. How many are having rice pudding for afters? she wonders, and is surprised when Dada's car slides to a halt beside her, her mother's furrowed face peering from the window. Jumping out, she runs to Tirzah. Quick, Gwyll, she calls, and between them they help Tirzah, still clutching the cat, on to the back seat. The purring engine sounds familiar to Tirzah. Mama? she murmurs, almost asleep. Are the blessings in your apron for everyone, or just for you?

Make Thee Mourning, As for an Only Son

(Jeremiah 6:26)

Biddy brings in a plate. Wrap your laughing gear round this, she announces. Tirzah is lying on a new, prickly sofa in Biddy's lounge. Thanks, she says, reaching for a handful of Ritz crackers. What's happened to your posh brown settee, Bid? Mam got fed up with it, Biddy says through a mouthful. And is that what's happened to your telly? Or did your dad have another change of heart and burn it on a pyre in the garden? Biddy pops a cube of cheese in her mouth. Sort of, she answers. They were convicted of their sin, and off the poor old telly had to go again. Honestly, I wish they'd make up their minds. I miss it, though. The girls munch, thinking. I really, really loved Robinson, Tirzah says. Who didn't? Biddy asks, her mouth full of Ritz. Tirzah remembers Robinson's beautiful hair and smooth, gleaming chest. Mostly she'd loved his arms. What would it be like, having those arms embracing you? He had the most gorgeous legs, Biddy says. But shove Robinson, I'll miss Scooby Doo. They lie either end of the sofa and silently make their way through the goodies Biddy has filched while her mother

330

is out. Tirzah tries several times to frame the question she needs to ask. What's the matter with you, Tiz? Biddy asks eventually. Have you got a pain?

Tirzah decides just to come out with it. Would you help me do something? Even if you thought it was stupid or wrong? she asks. Yes, Biddy answers. Tirzah explains about the parcel she left in the woods. You know the scruffy boy we saw by the stream that day we were picking bluebells? The one you said you fancied? she asks. Biddy slowly nods. Well, he's been living in the woods for months. Biddy narrows her eyes. Anyway, Tirzah continues quickly. He's still there, and it's getting cold, and his boys have left him. So? Biddy says. So I want to leave him some food and a blanket. It's going to be winter soon, but I don't think he wants to leave the woods. Will you help me? I daren't go on my own now, in case I fall over or something. Biddy shakes her head as if in disbelief. Tizzy, you are nuts, she says at last. But yes, of course I will help you. Shouldn't we try and talk to his mother first? See what she says about him? Tirzah realises this is a good idea. We could do it now, Biddy suggests, jumping up. I know where she lives. What's his name, anyway? For a moment, Tirzah struggles with a strange reluctance to tell her.

The girls go into the kitchen and look through the cupboards. Biddy puts the half-full Ritz box in a carrier bag, and the cheese. Let's make sandwiches for him, she says, and quickly butters four slices of bread, spreading them with Bovril. Tirzah keeps watch at the back door. In the pantry Biddy finds a bottle of dandelion and burdock pop. This'll do, she says. Come on. Tirzah runs round to her own kitchen and stands, listening. Her mother is upstairs changing the beds, so she dashes to the pantry and takes a handful of Welsh cakes out of the tin, then runs back to where Biddy is waiting. Biddy insists on carrying the bag. Tirzah looks at the shiny tip of her nose and bouncing hair. You're enjoying this, aren't you? she asks. Biddy nods. But I'm also sorry for him, she says. The poor dab. She stops and looks as if she is about to ask Tirzah a question. What? Tirzah says. But Biddy shakes her head. Nothing, she says. Let's go.

They walk through the village to the area where Brân's mother lives. The alleyways are stony and sharp with the smell of pee, clogged with nettles, holed saucepans and torn wellies. Tirzah realises this is not far from the place she found poor Osian crouching. Biddy leads the way and ignores the groups of children who watch them. This is it, she says, putting the carrier bag down. You wait here, I'll go and investigate. But Tirzah brushes past and walks to the front door. Up against the mottled glass she can see piles of mail held in a bulging swathe of net curtain. Biddy stands behind her as she knocks. They can hear music blaring in a distant room, and Tirzah bangs again. The door opens a few inches, and a little girl with a sore at the corner of her mouth peers through her fringe. A strong smell of frying fish billows out. Tirzah smiles at the blank-eyed girl. Are you Brân's sister? she asks. The girl nods, but before Tirzah can get any further a woman with mottled bare legs appears and grabs the girl, thrusting her out of sight. Biddy quickly moves to shield Tirzah from view. The woman surveys them, arms folded and legs planted wide. Whatever you're selling, we don't want it, she says, and puffs on the stub of a cigarette. Bugger off afore I sets my dog on you.

Tirzah's heart is jumping in her chest. Excuse me, she says over Biddy's shoulder, but we are friends of Brân and wondered if you could tell us where he is? I dunno nobody called Brân, the woman shouts, ash dropping to her cleavage. Now fuck off, the pair of you. And she slams the door on them. The girls hurry down the path, only slowing for Biddy to pick up the bag. When they are safely in the alley again they stop. Well, Biddy says, blowing out her cheeks, she is what my mother would call *a slummocky piece*, and they laugh weakly, holding on to each other. When they've sorted themselves out, they set off for the woods. It'll be getting dark before we know it, Biddy says. So they walk briskly, the air chilly and overlaid with the smell of rotting moss and dying allotment fires. Biddy helps Tirzah manoeuvre over the stone walls until the woods appear. They decide she will wait while Biddy climbs down the bank and finds a spot to leave the bag. You know where he built his wigwam, don't you? Tirzah calls. That's the place. Biddy is already making her way towards the rustling, coppery branches, and soon she has ducked under and disappeared.

A layer of dewy air rises from the grass and plays around Tirzah as she sits. Overhead, two crows swim through the grey sky, making for the woods. A spider with long, hair-thin legs and a tiny body skitters across her folded hands. How can Brân live in the woods with just his birds for company? she wonders, trying to imagine having absolutely no one to talk to. How does he clean his teeth and wash? The next time she comes she will bring toothpaste and a toothbrush, even some soap. Silence nudges her from every direction, and she begins to become uneasy. Just as she's struggling to her feet, Biddy is back, holding the tablecloth Tirzah packed everything in last time. This was neatly folded on the ground, she says, handing it to her. At the sight of it, Tirzah's eyes blur; the thought of Brân finding the bundle and rooting through, ravenously eating, turns her heart to a plummeting stone.

Laboriously, they make their way back across the fields, and Tirzah can barely carry the weight of her laden heart, but soon they are amongst the lamplit streets. Curtains are being drawn against the evening as they come down the road. This is a secret, mind, Tirzah whispers when they stand outside Biddy's house in an oval of yellow light. Promise? Biddy kisses her, and Tirzah watches until she disappears before going in through her own door. Where on earth have you been? her mother asks, stopping to take in her damp, tendrilly hair and red cheeks. I'm all over the place, she adds, not waiting for an answer. We have a visitor, in the front room. Tirzah washes her hands at the kitchen tap and rearranges her hair, fighting the desire to climb the stairs and fall on her bed. In the front room, sitting pressed into a corner of the sofa, is Osian's mother. Tirzah is so taken aback that for a moment she says nothing. The gas fire is glowing, and Mrs Evans seems fascinated by the tiny blue and orange flames. Hello, Tirzah manages to say. But Mrs Evans does not respond. She is busy twisting her undone black hair into a long rope. Grouped beside her are three stuffed shopping bags.

Tirzah waits for her mother to come in. When she does, the room seems to warm up and grow lighter. Marg, she says, smiling and pulling out a little bent-legged table from the nest of three, what you need is a nice cuppa and a bite to eat. Her mother has made some dainty sandwiches. On another plate are buttered scones. Tirzah offers a plate, but Mrs Evans goes on gazing at the fire, so they busy themselves with cups and pouring. Tirzah's mother sits and the cushion makes a sighing sound. Now, dear, she says gently, please have a little sip. Go on. She offers the cup and saucer, and Mrs Evans takes them. Then she picks up her own cup and raises it to her lips, overemphasising her movements, as if teaching Mrs Evans what to do. Good, she says. Now a sandwich. Mrs Evans takes a triangle and nibbles the edge. Soon she has eaten it and drunk half her tea. How are you now? Tirzah's mother asks, taking Mrs Evans's limp, empty hand in her own warm hands. Mrs Evans nods. You are missing your lovely boy, I expect, she goes on. And that is natural. But you must look after yourself, for his sake at least. It is good he is at his aunt's and still getting on with his studies. There is a pause. Would you like me to get some hair clips and a brush? she goes on, her voice coaxing. I could put your hair up nicely for you.

Mrs Evans is listening, Tirzah can tell, even though she is unresponsive. She is still wearing Osian's T-shirt. The fire makes small popping sounds and the purple evening waits calmly outside. Mrs Evans begins to stir. Rest a while longer, Margiad, Tirzah's mother says. I will get Gwyllim to walk you home. But Mrs Evans wants to leave. Tirzah watches the two women in the hallway. While her mother fastens her coat, Mrs Evans stands patiently until all the buttons are done up. Dear sister, she can hear her mother say. I will pray for you. Then Mrs Evans is gone. The bags shift by the side of the sofa, and Tirzah sees one of them has a note pinned to it with her name written in red biro. As she sinks to the rug, pieces of Osian's train set clatter out. Picking up a red carriage and a bundle of signals, she remembers Osian's onion-scented mouth on hers in the attic, and the way that had all ended. Then she sees something half-hidden under the sofa and snatches it up. It is the tiny girl with the auburn ponytail who waited on the platform for a train that never took her anywhere, still carrying her empty basket.

He Had Prepared for Him a Great Chamber

(Nehemiah 13:5)

October moves forward in a haze of garden fires and misty evenings, and Tirzah tries to read the textbooks that have been delivered from school. Her mother's cleared the dining-room table for her to work at and given permission for the heater to be used on cooler days. Now that last month's despondency has lifted, Tirzah feels a sense of urgency about keeping her brain on track, ready for next year. Apart from anything else, studying gives her jumpy mind something to worry at; when she has spent the morning taking notes and reading, it's smoothed out. But some days Tirzah spends her time looking out from her bedroom window at the hemmed-in street, her mind like a jagged rock rattling about inside her skull. Some days, thrumming, poker-straight rain falls in concentrated intervals, and when it lets up, spoilt leaves are flung around on the gusty breeze, their faces splatting briefly on to her window before being snatched away again. On those days, she doesn't read or talk; nothing she could say would be of any interest to anyone, she thinks. I am waiting for this child to be born. That's enough. Her mother leaves her be. On Sundays, they all go to chapel. Now Tirzah can wear a coat, she doesn't feel so utterly naked amongst the fellowship.

Today she is lying down, her mind working its way through the usual groove. How can it be that my brain will only think about Osian, Brân, my parents, my bump and blimmin' chapel? she wonders, dog-tired of them all. She shifts position on the bed. Knock, knock, Biddy calls. Tirzah doesn't respond. Well, look at you, Biddy smiles, walking over to the foot of the bed. What a sight. And she squeezes in beside Tirzah. Not much room in by here now, is there? she asks, giggling. After a little silence, she raises herself on one elbow. How's the studying? she asks. Next year you will be the most brilliant girl in the whole school. Tirzah eyes her, unimpressed. How are you getting on, Biddy? she asks, hoping Biddy doesn't complain about school. She'll punch her if she does. Biddy flops back down. It's blimmin' hard, she answers. But I think I'm all right. Tirzah is silent. Seriously, Tizzy, Biddy says after a few moments, as if continuing an interrupted conversation, you must get up and doing. Your mother is worried about you. Tirzah gives her a narrow glance. She's down there, she adds. Crying her heart out.

Tirzah struggles to get up. What has she got to cry about, may I ask? she says, dressing hurriedly. I'm the one who should be crying. I'm the one having a wretched baby. I'm the one who can't go to school. She stops abruptly and closes her mouth; there are so many other things wrong that she can't explain. Biddy sits back, her hands behind her head, watching as Tirzah hops about, trying to find a lost slipper, looking for her hairbrush. When she is struggling with her knotted hair, Biddy gets up and gently steers Tirzah to the stool near her desk. Let me do that for you, she says, taking the brush. You're going to be bald, pulling at it. Just sit still, for goodness' sake. She begins to work through the confusion of Tirzah's curls. What a flipping fusspot you are, she goes on, tapping Tirzah on the head with the brush handle. They look at each other in the mirror. Now, what's been happening? Tirzah shrugs. She is thinking of her little mother weeping in the kitchen. And of her dada, going to work, coming home, going to work, coming home, even if he doesn't want to. No one asked them what they wanted. But you can be sure it wasn't a pregnant daughter who got them thrown out of chapel. I am a selfish pig, she says at last. Selfish piglet, Biddy corrects her. Piglets are much cuter. There's nothing very cute about me now, Tirzah murmurs, her nose congesting.

Biddy concentrates on braiding Tirzah's hair. When it is a thick, knobbly column she ties the end with a thin black ribbon. There, she says. Lovely. Your hair is so much thicker than mine. Tirzah examines her reflection, but all she can see is a suety face, a swollen mouth and a double chin. I'm so fat, she says, even my nose is fat. Biddy leaves the room while Tirzah glares at herself in the mirror, filled with an urge to scratch her own stupid, doughy cheeks. She remembers a time, not that long ago, when her face was pointed and her hair lively. Where has this podgy, indoor person come from? Suddenly, Tirzah wants to get out of the house and feel the rain-laden wind on her neck. She avoids looking at her blotchy eyes and wipes her face with a corner of the bed sheet. When she turns, her mother is standing in the doorway, tear-stained and red-lipped. What are we going to do with you? she asks, and makes a helpless, open-palmed gesture. Oh, Mam, Tirzah says, and runs to her mother's side. Words spill up into her mouth, but she is incapable of putting them in order. Against her cheek, she feels the worn fabric of her mother's pinny, and inhales the smell of fresh ironing she always seems to carry with her. When Biddy calls them, they wipe each other's eyes and go down.

I've got a great idea, Biddy announces, after they have been at the table for a while. She reminds them it will be half-term soon. Tirzah nods. So why don't the two of us arrange to stay at Granny's? she finishes. Ta dah! No need to thank me. Tirzah thinks this is a wonderful idea. We'll see, her mother says, smiling. Tomorrow I will arrange it, if I can.

The next week, Tirzah's father takes the girls to their grand-mother's. He leaves the big car's engine growling in the lane to carry Tirzah's case. Two girls for you, he announces, and puts the case down in the conservatory where Gran is having five minutes with the paper. Her old mousing cat draws itself into a plush black pool under the chair. And may the Lord give you wisdom, he adds. I have a bit of wisdom of my own, thank you, Gwyll, she says, heaving herself out of the chair. Look, you've scared Queenie with your pronouncements. Goodbye, Mother, he says, and she flaps him out with the newspaper. The girls kiss her on the cheek and rush upstairs, each want-ing to be first through the door of their room. Biddy wins. Oh, hallelujah, praise the blimmin' Lord, she shouts, laughing.

Tirzah takes off her dress and long socks and lies on the bed, welcoming the way the house washes over her. Here is the rag rug and the flower-wreathed bride in her frame on the mantelpiece. A coal fire is fizzing in the small grate. Biddy twirls around and then runs downstairs again. Soon Tirzah is asleep, and when she wakes, it's as if the little bedroom has delivered her to a simpler, scrubbed-clean place, where no one is looking for her to do anything at all. She rests on the pillows and listens to the gentle, living hum of the house. Outside it is dark, and the wind screeches over the garden's high stone walls, battering the dying dahlias in the borders. She can make out the sounds of Biddy and her grandmother in the scullery, laughing and clinking plates. She lets out a deep breath, allowing her whole body to relax. Just as she's thinking about moving, the door opens.

Biddy jumps up next to her. You're not to stir, she says. We are going to have a picnic. Tirzah watches as her grandmother mends the fire and Bampy brings up cheese and bowls of soup. Gran and Bampy sit in the easy chairs and Biddy is cross-legged on the rug. Bread rolls, Gran announces, I knew there was something, and Biddy runs down to get them. The cat slinks in and sniffs the air, then turns and struts out. Queenie doesn't like soup, Gran says. Fussy little bugger, she is. Tirzah isn't hungry; it is enough to sit and watch the others, and listen to the shifts and purrs of the fire. Thank you, she says. For doing this. They all gaze at her, waiting for what she will say next. She wishes there was something she could do to show them how much she loves them. As they sit watching her, soup bowls in their laps and bread on their plates, it feels as if they are expecting her to carry on.

Tirzah settles herself. I have something else to say, she announces. Biddy puts another morsel of bread slowly in her mouth, and Gran quirks an eyebrow. Tirzah swallows and blurts out that she knows they would like to know who the father of her baby is. She senses them all lean forward. So I can tell you honestly that it is not Osian. Nor is it Derry. They continue to wait. And that's all, Tirzah says, trailing off. Her grandparents start spooning soup up again and the point of

Biddy's nose goes pink. Is that it? she asks. Is that all you are going to say? Tirzah nods, her lips folded tightly. Well, save your breath, Biddy goes on. Keep your flipping secrets if you want to. I don't care. I'm fed up of the sight of you. And anyway, Osian swore it wasn't him, and I could tell he was speaking the truth, so that's yesterday's news. She turns towards the fire with her arms crossed, slopping her soup. Now, now, Bampy says, pulling out his hankie to wipe his mouth. If this is all Tirzah can tell, so be it. He gets ready to stand up, shifting himself back in the chair. Although, dear, he goes on in his usual dry voice, that is very slim pickings. Tirzah tries to speak. Don't be a-worrying, he goes on, I'm sure you have your reasons. And we must respect them. Though why you won't trust your own family is beyond us all. Tirzah is soon alone again and too dispirited to do anything but lie in bed.

For the rest of the time away, Tirzah cannot shake the feeling she has disappointed everyone. Biddy is unhappy with her, but Tirzah knows she will come round. It's Gran and Bampy she's heart-sore about. Throughout the quiet days, in the garden helping Bampy tidy his borders ready for winter or sucking boiled sweets and reading old *Woman's Realm* magazines with Gran, Tirzah tries to discern what they are really thinking. Biddy is giving her the cold shoulder. In the end she is exhausted. It's like climbing up a huge slippery boulder only to fall back each time; with nothing to hold on to she makes no progress. Soon it is time to go home. When they are packed and ready, she sneaks out to the scullery where Gran is making jam. Finished my onions, she says, nodding towards the pantry. Jars crammed with white orbs are lined up on a shelf like specimens in a laboratory. Heated, blackberry-laden air catches in Tirzah's throat as she tries to explain. No need to utter a word if you don't want to, Gran says, taking off her glasses to wipe them. She gives Tirzah a brown paper bag. This is a special drink I have made up for you, she says. Make sure you take it twice a day, there's a good girl. In boiling water. Off you go now. Tirzah walks up the long path fringed with orange-red rose-hips and seeded flower heads to the garden door. Looking back through the car window she sees her grandparents waving, and quickly turns to face the front; never before have they looked so small and old.

The short journey back is like the slide down a chute. Tirzah stares so intently from the window that the view blurs. Biddy is still angry with her, and in such a hurry to be gone she jumps out of the car when they arrive, gets her things and barely manages to throw a goodbye over her shoulder before she runs home. Tirzah leans against the car door for a while after her father carries her case in. The street is just the same: the neighbours' curtains twitch as always, the lights shine through the small rectangles above each front door, the same stray dog cocks its leg against a lamp post. In the empty kitchen, the table is laid for a meal, the radio tuned to her mother's special programme. Tirzah is wondering where her parents are when she hears her mother's Yoo hoo! From the bottom of the stairs she sees them both smiling down at her. They beckon, flapping their hands. Tirzah climbs each step slowly. The three of them seem a crowd on the landing. Well? she asks, out of breath. We have something to show you. Close your eyes, her mother orders, so she does, and two sets of hands guide her forward. Now, open them! her mother cries, in a voice throaty with excitement.

Tirzah stands in the doorway. Before her is the old box room, but now it is like a glowing, cream-coloured cave; the walls give off a soft light, the carpet's pile is deep and speckled. Tirzah gasps and steps forward to breathe the smell of new things. Well? her father asks. But Tirzah is rapt. She is taking in the freshly painted old wooden crib and the sprigged curtains. There is even a toy box with teddy bears stencilled on the lid. For a moment, she soars above it all, she is so full of sudden joy. Then she turns to look at her mother and father huddled in the doorway. You darlings, she says, stepping towards them with her arms open, her heart uncreasing. Later, when they sit together in the kitchen eating golden-crusted cheese pie and fried bacon, she thinks for the first time about the living, breathing baby whose toys will soon be in the box her father made. She sees a picture of its small, sweet body snuggled up in the crib, warmed by the blanket her mother has knitted, and realises everything is now ready.

And Thou Shalt Rejoice in Thy Feast

(Deuteronomy 16:14)

Tirzah's mother has been what she calls *bottoming out* the house. We can't wait for spring to do our cleaning this year, she says, head tightly wrapped in a scarf. This place was due for a good session anyway. She's allowing herself a breather with Tirzah before tackling the front room. We'll soon be ready for your birthday and Christmas and, more importantly, the baby's arrival. Tirzah has her legs up on a kitchen chair and is balancing a cup on top of her belly. Mam, I'm frightened, she says. What is having a baby like? Her mother pulls the corners of her mouth down. It hurts, love, she says. It hurts a lot. The contents of Tirzah's cup slosh around as the baby kicks. You will recognise the pain when it comes, her mother adds. How? Tirzah asks. You just will, her mother says. Now, I must get cracking. You go on sorting that sewing box for me, there's a good girl. Tirzah is puzzled by her mother's answer. Why did she rush off like that? She can't imagine pushing a huge baby out through such a small opening. I won't think any more, she decides. Or I'll only go off my onion.

It takes a few days for the smells of bleach and polish and paint to subside. Tirzah is planning her birthday party. Of course, it will be a small affair, but still, she is excited. If only Osian could come, she thinks, sucking her pen at the kitchen table one November day when the cold air has deadened all normal sounds in the streets. It will not be the same without him. But she realises she is thinking of the old, gently amused and sweet Osian. The one who enabled everyone to have fun. He has gone just as truly as the new, strange Osian has. She's working her way through a chunk of fruit cake and takes a bite. As she does, the thought of Brân flashes like a startled bird across her mind. We must do something, she thinks, glad that Biddy is her friend again. She has already found a good, warm coat for him in a local jumble sale. And a pair of walking boots. Tirzah starts to make a new list. Candles, matches, socks, a roll of strong plastic for lying on, food in tins and a tin opener. They will have to use rucksacks to carry it all. Then she writes down toothpaste and toothbrush. She is waiting for Biddy to come for tea after school. Quickly she finishes her lists, puts the notebook away and lays the table.

After their meal, the girls are allowed to go in the front room and put the gas fire on. Biddy has described her own birthday trip to town and the film she saw and the food she ate. Now she is talking about how funny Ffion is. You would die at some of the things she comes out with, she says. Really? Tirzah answers, not looking at her. She never used to strike me as the comic type. Well, she is when you get to know her, Biddy goes on. She's a laugh a minute, that one. After a short silence, she scrutinises Tirzah's flushed face. Hang a banger, though, she says slowly. Are you jealous of Ffion? Tirzah nods. Oh, you thick twit, Biddy says. I love you more than anyone in the world. So put that in your pipe and smoke it. Tirzah reaches to give her a hug. Gerroff me, Biddy shouts. Honestly! When they are settled again, Tirzah gets out her notebook and explains her plan to take stuff to the woods. Maybe we'll need Ffion as well, she suggests. Things will be so heavy. They think for a few moments. No, Biddy says. I will do a few trips. That will be safer. Tirzah throws her a look. Truly, Tiz, I don't mind. I'm very strong, you know. The fire gives a series of soft hiccups. They are both picturing Brân somewhere out amongst the dying bracken and silent, leaf-shedding woods.

I will do it on one condition, Biddy says. Tirzah knows what Biddy is going to say, but she keeps quiet. You must answer me truthfully, Biddy says, coming to kneel in front of the fire. Is Brân the father of your baby? Tirzah is hollow, she is so ashamed. Yes, she answers, keeping her eyes fixed on the gas flames. Biddy is silent. Oh, Tizzy, that wild boy? she says eventually. How terrible. I sort of suspected it was him. But Tirzah cannot say another word, so she shrugs. Now she feels even worse. The memory of her furtive encounter with Brân makes her wince. I promise I won't tell a soul, Biddy says, peering at her. Now let's not dwell on it any more. The birthday party! That's what we should think about, and she claps her hands. So Tirzah makes a huge effort to wrestle her mind on to another track, and tells her she's going to invite Derry. He's such a sweetheart, he really is, she says. And Betty Palfrey, because me and Mam like her. Gran and Bampy, naturally. And we'll ask Osian's mother because she's so lonely, and Ffion, since she is so hilarious. Biddy nudges her energetically. Soon they are making a list of all the food Biddy likes best. I love party grub, Biddy shouts, jumping on and off the settee. Can we have roast potatoes? I love, love, love 'em. Tirzah watches her bouncing, pencil in mouth, still trying to get into the spirit of things. No, we cannot have spuds. Even though you love them. Anyway, you love most food, so it makes no matter. It's to be things like small sandwiches and cakes. Oh, and those cubes of cheese on sticks. There's posh, Biddy says, flopping down.

The next day, Tirzah takes the scrap of paper Derry gave her when they parted in the park, and walks to the telephone box. Inside, she is bewildered; she hasn't used a telephone much. Of the people she knows, only Pastor and Gran and Bampy have one. It's difficult to decide when to insert the coins, and the chirruping *brrr, brrr, brrr* is so nerve-wracking she drops her purse and has to start again. Twice her money comes jangling from the rejected coins slot, but finally she can hear the stupid thing ring, and she asks for Derry. Soon his raspy voice fills her ear. She can barely believe it when he asks her if he can bring his girlfriend. Tirzah clutches the handset. But, Derry, she hears herself saying into the receiver, I thought you were going to love me for ever and ever. You didn't waste much time finding a replacement. Well, o' course, he says, not losing a beat. I knew you'd never 'ave me, so I thought I'd carry on, see? Find someone more my dap. Tirzah is silent. I will still love you for ever, though, he adds. Just don' tell 'er that. Derry, you are an idiot, she says finally. And yes, of course, bring your girlfriend. She hangs up, balanced on the edge of laughter and tears. Someone is waiting to use the phone, so she pushes the heavy door open and walks home, still not knowing how to feel about Derry's fickleness.

On the day of her birthday she wakes early. The room is dark, and freezing air snakes out from the gaps between the curtains, burning her naked arm where it lies outside the bed-clothes. So, I have sent lots of things to Brân, she thinks with satisfaction, thankful to Biddy and her three treks to the woods. For the time being the burden of Brân is lighter. Sometimes her shoulders actually ache, she is so aware of him, and she wishes she didn't care. At least he has necessities to last for a while, she thinks. And I have organised the people who are coming to the party. We can let off the fireworks left over from Bonfire Night. When she was little she thought the explosions and spangles in the black sky over the village were expressly to celebrate her birth. So now they will be, she thinks. When they've had mid-morning coffee, her mother bans her from downstairs, so she reads on her bed. After lying down for a while she becomes aware of a strange pressure creeping over her belly, and pulls the bedclothes down to have a look at her bump. Over the stretched, unblemished surface of her skin she can see ripple-like tightenings, and sure enough, moving like strong currents of water under her spread hands, her muscles are contracting and letting go.

Tirzah pulls the bedclothes up to her neck and turns to lie on her side. She remembers Mrs Palfrey telling her something about the body doing practice contractions, and tries to relax. She is relieved, though, when the sensation gradually lessens. Her mother calls her for an early lunch, and afterwards she returns to her room to rest. When she awakes, it is already dark outside and the clock says six. With an effort she pushes herself out of bed and prepares. It's not complicated: her hair is already braided, so she changes the ribbon, and then climbs into one of her old maternity smocks. Then she goes downstairs. Hanging from the hall ceiling, bunches of balloons nudge each other, and when she opens the dining-room door to have a look, the table is laid with all kinds of party food. Dear Mama, she thinks. In the kitchen, her mother is taking a tray of sausage rolls out of the oven. Don't you look nice? she says, giving Tirzah a hug. There is a knock at the door and she rushes out to answer it. It is Gran and Bampy. Then someone else appears. Tirzah can tell by the way her mother is talking it must be Derry, so she sneaks a look. Derry and his girlfriend are standing in the doorway. Come in, come in, her mother is saying. Let's keep the cold out. Into the front room with you. She calls Tirzah to take their coats. Tirzah feels awkward, convinced they are both gawping at her growing bump, but she does as she's told.

Osian's mother arrives, then Betty Palfrey. Tirzah's mother and Gran are in full swing, greeting people and seating them, but Tirzah hangs back in the kitchen until her mother finds her. We're missing the birthday girl, she says, and drags Tirzah by the hand. The front room is crowded with people, but seeing their smiling faces, she starts to brighten; everybody wants to kiss her and say happy birthday. Derry's girlfriend's name is Jeanette, and she has perched herself on his knee. Tirzah realises she is quite a lot older than him. She strains to hear what Jeanette is saying to Osian's mother. While Jeanette talks to her, Mrs Evans's eyes wander around the room as if she is searching for something. Biddy and Ffion come in late, laughing, but Tirzah doesn't mind. She is just relieved to see them. Soon, her father gets home and it is time to eat. Let us pray, he says from the head of the table. When everyone's eyes are shut, Tirzah looks at them all bowing their heads, and then at the plates of filled baps and sausage rolls, the bowls of crisps and pickled onions, the orange halves covered in silver paper, bristling with cubes of cheese on sticks, until it all begins to blur. I mustn't blub now, she thinks, sniffing the tears away. Not while the party is going on. Tuck in and enjoy, her mother announces.

After the guests have eaten a second bowl of trifle each and Tirzah has blown out her seventeen candles, it is time for fireworks. In the garden, bundled in their coats, everyone breathes clouds of smoke and stamps their feet. Tirzah stands amongst them. She can see each dear person, and they can see her, but there is a membrane separating her from them all. At any moment she might snap her moorings and sail off into the star-pricked, crystalline darkness that crowns the valley. She is at odds with her own life now. And afraid she will not be able to manage her changed future. Her father lights the rockets, and with thrilling whooshes they ascend. Huge, bursting, orange flower heads spill down weightlessly on to Tirzah's face and drip showers of sparkling gold on the surrounding slate roofs. She watches as purple rosettes explode, and emerald light streaks overhead. The upturned faces around her change colour in the flashing night and become strange. Suddenly she feels a jolt, and puts out a hand to find something to hold on to; her belly is doing an altogether different sort of secret dance to the one it did earlier, and Tirzah knows she is feeling her baby move for the first time. Across the garden, Gran is tracing Tirzah's name in ragged, silver lines with her fizzing sparkler, and as the final rocket explodes with a deep boom, showering them in starry, scarlet petals, the baby shudders and flips in her womb.

Hast Thou Entered into the Treasures of the Snow?

(Job 38:22)

Throughout the month after the party, Tirzah can't shake off the sensation that she's acting a part. Here she is, walking to the shops, or lying on the sofa in the front room with Biddy, or eating with her parents in the fuggy kitchen, but more and more her life is turning into a sort of extremely dull pantomime; her family and friends are actors proficient at memorising their lines, while Tirzah is always tripping over her words or blanking out in the middle of a sentence. It will soon be Christmas and everyone has been planning presents, but Tirzah can only gaze hard at each person, yearning for a sense they see her and understand how alone and afraid she feels. No one will be still; they are busy and breezy, their eyes always sliding away from hers towards the next important thing.

I must get a grip of myself, she thinks, marshalling her strength to make sweets for everyone. Each morning she resolves to try harder to be normal and ignore the terrifying shell solidifying around her, only to flop into bed at night like a flung glove puppet. She can't stand the sight of her schoolwork these days. When she looks through the pages, she is unable to understand anything. It's as if her head were full of feathers. Then one night she wakes from a sleep so deep it takes long minutes for her limbs to unlock, and she realises the truth: she is alone. Even though they care about her, no one can help her now. Soon she and she alone will have to give birth to this child. That is why everyone is skirting around her. In the semi-darkness, listening to the profound silence lying on the valley, it is as if she has been abandoned to her task already.

Down in the kitchen, she lights the gas under the kettle and sits at the table, feet freezing in her felt slippers. Under the mutter of the heating water, another, unfamiliar sound is making itself heard. The noise is like a thousand voices whispering *hush, hush, hush* – dry, shale-like, falling away, building, then dying only to build again. It is as if some huge machine were throwing handfuls of tiny stones at the window and rubbing them in. Tirzah rises from the table and unlocks the back door. In the golden light falling over her shoulders on to the path, snow is moving in draping, undulating sheets. Innumerable icy flakes skitter on the broken concrete and strike the windows. Freezing air billows into the kitchen, pressing the folds of her nightdress to her body. She hears the snow spreading itself over the dug-up earth and quickly shuts the door on it. Automatically, she snatches the kettle off the flame with an oven glove and pours a scalding stream into a mug. Then she drops to one of the easy chairs by the damped-down fire. Oily warmth sneaks from the sleepy covering of coal dust her mother shovelled on last night, but Tirzah doesn't notice. Her mind is searching the whitening woods for Brân, the blood in her veins stuttering. She is lost, flitting through the trees, calling for him. At last, chilled to the bone, she stirs and moves to the table again.

By the time Tirzah fully comes back to herself, dawn, muffled and grudging, is pushing at the window, and the herbal drink is cold, but she swallows it, remembering the promise to her grandmother. Stiffly she walks along the hall and climbs the stairs. With her slippers on and dressing gown still tied tightly, she climbs back into bed and falls instantly asleep. When she wakes again it is late in the morning and her mother has brought toast and hot chocolate. Look! she says, and opens the curtains. Thick crusts of snow crown the slate roof tiles opposite and stand on the windowsills. The sky is grey and lowering. We'll be in for some more later if I'm not mistaken, she adds. I love a bit of snow, mind. But I hope it doesn't hang around too long. When she is alone again, Tirzah listens to the snow silence. Last year she would have been impatient to get out in the lane with her sledge and play late into the evening with all the others. Still, she is happy. And it makes things more Christmassy. She is pleased with her mint creams, all wrapped, ready in their ribbon-tied cellophane bags. The trays and trays of pale-green coins took days to do.

Tirzah lies in a deep bath and watches her bump surge. The ankle-skimming bath water rule has been relaxed for the time being. That's probably the only good thing about being pregnant. I wish for a baby girl, she thinks, surprising herself. In the middle of a contemplation about names, she suddenly realises that Brân needs a hot-water bottle or two. The idea of a little girl is so warming, even a stray thought about Brân does not concern her. It will be Christmas Eve in two days, and Granny and Bampy are coming, as well as Biddy, and Uncle Maldwyn and Aunty Ceinwen. Her mother ordered a big chicken in November and has been humming in the kitchen with the radio on, making sage and onion stuffing and mince pies. The pantry is full of good things. Everything will be lovely. And that's all I'm going to think about, she decides, pouring hot water from a jug on to her belly. Mrs Palfrey is calling later to examine her, and when that is done, and Biddy sent to deliver the hot-water bottles, she is going to enjoy Christmas.

In the afternoon, her mother comes into the front room with a Christmas tree. But, Mam, won't Dada be angry when he sees it? she asks. His majesty can stick what he feels up his jumper, her mother says, carrying the tiny tree in its pot to a space by the nest of coffee tables. I mean that with love, of course. We are having a tree this year. Then she shows Tirzah the ornaments she has been collecting. Together they decorate the branches, trying not to listen out for the front door. Tirzah looks at the tree and can hardly believe it. Never before has this happened. Her father always says no. When she was little, if she pleaded, he would start to get worked up and throw questions. Are we pagans? he would shout. What does the birth of Christ have to do with baubles and gewgaws? The only thing Tirzah was ever allowed to do was write a scripture verse on the mirror with a bit of dry soap. Once she drew some holly leaves at either end of the sentence, but her father insisted she wash them off. Shame on you, he'd said, watching her rub at them with a dishcloth. Give the Devil an inch. And now, here they were with a tree.

Tirzah inhales the smell of the fir branches and is whisked instantly to the forestry and a warm, still day when she and Osian fell asleep together in the crook of an old tree. How long ago that seems now. Then her mother comes back with a string of fairy lights. Never, Mama! Are we having lights as well? she says, filled with excitement and dread. They drape the cord with its multi-coloured lights around the tree and her mother switches them on. Turn the big light off, Mam, Tirzah says. Then they sit in the semi-dark with the little red, green, blue and yellow lights shining. Outside, large flakes of snow drift past the window. Let's have a mince pie, shall we? her mother suggests.

The gas fire hisses, and side by side on the sofa they eat warm mince pies together. At five o'clock they hear the sound of a key turning in the lock, and her mother rushes out, shutting the door behind her. Tirzah can make out her father's raised voice, and her mother's lighter, insistent tones talking over him. Then the row moves into the kitchen and fades. She half-closes her eyes and watches the lights spread and dazzle. She has a sense of this small, pine-scented room perilously perched on the huge curve of the world, surrounded by yawning, colossal tracts of nothing. Again, she wonders if any of this matters a jot. And instead of the thought making her sad or panicked, she finds it comfortable. Everything will be fine, in the end, she thinks, aware for a fleeting moment of the shining presence she has felt before, hovering over the house.

And I Will Turn Your Feasts into Mourning

(Amos 8:10)

By late afternoon on Christmas Eve, the heat in the kitchen is so unbearable Tirzah's mother opens the back door a little. Oh, that's lovely, she says, sniffing the chill, and fanning her face with an oven glove. Just for five minutes, and then we'll close it again. Gusts of icy snow skitter across the tiles, bringing with them freezing swathes that briefly carve gaps in the kitchen's savoury warmth. Her father is asleep by the gas fire in the front room, his open mouth like a bashed-in bucket rim. Every so often he lets out a throaty snort. Her mother has worn him out this year with her chattering about festive decorations. All right, all right, I give up, he'd said. This tree business is the final straw! I am a lone voice, crying in the wilderness. Yes, you are, Gwyll, her mother answered from atop the stool in the hallway. Now pass me some drawing pins, thou poor, ignored prophet of doom. Tirzah thought he didn't look too unhappy, though it was difficult to tell with Dada. He's been going around, pretending to bang into the decorations, knocking cards off surfaces, just to make his point. But Tirzah and her mother pick them back up and don't say a word. Now that all the work is done, they have put on tidy clothes and wait for the visitors to arrive.

The dining table is laid for a special supper; there are seven red candles. It's like Sunday, but better, with the holly boughs over the frames in the hall, paper garlands radiating out from the central lampshade in the dining room, and on its own little table in the front room, the sparkling tree. Tirzah quietly walks past her father and sneaks behind the curtains, worrying her grandparents will not make it. Putting both hands to the sides of her forehead, she presses against the frosted window, belly resting on the windowsill. Outside, around the glowing halo of the street lamp, snow masses like a swarm of flies. There is only a narrow walkway down the middle of the street now; on either side, solid, mauve-shadowed white piles rise to well over elbow-height. The space between the window and the curtains is a cold hinterland, and Tirzah feels like Jane Eyre, hiding behind the curtain at Gateshead House: neither inside the room nor outside, halfway between two worlds and not part of either. Gradually, shapes firm up through the teeming flakes, and Tirzah lets out a little scream, waking her father. It's them! she shouts. And she and her mother run to open the front door. Come in out of the weather, both, her mother calls, grabbing their arms and pulling them in as if they were drowning.

Her grandparents' coat fronts are white, and only their eyes visible in the gaps between scarves and pulled-down hats. They need help to get things off. Now, into the front room with you, her mother says, make yourselves comfortable. Tirzah kneels and helps both of them put their slippers on. Gran has scarlet cheeks and a white nose. You poor thing,

Tirzah says, touching it, your hooter is frozen. Nothing that a little mouthful of my famous pick-me-up won't cure, Gran says, winking, and she pulls a bottle of purply-black liquid from one of her carrier bags. Tirzah's father gives a sniff and folds his arms. Come now, my boy, Bampy says. It won't hurt you to have a swig of seasonal cheer. Soon they are all sipping the sloe gin's dark sweetness from stubby, gold-lipped glasses that Tirzah's mother keeps in the display cabinet. Made this myself, Gran says. Last year was a good one for sloes. When Tirzah goes out to the kitchen to fetch a bowl of crisps, pools of melted water already surround the two pairs of boots, and the sodden coats are steaming on the airer.

After supper, Dada distributes carol sheets and they all sing while Bampy plays the piano. Tirzah looks around at her family, and thinks about the houses lined along the valley sides and the serious, silent mountains above them, all slowly disappearing under a layer of glimmering white. Her heart thuds, and she stops singing. Brân is somewhere out there. Or maybe he has gone home to his mother. But just as quickly as that thought lights up, it falls to earth. She cannot imagine the mottled woman who had slammed the door on her and Biddy welcoming Brân back after all this time. At least Biddy had agreed to trudge over the fields with two hot-water bottles. The woods were silent, she'd reported, but there'd been a smell of smoke in the air when she'd dropped the bag in the clearing. Surely that was a good sign? Now they are singing *In the Bleak Midwinter*, her mother's favourite carol, and Tirzah cannot stand it any longer. She slips out as they harmoniously sing the bit about earth standing hard as iron, water like a stone. By the time she is in bed, she is so cold herself that it's impossible to push her feet down between the rigid sheets.

An uncomfortable pressure is building between her legs. Her mother comes in to say goodnight. I cannot find the hot-water bottles anywhere, she says. Have you seen them? No, Mam, Tirzah answers. I haven't.

On Christmas morning, Gran comes in with a tray. Wakey, wakey, festive greetings! she calls. It's a splendid day, if a bit nippy. Tirzah stirs. Is it still snowing? she asks. Gran opens the curtains. Tirzah sees a wan sky and a tiny, weak sun like a punched-out hole adrift over the houses. The temperature is dropping, Gran says. I predict more later. Tirzah falls back on the pillows, reluctant to move. By the time she gets up, her parents have already gone to Horeb for the Christmas morning service and her grandparents are busy peeling vegetables in the kitchen. She offers to help but is told to sit down and put her feet up, so she parks herself at the table and waits for the rest of the family to come home. At dinner time, Dada brings the Christmas chicken to the dining table. God bless, he says, and smiles around at them all. Tirzah has a portion of everything on offer, but her best things are sage and onion stuffing and the little golden sausages. Those, and gravy. This is lovely, Mair, Granny says. Well done. And everyone joins in until Tirzah's mother is blushing all down her neck. While they wait for Christmas pudding, they pull their crackers. Bampy puts his paper hat on upside down and pretends not to notice, and as a surge of laughter goes up from around the table, Tirzah suddenly shivers. In her mind's eye, an image of Brân has appeared. Briefly she meets Biddy's gaze, but then the picture of Brân reasserts itself. He is walking through the white village, his footsteps bloody and his head crowned with snow. She sees him looking in through the lighted windows, and rubs her eyes, trying to clear them, but he is still there, moving from house to house.

Excuse me, Tirzah says, and leaves the table. In the chilly hallway, Biddy joins her. Are you feeling poorly? she asks. But Tirzah shakes her head. She grips Biddy's hand. I have a feeling he is out there, she whispers, pointing to the street. In the snow. Who's out there? Biddy asks. What are you talking about? You're scaring me. Tirzah moves to the front door, but does not open it. Biddy comes close. Do you want me to look into the street? she asks. Tirzah nods. The girls look at each other for a moment, then Biddy opens the door and glances up and down, peering through the swirling snow. No one is out there, she says firmly, and comes inside, drawing snowy gusts with her. Look again, Tirzah says. No, Biddy answers. You imagined it all. Stop it. And she leads Tirzah back to the table. Tirzah puts her party hat back on, but her Christmas pudding has the texture of gravel, and all she can think about is the picture of Brân in tatters, stumbling past the house, trying to find her.

Consider Mine Affliction, and Deliver Me

(Psalm 119:153)

Tirzah lies on the sofa in the front room, surrounded by piles of opened Christmas presents, consumed by thoughts of Brân. It is as if her brain is made of barbed-wire fencing, and he's caught in the mesh like sheep's wool. She hates to be alone now, because that's when he appears and eventually blots everything else out. She struggles up and goes to find someone to talk to. Her mother is ironing, the kitchen soft with the smell of freshly pressed clothes. The kitchen window is busy with snow-flakes. Well, what a wet weekend you are, madam, her mother says, sprinkling water on to the dry shirt in front of her. But, Mam– Tirzah starts. But Mam me nothing, her mother chips in, flicking her with water. Buck up. The sight of you is enough to make a clown weep. Tirzah walks out. In her bedroom she sits at her desk. It's true, she thinks, fishing her notebook out of the drawer, I am an absolute drip. After sucking her pen for a while, she rests the book on her bump and writes *Things to Do* in twirly letters on a fresh page. Then she sucks her pen again.

Biddy comes round after tea. When they are sitting on her bed, Tirzah explains that she needs help thinking of things to keep her distracted. Easy-peasy, Biddy says. Let's brainstorm. What's that when it's at home? Tirzah asks. It just means firing off ideas, Biddy explains. Come on. Get your pen and paper. Tirzah can't think of anything, and listens, open-mouthed, while Biddy reels off some ideas. Write 'em down, Tiz, Biddy says. Honestly, being pregnant has made you a bit slow. After a while, Tirzah remembers to tell Biddy that she'd like to get a parcel of provisions to Brân each week. She asks if Biddy will take them to the woods for her, pointing helplessly at her large belly. Don't tell me anything about anything though, Tirzah says. I just want to know when it's done. I promise, Biddy says. After she leaves, Tirzah reads the list through, and decides to start in the new year.

Over the following weeks, Tirzah fills her days. It's still too snowy to go out so she writes to Osian, care of his mother, and invites Ffion and some girls from school for tea. She learns to make Welsh cakes and has lessons from her mother about how to pin nappies. She forces herself to work through her school books. Steadily the time creeps on, and Tirzah hardly notices, until one morning in the bath she is confronted by the size of her enormous belly, smooth as an egg, decorated around its sides with silvery hairlines. She strokes it with soapy hands, marvelling at her transformed body's firmness and girth. One of her mother's friends from chapel has a ten-month-old baby, and brings her round for Tirzah to look after while she goes to the weekly ladies' meetings. This is Tirzah's favourite new thing to do. She surprises herself. Babies never used to interest her, but Mrs Taylor's little one, Sioned, is so dimpled and soft that the times she plays with her in the front room fly by. Nothing bad can happen when Sioned is perched on her knees, dribbling over a rusk. She rocks Sioned when she's tired, pressing her cheek gently on the baby's petal-like cheek. You don't believe in bad things, do you, cariad? she whispers. You don't know about the woods yet, or wigwams, or anything.

January is nearly over, and Tirzah is in her room, bending down to pull something out from under the bed when a huge movement in her bump makes her cry out. Something has happened to the baby that doesn't feel right. She can tell it has shifted into a new position and is pressing on the roots of her belly. Gingerly, she lies on the bed and waits until the pressure lessens. Soon she begins to feel normal again, and decides to say nothing about it yet. In a few days Betty will call, and she will tell her then. In the meantime, she lies down a lot and reads her Christmas books. Every time she passes her baby's bedroom, she finds herself looking in through the open door with a kind of fascination, reluctant to step over the threshold.

On the day Betty is due to visit, Tirzah stations herself in the front room, listening for the door. Soon there is a commotion, and she arrives. Tirzah gets up carefully and stands in the doorway. Betty's hat is piled with fallen snow, and she is wearing her husband's wellingtons. Tirzah's mother takes her coat and lays it on the airer above the kitchen fire. Betty is out of puff and there is a wavy wet border of darker blue at the bottom of her uniform. That snow is definitely easing a bit, she says, pulling off her gloves and shooing Tirzah back into the front room. Still. A little bit of snow never stopped me, she adds, accepting a cup of tea.

Betty puts her cup down and listens intently, head to one side, as Tirzah described what happened a few days earlier. Her mother tuts. Naughty girl, why didn't you tell me? she asks, but Betty raises a hand. Mair, don't worry about that now, she says, dropping to her knees and shuffling to the sofa.

Let me have a gander. Tirzah examines Betty's face, but her mouth with its faint moustache has its corners firmly turned up in the usual smile as she puts her hands around the bump and gently rocks it. Does anything hurt at the moment? she asks. There's just a dull ache in my back, Tirzah says. As Betty scrambles up to sit on a chair, Tirzah looks at her mother. What if we have more snow and the baby comes, Mam? she asks. I won't be able to get to the hospital. Then what will happen? Hush, her mother says. Don't go down to Llantarnam looking for trouble coming up from Newport. What does that mean? Tirzah says. Sufficient unto the day is the evil thereof, her mother answers. Amen to that, Betty adds.

She gets out a bulging diary from her big black bag. Now, we must face facts, she says, looking at Tirzah. Your baby is due at the end of February, but it has already moved into what we call *the engaged position*. Tirzah stares at the buttons on Betty's uniform, and the small watch pinned by its half-strap to her large bosom. This means it is getting ready to be born. I won't lie to you, Betty continues. This child is on the move. Tirzah bites her lip and looks at her mother. Oh, Mam, she says. The two women move close to her. I know you're scared, and that is understandable, Betty says calmly, taking her hands and giving them a squeeze. But you are a healthy young woman, your pregnancy has been problem-free, and I am not scared. I'm not concerned one bit. And that's the main thing. I have helped hundreds of women give birth up and down this valley. Some of their babies have come early, some late. We will take care, and be fine. And the roads will be clear soon, thank the Lord. Bed rest for you now, she tells Tirzah. She turns to her mother. And, Mair, ring me any time, day or night. I will be back tomorrow.

After Betty leaves, Tirzah gets undressed and into bed. Her mother has gone out to telephone Gran; her father is not home from work yet. She closes her eyes and takes some deep breaths, thinking about all the other pregnant women who live the length of the valley, until she feels calm. The ache in her back comes and goes. Then she turns her bedside lamp on and starts to read her new book, *Ben Hur*. With a thrill she sees that his sister's name is Tirzah too. He and his mother and sister are all so happy, she just knows something horrible is going to happen to them, and after a while she closes it. Her mother has come back and is in the kitchen, cooking, and she can't resist going downstairs again.

When her mother sees her in the doorway, she puts down the chopping knife with a bang. Never in this world did I meet such a wilful girl, she says, flushing. What are you doing out of bed? She manoeuvres Tirzah into the front room, and makes her lie on the sofa. Now, stay there, she says, putting a blanket over her and turning the heater on. I will bring you some casserole in a while. She fusses with the blanket around Tirzah's chin. Gran is walking down to stay with us, she says in a calmer tone. Your dada is going to meet her. You would like that, wouldn't you, cariad? Yes, Mam, Tirzah says, smiling up at her mother. Alone in the quiet room, her mother's china sailor and parrots watch Tirzah. Nothing to see here, she tells them, aware of the pairs of painted eyes fixed on her. Curled up on the sofa, Tirzah is still, but inside, her body moves without her say-so. Her forehead prickles, and she holds her breath against the churning ache developing in her belly and lower back.

After a half an hour when the pain advances and retreats regularly and the pressure at the roots of her belly intensifies, Tirzah gasps. A new, sharper feeling forces her to scramble off the sofa. As she straightens, she senses a distinct pop in the very centre of her body, and out of the most private place between her legs, like an uncontrollable secret, rushes a cascade of cloudy liquid. She sees it splash all over the rug in front of the gas fire. Mama! she shouts, and her mother rushes from the kitchen, dropping the tray she is carrying as she gets into the room. Dammo di, she says, under her breath. I'm sorry, Mam, Tirzah sobs, looking at the chunks of beef and carrot strewn across the carpet. Not to worry, her mother says, and helps her to step over it. Together they take the stairs slowly, and Tirzah is ashamed of her wet pants and soaking slippers. Your waters have broken, cariad, her mother tells her. Remember Betty told you? But Tirzah remembers nothing.

When she has changed her nightdress and the plastic sheet is put under the two layers of flannelette, she settles her breathing to concentrate on what is happening. Small surges of pain, like the wavelets of an incoming tide, ripple through her belly. I will make believe I am a leaf on the surface of a lake, she thinks, picturing the smooth, mirrored surface of a vast expanse of water rimmed with dark trees. Above her, like a clouded silver bubble, the moon bobs. She imagines the water, slow as quicksilver, lapping her body as she lies suspended on the lake's surface. She lets the water penetrate, working its way strongly into her innermost places, and closes her eyes against the white moon's rays. Soon she is asleep. When she wakes again, it is dim in the bedroom, and warm, and she is aware of the presence of her mother and grandmother. Where is Betty? She asks. I'm here, Betty says, coming to the bedside. The three women lean in. What time is it? Tirzah asks. Late, her mother whispers. I suppose it's still snowing, Tirzah says, as if to herself. In the corner are the gas and air canisters. Betty pushes them on their little wheeled frame over to the bed. She offers the mask. Breathe deeply on this, she says, and Tirzah takes three breaths and is asleep again.

All through the night, Tirzah dreams she is being raised and lowered on a fretwork of grinding pain. There is a constant moaning sound, but she does not know where it is coming from. Then, towards dawn, she is forced into consciousness by a huge, final wave that sucks her up and flings her far out of reach. When she opens her eyes, the room is light, and her grandmother is asleep in the chair by the bedside. Granny, she calls. Gran? And her grandmother is instantly with her. Now, love, she says. Betty is going to check you over soon. She's popped home for some things.

Tirzah's eyes are huge and tear-filled. Just think, her gran goes on. Tomorrow this will all be over. Poof! In the past. And your baby will be here. Tirzah listens, but the idea of tomorrow doesn't make much sense, and a baby is unimaginable. She is trapped now, in this room, in this body that has turned against her. Her mother comes in with a mug of her gran's tea and some toast. Do you think you could manage this? she asks. Tirzah drinks the smoky, strange liquid and nibbles a crust, and all the while, pain claws at her insides, raking her back. The pains you are having are the bones and muscles moving, making room for the baby to travel, Gran says. That's all they are.

Tirzah shuts her eyes, thinking about the mysterious adjustments going on and trying to breathe smoothly. But all the time she lies quietly, there is another part of her that is desperate to jump out of bed and scream. This other version is terrified and wants to pull her hair till the roots rip from her scalp. Help! Help! Help! she screams, banging against the walls, punching her belly. With an exhausted effort, she shuts that person out and gazes instead at her mother's lovely face as she massages Tirzah's feet. In less than a day, this will be over, she tells herself, trying to think of the baby, as her gran said. All over, and a new, tiny person will be alive in the world. But the idea of a baby is drowned out by the pain dumping itself down all over her. The pain is building: it is as big as a shed, now as big as a house, now as big as a fir tree, and Tirzah can't help but cry out. She wants to push and push, but is unsure.

Now Betty is back, and as she enters the bedroom. Tirzah slumps on to her pillows, mutely gazing at her. You are being a wonderful girl, Betty says, wiping her sweating brow with a rough, damp cloth. Tirzah feels safer now Betty is here. Granny brings up another tray, and the three women sit quietly. Tirzah has a drink of water. Well, Betty announces, measuring with her fingers under the sheet, she is fully dilated, and I think ready to push. The rest is a flickering scarlet and black dream to Tirzah. She is struggling as she has never struggled before. She has to do this, she knows; she has to do it or die. Her legs are trembling and her lips swollen. Tiny maroon veins break through the white skin of her neck as she braces her feet against the bed frame, tucks her chin in, grips her mother and grandmother's hands and pushes and pushes. Then, at last, with a tearing scream, in a slither of blood and juice, her baby girl bursts into the world.

Your Sorrow Shall Be Turned into Joy

(John 16:20)

When the naked baby is placed in Tirzah's shaking arms, she dare not look. One lightning glance earlier had made her want to faint away. Cariad, someone is saying, here is your beautiful little one, but printed on Tirzah's eyelids is a picture of startled, cream-smeared limbs, swollen, bloody lips half-open to show an inch-long, stumpy tongue, and a hollow belly sprouting with a braided purple and cerise umbilical cord. The longer she keeps her eyes shut, the more difficult it is to open them. I cannot, I just cannot, she says, beginning to cry as she thinks again of the child's punched-looking eyes. The baby is like a warm doll in her slack arms, curiously heavy. There is a shifting at the side of the bed, and Tirzah becomes aware of her grandmother's presence. Now, dear, she is saying, you must open your eyes and say hello to your daughter. Tirzah stops sobbing to listen. You need to recognise each other.

Tirzah forces her eyes to open slightly, and through her lashes sees an almost transparent pink and gold creature blinking up at her with eyes bright as bluebells. She lets out a breath and has a proper look. The baby is studying her, its flower of a mouth softly closed, and for a few moments they lock eyes. Oh, Tirzah says. The baby opens an almost weightless hand and lays it on Tirzah's breast reassuringly. The women gather to have a good look. She's the image of you, Mair, Gran observes. Her little face is shaped just like yours. Her mother blushes. Oh, I don't know, she says. She has Tirzah's beautiful blue eyes, anyway. Betty helps Tirzah to give a first feed, but she is not sure anything comes out. Then her mother brings a tiny wrap-around vest and a nappy, and takes the baby from Tirzah. Already it looks more robust. Let's put some glad rags on, shall we? she says, swiftly covering the dimply body with its gruesome, stiffly poking umbilical knot, and topping everything off with an all-in-one. Gran gets the crocheted blanket, and they wrap her up so that just the crown of her blonde head and sweet eyes show. Then they hand her back to Tirzah for a moment. After a hesitant sniff, Tirzah looks at her grandmother and says: But she smells wonderful. Then she rests her mouth and nose on the velvet head, planting a series of kisses on the baby's eyes and nose. I wished for a girl, and here she is.

Betty comes to the bedside and lifts the baby out of Tirzah's embrace. Now we must make you nice and clean, she says, and Tirzah notices the dishevelled bed and stained sheets that cover her body. Her mother brings a steaming bowl and towels. This is a present, Gran announces, and hands a tin of talcum powder to her. Just a little something I thought you'd like. It's called Bluebell, Tirzah says, reading the label and thinking of the child's eyes. While she washes Tirzah, Betty explains she is pleased that she will not need any stitches. Stitches? Tirzah asks, her insides tightening. What stitches would those be? No need to trouble yourself about them now, Betty goes on, busy powdering. And your baby is fit and well, even if she is on the early side. In the next day or so the roads will be clear enough for you both to go down to the hospital. Soon Tirzah is presentable and fragrant. Can you stand for us to sort things out? Betty asks, and Tirzah nods, swinging her legs over the side of the bed and walking to the waiting chair. Oh, to be young, Gran says, laughing.

The room is different to Tirzah now. For those long, unspeakable hours when terrible things were happening, death had seemed to wait for her in the folds of the curtains. But the blood and screams, tears and sweat are all gone, and the room is light and clear, the air sweet with talcum powder. In the corner, the crib stands, with its little breathing mound swaddled in blankets. Tirzah settles back into the freshly made-up bed, and her mother brings cups of tea and hot, buttered crumpets for everyone. I don't know about anyone else, her grandmother says, but I am conked out. They all nod in agreement. Soon Tirzah begins to feel sleepy and is aware of someone taking the plate out of her hand.

When she wakes, Betty brings the baby to her. Here she is. All four pounds of her, she announces. She's a bit reluctant to feed, being so early, so we need to coax her. Time for another go, and together they get the baby latched on to Tirzah's nipple. Ouch, she says, her toes curling. There is a squeezing sensation in her breasts and a warm release as something begins to flow. But there isn't enough for her, she sobs. Look, I don't have any milk. Her mother moves to her side. This is the special milk that comes first, Betty says, and there's only a little bit of it. Very precious, it is, though. With lots of good things in it. The little one might not get the knack of feeding at first. Tirzah gazes at the baby sucking, its fingers resting like a strange, beautiful clasp on her open nightdress. Betty leans over. But I can see she's hungry and trying her best, she adds. If she has Tirzah's appetite we can all look out, her mother says. Oh, Mam, Tirzah sighs, a wave of love making her speechless. Yes, her mother says, stroking the baby's fair hair.

When Tirzah comes downstairs late the next day, her steps feel oddly weightless. She is back in her old clothes, but her tummy is like the shrivelled skin of an over-stretched purse, and she hates it. That will soon go, her mother says, but Tirzah can't quite believe her. Other things are just like they always were; her toes are thin again, and her fingers. The tracery of broken veins on her neck has almost disappeared. She doesn't want to think of how wet and spongy her other parts feel. But that too will tighten up perfectly, given time, her mother promises. Her breasts are like hot bags of ball bearings, sensitive to any pressure, leaking milk all over the place. She is yearning to go out into the freezing, dazzling morning, but no one will let her. She is sick of house air and longs to fill her lungs with the mountain's blustering breath. In the kitchen, her father is at the table, reading Spurgeon. Suddenly, Tirzah is shy. Dada? she whispers. He stands and wraps her in his arms. Well, well, he says into her hair. You have done a good job. Then he clears his throat and sits back down. It's off to the hospital in the morning, I believe, he continues, picking up his book. Now the snow plough has been round. I will get the car out. Thank you, Dada, Tirzah says, and drifts towards the front room, unsure of what else to say to him.

It's going to be a funny life, Tirzah realises: feeding the baby, changing her, resting. The snow has stopped for now and Betty has been to check the baby. Outside the world is pristine, and Tirzah is already stifled in amongst the piles of baby clothes and nappy cream and breast shields. It's as if she is only playing at being a mother. Each time the baby cries, her breasts harden, then spurt milk in a way she has no control over. The real part of her, the part she has always been able to tell what to do, would love to be striding out on the crystalline eggshell surface of the snow, baring her face to the icy wind. And she still hasn't thought of a name. Biddy keeps making suggestions, but Tirzah wants to get the hospital visit sorted first. She wants to know that everything is well with the baby. Then she can think about what to call her.

Give Her the Living Child ...
She Is the Mother Thereof

(1 Kings 3:27)

The next morning, Tirzah and her parents ready themselves for the journey down the valley. They gather round the baby while Tirzah's mother bundles her up. Go and get the car, Gwyll, her mother urges. Honestly, standing there, gawping like that. Tirzah is amazed at the way her father obediently goes off, jingling his car keys. I won't be a jiffy, he calls before closing the front door. The air is keen when they pile into the car. Tirzah can almost feel how the cold must be pressing on her baby's skin, even though she is so muffled in covers that only the smallest section of her face is visible. Her father drives slowly down the cleared road and Tirzah leans forward, trying to make the car go faster, eager to get this over so they can return home. In the empty hospital waiting room, they sit in silence. Have they forgotten us? Tirzah asks, just as a nurse appears. Mummy and baby, come this way, she says. Tirzah doesn't want to leave her parents, and lingers. Off you go now, her father says. We'll be here, waiting.

She is shown to a room where the nurse gently takes the baby from her arms. Tirzah watches as she walks away down the corridor and disappears through another door. Pop on the couch, she hears someone say. I will be back soon. For a moment Tirzah finds herself entirely alone, and reluctantly inhales the surgical smell of everything, eyeing the gleaming bits of medical equipment that seem eagerly to lean in at her from their hooks on the walls. But they don't frighten her like they used to. Her mind is not really in the room; it is following the invisible thread of her baby's cry down the corridor. By the time the doctor has returned and she has been examined, she is jittery. All fine here, the doctor says. You're healing nicely. You can get dressed now. Milk is seeping into her jumper, and she can still hear the baby grizzling from far off. The sound tugs more powerfully at her now, and pulling on her pants and long socks, she hurries down the corridor into a room whose door is ajar. The sight of her baby squirming in a little glass container hits her like a bolt of electricity and she rushes across to scoop her up, startling the nurse. With the baby in her arms, Tirzah instantly relaxes. The nurse smiles. Your little one is doing well, she says, and seems to be developing a lovely healthy pair of lungs. Keep her warm and bring her regularly to the clinic to be checked and weighed. We'll see you again in two weeks' time. As the nurse gathers her paperwork, Tirzah gets the baby wrapped back up for the cold, fumbling a little, her hands still shaking. In the waiting room, she can hardly pause for her parents to gather their things. Come on, she says. Let's go. Then she remembers she has forgotten her shoes, and thrusts the baby into her mother's arms to go and fetch them.

Back at home, Tirzah's mother puts the kettle on before taking off her coat. Well, that's a weight off my mind, she says. Thank you, Lord. Her father is holding the baby for the first time, a new expression on his face. Amen, he says, his voice thickened. There is a stamping of boots outside the back door and Biddy's voice calls, Anybody home? Come in by here, lovely, Tirzah's mother calls back. You girls go upstairs, she goes on. And take the baby with you, Tirzah.

The girls lie on Tirzah's bed with the baby curled between them. She has filled out all her little creases now and is smooth and pale, the early transparent look long gone. They watch as she sleeps, one hand cupping her chin like a person trying to work out the answer to a tremendously difficult question. So, Tiz, Biddy says. I think you should decide about names. She's getting on, you know. Tirzah kisses a perfect, squidgy foot. Something will come to me, she replies, adding: It's strange to think she shouldn't even be here yet. Tirzah pictures the growing baby, folded up in a dark, wet sleep all those months. She'd wanted to get to me as fast as possible, she thinks. That's why she came early. It's a wonderful thought. What about Angelique? Biddy asks. I think it's beautiful. Have you gone off your trolley? Tirzah says. Angelique? What sort of name is that? I've been reading a book about someone with that name, Biddy answers dreamily. She's French and has blonde hair and blue eyes. All the men are mad about her. Shut up, Tirzah says. Are you twp? Honestly. All the men? She's not even a week old, for goodness' sake. Yes, but she is blonde, Biddy goes on, and she has blue eyes. Tirzah starts to laugh. I know, she says, maybe I'll call her Bluebell. She puts her face close to the baby's. Little sky-eyed angel, she croons, suffused with relief that the eyes looking up at her aren't rain-grey. You are my lovely girl.

They both watch the baby, listening to her quiet, rhythmic breathing, and in the silence Tirzah tries to find the best way to explain how the thought of Brân has been pressing on her. She wants to tell Biddy how tired she is of thinking about him, but doesn't know what to do about it. She lifts the warm, floppy bundle and puts her in the crib. There is a knock at the door. Who's for a little snack? her mother asks, popping her head in. When she has left the tray, Tirzah brings up the subject of Brân. What if he's frozen solid in his hut? Biddy asks, biting into a sandwich. Don't say such a thing, Tirzah says, immediately picturing Brân encased in ice, his grey eyes like glass marbles. We've given him lots of things to keep warm, haven't we? Yes, yes, Biddy answers, swallowing. I was only joshing. Tirzah can barely keep still; her room is fuzzy and close, and the snuffling from the cradle is suddenly driving her mad. Oh, Biddy, I have to get out to the woods soon, she says. I understand, Biddy says, looking at her doubtfully. How, though? Your mother watches over you like a jailer. But I am just as good as new, Tirzah cries, jumping up. Look at me.

Biddy clears her throat and points to the two wet patches of escaped milk on Tirzah's blouse. That's nothing, Tirzah says. What I mean is I'm fit and healthy, aren't I? The doctor said so. And Biddy nods. People fuss too much. I know what I can do better than anyone, Tirzah goes on. I'm right, don't you think? Well, maybe … Biddy starts. Well, maybe what? Tirzah asks. Well, maybe nothing, Biddy answers. You only had a baby a few days ago, that's all I'm saying. Anyway, why do you care so much for that boy? He doesn't deserve a thing from you. Tirzah can't explain, even to herself, the burden she must carry. Is this what my mother meant about my ungovernable heart? she wonders. I don't love him, but there are ways I am connected to him. She shakes her hair out of her eyes. I can't explain, she says. It's just that I have to do something. She takes Biddy's hand. OK, Biddy answers, I just thought I'd ask. Now, let's think.

They discuss what to do and decide to leave things for another week. Even though a week sounds like a long time, Tirzah feels better having made a decision. How they will manage to escape she doesn't know, but she's not going to worry any more. They agree that Biddy will prepare another bag for Brân, so they can just take it when the time is right. Every day Tirzah looks for an opportunity, but no one seems to want to go out or leave her alone for a moment. At times she is so full of feelings she closes her bedroom door and howls into her pillow. Never has she cried so hard; her sobs are body-shaking. Has there ever been another mother who cries more than her newborn child? she wonders guiltily in the moments when she's calm. And then, suddenly, at the weekend, the way becomes clear. Her parents have decided to visit some house-bound folk for a few hours, and she and Biddy are to play Monopoly in the front room.

They sit either side of the gas fire and stare speechlessly at each other as Tirzah's parents fuss around, getting ready. Here are some nice crisps, her mother says, coming into the room again, this time with her coat on. And a bowl of grapes. Have some pop if you want. We will be back by five o'clock. The crib is in the corner, and she has a last look at the baby, rearranging the covers. You will be all right, won't you? she asks Tirzah. Betty is on hand if you need her. Don't worry, Mama, Tirzah says, stifling the desire to throw back her head and scream. Me and Bid and the dwt will be fine. As soon as they are gone, Tirzah feeds the baby and changes her nappy. You mind you wind her properly, she says, handing her to Biddy. Make sure she does some good burps. And give her a nice cwtch. She likes that. Biddy lifts the baby up to her shoulder and nods. And you be very careful, Tizzy, she says. I'm not sure this is such a good idea now. Oh, pish, Tirzah says, ignoring Biddy's anxious eyes. When she is bundled up and has slung the bag across her back, she hugs Biddy and kisses the baby before leaving by the back door.

The air is pure and sparkling, and the village silent. As she walks up the cleared road between the shrinking drifts she sees lighted windows, even though it is still early afternoon, and remembers that February is only a week old. Single, clumpy flakes start meandering down from the vast, pearl-grey sky. Tirzah sniffs the air, full of energy, and soon she is striding across the empty fields on the snow's untrodden white crust, her cheeks burning pleasantly and her forehead numb. With each step she senses her home-bound life falling away, and a resolution firms inside her: Brân can't be allowed to go on living alone like a savage. No one should live that way when there are houses and people so close by. She skims the snow's crisp surface. Over the woods ahead, amidst the moving snowfall, she thinks there is a whirling circle of crows, but when she stops to have a proper look, they are not there. The cold has killed every sound. All she can detect is the weightless flumping of snowflakes as they settle. When she gets to the rim of leafless trees, she is warm, and takes off her gloves, enjoying the frosted air between her fingers. Shaking the snow from the shoulders and arms of her coat, she hoicks the bag on her shoulder and pushes on.

Then Shall the Trees of the Woods Sing Out

(1 Chronicles 16:33)

Tirzah steps through the tangle of undergrowth, her coat catching on twisted, thorny branches, and immediately it is as if she has slipped into another time. Or maybe time is absent from these woods. The feeling intensifies as she makes her way down the bank. It's like wading through a knee-deep, fast-running current of water: each step is a struggle. The ground is close-covered with glossy ivy now, and she picks her way carefully through the black tendrils snaking underfoot. The bag on her back grows heavier, and the straps bite into her shoulders. There is a constant rustling amongst the seared brambles, and the air is noticeably colder as she descends. Tirzah has a sense there are no living, warm creatures left alive in the undergrowth, but she tells herself that is not true. Animals hibernate; they stay cosy and safe in their little nests. And there is Brân, somewhere about. The air smells powerfully of composting plants and fungus. Above, the beech trees rub their veiny branches against each other, although she cannot detect a breeze. There are no signs of the birds she thought she saw a while ago.

Tirzah is having difficulty seeing across the tinkling water. The stream's margins are fringed with hundreds of icicles, thin as pencils. Now that she is poised to cross, she hesitates, unsure of her plan. Her limbs are uncoordinated, and there is an unfamiliar weakness in her lower back. The winter afternoon is racing down to meet her in a glacial mist. She almost turns around, but is stopped by a sound. At once her reluctance becomes an urgent need to move forward, and she leaps across the stones, slipping and filling her boot with water so cold it's as if her instep has been stabbed. Then she is scrambling on the icy grass, bending double for a moment to keep herself from falling. Straightening up, she hears the noise again: a slow creaking, altogether out of place amongst the trees. Tirzah cannot stop now, and walks doggedly on into the clearing with its scorched earth. Barely any snow has fallen here. The creaking is closer, and the blood in the chambers of her heart stalls. She lifts her eyes, aware of a bitter gush of spit washing her tongue, and allows the bag on her back to fall. Brân, she says aloud, in a stranger's voice. Oh, Brân.

And there he is, hanging from the biggest beech tree, his body like a rotten bolster, his shaggy, ruined head wrenched to one side by the rope. She steps closer, and realises the crows are silently feasting on his semi-frozen flesh, their ragged wings flapping, their bright eyes unblinking as they jostle each other for space. One clings to the rope, wings knifing the air like black blades. There is a noiseless flip as the world overturns, and Tirzah sinks, suspended between the trampled earth and the high, grave sky, her eyes locked on Brân's icy, blood-black face and wounded scalp. She sees the empty eye sockets and lipless mouth, his devoured tongue and stiff, gnarled hands. Her throat contracts as if someone has grabbed it with a powerful fist. One of the boots Biddy left for him is lying open-mouthed on the ground. She looks at Brân's naked, filthy foot with its long, curved nails. The truth of what she sees pushes at her heart, and she cowers from it. Brân and his crows, she thinks dully. Brân, the Prince of Crows. And she lies on the perishing cold ground with a silence like the end of everything crushing her. When she comes back to herself she detects the creaking music of the rope and the feathered manoeuvrings of the feeding birds, but still she cannot move.

A ringing starts in her head, and her tongue is so dry it is stuck to her mouth's roof. The sweetly nauseating smell lying over the clearing permeates her lungs; she can taste it. The hulking trees lean over, and she struggles, inch by inch, to stand. When she regains her feet she sways, unable to clear her thoughts, and retches. She wants to expel the vileness that has seeped into her with the cold air, but there is no moisture in her. Her eyes are filled with Brân's lonely, shrivelled body. The crows continue to fight and feed, ripping strips of flesh efficiently from his face and neck. The biggest bird, the one she thinks Brân listened to on the night she stayed with him, is jabbing his horny beak into Brân's frigid eye socket, and after each successful jab, he turns his head to look at her, his gaze glowing and untroubled. Leave him alone! she screams, and the scream startles the birds into letting go and awkwardly flapping out of reach. She runs at the body, beating the air around him with her arms. But when she stops, exhausted, her face smeared with snot and tears, the birds resettle. Tirzah stands, gasping and shivering, unwilling to move in case Brân needs her, crushed by her failure to save him.

The minutes outside the wood tick on, and the invisible sun slips down the snow-laden sky. Eventually she becomes aware of the shadows growing in the hollows under the trees. Without knowing where she is headed, Tirzah starts to walk, leaving the bag where it fell. Soon she cannot hear the creaking rope any more. Around her tiny flickers appear, and she realises it is still snowing. The flakes whisper amongst the naked branches, and the air is laced with white skeins. On she goes amongst the trees, almost blinded, unmindful of where she is, and as she stumbles, images of Brân flash and twist before her: Brân with his spear and headdress in the leafy sunlight, Brân sharing his food, Brân showing her his grass-filled den, his sharp eyes glinting across the fire. The smell of crushed ferns as Brân lay between her legs, his unsubstantial body labouring. The tangy smell of him. Tirzah has to rest, and leans against a towering beech, unseeing, her leg muscles twitching. Gradually she becomes aware of something lighter ahead, amongst the tree gloom, and starts towards it. Coming nearer, she realises that here, in the woods she knows, is something she has never encountered before.

Behind the huge, mossy boles of the beeches, slim white birches hover like wraiths, and Tirzah walks eagerly towards them. In a huge circle they hold back the forest with pliant arms, and it is as if their coverings of silvery, fraying bark give out a faint light. The circle's empty centre is blanketed with untouched snow, and Tirzah hesitates, reluctant to walk any further. The open sky is mauve and subtly moving, the clearing an untroubled shield to hold against the terror behind her. Here there are no crows; there is nothing to fear. Tirzah stands, transfixed. She senses a kind of rapture amongst the radiant, delicate trees. On the edge of hearing, a voiceless song mingles with the snow-muffled silence, neither breaking nor filling it. Here again, hovering at her eye's corner, she is aware of the shining white presence that visited her on silent wings in the twilight one evening long ago. The open fields and wild places are its home, and yet she senses it inside her, gazing out from her own eyes at the impenetrable, secret woods.

So the boundless world is all things, both good and bad, she thinks, as snow feathers her hair and catches on her eyelashes. And I am part of it. And so was poor Brân, and so are all the people I love, and beyond them, all the folk I will never know. She thinks of Osian and the discarded train set, and his lost mother waiting. If only he'd understood about the valley, how limitless it is and full of mystery. Her mind darts to how she used to dream about other sorts of people, undiscovered yet, living their lives in the world, and she smiles at the girl she used to be. Finally, she thinks about the front room at home with its warm crib and sleeping baby. Her mother and father will be back soon.

The slender trees stand shoulder to shoulder with her. Reaching out to touch their papery skins, she knows she must go soon. A wave of energy flushes her cheeks and expands her heart. Snowflakes hiss and twirl, white on white on white, and the silver birches come and go in the dusk. Tirzah hears a sweet and lonely tune high up in the woods: thousands of branches are dancing in the chilly air. She turns her mind to the long rows of lighted red-brick houses and pictures Biddy standing at the bay window, watching the darkening street. From across the fields, on the cold wind, she can almost hear her unnamed baby girl crying for her, and feels milk spreading warm as blood from her breasts. Without a backward glance she leaves the circle of glimmering trees and the empty snow-spread clearing at their heart, and runs, surefooted, away through the woods. She is glad to abandon the feasting, ravenous crows and the husk of Brân swaying in his tree. Glad to forget even the lovely birches and the brilliant snow. I must go home, she thinks, as she runs effortlessly out of the woods and across the white fields. My whole ungovernable life is there, waiting to begin.

Acknowledgements

Many thanks to Juliet, all the wonderful folk at Oneworld and to Cathryn Summerhayes, my hugely supportive and unflappable agent.

I am grateful also to my writing group, Edgeworks, and to my neighbour Will for his advice about the spelling and use of some of the Welsh phrases in this book.

Also, to my family and friends, a heartfelt thanks.

Most of all, I am grateful to my husband, Norman Schwenk, without whose bolstering presence, unfailing humour and wide-ranging knowledge of *stuff* I couldn't have written this book.

Reasons She Goes to the Woods

Shortlisted for the Encore Award 2015

Longlisted for the Baileys Women's Prize for Fiction 2014

Pearl can be very, very good. More often she is very, very bad. But she's just a child, a mystery to all who know her. A little girl who has her own secret reasons for escaping to the nearby woods. What might those reasons be? And how can she feel so at home in the dark, sinister, sensual woods, a wonder of secrets and mystery?

Told in vignettes across Pearl's childhood years, *Reasons She Goes to the Woods* is a nervy but lyrical novel about a normal girl growing up, doing the normal things little girls do.

'Exquisite...to be marvelled at.'
Guardian

'Outstanding...every word is pin-sharp and perfectly in its place.'
The Times

ONEWORLD